ARREST

Titles by June Gray

DISARM

ARREST

ARREST

JUNE GRAY

BERKLEY BOOKS, NEW YORK

THE BERKLEY PUBLISHING GROUP
Published by the Penguin Group
Penguin Group (USA) LLC
375 Hudson Street, New York, New York 10014

USA • Canada • UK • Ireland • Australia • New Zealand • India • South Africa • China

penguin.com

A Penguin Random House Company

This book is an original publication of The Berkley Publishing Group.

Library of Congress Cataloging-in-Publication Data
Gray, June, 1979– *5415 4702* *06/14*
Arrest / June Gray.—Berkley trade paperback edition.
pages cm—(A Disarm novel)
ISBN 978-0-425-27213-8 (paperback)
1. Newlyweds—Fiction.   2. Police officers—Fiction.   I. Title.
PS3607.R39515A93 2014
813'.6—dc23   2014006150

PUBLISHING HISTORY
Berkley trade paperback edition / June 2014

PRINTED IN THE UNITED STATES OF AMERICA

10 9 8 7 6 5 4 3 2 1

Cover photo by Photoalto Photography/Veer.
Cover design by Lesley Worrell.

To the A-Team:
Amelia, Abigail, and Aarilyn.

ACKNOWLEDGMENTS

When I first started writing this book, I knew very little about law enforcement officers. They were just the stereotypical cops to me—doughnut-eating, coffee-guzzling, ticket-writing guys in uniform. But the more I dug into their lives, the more I came to understand and appreciate what it means to lay your life on the line day after day in order to keep the peace. More than that I came to empathize with LEO spouses, who are not all that different from military spouses. We all say a silent prayer in our heart every day to keep our spouses safe.

To my husband, Mark: I couldn't have written this book without your help and patience. Thank you for taking care of the girls while I'm locked away writing, and for putting up with me when I'm stuck in my head and can't carry on a conversation. I love you.

A big thank-you to my mom, Daisy, who came out to stay with us for a month and helped us unpack an entire house *and* watched the girls while I chased a looming deadline.

Thank you to my sister Liza, for reading my awful first drafts and yelling at me to finish the story; and to my sister Jeline, for being a kick-ass assistant.

To my beta readers, who have been with me from the beginning of this crazy journey: Beth, Lara, Shannon, Kerry, Gillian, and Margo. Thank you once again, ladies!

To Dyann: I'm sorry I forgot to mention you last time! Thank you for your help with *Disarm*, especially with information on deployments.

I'm so grateful to fan-turned-friend Victoria and her LEO husband for the valuable insight into the lives of law enforcement officers and their families. You have both been so accommodating and helpful, and any inaccuracies or errors are all my doing.

Thank you to Cindy Hwang at Berkley, for your enthusiasm and belief in me. To Kim Whalen at Trident Media Group: thank you for having my back! To Tara and Kristine: thanks for always answering my questions, no matter how inane.

Finally, I'd like to express my gratitude to you, the reader. None of this would have happened were it not for your love of books. Thank you for following me on this crazy journey.

For more information on me and my books, visit my blog at authorjunegray.com.

ARREST

PART ONE

ARREST

PROLOGUE

I ran my hands through soft waves of dark hair, the ends of which curled around my fingers. I looked up and into the blue eyes of the shirtless man staring at me through the wall mirror. "Are you sure it needs to be buzzed off completely?" I asked, disappointed that I'd once again have to cut off the very thing that had brought us together.

"Yes. Academy standards."

Call me sentimental but I loved Henry's hair, which was black and had grown long over the past months. For several years I'd only seen him with it cropped short, and it was only after he separated from the military that I was able to watch it grow again. Inch by inch, it felt as if the old Henry came back with each wavy strand, not only through appearance but also in attitude. The spark of mischief came back into his eyes, his smiles seemed wider, his laughter deeper.

I loved this unruly dark mess because it represented him as a teenage boy. It was a constant reminder that we had loved each other for nearly forever.

And now I had to cut it off. Again.

"Els?" Henry said, craning his head around to look up at me. "It's just hair."

"It's *not* just hair," I said, running my fingers through his dark locks again. "Once you start the police academy, then that's it. You'll never be able to wear it long again."

"I can when I retire."

"By then you'll be old and wrinkly and you won't look sexy with it anymore," I said, only half teasing.

He spun around in the computer chair and grabbed me by the waist. "You think I'm sexy?" he asked with a cocky grin.

"Always." I held his face in my hands, finding it hard to imagine his olive skin lined with age. It occurred to me then that I had the rest of my life to witness the transformation, and the thought filled me with joy.

"Okay, old man," I said, spinning him back around and reaching for the clippers. "Let's get this show on the road."

I took the first swipe in the center of his head, going all the way to the back. I grinned at him in the mirror, pausing long enough to chuckle at his odd appearance, then went back to the task with more care.

As his dark hair fell quietly away, I thought of Henry's words in his therapy tapes, when he'd talked about the first time I cut his hair back in high school.

That was when I knew I was a goner. This girl in front of me was going to be my happily ever after.

I bet when he made that revelation he never would have imagined he would somehow find himself in nearly the exact same place many years later, with our happily ever after no longer a whispered wish but a reality.

"You're so beautiful," Henry said in a soft, raspy voice, drawing me away from my thoughts.

I looked up and studied my reflection, my curly brown hair, hazel eyes, and light skin that Henry had once likened to milk. I'd always considered myself somewhat average in the looks department, but nobody else made me feel gorgeous with just one look. Nobody but Henry.

I met his eyes through the mirror, and for one brief moment, I saw that kid again, the one who wore braces, who stole trinkets from people's houses, who went home night after night to an empty house. Who could have guessed that kid would grow up to be this noble, honest, caring man?

"I think you're good to go." I rubbed his bristly head, brushing hair off his bare shoulders.

Quick as lightning, his hand shot out and captured one of mine. He brought my palm to his lips, pressing a soft kiss against my skin. Then he stood up and turned to face me, standing so close my breath ruffled the hair on his chest. "This is what I should have done back then," he said and kissed me like we were just two kids in love, without a clue what the future held. "This time last year, I was in Korea, thinking I'd lost you for good. And now I'm here with you, building a life together," he said. "I could ask for nothing more."

"I'd say we got pretty lucky."

He shook his head with a tender smile. "Luck has nothing to do with it," he said. "We're just two willful people who moved mountains to be together."

As he held my face in his large, capable hands, I wanted nothing more than to freeze that moment and preserve the memory, knowing that we were about to embark on an adventure that would change us both in ways we'd never imagined.

1

———

Several months later . . .

"Honey, I'm home." I unloaded my purse and laptop bag on the floor as soon as I shut the front door. When I didn't hear a reply, I kicked off my shoes and carried them through the living room and to the kitchen. Still no sign of Henry. "Hello?"

"I'm up here."

I eyed the cold pasta salad on the counter wistfully, my stomach reminding me that it was past eight o'clock and I hadn't eaten dinner yet. I grabbed a fork and took a few mouthfuls, chewing quickly before heading upstairs.

I found Henry in our master bathroom, folding a box and stuffing it into the small trash can. "Hey," he said planting a kiss on my mouth. He pulled away, licking his lips. "You taste like Italian dressing."

I looked around the bathroom, trying to figure out what he had changed now. We had lucked out in finding an older two-story home on the southeast side of Cherry Creek that had been priced way below market value. Since closing in August, we had been slowly trying to update the outdated interior. But with Henry's long days at the police academy and my hectic hours at work, we hadn't been able to do much at all. We were nearing Thanksgiving and all we'd accomplished was replacing the dingy carpet, painting the trim white, and changing the color of the walls.

Too tired to keep playing sleuth, I finally asked, "Okay, what did you do?"

"Here, let me show you." He pulled his T-shirt over his head then reached out and started to undo the pearl buttons on my teal shirt.

God, even nearly bald, Henry possessed a stark beauty that never failed to strike me. Even at this time of night, when I was so tired I could barely stand, the very nearness of him sent ripples of arousal across my skin. "How do you do that?"

"Do what?" he asked, reaching behind me and unclasping my bra.

"Wake up at six in the morning and still manage to be so perfect by the end of the day?"

His hands cupped my breasts, thumbs flicking at my nipples, then slipped down to tug my skirt and panties. "I skipped the gym and took a nap."

Well, that answered that. I bet I'd look gorgeous too if I'd had some beauty sleep.

"Then I went out and got something for you." His eyes glittered as he pulled the gray shower curtain aside and motioned to the new chrome fixture with two showerheads, one of which was on a handle. "You've been complaining about the old one for the longest time."

I stepped in the tub and turned on the water, nearly squealing with delight when the stream was strong and straight. Henry undressed and stepped in behind me and reached for the handheld fixture. He twisted the control valve and then held the pulsating stream of water against my shoulder. "Oh, that feels good," I said, bowing my head and closing my eyes. When he kneaded my other shoulder I nearly melted.

"So how was your day?" he asked, continuing the water massage.

"Not great," I said. "My computer froze, so I had to restart, but then I got the spinning ball of doom. I had to work on the old iMac for the rest of the day, which is an exercise in frustration."

"I hope you didn't lose any work."

"No. Thankfully everything's saved on the servers. It was just a little stressful since we're still working on that Go Big campaign." Go Big Sports was Shake Design's largest client to date and a lot of resources and man power were being utilized to make sure the company was happy. We were in the middle of a complete brand over-haul as well as a new webstore design. The entire project was already a daunting and exhausting task, but as head of the team, I was under extra pressure to perform. The death of a computer was not a huge deal in the grand scheme of things, but it was added strain to an already stressful day.

Henry pressed a soft kiss to my neck, pulling me away from thoughts of work. "Hey, come back. No more thinking about work for the rest of the night," he murmured.

"Easier said than done," I said and was about to launch into the next day's long to-do list when water was suddenly pelting me on my stomach, due south.

"Open up," he said, nudging my legs apart with his foot. He brought a palm to my back and bent me over, exposing my backside as I planted my hands on the wall. "I'm going to make you forget about everything for the next half hour."

"Half hour? We'll run out of hot water long before—Oh!"

He changed the spray to a stronger, more concentrated stream and aimed it directly onto my clit.

"I love this showerhead," I said between moans.

"Me too." The water disappeared and was replaced by the wholly different sensation of his tongue sliding between my folds.

I peeked between my legs and saw him palming his erection as he lapped at me, sending an energizing jolt of desire through my core. "I want you."

He stood up and loomed over me. "You want me where?" he asked, pumping his length along the crevice of my ass.

I reached back and wrapped my fingers around him, guiding him to my entrance. "In here, filling me up."

"Slow or rough?"

I sat back against his hip and sighed as the head of his cock penetrated my cleft. "Rough. Hard."

He gripped me around the chest and with one swift thrust was completely inside me. "Like this?" he rasped against my ear, sliding out and driving home again, causing me to lurch forward from the force.

"Hell yes."

He obliged, kissing along my neck and nipping my skin with his teeth as he continued the assault. He kept murmuring sweet and nasty things as he pummeled me, the noisy slapping of skin intermingling with the sound of running water.

I closed my eyes and surrendered, content to give Henry full control of my pleasure. The man did not steer me wrong; he knew all the right ways to touch me so that I was racing toward orgasm, my muscles coiling, grasping for a tighter hold. When he held the strong stream of water against my clit once again, I broke apart. "Henry," I hissed as my inner walls convulsed around his shaft.

"Here," he ordered, pressing the showerhead into my hand. With both hands free, he gripped my hips and drove into me faster.

I flicked the water setting to a softer stream and pointed it between my legs and directly onto his balls. He made a pained noise, but when I pulled it away, he growled, "Keep it there. Keep it there. Don't stop. Fuuuuck . . ." His hips bucked wildly as he climaxed, thrusting into me one last time.

I could feel his heartbeat thudding on my back as he gasped

against my ear. It took him several long seconds but when he recovered, he pulled out and reached for the shampoo bottle.

My scalp tingled as his fingers massaged the shampoo through my hair, turning all the bones in my body to jelly. I leaned my head into his firm but gentle touch and sighed with pleasure.

Then he soaped up the loofah and washed my entire body, spending a long time washing between my legs. I noticed his mind was no longer on cleansing when his fingers probed me, sliding inside and finding that sensitive nub.

"I can't . . . I have no energy to come again."

"I'm just making sure you're completely clean," he said, his fingers rubbing and kneading. He brought his mouth down to mine and kissed me, his tongue bringing me back to life.

I squeezed at his fingers, feeling warmth spread throughout me, and inexplicably, I started to come again. I leaned against the tile wall when my legs buckled, Henry's hand keeping me from crumbling to my knees.

When the last of my orgasm subsided, he turned off the water and reached for a towel then handed it to me.

"I don't think I have any energy left for work," I said, wondering how I was going to manage drying my hair let alone do anything else.

"That's the point. You go to work early, get home late, and then do more work until nearly midnight." He swept me off my feet and carried me to the bed. "Tonight, you deserve some rest."

"I'm still wet," I laughed, trying to sit up.

He held me down by the shoulders, a laugh playing in his eyes. "Then we shall have to dry you off, won't we?" he said and swept his tongue along the length of my stomach, lapping up water droplets.

I grabbed the back of his head, too worn out to do anything but moan. "You're going to give me death by orgasm."

He looked up and grinned. "Can't think of a better way to go."

"Sherman." The deep voice of my boss, Conor McDermott, echoed over the block of cubicles as he stood outside his office with his hands on his waist. "My office."

Kari, a senior designer on my team, peered over the wall. "What did you do?"

"I have no clue." I saved my file, straightened my blouse, and prepared myself for what was to come.

When I entered his glass-walled office, Conor was leaning against his desk, his hands folded across his chest. "Sit down, please."

I perched on the curvy chair made out of one thin piece of wood, uncomfortably close to where Conor stood. The Irishman was in his midthirties and had dark auburn hair and lovely green eyes, which were currently fixed on my face.

"My last name is Logan now," I said, trying to diffuse the tension. It was no secret that Conor was a ladies' man with a natural charisma that made him seem flirty without trying. Being the CEO of Shake Design, he wore expensive suits but rarely shaved so that he was a compounding mixture of crispness and scruff, professionalism and impudence. It was no wonder women fell at his feet.

"I'm sorry, I forget sometimes," he said with a slight Irish brogue. He crossed one foot over the other and regarded me for another few uncomfortable seconds.

I tried to hold his gaze but felt a little strange doing so, as if simply finding another man attractive was an act of adultery.

"Are you happy here?" he asked, a question that took several seconds to sink in.

"Yes, very." I raised an eyebrow. "Why?"

"I've been keeping an eye on you. You've been working really long hours, showing a lot of dedication to Go Big. I just wanted to make sure that you're happy." He gave me a roguish grin. "Basically, I want to make sure no other companies try to steal you away."

I returned his smile. "I'm happy to hear that."

"So what can I do to make your life easier?"

"Make the Go Big execs agree on everything from here on out?"

He chuckled. "I suspect nothing short of a miracle can do that."

"Can I have one more designer on the team then?" I asked.

He let out a long breath through his nose. "I was afraid you'd say that. I can't do that, however, as all of our designers are busy with other projects. But I will look into hiring a freelancer."

I shrugged. "How about a slushee machine for the break room?" I joked.

"That I can probably arrange," he said with a deep laugh.

"How about giving us all the entire week of Thanksgiving off?"

"Now you're just pushing your luck."

I shrugged. "Worth a try."

Still smiling, he stood up and motioned to the door. "Well, if there's anything else you need—within reason—my door is always open."

"Thank you, I will keep that in mind," I said, walking past him and catching a whiff of his expensive cologne.

"Elsie," he said with a smile that could have held a thousand meanings. "I'm glad you're on my team."

"Me too," I said quickly and walked out, feeling a little out of sorts. When I got back to my desk, my phone immediately rang.

"Psst," Kari said into the other line. I stood up to look over the cubicle wall and found Kari holding the phone against her ear and using a hand to cover her mouth. "What did Sex on a Stick want?" she whispered, winking up at me.

I snickered. "Nothing. Just making sure I was content here."

"So he didn't bend you over his desk and spank you for not getting those mock-ups done to perfection?"

I sat back down, stifling a surprised laugh. Kari and I had spent many hours together in the past several months and had become good friends. One thing I really loved about her was her unabashed love for erotic romance novels, one about a troubled billionaire in particular. "You are a sexual harassment lawsuit waiting to happen," I said in a low voice. "Conor is *not* Christian Grey."

"But he could be," Kari said, giggling. "You never know what he's like behind office doors."

"He's got glass walls."

"So he's an exhibitionist too."

"You're crazy."

"You love it."

"You're projecting your fantasies onto a mere mortal."

"Give me one night with him and I'll turn him into a god."

"You're nuts." I wished her luck with her plans of seduction and hung up, still laughing to myself even after I went back to work.

————

That night, Henry was already starting dinner when I walked in the house.

I kicked off my shoes and washed my hands at the sink before standing on my toes to give him a kiss. I pulled away, noticing the redness around his eyes. "What happened?" I asked as I started to chop the bell peppers by the cutting board.

"We were pepper sprayed at school today," he said, pouring oil into the wok. "We stood there one by one and got sprayed in the face. It was . . . not fun."

I looked down at the ingredients on the counter. "So you didn't get enough peppers? You wanted to eat them for dinner too?"

He shrugged. "Next week we get Tasered."

"Where? In the balls?"

He coughed. "Let's hope not. Ugh, that sounds like the worst pain known to man."

"Then we can have Rocky Mountain oysters that night," I teased, jabbing him in the side.

"You're sick," he said, pulling me in for a noogie and making a mess of my hair.

"Stop that," I said and held up a sliver of pepper. "I'll spray you again if you're not careful."

He held his hands up in defeat. "I surrender."

The good mood continued on into dinner as we talked about our days while eating chicken stir-fry. I knew it wouldn't always be like this, that once he became a LEO—law enforcement officer—our times together would be unpredictable at best. So I held on to the moment, completely immersing myself in the simple joy of being with the love of my life, and I tried to avoid thinking about the future.

Henry and I didn't go back to California for Thanksgiving. Instead, we spent a fair amount of the day in bed, snuggling while watching the Macy's Thanksgiving Day Parade on television. There was something romantic about spending the first holidays alone together as newlyweds and starting our own traditions in our new home.

"How long until we eat?" Henry asked, his arm around me.

I stretched my limbs, straightening my toes and fingers. "The turkey's not even done thawing yet. And we haven't cooked anything else."

"But. I'm. So. Hungry," he said, grabbing his stomach for effect.

I laughed at his theatrics and pinched at his side, unable to find an ounce of fat anywhere. "Poor baby, starving on Thanksgiving."

"It wouldn't be the first time," he said. "Remember that Thanksgiving when we went skiing and Jason forgot to make restaurant reservations?"

I nodded, feeling a sudden rush of emotion at the mention of my brother and that time long ago before death and heartache had touched our lives. Jason, Henry, and I had all gone to Vail, Colorado, to spend the holiday weekend skiing. Without dinner reservations, we had ended up going to the grocery store and buying bread and sliced turkey, eating the sandwiches in our hotel room instead.

"How could I forget? Jason poured jarred gravy on his sandwich thinking it would taste good. It was nasty but he ended up eating that sandwich anyway," I said, laughing as the memory of my brother filled me with warmth.

"I tried it. It wasn't so bad," Henry said. "Though it would have been better if we'd had a microwave to warm it up in."

"No way. It was gross."

"That was a fun vacation," he said, his voice taking on a wistful tone.

"Yeah it was." I sighed. "I miss him."

Henry cleared his throat and turned his attention back to the television, only grunting out a soft, "Yeah." But despite his nonchalant attitude, I knew he still missed his best friend. He and my older brother, Jason, had grown up together; they had gone through ROTC, college, and even the Air Force together. Jason was a part of Henry as much as he was a part of me, and even now, nearly six years after Jason's death, his memory was like a phantom limb, a daily reminder of the person we'd loved and lost.

Sharing the death of a brother—whether he was by blood or by bond—bound Henry and me together, made certain that we were always linked by that common loss.

Determined not to keep dwelling on the past, I slid out of bed and pulled on some yoga pants and a T-shirt, and twisted my hair up into a bun. "Come on, let's get cooking."

He was pulling on a pair of gray Air Force sweat pants when the phone rang. He read the name on the caller ID before answering. "Hello?"

I raised my eyebrows at him, trying to decipher by Henry's tone if the caller was my mom, or maybe Julie, the woman my brother had intended to marry.

"Bergen!" Henry said, his voice taking on the brash tone he used with his male friends. "What the hell are you up to, man?"

Satisfied the call wasn't for me, I went downstairs to start preparing the food. Several minutes later, Henry followed. "That was my old buddy Bergen. We were stationed together in Korea," he said, standing by the counter and snapping the green beans with his fingers.

I slipped my hand inside the turkey, reaching around for the elusive giblet packet. "Where the hell is it?" I mumbled, grimacing from the cold, clammy things I was touching.

"Is it wrong that I find your turkey fisting incredibly hot?"

"You should see what I can do with a duck," I grumbled, my fingers making contact with something plastic.

"Please tell me it rhymes with 'cluck.'"

I came up with the plastic package and threw it into the sink. "What's Bergen up to today?" I asked, placing the small turkey inside the pan and rubbing two entire packets of French-onion-soup mix all over it, a trick I'd learned from my mom.

"He's driving through Denver on the way to Colorado Springs. Do we have enough food for another person?"

"Oh definitely," I said, helping him with the green beans once the turkey was in the oven. "You want to invite him over for dinner?"

He grinned sheepishly. "Already did," he said and crunched on a green bean.

———

Several hours later, the doorbell rang while I was still getting ready. I could hear Henry greeting his friend downstairs, their deep, masculine voices echoing through the house.

I hurriedly dressed then applied my makeup. I looked at myself in the mirror, trying to decide what to do with my hair, but laziness won out so I just pinned it up and left a few tendrils down. "Good enough," I said and went to meet our guest.

Bergen, a tall man with beautiful chocolate skin, a shaved head, and a bright smile stood up when I entered the room. "You must be the lovely Mrs. Logan," he said, holding out a hand. "Henry has been talking about you for years."

I smiled and returned the handshake. "And you must be the mysterious Mr. Bergen."

"Major Jackson Bergen, ma'am." He waited until I sat down before following suit.

"I'm glad you could make it, but if you call me 'ma'am' again, you're not getting any pie."

"Yes, sir," he said with a tiny salute, the skin around his eyes crinkling as he smiled.

"At ease." I grabbed Henry's beer from the coffee table and took a sip.

"Hey now," Henry said and touched his cold fingers to my neck in retaliation.

"Whipped," Bergen coughed into his hand.

Henry laughed, leaning back into the couch and resting his arm across my shoulders. "I guess I am."

Bergen smiled. "That's good to hear, man."

We ate our Thanksgiving meal at around four thirty p.m., passing serving dishes around the table wordlessly as we heaped food on our plates. Years of cooking with my mom had conditioned me to prepare more food than was necessary so we thankfully had enough to share with even a large man with an equally large appetite.

"So, Bergen," I said after we'd been eating for several minutes. "What was Henry like at Osan?"

The two men exchanged a quick look that sent my spidey senses tingling. "He was a mess when he first got there," Bergen said nonchalantly. "He was one depressing peckerhead, always talking about the meaning of life and finding oneself."

"Ah, I wasn't so bad," Henry said, washing his food down with beer. "So anyway, what are you doing in Colorado Springs?"

Bergen took the hint and moved on, talking about his new job at NORAD, the U.S. North American Aerospace Defense Command. I sat back and listened, chewing thoughtfully and watching Henry's face as they exchanged stories. Something about the way he talked—carefully, with every word thought out—gave me the feeling that Henry was being extra cautious about what was being said.

There was something the man wasn't telling me and I, being who I was, intended to find out what that was.

————

After dinner, Bergen and Henry cleaned up while I was banished to the living room for some R and R. I turned on the television and burrowed under a blanket on the couch in a pleasant state of drowsiness.

My eyes were starting to get heavy when I remembered something. With great effort, I pushed up off the couch to remind Henry to put the pie in the oven but the sound of their hushed conversation froze me where I stood around the corner.

"She doesn't know about what happened at Osan," Henry said in a low voice, almost inaudible under the sound of running water.

"You never told her?"

"No. It's not exactly something you want to tell your wife, you know?"

I entered the kitchen, deciding that getting the answer directly from the horse's mouth was a better alternative to eavesdropping. "What is this big secret?" I asked the two men, who were behind the sink with identical looks of *busted* written all over their faces.

Bergen took a deep breath. "I need to use the restroom," he said and left the room, not bothering to slow down or ask for directions.

I folded my arms across my chest, staring down my husband even as he towered over me.

He scratched his forehead. "It's not a big deal."

"Then why are you keeping it from me?"

His jaw tightened and his eyes turned wary, reminding me of that same stranger who came back from a six-month deployment to Afghanistan. "I'm not keeping it from you to hurt you, okay?" he said, his voice taking on a frustrated edge. "It has nothing to do with you."

"Really, Henry?" I asked. I glanced down the hall to make sure our guest was still out of earshot. "This is how it's going to be again?"

He ran a palm across his scalp, a nervous habit that persisted even without his long hair. "There are some things that I can't tell you, Els."

"Is it classified?"

He blinked a few times then said, "No."

"Then why can't you tell me?"

"Because it's personal."

"I'm your wife. I think I've earned personal."

"There are some things between us that need to be kept secret."

"Why? What's the purpose of that?" I asked. "I tell you everything."

He latched on to that subject with gusto. "Am I supposed to believe that you've told me every little thing about you, every shameful detail of your past?"

"Yes, for the most part." I shook my head. "Anyway, this isn't about me. This is about you keeping secrets again."

He dodged around the counter and came toward me with an exasperated look. "Els, can we please just drop it for now and enjoy the rest of the day?" he asked, rubbing my arms.

"Why can't you just tell me? Whatever it is, it can't be worse than what my imagination can cook up."

His eyebrows drew together as his eyes roamed over my face. "Yes, it can," he said and left it at that.

———————

Bergen stayed until late into the night. He and Henry pounded beer after beer while they exchanged stories, and by the time midnight rolled around it was clear Bergen wasn't going to be driving anywhere. I offered him the guest bed and he accepted readily, if a little ungracefully, kicking off his shoes before stumbling face-first into the pillows.

Henry was usually a chatty and affectionate drunk, but he sensed my foreboding mood and didn't try anything in bed. I turned away from him, the ball of frustration growing in my belly. How many times had he kept secrets from me only to have them blow up in his face? You'd think he'd have learned his lesson by now.

I stared at the digital numbers on the clock, seething. When I could no longer keep it in, I sat up and shook his shoulder. "Wake up."

He stirred and immediately took in his surroundings. "What? What is it?"

Trying to take advantage of his inebriated state, I said, "Tell me what happened in Korea."

He rolled onto his back with a sigh, covered his eyes with one arm, and groaned. He was quiet for so long, I thought he'd fallen asleep, but he finally gave a deep sigh and said, "I was cornered in an alley and assaulted by a group of men."

"What? Why?"

He shrugged. "Money. Maybe because I looked like a big, dumb American."

"Were you badly hurt?"

"Bad enough to be hospitalized," he said with anger in his voice.

"Where? How?" I couldn't find words beyond those breathless questions. How had I not known that Henry had been so badly hurt? Wouldn't I have felt it in some way?

"I don't want to talk about it anymore, Elsie. Please," he said. "I told you what happened, don't make me relive the entire night again."

I couldn't sleep afterward, imagining Henry being attacked and unable to defend himself, and when my alarm rang at six, I decided that it was just as well because my sleep would no doubt have been riddled with ugly, violent images anyway.

2

A week after Thanksgiving, Henry and I finally had time to put up our Christmas decorations. Since it was our first Christmas together, we went to the store and bought a fake seven-foot tree with twinkle lights already installed. Henry wanted a real tree but for the same reason I disliked receiving fresh flowers, I preferred a tree that would last and didn't need to be replaced year after year.

After we hung the ornaments, we turned off the living-room lights and, with our hot cider in warm mugs, sat on the couch basking in the cheery display.

"You're being really quiet," I said, blowing into my mug.

He dropped a few Hot Tamales candies in his cider, something he and Jason had learned to do back in high school, and stirred it with a teaspoon. He popped a candy in his mouth and chewed for a few moments before saying, "It's nothing."

I squeezed his thigh. "No, tell me."

He chewed some more. "My parents never bought a real tree. They always just threw up that white fake Christmas tree and called it good. I hated it. It was so . . . phony. I always told myself that once I had a house of my own, I would finally get a real tree. Maybe then Christmas would feel real."

The faraway expression on his face as he stared at our impostor tree hurt my heart, making me feel like the most selfish person in the world. Hell, I could be such a self-absorbed jerk sometimes. "Then we'll return the tree," I said, my mind made up. "You'll get your real tree."

He shook his head. "Hell no. That monstrosity was a motherfucker to strap onto the Volvo."

"But I want you to have your fresh tree."

He waved the idea away. "It's okay. Maybe next year."

"Yeah, maybe," I murmured into my mug, unable to quell the feeling that I was the world's worst wife.

————————

The next workday was busy but felt like nothing was getting accomplished. Every time I sat down and began a project, I'd get interrupted without fail and have to solve another problem or put out another fire. The freelancer Conor had hired was not much help either, all ego and no common sense. By eleven, I was already reaching for the bottle of Advil I kept in the top drawer of my desk.

During lunch, I managed to talk Kari into helping me with a personal project that took the entire lunch hour and then some. Thankfully Conor was out of the office for the rest of the day and didn't see us sneaking back to our desks with pine needles still stuck in our hair.

That night, I sat in the darkened living room with a bottle of hard cider and greeted Henry with forced nonchalance when he walked in the door.

"Why is it so dark in here?" he asked, flipping on the switch, filling the room with white light.

I watched his face, waiting until the moment his eyes landed on the tree at the far side of the room. The corner of his mouth twitched as his gaze swung down to me.

"What did you do? That's not our tree."

I took a casual sip of my drink. "I don't know what you mean."

The smile on his face grew. "That's . . . a real tree." He walked over and touched it for confirmation.

"Oh, is it? I hadn't noticed."

He whirled around and took slow, deliberate steps toward the couch. "Did you get me a real tree?" he asked, taking the bottle from my hand and placing it on the coffee table.

I gave up the pretense. "I want you to have the Christmas you've always wanted."

He grabbed my hands and pulled me up off the couch and into his arms. "How did you do this?"

"My friend Kari helped me during our lunch break. She has a pickup truck, so we took the fake tree back and got a new one at the place by the gas station."

He glanced at the tree again, which was already decorated with string lights and ornaments. "You did this? For me?"

"Of course," I said, beaming. "I would only place a tree corpse in our living room for you."

Henry, still smelling like the gym, suddenly scooped me up in his arms and lifted me off the floor. "This is . . . really sweet," he said against my hair. "Thank you."

"You're so welcome," I said. "And oh, Kari said this gives her a free pass on a future speeding or parking ticket."

He chuckled. "I'll see what I can do."

"We should make some popcorn so we can thread it and put it on the tree," I suggested, enjoying the way his face was lit up. "But you should probably take a shower first, buddy."

Halfway up the stairs, he paused and gave me the largest, most boyish smile I had ever seen. I knew in that moment that I would do anything in my power to keep that smile where it belonged.

———

The next morning Conor wandered down our row of cubicles with a stack of manila folders in his hand. He stopped when he caught a glimpse of me and turned around deliberately to give me a second look.

"Top o' the mornin'," I said, tipping my imaginary hat, even as I felt the first stirrings of a headache.

He rolled his eyes at my lame joke then regarded me quietly. "You feeling okay?"

"Do I look that horrible?" I asked, rubbing my eyes.

"No. You're just frowning, like you're really mad at your computer."

I shook my head, pinching the bridge of my nose. "No, just a headache."

He rumpled his dark eyebrows, which were the same auburn as the stylishly messy hair on his head. "Does that happen often?"

"No more than usual." I waved his concern away. "Everybody gets headaches."

"No they don't," he said. "I almost never get headaches. When I do it's because something's off."

I sneaked a peek at his face and saw that he actually looked genuinely concerned. I supposed that was his charm, his way of making it seem as if you're the most important person in the world, at least for that moment. And for my part, I felt like I needed to ease his mind. "I think it might be my eyes. I've been meaning to see an optometrist one of these days."

"Yes, definitely do that," he said. "Go today. You can have the afternoon off."

"I can't," I said, gesturing with my hands at the mess in front of me. Somewhere underneath the folders, notes, and papers was my desk, I was sure of it. "I have a ton of work."

"Email it to me and I'll get it done," he said. He smacked the top of the cubicle wall and pointed at me. "Then it's settled. You are seeing an optometrist today."

He started to walk away, his attention somewhere else. My fleeting time in the warmth of his regard was now over. "Thank you," I called out, reaching for my phone to search for an optometrist nearby.

He didn't turn around. He just threw a wave over his shoulders and continued on his way.

———————

Later that day, I went home and logged onto the company server to look over the work that Conor had done. True to his word, he had completed my list of tasks. I was struck then by how lucky I was to have a boss who not only cared for his employees but helped out with the workload whenever necessary.

I left the home office when I heard the shower turn off in our bathroom, and walked to the bedroom with the new pair of glasses in my hand.

Henry was naked when he came out of the bathroom, affording me ample view of his muscled body before slipping into his favorite pajama pants. He kissed me on the cheek, patting my butt through my pencil skirt. "You had a meeting with a bigwig today?"

"Yeah, this morning. How did you know?"

"You always wear that skirt with a nice shirt or sweater when you're meeting with a client."

I laughed. Even after all this time, he still surprised me with how observant he was. "True. I didn't think the company would appreciate me wearing jeans to a meeting."

He gave me a sliding look that warmed every inch of skin from my face to my feet. "You underestimate the power of your jeans," he said, his voice taking on a husky quality. "Or maybe just what's underneath them."

"You are a hornball today, aren't you?" One glance down at the bulge forming in his pants confirmed as much.

He grinned without shame, advancing toward me with one eyebrow raised. He grabbed me around the waist and pressed a kiss to my neck, tickling me with his five-o'clock scruff.

I squirmed out of his grasp. "I want to show you my new glasses." I sat down on the bed and slipped them on, feeling a tad insecure. "Turns out I'm a little nearsighted, which was causing the headaches."

Henry said nothing, only stared at me with a dumbfounded expression on his handsome face.

"What?"

"Stand up," he said. I went to kick off my heels when he said, "No, keep those on."

I stood up, putting my hands on my hips. I raised my eyebrows in question.

"Hold these," he said, coming closer and handing me a pile of law enforcement books from his bedside table. "Hold them like you're about to put them back onto the shelves."

"Oh my God," I said, laughing. "You have a librarian fetish!"

He grinned and cocked his head. "I didn't. Until now." He came closer and his blue eyes flew all over my face, making me flush with his intensity. "I didn't think it was possible, but you are even sexier with those on. Can you frown and pretend I'm returning my books a week late?"

I laughed and smacked the pile of books against his chest. "You are one strange man."

He gripped me by the elbows and pulled my body against his. "Go on, Mrs. Logan," he said huskily. "Recite the Dewey Decimal System for me."

The laughter died in my throat when I felt his hard length against my abdomen. He reached between us and plucked the books out of my hand, flinging them onto the bed.

Without warning, he bent down and swept me up in his arms, walking out of our bedroom at a fast clip. He entered the office and deposited me in front of the large bookcase that took up nearly the entire wall.

"I was wondering if you could help me find a book," he said, his eyes glittering with mischief.

I acted along. This was not the first time we'd played pretend. "What can I help you find?" I asked, adjusting my glasses.

"I was looking for a book called . . ." He looked up at the top shelf and said, "*Adaptive Web Design.*"

"Ah, I believe I know where that is," I said, turning around and reaching up to retrieve the book, standing on tiptoe and lifting one foot back.

Immediately I felt his hot palms land on the back of my thighs. I continued to stretch as his hands slid upward and under the hem of my skirt.

"Now, I don't think that's appropriate library behavior," I said in a prim tone.

I felt his large frame looming over me as he pulled on the stretchy material of my skirt, gathering it up and over my ass to reveal my black thong.

"Forget the book, I want something else," he rasped against my ear then landed a quick slap on one cheek that sent a throbbing ache right to my crotch. I arched my back and pressed my ass into his groin, noting his rock-hard erection in his drawstring pants. His hands traveled up, skimming along my waist and up my arms. He gripped my wrists, holding them above my head, trapping my over-heating body against the bookshelves.

"Keep your hands up here," he said, hooking my fingers onto the highest shelf before his hands moved back down, sliding my thong down my legs. He traced a finger from the base of my spine to the crease of my butt and down to my slick folds. "Are you always so turned on, Mrs. Logan?" he asked, slipping one finger inside me.

I closed my eyes and nodded, squeezing at him.

"Do books turn you on?" he asked.

"No," I breathed. I twisted around, keeping my hands on the shelf above me. "You do."

He pulled his pants down, revealing his engorged shaft. I glanced down at it, licked my lips, and swung my gaze back up. His face was dark with desire and his chest was rising and falling. "Do you want me to fuck you right here in the library, Mrs. Logan?"

I spread my legs apart. "Yes, please."

With that, he grasped my ass and lifted me up, plunging into me with a loud groan. His fingers dug into my skin as he held himself still for a few moments before sliding almost entirely out then entering me again. He moved slowly, torturing me with pleasure and anticipation. Each drawn-out stroke strummed against my sensitive nerve endings, slowly but surely driving me to insanity.

I opened my mouth to speak, to ask him to speed up, but only a sigh escaped when he hit a particularly sensitive part. I could feel his ragged breaths against my cheek, smell our arousal in the air. I pulled myself higher on the bookcase and wrapped my legs around his waist, meeting him thrust for thrust.

"You feel so incredible," he rasped.

I closed my eyes and imagined my body as a piece of string, stretching, stretching, until I could bear no more. I snapped, throwing my head back as I cried out, my sex pulsing as he continued the languid assault. My orgasm went on and on, one long bout of ecstasy. Just when I was starting to recover, he slipped his hand between us and massaged my clit, sending a jolt of shock and pleasure through my entire body. My head fell onto his shoulder as I came again, my arms trembling from the strain.

Then he sped up, driving into me with force until he climaxed.

With several long groans, he pushed up from the floor and speared me with deep little thrusts from his hips.

When he was done, he set me back down on my feet and adjusted my skirt. "Thank you for helping me find that book, Mrs. Logan," he said between breaths as he kissed my neck. "I'll be back to return it tomorrow."

3

As the Go Big website launch neared, the days got longer. One of our designers left for a change of career, and the rest of my five-person team was left to pick up the slack. A week before launch, we stayed at work until late into the night, scrambling to do perfect work, a fact that didn't escape Conor's attention. Even with the help of the freelancer—who was nearly useless—Conor stayed each night, taking on any excess work that needed done, even ordering dinner for everyone.

It was on a Tuesday afternoon, a week before Christmas, when Go Big signed off on the project and the website was softly launched, giving us a few days to troubleshoot any problems. The grand opening occurred on Friday and proved a rousing success, impressing even the surliest Go Big executive.

On Saturday night, Conor rented out a bar in downtown Denver for the annual Christmas party. After spending a much-needed day in bed together, Henry and I arrived at the bar at six o'clock to find it had been transformed into someone's idea of a winter wonderland on crack. Twinkle lights hung in thick tangles from the ceiling, a large Christmas tree with gifts underneath sat in the corner, and the floor was covered in something white and crunchy that was supposed to resemble snow. Off to the side was a long white table covered in staple holiday fare, complete with a large honey ham in the center.

"Hello!" Conor called from across the room. He came over, looking very casual in a black sweater that clung to his frame and a pair of dark jeans. He held out a Santa hat, which Henry accepted. "Merry Christmas."

"This is my husband, Henry," I said, waving my hands between the two men. "This is my boss, Conor."

Two strong, masculine hands shook.

"Nice to meet you, man," Henry said, perching the hat on his head without an ounce of self-consciousness. "I can't tell you how happy I am that the website is finally done and I can have my wife back."

Conor grinned, oozing with effortless charm. "Elsie is a wonder, a godsend. You are one very lucky man."

Henry beamed down at me and squeezed me to his side. "Don't I know it."

My face warmed with discomfort as both men turned to look at me. "I need a drink," I declared, inexplicably uncomfortable with my husband meeting my charismatic boss.

Conor waved a hand to the bar and nodded to the bartender. "Darius will take care of you."

When we reached the bar at the other side of the room and sat down, I was finally able to breathe a sigh of relief.

"How old is Conor?" Henry asked as he tried his beer.

I glanced at my boss, who was greeting people at the door. "I think he's thirty-five?"

"And he built the company on his own?"

I nodded. "His family immigrated from Ireland when he was in his twenties, and he started the company from his basement with a friend. When it got bigger, he bought his friend out and has run it by himself ever since."

"That's impressive."

I noticed Kari arriving so I twisted around in my seat and waved her over. "You look so nice," I said, noting that she had taken the time to curl her long brown hair and was actually wearing makeup, not that she really needed it. Kari was one of those effortlessly attractive women, with her Swedish side lending her incredible bone structure and her Salvadoran side giving her beautiful caramel skin and dark features. I'd asked once why she always downplayed her looks. "Because I'd rather be regarded for my work than for my appearance," she'd replied.

Now, looking at her in her tight jeans and slinky tank top, it appeared that, for the time being at least, she was ready to be regarded for something other than work.

"Henry, meet my partner in crime, Kari," I said, motioning to her.

"Well, technically you're my boss," Kari said, shaking Henry's hand then taking the stool next to mine.

I tossed a dismissive wave in the air. "I see you more as my right-hand man."

Kari's eyes flashed with amusement as she gave Henry a pointed once-over with one eyebrow raised. "Now I see why your left hand is always so busy . . ."

Henry laughed. "In any event, thank you for helping with the tree."

"No problem," she said then winked. "Thanks for helping me out of a future speeding ticket." She twisted on her barstool and turned her attention elsewhere, to the Irishman in a black sweater across the room.

I leaned across and whispered to her, "You're trying to get laid, aren't you?"

She turned to me with wagging eyebrows. "Laid across his knees? Definitely."

"Wouldn't it be such a surprise if he was actually just vanilla?"

She rubbed her hands together. "All the better. I'd mold him into my perfect Dom." She looked around the room and gasped. "Okay, who the hell is that?"

I followed her gaze and found her staring at a mountain of a guy with curly black hair down to his shoulders and a dark beard. "That's Julian, Conor's friend," I said. "He came by the office last week, don't you remember?"

She shook her head. "I think I'd remember someone who could make my ovaries explode."

"Maybe you'd gone home already." I nudged her in the side. "So go talk to him."

"Hello, have you met me? I'm Kari, all bark and no bite," she said keeping her eyes trained on Julian in his thin, gray shirt, his sleeves pushed up to reveal black tattoos swirling down one arm.

"Hello, have you *seen* you?" I asked. "You just have to walk by him and *his* ovaries will explode."

"What if he's a total dillhole? I don't want to ruin the fantasy," she said. "Or worse, he could have a high-pitched, nasally voice. Can you imagine him saying my name in that voice? *Kaaari*."

I placed a palm on her back and pushed her off the stool. "Then put a ball gag in his mouth. Just go."

She took one last gulp of liquid courage and, with one more fortifying intake of breath, walked off.

I turned back to my husband, who was having a conversation about hops with the bartender, and gave him a peck on the cheek, glad that I was done with the dating scene and the uncertainty that came with it.

A little while later after a trip to the bathroom, I came upon Henry talking with a group of people, that ridiculous Santa hat still on his head. I watched him from several feet away, admiring his utter confidence, the way he stood tall and relaxed as if he had easy command of the entire room. He had a way of talking to people as if he was genuinely interested in what they had to say, and when he smiled, I noticed Shelly, one of the junior designers, sigh a little. I couldn't blame her. Some days I still found myself struck that this beautiful man was now my husband.

"So that's the guy who changed your name," a voice whispered much too close to my ear.

I spun around and away, my heart thumping in my chest. "You scared me, Conor."

He stuck his hands in his pockets and grinned, setting off those deep dimples in his cheeks. Judging from the slight droop of his eyelids he'd had a few too many trips to Darius's corner of the room. "Sorry," he said, looking anything but. "I just never pictured you with a man that ... wholesome," he said, his eyes watching me closely, but whatever reaction he was looking for, I gave him nothing. "Put some glasses on him and he could be Clark Kent."

I glanced at Henry. "Sure. Why not."

Conor cleared his throat. "I just wanted to thank you for all of your hard work the past few months. The Go Big execs are thrilled. They are already reporting huge sales through the website."

"You're welcome. Thank you for giving me and my team the opportunity to prove ourselves."

He held out a white envelope. "Here, I wanted to give you your Christmas bonus personally."

I looked inside and found a check with way too many numbers. "Wow, thank you. That's very generous."

"Nothing you don't deserve." He fixed that intense stare on my face. "I've enjoyed working with you."

"You too," I said uncomfortably. I started to walk away when he said, "Would you like to dance?"

I glanced across the room. "I'd rather not."

"Why not? Are you afraid of me?"

I took a deep breath. "No, but I'm married."

"Dancing with another male is not considered cheating, you know," he said. "Besides, your husband is right there. He can see everything."

"That's precisely why I wouldn't do it."

"But you would dance with me if he weren't in attendance?" Conor asked with a teasing grin.

"That's not what I meant."

Conor held up his hands. "Relax. I'm just teasing." Suddenly, he looked over my shoulder and gave a friendly nod before turning away.

"Everything okay?"

I spun around to face my husband, my heart pounding in my chest. "Yeah, fine."

He looked toward the bar, where Conor was ordering another drink. "He has a thing for you, doesn't he?"

I sputtered at Henry's words but I couldn't deny them. "I don't know. Maybe." I took a peek at Henry's face, afraid of what I'd see there. "You're not worried, are you?"

His face was a picture of serenity as he gathered me close to his body. "No," he said simply, swaying with the music.

I gaped up at him. Was this the same man who'd been furious with himself a year ago because I'd dated and slept with another guy? "Really?"

He cupped the sides of my neck with his hands, his thumbs rubbing along my jaw. "No man can take you away from me."

A little surprised by his overabundance of confidence, I said, "Oh, is that right?"

He leaned down and pressed a soft kiss on the side of my neck, lingering to nibble at my earlobe. "That's right. You're mine. And if anyone tries to steal you away, I will shank a bitch."

I burst out laughing, remembering my words from what seemed

like a lifetime ago. "And what would you do if I told you that I'd spent every night having sex with him for the past few weeks?"

He grinned with a dark expression. "Then I'd have to punish you. Perhaps lay you across my knees and spank you for telling lies."

"Like you could." I smacked him on the arm, frustrated that I couldn't break through his confident facade. "Just once I'd like to see you get jealous."

All amusement slid off his face. "No, you don't. And I hope you never give me a reason to be." He kissed me then, taking no notice of anyone else in the room, tilting my head up to deepen the contact. "I trust you, Elsie," he said, his lips brushing lightly across the length of my jaw.

Only later did I realize that he was not so unshakable, that his actions, however innocent they seemed at the time, had branded me in the eyes of everyone at that party, letting all know that I was completely and utterly spoken for.

4

From a faraway place, I heard Henry's voice. "Merry Christmas," he said and I felt the tickle of his scruff on my neck as he nuzzled into me. I stretched, enjoying the sweet spot between realms, when the magic of dreams spills over a little into the real world. In that perfect moment, the entire planet was quiet and in complete harmony.

We made slow love that morning, in that sleepy state when it's hard to be sure you're not just dreaming the sensations, but the orgasms were real and so too was the man who put my pleasure above his own.

A few hours later, when we finally untangled ourselves, I pulled on a T-shirt and yoga pants and retrieved the cordless phone.

"You needed to get dressed to talk on the phone?" Henry teased, sitting up with a yawn and grabbing his laptop.

"Do you talk to your parents on the phone naked?" I asked as I dialed.

"I don't talk to my parents at all."

My mom answered after three rings, leaving me no time to dwell on Henry's words. I wished her—and my dad, who joined on the other line—a merry Christmas and apologized for not coming home for the holidays.

"Oh, we completely understand, honey," my mom said. "You have your own traditions to start."

"Tell Henry congratulations on his graduation," Dad said. "I'm proud of that boy."

"That's Officer Boy in a month," I said, grinning when Henry looked up. We chatted for nearly half an hour before we said good-bye. I hung up and held out the phone.

"What?" Henry asked, looking as if I was handing him a turd.

"Your turn."

"Um, no. We don't do that in our family."

I shook the phone. "Come on, Henry. If you want to fix this rift, then it's clear you need to make the first move."

"How many first moves do I need to make?"

"Just call them, please. It's Christmas," I said. "At the very least to find out if they are going to come to your graduation."

He sighed through his nose but took the phone anyway.

While he dialed, I padded downstairs, eager to put my Christmas gift to use. I turned on the single-serve coffeemaker—the fancy kind that used pods—and slid a cup underneath, excited at the prospect of never having to buy or empty coffee filters again.

When I came back upstairs with two mugs in hand, I found Henry staring hard at the computer with the phone lying on my pillow.

"What did they say?" I asked, handing him his favorite Air Force mug.

"They're not coming."

"Oh."

"Mom's got a big case she's working on and Dad apparently is trying to land this one job for the municipality."

His facial features were in neutral, but I knew Henry better than anyone, better than himself sometimes. "I'm sorry," I said.

"Don't be. I'm not surprised. The real surprise would have been if they'd said they were coming." He looked over at me and gave me a reassuring smile. "It's fine, Els. Really."

"It's *not* fine," I said, unable to quell the frustration, wishing I could shake some sense into his parents. "They ought to see what their son has accomplished. You're one of the top three cadets, for crying out loud. You've been offered a job at the highly competitive Denver PD. I don't know what else would impress them enough to get their asses out here. If you were elected president, would they be too busy to attend the inauguration?"

He set the laptop aside and took my face in his hands. "It's okay," he said, pressing a kiss to my forehead. "Simmer down."

I huffed, doubly angry that he'd dealt with it for so long that their indifference no longer fazed him. Henry worked his ass off for the past twenty-seven weeks; he deserved to have someone there for him, someone who would be proud of the man he'd become.

Struck with an idea, I took the phone and headed out of the room.

"Where are you going?" he called out.

"I'm just making a quick call," I said, heading to the office. I shut the door behind me and started dialing, having already decided on what I was going to spend my Christmas bonus money.

A while later, I came back to find Henry still playing on the computer. He looked up when I entered the bedroom. "Where did you go?"

"I was just making some calls," I said casually.

"To?"

"A few other people." I went into the closet and retrieved my gift, hoping it would redirect his curiosity. I handed Henry the large package and he ripped into it with the enthusiasm of a child.

Inside was a large shadow box with black velvet backing. I had arranged his medals, ribbons, unit patches, and coins around a portrait of him standing in front of the American flag in his dress blues.

He stared at it for a long time, his gaze landing on every piece of his history, reminders of his past life as an officer in the Air Force. He took a deep breath before looking up at me. "Thank you. This is . . . awesome."

"You're welcome. It took me forever to find all of those things. You're not the best at organization." I sat beside him as we looked at the frame again, at the handsome officer in the photograph, his smile still untouched by death and loss. If only I could go back in time and tell that fresh-faced young man that despite the loss he will suffer—his best friend, his girl, his sense of self—he will fight back and find a way to make his life right again.

But if he had known that back then we might not be here today. Sometimes the past is better off left untouched.

The day of Henry's graduation arrived. I woke up early out of excitement and retrieved a box I'd hidden in my sock drawer. I'd bought it for Christmas but decided that his graduation was a more apt time to give him the gift. I pulled the object out and wrapped my fingers around it, breathing a prayer into it.

I stood over Henry and looked at his naked form through the early light of day, his arms flung over his head. His body was bare— save for the sheet that was strategically covering some parts— affording me the opportunity to study the effects of his workouts. Henry had always been muscular, but since separating from the military, he had lost a little definition and edge. The rigorous schedule of the past several months at the academy, plus the mandatory after-hours workouts, had once again sculpted his body back to glorious definition. Even his face showed the results as his cheeks seemed carved in, his square jaw more prominent.

My roving eyes caught on two thin white scars to the right of his stomach, each about an inch and a half long, but before I could bend down to study them, Henry said, "Pervert."

I tore my eyes away from his muscular body and found him watching me with a sleepy grin.

"But you're welcome to keep looking," he said as he slowly pulled the sheet away from his crotch, revealing his growing erection.

I crawled on the bed and straddled him, resting the heat of my sex right on him. "We don't have time for that," I said, even as I rocked on him a little for torture.

His nostrils flared as he sat up, grabbing me around the waist. "There's always time for that."

I evaded his lips. "I have to give you something."

He raised an eyebrow and glanced down between us.

"No, not that." I held out my open palm to reveal a silver oval medallion with a relief of Saint Michael—patron saint of law enforcement—on the front. "I have a small graduation gift for you." I lifted it by the chain and pulled it over his head, the medallion coming to rest neatly in the ridge between his pecs. The necklace looked at home there, a fitting successor to his dog tags.

"Thank you," he said, studying the medallion.

"You'll need someone to watch over you when I'm not there." I pressed my palm over the oval piece of silver and over his heart, trying to keep from thinking about the reason why he'd need a saint's protection in the first place.

"Els," he said gently, and it was then that I realized my fingers were trembling. He lifted my hand up to his lips and pressed a kiss on each fingertip. "I'll be okay."

I nodded and pushed away all negative thoughts in my head. This was Henry's graduation day. In a week, he'd be starting his new job as a patrol officer at the Denver Police Department. Today was the culmination of several months of hard work; it was a time for celebration, not despair. "Have I told you how proud I am of you?" I asked. "I wish your parents could see you now."

He gave me a rueful smile. "You're the only person I need with me today."

I wrapped my arms around his neck and hugged him tight, smothering my secret smile against his skin.

I left the house early that morning, telling Henry that I needed to run a few errands and I would just meet him at the auditorium. My *errands* involved going to the airport, but he didn't need to know that.

And so it was that at fifteen minutes before the ceremony began, I led the way into the auditorium and found seats close to the center aisle. We didn't have to wait long. Soon after, my guests and I stood up along with the rest of the assembled crowd—all of us nervous with anticipation—when the doors opened.

The silence in the room was thick with pride and deference as the cadets marched in and took their seats on the stage. Henry passed by, flashing me a quick look, then doing a rapid double take when he saw who I had brought with me.

A little hand tugged on my shirt. "Do you think he saw us?" my nephew, Will, whispered.

I winked at him then smiled at his mother and my own parents, all of whom had flown in just for the ceremony. "He did."

The cadets stood still as stone—their spines erect, one hand by their heads in a salute, chins held high—while the flags were brought in.

I couldn't take my eyes away from Henry's rigid form throughout the ceremony. When his name was called, he walked up to the stage and received his certificate from the director, then proceeded down the line to the chief, who presented him with the badge. After every cadet's name had been called, they all stood facing the auditorium and were sworn in.

When families and significant others were invited to come onstage to pin badges on the officers, I stepped out into the aisle and walked up with others. We threw quick smiles at one another, knowing that we'd been chosen as the most important person in our officer's life. We would be there throughout the triumphs and inevitable heartbreak. And as I pinned that silver badge onto Henry's uniform, taking care not to prick him in the chest or put it on crooked, I felt a surge of pride for this man before me.

It struck me then, as he smiled down at me, that it takes a special kind of person to commit oneself to service to one's community or country. It's not easy, and God knows it's not always appreciated, yet there are still people willing to do it.

I just hoped it would be worth it.

After the ceremony, we stood outside in the crowded hallway where people were congratulating and taking pictures with cadets. We craned our heads, looking for Henry but the man was nowhere to be found.

"He knows we're here, right?" my dad asked.

I checked my cell phone and found a text message from him. "He said he'll be right back."

"Maybe he had to pee," Will said. A second later, he squealed as he was scooped up into the air and swung into the arms of a man in black uniform.

"Hey, buddy," Henry said, ruffling Will's blond hair.

When Henry set Will down, I was finally able to get a good look at him, at his black long-sleeved shirt and pants, black tie, duty belt, white gloves, and hat. His airman battle uniform will always hold a special place in my heart but he looked absolutely gallant in this new attire. Damn, the man could sure wear the hell out of a uniform.

"I didn't have to pee," Henry said and glanced at me. "I just had to get something out of the car."

"Elodie, John," Henry said with a wide smile, greeting my parents with hugs as if they were his own. Considering he had spent the better part of his adolescence in our house, they might as well be.

Mom embraced him warmly then held him an arm's length away. "Congratulations, Henry," she said. "Look at you, looking all heroic."

My dad thumped Henry on the back. "So proud of you, son."

"Thank you, sir," Henry said, beaming. I wanted to tell him then that even if he felt like an orphan sometimes, he would always have my parents. Even after all the heartache he put me through the past few years, they had welcomed him back into the fold, never once losing faith in him.

Henry owed a lot to my parents; not least of all is my ability to forgive.

After greeting Julie, Henry wrapped me in a tight embrace. "That was such a surprise, seeing everyone here," he said. "I had the hardest time not looking back during the ceremony to make sure I wasn't just hallucinating."

I beamed. "Surprise."

We took turns taking pictures with the graduate in his starched uniform. I'd never felt prouder as I stood beside him, never felt safer in the fold of his arms.

He pulled me aside as we headed out to the parking lot. "I have something for you," he said, coming to a stop beneath a tree. He reached into his pocket and retrieved a navy blue box. Inside was a ring; a line of tiny blue sapphires held together by a platinum band.

He slipped the ring on my right hand to mirror the one on my left. "The thin blue line," I murmured, my heart racing once again. This was it. From here on out I was an LEO spouse. "Thank you."

He lifted my hand to his lips and pressed a kiss there, so formal and yet so intimate. "I should thank you, for bringing everyone out here. I didn't think I needed anyone else here, but to see them as I walked in, to see the pride in their eyes . . . that was . . . unexpectedly good."

"I wanted you to have family here."

He wrapped an arm around the back of my head and brought me close, pressing his lips to my forehead. "I don't know why you think that I need anything more than you," he said huskily. "But thank you."

Later that night, after our guests had gone to sleep, I lay in bed, staring at the blue ring by the light of the lamp. Up until today I'd been able to push away thoughts of police life, but with that ring on my hand and the graduation certificate in Henry's, I couldn't ignore it anymore. It was true that he wouldn't be deploying for six months at a time anymore but in some ways, this was worse. This was his life now, twenty-four seven. He would be in danger every time he put on that uniform, every time he was dispatched to another scene. Every morning for the rest of our lives, I would kiss him good-bye not knowing if it would be our last.

The sparkly bauble on my hand essentially married me to that life of fear and the unknown; so naturally, the uncertainty scared the shit out of me.

Henry came out of the bathroom after brushing his teeth, wiping at his mouth with the back of his hand. "Do you like it?" he asked, stripping down to his boxer briefs.

I opened my mouth to breathe air to my fears but said instead, "It's beautiful."

He snuggled beside me under the covers, wrapping an arm around my waist. He proved that he wasn't completely oblivious when he said, "I'm going to make you a promise, Els."

I shifted around to face him.

"I know you're worried about my job, but I promise you that I will always do my damnedest to make it home safe each day. I'm not planning on dying anytime soon. I want to spend an entire lifetime with you."

I kissed him, believing in his conviction. But the thing about promises is that, no matter how much you mean them, sometimes fate will find a way to intervene.

5

The next day, my parents borrowed the Volvo to visit with friends in Longmont. Henry challenged Will to a game on Xbox and both males became quickly engrossed, which left Julie and me sitting around with nothing to do.

"You want to go out? Do something?" Julie asked, sitting on the couch beside her son.

Despite feeling sleepy, I agreed. "Please. I need some girl time."

We went to a sushi place in the Cherry Creek Shopping Center, a cute little restaurant with contemporary decor and a reputation for the best sushi in town.

"So how is Will doing in kindergarten?" I asked as we sat down at a table.

"Great. His teacher says he's very smart and that he's really good at math but has a bit of a habit of getting distracted and not finishing his work." She paused. "Was Jason that way?"

"I can't remember. He was smart and good at computers and math, but I don't know about the tendency to daydream."

"Maybe that came from me," she said with a rueful smile. "He's always daydreaming. A few times I've caught him in his room, talking to an invisible friend."

"I had one of those too," I said with a soft chuckle. "His name was Bernie and he was a bus driver," I added, pinching the bridge of my nose.

"What's wrong?"

"The headaches are back. I thought getting glasses would help, but it hasn't really."

Our food arrived then; we picked up our chopsticks and readied our bowls with soy sauce and wasabi. But as I took my first bite, a wave of nausea hit me and I very nearly spit out a piece of my spider roll. I managed to swallow it down with some tea but suddenly the thought of eating another piece made me want to gag.

"Excuse me," I said and practically ran to the bathroom, getting to a stall just in time to vomit rice and fish into the toilet. I retched a second time when a reason for my nausea planted itself in my head and started to grow.

My hands were shaking and my mind was whirling as I stood back up, kicking at the flush handle. I wiped my mouth with hastily ripped pieces of toilet paper and closed my eyes, leaning my throbbing head against the door and cursing fate and her awful timing.

It took me a few minutes to gather my nerves and go back out to the table. Julie's light blue eyes watched me as I sat down. "You okay?" she asked.

"Yeah," I said, busying myself with placing the napkin on my lap just right. "I think I just got a bad batch of sushi."

She plucked a piece off my plate and chewed on it. "The sushi tastes okay."

I lifted the glass up to wash the taste out of my mouth then quickly set it back down when I remembered it was filled with sake.

Julie's eyes got wide. "You're not"—she looked around then mouthed the rest of her words—"pregnant, are you?"

My head spun and I held on to the table for support. "No. I don't think so."

"Have you been dizzy? Tired a lot? Headaches? Peeing more than usual?"

I swallowed hard. I didn't have to say anything; my horrified expression confirmed it.

She covered her mouth with her hand. "Elsie . . ."

"I'm not pregnant. I've been taking my pills religiously!" More or less.

"But there's always a chance with any kind of birth control," she said.

Tears sprung to my eyes, adding to the mounting evidence that I might indeed be with child. "I can't be pregnant," I said, shaking my head. "I mean, Henry and I haven't really discussed having kids. I don't know if we can even afford a child right now."

Julie reached across the table and gripped my hand, trying to hold me together. Maybe because I looked like I was ten seconds away from falling apart.

"And at this stage of my life, I don't really feel like I need a baby, you know? I have Henry, my career, our house. My life is full. My heart is full." I dabbed at my eyes, my stomach a blender of amplified emotions. "I don't know if we're ready."

"I don't think you can ever be ready."

"What if Henry doesn't want this?" The thought horrified me, stopped me dead in my tracks.

"Of course he does. Have you seen him with Will? He *wants* to be a dad."

"What if—"

Julie squeezed my hands. "Look, we'll get a pregnancy test at the drugstore on the way back. Then you'll know the answer either way."

I drank water and chewed on edamame for the rest of the meal. Afterward, we went and bought the pregnancy test. Julie said I needed to use early morning pee to get the best results, which meant I'd have to wait until tomorrow.

"I wish you didn't have to leave this afternoon," I said, staring at the box in my hand, wondering how I was going to survive the next sixteen hours.

"Call me tomorrow and let me know, okay?" she said. "I don't care what time it is in Texas, I want to know the results."

When we got back home, we found Henry and Will still playing. Will jumped up, the controller in his hand, and cried, "I beat Henry! Mom, I beat Henry!"

Henry picked him up and held him upside down by the legs. "You weren't supposed to tell them, you little squirt!" he said, making Will laugh uncontrollably. After setting him down, Henry turned to me. "What do you have there?"

I panicked, clutching the bag tighter in my hand.

Julie, thankfully, was on the ball. "We brought you back some sushi." She carefully reached into the bag for the plastic box that held my nearly untouched spider and Philly rolls.

"Will, you like sushi?" Henry asked.

The boy made a face. "Ew. I don't like fish."

Henry opened the box and showed him the round pieces. "Try one. If you don't like it, I can make you a peanut butter and fish sandwich."

"Ewww!"

"How about a peanut butter and seaweed sandwich then?"

I felt a hitch in my chest as I watched Henry lead Will into the kitchen, but for the life of me, I couldn't decipher what emotion was going through me. All I knew was that tomorrow morning everything was going to change.

———————

"Henry, wake up." I poked him in the arm but he didn't stir. I pushed at his side but still nothing. So I flicked his nose.

His eyes flew open and he sat up, assessing his surroundings. "What's wrong? What's going on?"

"There's no emergency," I said.

He glanced at the clock as he lay back down. "Then why are you waking me up at four in the morning?" he asked with a croaky voice.

"Because of this." My fingers were trembling and my heart was pounding when I pressed the white stick with the pink cap into his hand.

"What . . ." He stared at the object in his hand for long moments. I guess he'd never even seen one before. He rubbed his eyes then looked at it again. "Is this what I think it is?"

My voice trembled when I said, "Yes."

He sat up and stared at that stick, as if he was trying to glare holes into it. His body revealed nothing about his reaction; his breathing was normal, his posture relaxed.

"Henry?" I finally said when the silence became too much. "What are you thinking?"

"Well," he said, his Adam's apple bobbing up and down. "I'm wondering if I'm holding the end of the stick that you peed on."

I let out a surprised laugh and smacked him on the arm. "Be serious."

His face split into a wide grin. "We're going have a baby," he said and pulled me on top of him. Kisses rained down my face, making me wonder if I was wired wrong. Shouldn't I feel overjoyed too?

I pulled away and sat up, straddling him. "Aren't you even a little bit scared?"

"Why?"

"Because!" I threw my arms out to express how monumental it was. "A baby!"

He sat up and wrapped his arms around my back. "I know, it's huge. But right now, the only thing I'm feeling is incredibly lucky."

"But . . . what if I'm a bad mom?" I asked.

He shook his head. "Not even possible."

"I like my career, and I sometimes have to work long hours when we have a big campaign. I don't want to be like . . ." I looked up at him, afraid of giving voice to my fear: that I'd somehow become like his mother. Helen had worked hard and was a sought-after lawyer, but at the expense of her relationship with her son. I admired her work ethic but in no way did I want to be like her.

"You won't be like my mom," he said with all certainty. "Just the fact that you're worried about it means you'll never be like her."

"What about you? Are you ready to be a dad?" I asked. "It's a lot of hard work. It's not like with Will, where you just hang out and have fun all the time. There are diapers to contend with, and crying, and puke, and interrupted sleep."

He took my face in his hands and gave me a solemn look. "We're having a baby, Elsie. We made a human being together. I would do anything and everything for you and for that little miracle inside you," he said, his hand sliding down to rest on my belly. "The rest we can deal with as it comes."

I had my doubts but I let him pull me down on top of him, still wishing I could share his enthusiasm.

"Aren't you the least bit excited about it?" he asked, running his fingers up and down my back.

A guilty tear squeezed out the side of my eye. "I'm . . ." I stopped, searching for words. "I wasn't expecting this yet."

"You might be in shock," he offered. "Sometimes people in shock react in unexpected ways."

"'Shock' is the correct word for it."

Henry's soft words reached me through the darkness: "You do want this baby, right?" he asked, the joy gone from his voice.

I tried to think but my brain refused to cooperate. I wanted to give him a real answer, but the truth was that I didn't have a choice whether I wanted the baby or not. The choice, for better or worse, had already been made. "I want to say yes."

Henry didn't say anything else. He just wrapped himself around me, pressing his face into the side of my neck, weighing me down with his silent disappointment.

———————

The next few days, I felt wretched both physically and emotionally. The nausea hit hard and fast, occurring at random times in the day so that all I could keep down was crackers and water.

Then there was the emotional toll, the guilt that I was somehow letting Henry down with my lack of enthusiasm. That was coupled with the knowledge that women every day were struggling to get pregnant, even spending hundreds of thousands of dollars for in vitro fertilization, and here I was, knocked up and not even happy about it.

The guilt I wrapped around me like a blanket was thick. Nobody, least of all Henry, was making me feel this way. It was all self-inflicted, and I needed to find a way to make peace with this thing inside me before I suffocated.

———————

On Thursday, we were finally able to get an appointment with an OB-GYN. While getting ready, I stood in front of the mirror in my underwear, contemplating how my body would change. I turned sideways, imagining how my stomach would swell in the coming months. I had to admit, the thought terrified me.

Henry came up behind me and pressed a kiss on the back of my neck. "You're beautiful, you know that?"

But I didn't feel beautiful. I felt in shambles.

"Henry, are you sure about this?" Because I sure as hell wasn't.

"I couldn't be more sure," he said, resting his chin on the crook of my neck. He wrapped his arms around me and faced us toward the mirror. "Do you remember the last girlfriend I had in Oklahoma?"

"Shelly? Kelly? I can't remember."

"Melanie," he said with a grin. "We went out for a few months."

"What about her?" I asked, feeling a prickle of jealousy. I hadn't really liked her—she'd been too possessive—and had been glad when Henry ended the relationship.

"Did I ever tell you why we broke up?"

"You just told Jason and me it didn't work out."

His eyes held mine in the mirror. "Because she wanted something serious. She wanted to get married, settle down, have kids. And for a guy in his twenties, that's the last thing he wants to hear from a girl he's not that sure about." He straightened but kept me tucked into his warm body. "I tried to picture a life with her but I couldn't see her in my future. When I think of the mother of my children, her face is not the one that comes to mind."

His hands slid up to my jaw and lifted the hair away from my face, tilting my face slightly upward. "It was always you, Elsie," he said against my ear. "The person who walked down the aisle, the woman bearing our child, the face I'll wake up to every morning for the rest of my life."

I closed my eyes, leaning into the solidity of his body. "I wish I had even half of your conviction," I said. "I'm sure about you too. Just not about a baby."

I could feel him nodding behind me, knew that he wanted more than anything for me to share in his excitement. But I couldn't give him something I didn't have.

———————

Later, Henry and I sat in the waiting room of the clinic, tense but putting on a happy face for others. I glanced around the room and seeing the contentment radiating from these pregnant women made me wonder again what the hell was wrong with me.

"Hey, ease up there," Henry whispered. "Or they'll have to X-ray my hand for broken bones."

I looked down and realized I'd been gripping his hand for the better part of an hour. "Sorry," I said, feeling the blood rushing back to my fingers when I let go.

"Els, it'll be fine."

My eyes flew across his face. "What if . . ." But I couldn't finish the sentence, couldn't breathe aloud the thought of what we'd do if I really didn't want a baby. I was afraid to mention the two *A*'s—*adoption* and *abortion*—still unsure of what I really wanted.

Henry gave a slight shake of the head. "Don't say anything right now. Let's just talk to the doctor and make our decision then."

A nurse drew my blood in the back then sent me out to the waiting room again. Several minutes passed before my name was finally called and we went into the exam room together. I changed out of my clothes and into the gown in front of Henry, and I pretended not to see how he was avoiding looking at my stomach.

I lay down on the exam table, ripping a bit of the thin paper cover in the process, and answered questions from Dr. Harmon. Henry sat in the corner of the room, quiet and observant. I could tell he didn't want to be stuck there, that he wanted to be more of an active participant, but it was my body on the exam table, not his.

Henry scooted closer when Dr. Harmon turned on the ultrasound machine and inserted the wand into me.

I was about to make a nervous joke about how she needed to buy me dinner first when she pointed at a tiny dot on the screen. "Right there," she said, stilling the wand so that we could get a better look at the black shape that was my uterus, inside of which was a tiny gray blot.

My heart stopped. It was so small, so helpless, seemingly cling-ing to me for dear life.

"It's tiny," I breathed.

Dr. Harmon nodded and pointed at a rapidly blinking spot on the fetus. "And that's the heartbeat."

And in that moment, as I stared at that peanut-shaped spot with its little heart thrumming along, I felt my entire world shift beneath me.

"It looks like you're around six to eight weeks along," Dr. Har-mon said.

I couldn't take my eyes off the screen, at this tiny being sprout-ing inside me. Henry moved closer, his hand caressing my hair. "There he is," he said. "Or she."

I reached above my head and grasped his wrist, the emotion finally welling in my eyes and bursting forth onto my cheeks.

Henry bent down and kissed my forehead and it was then that the tightness in my chest finally began to ease. I knew in that moment there was no way I was going to let this baby down. It was a part of me, but most important, it was a part of Henry. How could I have even entertained the thought of not keeping something he and I had created together?

Later, back in the car, Henry turned to me and asked, "Well?"

I smiled at him, my mind and heart at ease. "I guess we're having a baby."

PART TWO

ASSAULT

1

I wasn't there to send Henry off on his first day as a police officer. His shift started when I was already at work, which was probably just as well so I didn't have a chance to dwell at home.

Still, that didn't stop me from dwelling at work.

I kept my cell phone by my keyboard and even though I was trying to concentrate on work, my eyes kept flitting back down to the phone's glass surface, halfway wishing it would ring and yet hoping it wouldn't. A phone call from Henry would be good; a call from the police station would be grave.

I came home to a dark, lonely house. It would be the first time I'd spend the night alone there, and though I wasn't one to be afraid of being by myself, it was the first night I'd be safe in my bed with the knowledge that my husband was out there with criminals and lowlifes. It was unnerving to say the least.

Henry called around ten fifteen, halfway through an old episode of *The Walking Dead*. "I just wanted to say hi," he said, his deep voice soothing the worry that wound the muscles in my shoulders tight.

"How's it going?"

"Fine, so far. My FTO and I are out on patrol. She's out taking a smoke break and getting coffee right now."

The questions came firing out of my mouth. "Patrol already? And FTO? And *she*?"

Henry chuckled softly. "Yes, I'm on patrol already with my FTO, which stands for 'field training officer.' I will be with her for the next twelve weeks."

I swallowed down a nugget of jealousy, determined not to resent this woman who would get to spend every night of the foreseeable future with my husband.

"Her name's Sondra Jones. She's abrasive but certifiably badass, and she's married to a doctor," Henry said. "There's nothing to worry abo—Hold on a sec, okay?" He disappeared from the line for about thirty seconds then came back. "Els, I gotta go. We've been dispatched to a scene."

"Okay, be safe."

"Always."

Then he was gone.

I had plenty of time to kick myself that night, realizing too late that I should have told Henry I loved him, hoping I hadn't just given up my last chance to do so.

Henry crawled into bed sometime in the morning, wrapping his bare body around me with a long sigh. "I missed you," he said, splaying a hand on my stomach. "Both of you."

I twisted in his arms and took his face in my hands, kissing him with everything I'd felt and dreamed the previous night. "I love you," I said, pressing kisses on his eyelids, then along his nose, down his chin, and to his scruffy neck. He moaned when my lips continued to travel down his chest, as I paused to nip and tease his dark nipples.

His fingers tangled in my hair, pulling the band away to release my curls.

"How was it?" I asked, my lips dragging along the ridges on his taut abdomen.

"We answered a call for a noise complaint and I gave a ticket for a DUI."

I stopped my seduction to listen, resting my arms on his abdomen and giving him my attention, ignoring the hard length pressing into my chest.

"I thought the guy was going to run but he just pulled over," Henry said. "I didn't even get a chance to handcuff anyone."

"Well, I've been a bad girl, Officer," I said, once again touching my lips to his bare skin.

Henry grinned and began to rock his hips, his erection sliding along the crease of my breasts. "Oh yeah?" He sat up, taking me with him as he stood. When he towered over me, he moved down, his lips and fingers hovering above my skin so that all I could feel was a whisper of his touch. He sank down to the floor and, without taking his eyes off me, reached into his workbag.

The sound of metal clinking sent a bolt of excitement rushing through me. My suspicion was confirmed when he flashed the handcuffs at me, dragging the cold metal against my skin as he rose back to his full height. He dangled the cuffs on one finger, and with a soft but commanding voice said, "Get on the bed."

I lifted my chin, playing the part of the defiant felon, and bit out, "Make me."

He spun me around so quickly, all I could do was gasp in surprise as he took hold of my arms and cuffed them behind my back. "You have the right to remain silent," he said and pushed me facedown onto the bed, leaving my ass up in the air. But remaining silent became impossible when he pulled my cheeks apart and dragged his tongue through my folds in one long stroke.

I groaned into the sheets, knowing I was at the mercy of this man and loving it. I twisted my head around and saw him crouched behind me as he worked me over with his mouth. My legs trembled at the sight, threatening to take me down.

Then he was gone and I was left cold and bereft. From my vantage point, all I could see were his legs as he stood behind me in silence. "What are you waiting for?" I asked, nearly breathless from want.

"I'm just admiring the view." Then his hands were back on me, his hot palms sliding across my skin. On and on he touched me, worshipping me with his big hands, making me burn in anticipation.

I couldn't take it. Patience is not my strongest suit. "Get on with it."

All of a sudden, he grabbed me by the waist and threw me onto my back, my hands still trapped beneath me. The complete change in his demeanor unnerved me, the way he stood over me with his hands on his waist inflaming me even more. If I wasn't wet before, I was definitely gushing now.

He bent over me and, resting his elbow by my head, touched his thumb to my lower lip. His hard gaze bore into mine as he pulled my lip down and took it between his teeth. "I'll get on with it when I'm ready," he said in a gritty voice.

I twisted my head away, wrenching my lip from his hold. "Fuck me already, Officer."

He reached down, took hold of his shaft, and thumped it on my mound. "Is this what you want?" When I nodded, he said, "Put your legs up on the bed."

I lifted my feet off the floor and hooked them on the edge of the mattress, Henry settling in between. I'd opened my mouth to rile him up again when his hand landed over my lips at the same time he speared me with his cock.

I gave a shout against his palm, but his fingers tightened on my face as he withdrew and slammed back in. My muscles clamped down on him as he conquered me with steady, ruthless thrusts.

I couldn't touch him, couldn't kiss him. I was powerless to do anything but wind my legs around his back and urge him to move faster, harder.

Henry didn't relent. He kept the pace, pulling out slowly, slamming back in, then pausing for a breath when he was deepest in me. Each drawn-out stroke rubbed my most sensitive area, pushing me closer to the edge of climax.

I watched his eyebrows squeeze together, his mouth forming a thin, hard line as his breathing grew more ragged. He dragged his hand away from my face and brought it down between us, his fingers rubbing frantic circles around my clit as he ground out, "Come with me, Elsie. Come with me."

There was no way I couldn't. I clenched around him and exploded just as he cried out, "Fuck!" He slipped his arms under me and wound his fingers through mine as he thrust one last time, seated deep inside me as his cock surged with seed.

Even before he could catch his breath, he pressed a gentle kiss to my mouth then rolled us over to take the pressure off my hands. Later, he took the handcuffs off me and lifted my wrists to his lips, pressing gentle kisses to the marks they'd left behind.

"I'm sorry," he said, his fingers tracing over the red welts.

"I'm not."

"People might wonder how you got bruises."

I grinned. "I'll just leave it to their imaginations."

Nights without Henry became the norm. I quickly got used to eating dinner alone, to going to bed alone. He often tried to call before I fell asleep, and the first few times he failed to do so, I stayed up with worry, but that too quickly wore off. I had to just stop thinking about what he could be doing so as not to drive myself crazy.

The only time we really saw each other during the week was

when he'd stop by my office and take me out for lunch. But I was often still too nauseous to eat. Regardless, I was grateful for what little time we had together, even if it consisted of me just watching him eat while he talked about the crazy things he bore witness to on patrol.

"So what do you do at home all day?" I asked one afternoon, watching with envy as he ate a large bowl of clam chowder and wishing creamy soups didn't make me so ill. "Do you just eat pizza and play Xbox all day?"

"In my birthday suit," he said with a grin. He took a large swig of his iced tea. "Actually, I've been working on a surprise."

"What surprise?"

"You'll see." But he said nothing else about that damn surprise, delighting in keeping me in suspense.

———————

One Saturday, Henry and I went to bed to take an early afternoon nap together, but I could tell something was on his mind when his body refused to relax.

"What's going on?" I asked grumpily, reaching a hand back and grasping his thigh to keep him from moving it again.

"I'm not really all that sleepy." He got up and drew the sheet over my shoulder before closing the door behind him.

Exhaustion took over and I fell asleep almost immediately, but a loud thud woke me up. I listened and heard some more banging from the home office.

When I couldn't take the curiosity anymore, I crept out of the room and into the hall, watching quietly as he took books off the bookshelf and stacked them on the other side of the room, where he'd pushed the desk and chair against the far wall. He worked methodically and with precision, putting the books in near identical piles on the desk. When the large bookshelf was cleared, he took hold of one side and pulled it away from the wall, sliding it with little effort across the room.

Then his eyes found me. "Did I wake you?" he asked, coming out to the hallway and closing the door behind him.

"You didn't," I said with a smile. "But the desk banging into the wall did."

"It's a heavy desk."

"What were you doing?"

"Just redecorating," he said with a nonchalant shrug. "I figured I'd move stuff out of there to make room for the crib and changing table."

I tried to smother a smile, my heart warmed at how eager he was for this baby. There's nothing quite like a man who's looking forward to being a father. "You already have the room planned out? Is that the mysterious surprise you're working on?"

He grinned. "Yes, so stay out of there until I'm done."

"Okay."

He pinched my nose. "Promise? Because your curiosity will ruin the surprise."

"I can stay out of there if I want."

"Really? Who was it that couldn't even wait until the clock struck twelve before unwrapping her Christmas presents?"

I was about to issue a denial when I felt a now familiar wave of nausea hit. I turned on a heel and ran to the bathroom, kneeling in front of the toilet as I heaved up breakfast. Henry appeared beside me and held my hair back, his palm warm and comforting as he rubbed my back. "I thought it was called morning sickness," he muttered. "This is more like all-day sickness."

"It's supposed to go away after the first trimester," I croaked, my voice echoing inside the toilet bowl.

"You want me to make you something?" he asked. "Tea and crackers?"

I sat back on my heels and nodded lamely. He wrapped a hand on the back of my head and pressed a wet towel to my face, wiping at the corners of my mouth. I grabbed his wrist and held the towel against my forehead, enjoying the warmth against my chilled skin.

I looked up to find his face full of worry.

"If I could bear this for you, I would," he said.

"And I would totally let you," I said without missing a beat. I stood up, and trailed my fingers along his scruffy cheek. "I think I'll get back in bed."

Henry came back a few minutes later carrying a tray with my favorite large mug, a plate of saltine crackers, and a fake flower in a tiny white vase. He set the tray on the nightstand but didn't linger. He only made sure I had everything I needed, going so far as to retrieve my laptop from my bag, before closing the door behind him and returning to the office.

———

One night after work, I felt good enough to go for a run on the treadmill. Afterward, I filled the bathtub with near-scalding water and lavender bath salts. I slid into it with a sigh, feeling every muscle in my body unwind as I acclimated to the temperature. I closed my eyes and leaned my head back onto a rolled-up towel, imagining what our baby would look like, if she'd have my curly brown hair or Henry's dark waves. Either way, the kid was destined to fight the frizz all her life.

A noise downstairs got my attention and I sat up, stilling to better hear, when I heard the front door slam. I jumped out of the tub and grabbed a towel, nearly slipping and busting my head open. Footsteps thundered up the stairs as I ran to the closet, frantically trying to remember where Henry had stashed the handgun. In my haste and complete terror, I dropped a shoe box just as the bedroom door burst open.

"Elsie!" Henry's voice boomed.

I sagged to the floor in relief. "In here," I said weakly.

He appeared at the door of the closet, breathing hard. "Are you alright?"

I took a few moments to compose myself, scrubbing a palm down my face. "I was fine until you burst in here, scaring the shit out of me," I said, getting to my feet. "What are you doing here?"

"I was calling you to let you know that I was coming home for my lunch hour, but you wouldn't answer either phone."

"I was in the bathtub."

"I see that now," he said, his mouth twitching.

I put my hands on my hips. "Something funny?"

His eyes flicked down to the towel around my body. "I'm glad I was the intruder, that's all."

I looked down and realized that the towel was halfway down my breasts, exposing one nipple. I stalked off, the adrenaline still rushing through my veins, and continued my bath.

Henry was right behind me, undressing quickly and sliding in behind me. He wrapped his long legs around mine and pulled me down onto his chest.

I closed my eyes and melted into him, finally relaxing. His hands slid up my sides and kneaded my breasts. "Mmm, I was hoping I could eat dinner with you," he said, rolling my hardened nipples between his fingers. "But this is so much better."

"You still need to eat," I said with my eyes closed.

"I'll grab a sandwich on the way out. There's no way you're getting me out of the tub right now." He paused and twisted around, reaching for something outside the bathtub. "Oh, I wanted to give you this," he said, pulling out a small book from his pants on the floor.

"*The Little Book of Baby Names*," I read, studying the tiny book in my hands and noticing a few of the pink pages were folded in.

"I marked the names I liked."

I flipped open to one page and saw he'd drawn an asterisk next to a girl's name. "Hope," I said. "So you're *hoping* for a girl, I take it?"

I felt him shrug. "I've just always liked that name. It's very optimistic, and I like to think our child will be full of dreams and conviction."

"Yeah, that sounds nice," I said, nuzzling my head into his neck.

"Els," Henry said, his voice taking on an uncertain edge. "Have you ever . . . I just want to know, is this the first time you've been pregnant?"

I sat up and twisted around. "Of course!"

His face relaxed.

"Though there was one time in my junior year in college, when the condom broke and I thought for a few weeks that I might be pregnant."

His muscles turned to stone beneath me. "Who?"

"Some guy in my HTML class named Scott Kersey. He and I had been dating for a few weeks when we finally had sex. Wouldn't you know it, the condom broke on the first time." When Henry didn't say anything, I continued. "My period was always unpredictable so for a while there I was seriously worried that I had gotten pregnant. I took the morning-after pill and had an STD screening and everything, but still, the worry was always there. I was only able to breathe a sigh of relief when my period finally came."

"What did *he* do?"

"He was a nice guy and stood by me. Offered to marry me if I was truly pregnant."

"Like hell," Henry growled.

I laughed and touched his thigh for reassurance. "I told him thanks, but that I wasn't going to marry someone just because I'd gotten pregnant. We broke up about a month after because he didn't want to stay in a relationship with someone who didn't really want to be with him. Not in the long run anyway."

And God, wasn't that the story of my life? All of my previous relationships had been placeholders until Henry came along and claimed his place beside me. Even back then, every single one of my boyfriends had been able to sense that, even if I hadn't.

"How come I didn't know about it?" he asked.

"Because I didn't tell you."

"Did Jason know?"

"No. I never told him. Nobody knew."

"Huh, who's keeping secrets now?"

I twisted around, sitting on my legs, and faced him. "Nothing happened, at least nothing significant enough to worry my family." He opened his mouth, most likely to argue that it was no different from his Korea secret, when I put a finger on his lips. "The difference is that I'm telling you willingly."

He turned his head and said, "I wasn't going to argue that. I was just about to say that there's so much about you that I still don't know."

"Oh. Well, ditto."

His eyes flicked across my face. "I'm glad you weren't pregnant back then," he said after some time.

I pressed a kiss on the tip of his nose. "Me too. Otherwise I might be Elsie Kersey right now."

He snickered, pulling me close. "Over my dead body."

"What would you have done?"

"Married you immediately."

"No," I laughed. "I mean, if I'd been pregnant with Scott's baby."

He was quiet as he mulled it over. "I would have tried my best to talk you out of marrying him, that's for sure."

"Would you have tried to talk me into an abortion?" I asked.

His eyebrows furrowed. "No. Hell no," he said. "That's not my call to make."

"Then what?"

"I would have stepped up and helped you raise that baby the best I could."

I pressed a soft kiss to his lips, in awe of this man before me.

2

Late one Saturday morning, Henry came home a few hours later than normal. I was already awake, worrying the edges of my sweater, when he came in the front door, dropping the bag with his uniform by the front door.

I threw my phone onto the couch and made my way to him, wrapping my arms around his neck. "Thank God." I pulled away, immediately noticing the dark bruise on his cheek. "What happened?"

He ducked his head and walked past me, shaking his head wearily. I followed him upstairs and watched as he methodically took off his civilian clothes. When he bent down to untie his boots, I saw that his knuckles were swollen and red, with a few scabbed gashes.

Not asking him what happened was a hard task, but experience had taught me that I would push him further away if I pried. So I sat on the edge of the bed and watched him awkwardly try to undo the buttons on his shirt. "Do you want some help?" I finally asked.

"I got it," he said, gritting his teeth as he stubbornly made his way through the first two buttons.

I couldn't take it anymore, so I stood before him and undid the buttons myself. "You should put ice on that," I said, pushing the shirt off his shoulders. I yanked the hem of his undershirt from his pants and he lifted his arms to allow me to pull it over his head.

I gasped when I saw a large dark purple bruise on the side of his rib and reached out to touch it. Henry flinched at the contact. Swallowing down my agonizing concern, I turned away from the bruise and undid his pants, pushing them down to his ankles. When he stood in his boxer briefs, I did the nearly unbearable and turned around, ready to walk away without asking him what happened.

Still, I took my time getting to the door in hopes that he'd somehow speak up, but the man retained his stony silence. I closed the door behind me and simply tried to breathe through the hurt in my chest, feeling as if all of my worries had come to life.

I realized my hands were shaking in the kitchen as I made my second cup of coffee for the day. To hell with doctor's advice. My husband had just come home several hours late, beat up and tight-lipped. I needed some damn caffeine.

As I lifted the mug up to my lips, Henry walked into the kitchen and sat down, setting his elbows on the table and hanging his head. "Jones and I were on patrol when we tried to pull this car over. The driver decided to run, so we gave chase. We must have tailed him for ten whole minutes before he hit a curb and blew a tire." Henry looked up at me and it was then I realized I was holding my breath. "He jumped out and we pursued him on foot, jumping over fences and all that crap they show on cop shows. Only this ended with the guy turning and attacking me. We went at it before Jones Tased him. Apparently the perp was a former mixed martial arts fighter."

I couldn't speak, and even if I could, my brain was in no condition to form coherent sentences. So I fetched the ice pack from the freezer, wrapped it in a dish towel, and pressed it onto the hand of my wretched-looking husband.

"I got in a few hits myself," he said gruffly, clenching and unclenching his fingers. "The Krav Maga really helped."

I went back to my coffee, filling my mouth with the bitter liquid to keep from screaming.

"I'm fine, Els. The doc looked me over and said it was just bruising, though I could have done without all the extra paperwork."

Underneath my sweater sleeves, I fingered the sapphire ring. I didn't know how to act, how to feel. Relief and worry and anger and nausea roiled inside me. I had seen Henry with mental wounds before, but never with physical injuries, and honestly, I couldn't say which was worse right now.

"Say something."

"I can't," I said, pulling on my sleeves to hide my trembling fingers.

Henry stood up and wrapped me in his arms, kissing my forehead. "I'm sorry I worried you. I should have called. I didn't realize I'd be so late."

I pressed my face into his chest, taking in his day-old scent, and nodded.

"This is the nature of the job. I'll get roughed up once in a while," he said into my hair. "But at the end of the day, I come home knowing I've taken one more crack-selling, house-robbing asshole off the streets. Don't you think that's worth it?"

God, I wanted to say yes. Of course the answer was yes, but when faced with my bruised and battered husband, it was hard to remember why. He'd already given up so much for his country; did he need to give this too?

With his swollen hands, he tilted my face up to meet his. "Talk to me."

"You're too valiant for your own good," I finally said, but didn't add that I thought it wasn't an asset but rather his failing.

On Saturday night, Henry and I attended a cocktail party at his FTO's place. Sondra Jones and her husband lived in a third-story condo in the affluent Cherry Creek North neighborhood.

Sondra was tall—only a few inches shy of Henry's six-two—and wore a one-strap dress that encased her curvaceous body. Her features, especially her lips, seemed too bold, too big, and yet all put together, they created an aggressively compelling face. She wasn't attractive in the traditional sense, but she had sex appeal in spades.

"Great to meet you, Elsie," she said, giving my hand a shake, and even though I usually try to give a firm handshake with people I wanted to impress, Sondra's grip nearly made me wince. Somehow I got the feeling she wasn't trying to impress me. "Henry has told me all about you."

"I hope good things," I said, squeezing back a little harder.

One corner of her mouth curled up as she raised an eyebrow, a look that made me put up my guard. "Of course."

She led the way into her beautiful home, stopping to introduce us to a few people, because apparently, when the woman wasn't busy chasing and Tasing bad guys, she was throwing lavish parties in a fancy-dancy condo. I met a few other police officers and their wives. Most of them referred to Henry as "Rookie."

"How much do you really tell her?" I whispered to Henry sometime during the night.

Henry glanced down at me. "What do you mean?"

"Have you told her everything? Does she know about—"

A loud clinking grabbed our attention and we turned, as did the rest of the guests, to the source of the noise. "I just wanted to make a toast," Sondra said, laying the bread knife back on the table and lifting her champagne flute. "To Rookie and his wife, who are expecting their first child together, even if Elsie wasn't sure about it at first. Congratulations, you two!"

I tried to keep from glaring at Henry, but I wasn't sure if I was successful. When everyone's heads turned, I wiped my expression clean and pasted a smile on my mouth as people congratulated us. Henry wrapped his arm around my shoulder and kissed my head, his chest swelling with pride.

———

"I didn't realize we were telling people yet," I said to him after we got back from the party. "Only our family until we're past the twelve-week mark, remember?"

Henry pulled me close, unconcerned by my irritation. "I can't help it. I want to stop and tell strangers on the street."

I shook my head in disbelief, my irritation in full bloom now that we were in the privacy of our home.

"I spend a lot of time with Jones. How was I not supposed to tell her?"

"And what about my hesitation about having a baby? Did you have to tell her about that?"

He pursed his lips, unable to say a thing.

I crossed my arms over my chest. "She's judging me for it."

"She's not."

"She is. I can feel it." How could I explain the strange way Sondra's eyes followed me, the way she practically sneered at everything I said? Henry would just say I was being paranoid. "That woman doesn't like me."

He bent down and kissed my neck. "I don't know why she wouldn't. There's nothing to dislike about you."

"There's plenty to dislike about me. Like that I'm a moody bitch. I bet you've told her that."

"Hey," he said suddenly, his eyebrows drawing together. "I don't know where this is coming from, but I would never say that about you."

"But you think it."

He closed his eyes as his jaw muscles worked. When he looked at me again, he said, "This is just pregnancy hormones talking, right?"

"Right, because every time a woman gets mad it's due to hormonal imbalance, not because she actually has something legitimate to be angry about." I refrained from stomping my feet, even if what I really felt like doing was to throw an all-out tantrum.

"It's not . . . that's not . . ." Henry shook his head and held out his hand. "Come with me. I have something that might cheer you up."

Still seething, I allowed him to lead me up the stairs and down the hall, to the closed office door.

"I was going to wait until it's done, but I think you need cheering up right now," he said. He opened the door, but the nursery I'd been picturing was not the sight that greeted me. The computer table was still pushed up against the far wall, books still lying in piles all over it. Only the bookshelf was missing.

I took a step inside, opening my mouth to ask what the surprise was, when he grabbed me by the shoulders and pivoted me to the left, toward the wall where the bookshelf had once stood.

There, taking up the entire wall, was a mural of gray-blue, rendered darker around the edges to give it depth. To the right was a large, bright moon and to its left was the silhouette of a small child—with a skirt and pigtails—lit only by the golden glow of the moon. The gauzy horizon cut the wall halfway down, and the entire scene was reflected below in softer brushstrokes, making it look as if the child was standing on the water's edge.

The painting before me stole the anger from my lungs and replaced it with awe.

"It's not finished yet. I still want to add more detail to the moon.

And if the baby is a boy, I can just paint over the skirt and hair," Henry said, his hands in his pockets. He turned to me with his eyebrows raised. "What do you think?"

I looked at Henry standing almost bashfully beside his labor of love, and felt myself fall all over again. I mean, how could I stay mad when the man's excitement was exhibited all over the wall?

I touched a finger to the girl and her pigtail. "It's beautiful."

———————

"Kari, have you finished with that file yet?" I asked, looking over the cubicle wall to find her tapping away at her keyboard.

She held up a finger and finished typing, her fingers flying across the keys. "Sorry, I had to send off an email," she said. "I'm done with the file. You can work on it."

"Thanks." I winced, feeling a strange cramp but in the next second, it was gone.

"What's wrong?"

I shook my head. "Nothing. Just a cramp."

"You have your period too?" Kari mouthed.

"No. Just a weird twinge, I guess." I went back to work, opening the file from the server, rubbing my stomach and feeling a little guilty I hadn't told her about the pregnancy yet.

After lunch, Conor held one of his monthly meetings to discuss events on the horizon. "And finally, we are trying to woo Lombart."

"The pharmaceutical company?" James, one of the junior designers, asked.

Conor didn't even bother hiding his excitement. "The very one," he said, his face lit up by a wide smile. "They are looking for a brand refresher. Something to modernize their image."

"That's huge," James said with a whistle.

"That it is. In a few months, we are going to be ramping up, working on a concept." Conor looked around the room, giving each one of us a meaningful look. His eyes landed on me. "Sherman, I want you to head it."

"Logan," I corrected with a grin. "And thank you."

Kari nudged my leg under the table, flashing me excited little smiles. After the meeting she said, "Please bring me into the team if he gives you the choice."

"Of course I will," I said as we walked to our desks. "Late nights wouldn't be the same without your dirty jokes and Photoshop expertise."

"Damn straight."

Suddenly, I stopped and clutched at my stomach as intense cramps racked my insides. Short of breath, I turned on a heel and ran to the bathroom.

"No, no, no," I whispered as I locked the stall and pulled down my pants, wondering why I hadn't noticed the dampness before. The breath caught in my throat when I saw the blood—not a lot, but enough to send an arrow of fear straight through my heart. "No."

I grabbed handfuls of toilet paper and wiped, horrified to find even more blood. I kept wiping with fresh toilet paper, willing away the blood.

"Elsie!" Kari yelled, her voice echoing in the small space of the bathroom. "You in here?"

"I'm here," I said in a shaky voice.

"What the hell happened?" she asked, her voice much closer and quieter. "Are you okay?"

"C-c-could you please get me a pad?" I stammered, the tears welling up in my eyes.

"So you *do* have your period," she said, and a second later, I heard the quarter clink as she turned the knob on the wall dispenser.

"I—I guess." I grabbed the pad she held over the door and said, "Thanks. I think I'm good."

When I walked out, Kari gasped. "You're white as a sheet."

I wiped my eyes and took a deep breath, trying hard not to sniff. "I think I need to go to the hospital."

"What? Why?" She touched my arm, looking me over for any obvious signs of injury.

"I think..." I swallowed hard, finding it difficult to say the words aloud. "I think I'm having a miscarriage."

———————

"I can't believe you never told me!" Kari yelled as she drove to the Denver Health Medical Center in her truck.

I looked down at my phone, willing it to ring. I'd called Henry several times and left nearly twenty text messages but all I'd gotten was radio silence. "I'm sorry," I said to my friend. "We were waiting until we were past the twelve-week point."

"And how far along are you?"

I wiped at my cheeks. "Eleven."

Kari shook her head, swerving around a driver. "Get out of the way, shithead!" she cried, flipping him off.

It took us twenty-one excruciating minutes to get to the hospital. Kari dropped me off at the ER door and went to park the truck, and I hobbled inside, trying to quell the panic that had taken hold of my muscles.

While in the waiting room, I tried calling Henry again but received no answer. "Fuck, Henry, answer your fucking phone," I said under my breath. I needed my husband beside me during this critical time and he was nowhere to be found.

Kari sat beside me, holding my hand, trying her best to be Henry's substitute.

Another round of cramps racked my insides, and I doubled over, trying not to cry out.

Kari stood up and stalked over to the front desk. "My friend over there could be losing her baby. Is there any way we can hurry up and get her seen already?"

The nurse shook her head and motioned to the several other people in the waiting room.

Dr. Harmon finally called me back on my cell, telling me that she couldn't get out of the office. "I've already called the hospital. They'll test the HCG in your blood levels and do an ultrasound."

"Am I going to lose the baby?" I asked, trying to sound strong and not sure I'd succeeded.

"I don't know, Elsie," she said gently. "But bleeding during pregnancy is actually quite common. Many go on to carry full term. It could be a number of things, so don't worry yet."

That wasn't really comforting to me; in fact it had quite the opposite effect.

"Are you filling more than one pad an hour?" she asked. "Pain?"

"No. I don't think so. The bleeding just started. But the pain is intensifying."

"I don't know if they'll send you back home, but stay positive, Elsie. I'll be there at six."

"Thanks." I hung up just as Kari came back with a few more pads in hand.

"They told me to sit tight and wait, but gave me these just in case," she said, handing me the packages.

I stood up to go to the bathroom when I felt a gush, as if gravity had wrenched out a part of me. I looked down to find blood saturating my pants and dripping at my feet.

The last thing I remembered was my vision graying as the linoleum floor rushed at me.

3

I was disoriented when I woke, not recognizing the room or the bed I was in.

"How are you feeling?" a male voice asked. I was about to breathe a sigh of relief when I turned my head and saw that it wasn't my husband standing by my bed but my boss. "Sherman, you gave me a fright," Conor said, taking hold of my hand.

"What are you doing here?" I looked around the room, finding Kari in the corner and nobody else. Still no Henry.

"I called him to say we were going to be gone the rest of the day, and he demanded to know the reason," Kari said, stepping forward. "I had to tell him, Elsie. I'm sorry."

I nodded, tears blurring my vision once again. "And the baby?"

Kari bit her lip and looked away, not needing to say any more.

I closed my eyes but the tears fell anyway, fat drops rolling down the sides of my face and onto the pillow. "Are they sure?" I asked in a near whisper.

"They did an ultrasound and blood test," Kari said. "If you want, I can call the nurse in and she can explain it better."

I shook my head, unable to bear the thought of hearing in cold, medical terms exactly how my baby had died.

"They asked us to call them as soon as you're conscious, to get your consent on performing a D and C."

A nurse came in then, an elderly woman with dark skin and even darker circles around her eyes. "Oh good, you're awake," she said, grabbing the clipboard at the end of my bed. She turned to Kari and Conor. "Would you two please wait outside?"

"We'll be right there if you need us," Conor said and followed Kari out the door.

When they had gone, the nurse closed the curtain and turned to me with a grave look. "I'm sorry about your loss."

My lips quivered as I tried my damnedest to keep from bursting into angry tears. "Are you sure?"

She closed her eyes and nodded. "When you're ready, we need to talk about a D and C," she said. "It's a procedure where your cervix will be dilated and then the doctors will remove the contents of your uterus to make sure everything is out to prevent an infection."

I lost control of my emotions and, despite the ache in my stomach, I sobbed hard.

She sat on the side of the bed and patted my hand, careful not to press on the IV needles, and sat quietly with me for a long while, giving me the comfort of her presence until I was ready to sign the forms.

In the end, the procedure was over in a blur. What I had carried inside me for eleven weeks was gone in twenty minutes, and soon I was wheeled back to the recovery room to take in my loss in private.

At nearly ten, Kari and Conor finally went home at my insistence. "Take a few days off if you need," he said, his brows knitted with worry. "Take care of yourself, Sherman," he added before they left.

In that dark room, with only the soft humming of medical

equipment, I stared up at the ceiling and tried my hardest to keep from falling to pieces.

I'd never felt more alone in my entire life.

———————

I woke up to knocking on my door. I opened my swollen eyes to find Henry standing at the door, his solid frame illuminated by the fluorescent lights behind him.

"Elsie," he said, crossing the room in three long strides and bending down to gather me in his arms, pulling me up off the bed. He buried his face in my neck and I felt his hot tears land on my shoulder but my insides were numb and so I felt nothing but the gaping hollowness. His shoulders quaked as he held me, rocking me back and forth, holding me tight.

After what seemed like forever, he finally pulled away. He grabbed my face and planted kisses on my lips. "I'm sorry," he said over and over.

Unable to bear his touch, I pulled his hands away. "Where were you?"

"My phone was out of battery," he said, stung. "Why didn't you call the station? They could have radioed me."

"You never told me I could." I looked at him still in uniform, at the bags under his red eyes, and realized he hadn't had any sleep yet. "Go home and sleep, Henry."

He frowned as hurt and anger flew across his features. "I'm finally here. Why the hell would I leave?"

"Because you haven't had any sleep," I said simply, lying back again.

"I'm staying," he said, taking my hand.

I turned away. "It's okay. They just wanted to keep me overnight for observation. I'll be released later today."

"Then I'm leaving later today. With you."

"Henry, you have to work tonight. So please, go home and get some sleep."

He wrapped his fingers around my jaw and turned me to face him. "Why the hell are you pushing me away right now?"

I turned my eyes to the dark stubble on his cheek, unable to meet his angry gaze.

"Fuck sleep. Right now, I want to be with you," he said in a rough voice. "I'm sorry. I should have been here when . . ."

His unspoken words undid me, and my face crumbled in on itself.

"Come here," he said, reaching out with one hand to pull me into his chest. He curled over me and we grieved together in the dark.

———

I survived the next few weeks by tucking the hurt and the sadness inside, pasting on a fake smile in hopes that acting the part would somehow convince my heart to feel it.

Any day now, I was sure of it.

Henry seemed everywhere and nowhere at once. He still worked a lot, leaving me alone for long periods of time, but when he was at home he practically suffocated me with his presence, constantly cuddling me, offering to make me tea, anything to ease the blow of his absence that night. His constant pandering irritated me until I finally couldn't take it anymore and just told him to back off.

"I don't need you to treat me like an invalid, Henry," I told him one day after the third time he suggested we go shopping or watch a movie.

He frowned at me as his nostrils flared. "I'm not. I'm just trying to get you to leave the house. Maybe it'll make you feel better."

I gestured at my perch on the couch, the blanket over me with my e-reader and a cup of coffee nearby. "I'm fine right here."

"Where you've been for the past three days."

"If you want to go shopping so bad, why don't you go call Sondra and make a day of it? Get a mani-pedi and talk about your poor wife who can't even get herself up off the couch," I said, relishing the fact that I was getting him so riled up.

His nostrils flared again. "I haven't told her about . . . it."

"It?"

He averted his eyes. "You know what I mean."

"It's easy for you, isn't it? To just pretend the baby wasn't real, so you can deal with it?"

"You think this is easy for me?" he asked, his features clouding over. He paced in front of me, the veins in his forehead popping. "I'm trying to be the strong one here even though it's tearing me apart. I'm trying to be here for you."

"You're here for me? Where were you when it really mattered?" I asked, pushing the blanket away and rising to my feet. "I needed you, Henry, and you weren't there. You were out there saving Denver when you should have been with me, saving our child."

"That's not fucking fair!" His voice boomed like thunder throughout the house, surprising me with its force.

I knew it wasn't fair—I knew that—but it didn't stop the words from coming out of my mouth. Maybe I just wanted to hurt him as much as I was hurting.

He grabbed me by the shoulders, his fingers digging into my flesh. The unmasked look of resentment in his eyes filled me with regret and worry. I had never seen him look at me like that before, and it made me feel absolutely wretched. "You're not the only one who lost something that day, Els."

I turned away, ashamed of myself but unable to voice my regret. "Maybe you're right. Maybe we do need to get out of the house," I said instead.

He wanted to say more, I could see it in the hard set of his jaw, but he said nothing else. He just nodded, the look still on his face.

We ended up going to a nearly-deserted matinee movie—I couldn't even recall which one now—but it felt as if something had shifted between us. We didn't touch, barely even acknowledged each other. We simply sat together like two strangers who just happened to be in the same place at the same time.

As we sat there in the darkened room, I looked down at our hands resting on our own laps, neither one of us even daring to use the armrest. It was as if we didn't know how to act around each other anymore. We, who had grown up together, who had braved the death of my brother together, suddenly couldn't figure out a way to deal with this kind of grief. Instead of drawing us closer, the loss of our baby was tearing us apart.

Unable to bear the thought of losing him too, I leaned over and reached for his hand in the dark, holding my breath as I waited for a response.

After a few tense moments, I closed my eyes in relief when his fingers curled around mine. That one gesture filled me with so much hope, my sight immediately blurred with tears.

"I'm sorry," I whispered, bringing his hand up and kissing his knuckles.

His eyes flickered from the light of the movie screen as he gazed down at me. Then he bent down until our foreheads were touching and granted me a rueful smile.

"I shouldn't have said that. I was out of line," I said.

He nodded gently.

"I just . . ." I swallowed. "I've been carrying around all of this guilt, and I think I needed to just give it someone else to carry for a while."

"It's not your fault, Elsie. You heard the doctor. She said it happens to one in five women. You couldn't have done anything differently to prevent it."

"I could have loved it from the very beginning." My voice broke at the end, and before I had a chance to blink, Henry lifted the armrest out of the way and gathered me into his side.

"Hey, don't do this. Don't even think that, okay?" he said, brushing hair away from my face.

I buried my face in his neck. "Sometimes I feel so weak, like I've fallen to my knees and can't get back up."

He touched my chin and lifted my face up to meet his. "Then lean on me, Elsie," he said, determination and love in his eyes. "I'll hold you up until you're strong enough to stand on your own again."

4

Time heals all wounds, but only because the brain is a forgetful thing. We forget on purpose in order to leave the past behind and move on; it's human nature. And since I'm only human, the hurt subsided with each day that passed.

After a month, I had almost completely convinced myself that the miscarriage was for the best, that there was a valid medical reason why my body decided to terminate the pregnancy. Whenever I felt myself spiraling into sadness, I'd remind myself that there was nothing I could have done to change what happened, that it wasn't my fault.

When you tell yourself something enough times, eventually, you start to believe it.

Conor came by my cubicle one day, hanging his arms over the low wall. "How are you, Sherman?"

I smiled up at him. "Logan. And I'm doing fine."

"I noticed you've been keeping your head down and working hard on the presentation."

I nodded, glancing back at my screen, hoping he wouldn't come farther into my cubicle and see that I was actually just looking at funny pictures on the Internet.

"I just wanted to tell you that I appreciate your work ethic, that you didn't bring your personal issues with you to work."

I felt my face warm up, from the compliment and from the fact that he had seen me at my worst. "Thanks for not telling anyone."

"It's not mine to tell." His eyes assessed me quietly for a long, uncomfortable moment. "I'm sorry it happened."

"Me too."

"Anyway, if you wanted to get out of here early today, then go ahead."

I glanced at the stack of folders on my desk and the to-do list pinned to my wall. "That might not be possible."

"Do it Monday," he said with a nonchalant shrug. Something caught his attention across the wall of cubicles for a moment and he straightened. "Seems you have a visitor," he said, his mood changing.

I stood up and found Henry walking down my row, making the breath catch in my throat. He looked intimidatingly gorgeous in his black leather jacket and jeans, with day-old stubble on his face and sunglasses covering his eyes. He walked toward us with long, comfortable strides, ignoring looks from my coworkers, his attention aimed directly at me as if I was his prey and he had all the time in the world to catch me.

I had to admit, seeing him like that rekindled the fires that had once burned low in my belly. I hadn't seen him much the past few days, except when he was asleep, and seeing him this way was like a punch to the gut. Sometimes even I forgot how magnetic and beautiful my husband was.

"Hi," he said, coming to a stop at the entrance to my cubicle.

Conor gave him a slap on the back. "Nice to see you again."

"Same to you." Henry took off his sunglasses and aimed his

attention to me. "Hey." He reached out and touched the small of my back and gave me a quick, warm kiss.

"What are you doing here?" I asked, my lips tingling. It had been over two months since we'd last had sex, and all of a sudden, it was as if he was sending out pheromones that my body was picking up.

"It's a nice day. I wanted to see if you were available to go for a ride on the Harley with me." He glanced down at his watch. "Just for a while."

"I was just telling her to get out of here," Conor said, stuffing his hands in his pants pockets. "To take the rest of the day off. She's been working too hard."

Henry raised a dark eyebrow at me. "Well?"

My eyes flicked between the two men but eventually landed back on my husband. "You're lucky I'm wearing jeans and boots," I said to Henry. "But I don't have my jacket."

The corner of his mouth lifted. "I brought it with me."

Conor started to back away. "See you on Monday, Logan," he said and walked off toward his see-through office.

———

In the parking lot, Henry pulled my jacket from a saddlebag and came around to me. I slipped into the sleeves while he held the jacket out, then he gently tugged my hair out from the collar. I was acutely aware of his gaze on my face as he zipped up the front of my jacket and closed the snap at my neck, his fingers touching the skin at my throat for the briefest moment.

"What's the special occasion?" I asked as he handed me my helmet.

"The sun is out," he said. "What better way to enjoy the approaching spring than to ride together?"

Spring, the time of year when animals answered the mating call. That explained it all.

He gazed down at me, his blue eyes warm with sincerity. "But mostly you. You're the special occasion." He swung a leg over the bike and turned to me. "Ready?"

I pulled the helmet over my head and sat on the bike, wrapping my arms around his torso. "Ready," I said and the bike roared to life.

We rode around downtown Denver then headed west on Sixth Avenue toward the mountains. Even though I didn't have to, I held on tight, pressing my body into his back. Every now and then I caught a whiff of his scent, and it was all I could do not to hump him right then and there.

The fresh air and the sunshine were like bleach to my soul. With each mile we traversed, I felt as if the tethers that had been holding me down were loosened, flapping behind me in the wind until they tore off one by one.

By the time we stopped at a scenic lookout and I climbed off the bike, I could almost imagine that I was the old Elsie, whose only worry was whether following her brother to Oklahoma was the right thing to do. That girl was still excited about life's possibilities, still woke up with a smile on her face. She didn't know yet about the pain of losing her only sibling, didn't know yet the highs and lows of loving the boy of her dreams, of the mental anguish a man can go through when he realizes he's not the man he thought he was. She didn't know that marrying the love of her life did not guarantee a happily ever after, that heartbreak could still occur on the other side.

"What are you thinking?" Henry asked, coming up behind me and wrapping his arms around my waist.

I looked out over the view of the jagged mountains, and decided that, for today, I could be that old Elsie. I twisted around in his arms and looked up into his face as I unzipped his jacket and slipped my arms inside. "Absolutely nothing," I said, molding my body against his.

He raised an eyebrow, intrigued. "You sure?"

I stood on my tiptoes. "I lied," I whispered against his ear, my lips brushing against his lobe. "I was thinking about how I want you to bend me over this bike, spread my legs apart, and fuck me hard."

My words hit their intended target; I felt the stirring in his pants almost immediately. He gazed down at me with a dark, heated expression and said in a rough voice, "God, I want to."

"Then let's do it," I said, knowing that the old Elsie would have had no reservations, even if this new one did.

"Has it been long enough?" he asked, uncertainty tainting his desire.

Dr. Harmon had originally advised we wait for a month before trying again with the caveat that sometimes it took longer to heal emotionally. I wasn't entirely sure about the stability of my emotional state, but my body was definitely raring to go. "Hell yes," I said without hesitation.

The ride back to our house was long and gave me ample opportunity to question myself. Slowly but surely the old Elsie flew off into the wind, as if returning to the vicinity of our house brought us back to our issues. By the time Henry parked the bike in the garage, I had almost convinced myself that it was too soon, that I wasn't ready yet.

I climbed off the bike the moment Henry killed the ignition, immediately taking my helmet off and placing it on the shelf. I held out a hand, waiting for Henry to hand me his helmet too. I stood by the shelves, my back to the bike, taking my time, uncertainty clouding my thoughts.

"Hey, come here," Henry said gently. He leaned against the bike's seat and pulled me between his legs, setting his hands on my waist. "You okay? Having second thoughts?"

He knew. Just one look at my face and he knew. "How do you do that?" I asked, more to procrastinate than from actual curiosity.

He flashed a crooked grin. "Give me some credit here. I've known you since you were twelve." He guided me closer and gently touched his lips to mine. One hand slid up my back and tangled in my curls. "I've missed you, Els."

"I've missed you too." I leaned into another kiss, cocking my head to get deeper inside him, feeling my desire roaring back to life. With that kiss, all my worries melted away.

I straddled one thick thigh and ground myself into him, struggling to ease the ache between my legs. He groaned in appreciation, flexing the muscles on his leg to give me more resistance.

"Fuck, Els," he rasped against my lips.

His words sent arrows of lust directly to my loins. I took a step back and shrugged off my jacket; he followed suit then reached behind his head and pulled off his T-shirt. He raised one dark eyebrow, waiting for my next move.

"Strip me," I said, giving him access to my body once again. His hot palms slid under my shirt and up my back, undoing my bra clasp even as they moved up to pull my shirt over my head. "Smooth," I said with a smile.

"It's a gift." His hands moved down to the waistband of my jeans, undoing my button and fly. Then, with nostrils flaring, he slid them down my hips, hooking his thumbs in my panties and taking them along for the southbound trip.

I kicked off my boots and stepped out of my pants, standing completely naked in the garage and loving it. Henry's hands roamed around my body as his eyes drank me in with lust and adoration, kneading and spanking and pinching at will.

"I want to see you straddling the Harley like that." He stood up and lifted me onto the bike. The cool bite of the leather was a nice contrast to the heat of my crotch. I gave him a seductive smile and leaned over to grasp the handlebars, arching my back to improve the visual.

"Like this?" I asked with a raised eyebrow.

He took a deep breath, his nostrils flaring. "Fuck, that's sexy," he ground out. "I'd like to do you right there on the bike."

"Then do it."

It didn't take him long to kick off his shoes and pants. Don't let men fool you; they can actually move quite fast when there's sex on the line. In less than a minute, he was standing beside the bike completely nude, ready for action. "Lean over a bit more." He palmed his erect cock with one hand while the other reached over and started the bike.

The effect was instant, like turning on a massive vibrator between my legs. I shifted around, trying to find the best angle, moaning when I found it. "Oh!"

Henry climbed on behind me, sliding me forward onto the red gas tank. He grasped my hips and lifted my ass up, then guided me to his shaft. I sank onto him almost immediately, eager to feel the bike against me again.

He made an indistinct noise through his teeth, no doubt also experiencing the bike's thrums against his balls. "Fuck, this feels good," he barked out. "Why haven't we done this before?"

We sat still for a few moments, enjoying the tremors that racked our bodies. Then he gripped my hips and lifted my ass before he began to rock into me. I reached out and grasped the handlebars to steady myself, standing on the pegs for better leverage.

I felt so wanton and wild, being fucked on a motorcycle by my big biker man, with my hair over my face and my breasts bouncing around. In that moment, nothing outside this garage mattered. Only Henry and me and the bike below us.

I started when he slapped my ass hard enough to sting. I lifted my butt higher, asking for more.

"You like that?" he asked, stroking my heated skin a moment before smacking me again.

The sting was a welcome distraction, the kind of pain that didn't go past the surface of the skin. I welcomed it, wanted more.

Henry moved to the other cheek, slapping the flesh as he said, "You've been shaking this ass at me for years. Now it's all mine." He smacked me again before taking both cheeks in his hands and kneading them. All the while, he was thrusting into me, pushing me closer and closer to the edge.

I heard him start to pant, felt his fingers dig deeper into my flesh. I tightened around him, hoping to chase his climax down.

"I'm about to come," he said and as he did, he pressed me back down onto the bike, shocking me into an intense orgasm. I tried to push up but he held me down, the strong vibrations wrenching another miniorgasm out of me.

I was shuddering by the time he reached over to turn off the bike. He bent down and planted kisses up my spine, lifting my hair out of the way, and stopping at my nape. Goose bumps broke out over my skin as he whispered, "It's good to have you back."

5

"Elsie, can you come up here?" Henry's voice boomed throughout the house as I cleaned the downstairs bathroom. We'd decided to spring-clean the entire house that Sunday afternoon, Henry taking the upstairs while I tackled the downstairs.

I stuck my head out of the bathroom and called out, "Hang on, I'm not done yet."

"Now."

"Yes, sir. Right away, sir," I muttered to myself, performing a sarcastic little salute in his direction. I took my time wiping down the bowl, not in the mood to be summoned in such a manner. I figured if he needed me so badly, then he could come to me himself.

And come he did. "What the hell is this?" Henry said, appearing in the doorway with a round plastic case in his hand.

Shit. "Where did you get that?"

"I was looking for some aspirin in your drawer and found it," he said, his lips a thin line of aggravation. He opened the case, seeing that each pill had been taken up to today. "Why are you taking them again?"

I put down the cleaning spray and wiped my hands on a paper towel to buy some time while I thought of a suitable explanation.

But in the end, I had nothing but the truth. "You know why," I said softly.

He snapped the case shut. "Why didn't you tell me?" he asked, his face red.

"Because . . . I don't know. Because I knew you'd disagree."

"I thought we were trying again."

"You just assumed we would."

"Don't you want to?"

I put the toilet lid down and sat on it. "I do, but . . ." I looked up at him, feeling like I was once again disappointing him. "I didn't think I was ready yet."

He kneeled between my legs and set his hands on my thighs, his long fingers splayed. "If you need more time, then just say so," he said, giving my legs a gentle squeeze. "Just . . . don't leave me out of the decisions."

I nodded, kissing the tip of his nose. I hated that he was mad at me, particularly when we'd just arrived at a good place in our relationship again. "I promise you won't be," I said.

He sighed. "It's been awhile, Els. Doc said we were ready to try again after a normal cycle. You're sure you're not ready yet?"

Easy for him to say; he wasn't the one who went through the harrowing ordeal. "I don't know . . ." I reached up to run my hands through my hair when he captured my wrist.

"We can just call it nonprevention," he said. "To take the pressure off."

I bit my lip. "I guess so."

"Doesn't mean you'll get pregnant right away."

I looked at him, at the unabashed determination on his face, and decided to push myself beyond my comfort zone. For him. "Okay," I said. "I'll make an appointment with Dr. Harmon first for a checkup."

"Really?" he asked, the smile spreading slowly, cautiously. His hand slid up my thigh. I nodded and he let out a relieved laugh, giving me a quick peck on the lips. "God, I love you."

I wanted to return the sentiment but was too filled with anxiety to speak, so I simply pasted my lips to his and hoped for the best.

———————

My appointment with Dr. Harmon took place a few days later. She was a well-respected OB-GYN, often booked for weeks, but she made sure to squeeze me in during her lunch break.

"I've been wondering about you," she said inside the exam room. She looked at her laptop, where her patients' files were held. "So you had an emergency D and C and were released the next day."

"Yes."

"No complications, correct?"

"Correct."

"And you're here because you want to try again?"

"Right."

She stood up and slipped on latex gloves. "Okay, lie back and I will examine you."

I got into position, sliding down to the very edge of the table and slipping my feet into the stirrups. I hated being in this position and what came right after it, but it's one of those things every woman must endure repeatedly. It was best to just go to my happy place until it was all over.

So I thought of a time in Oklahoma when Jason, Henry, and I had gone camping at Red Rock Canyon. We shared a four-man tent, which really meant four people had to lie side by side in order to fit. I somehow ended up in the middle (for man-spacing purposes), which meant sleeping beside Henry. I hadn't thought of him as anything more than my brother's best friend in years, so when I woke in the middle of the night and found him watching me, a frisson of excitement ran up my spine. But the irritating guy didn't say anything. He just got up and went outside, pretending he simply needed to pee. But I saw the way he looked at me, felt the warmth of his gaze on my face . . .

Dr. Harmon pressed on my stomach and I flinched.

"Pain?"

I nodded. "I've had some cramping the past few weeks."

"Bleeding?"

"Beyond my normal period? A little." At her concerned expression, I asked, "What is it?"

She ignored my question. She simply took off the gloves and picked up the phone from the wall, speaking to one of her staff for a few minutes. "Yes, bring the ultrasound machine to room three, please. Also, saline and a catheter."

After she hung up, I leaned up on my elbows, my heart beginning to hammer. "What's wrong?"

Dr. Harmon turned back to me. "If you have about thirty to forty minutes to spare, I'd like to perform a sonohysterogram."

"A what?"

"Sonohysterogram. It involves inserting a catheter into your uterus, which will pump saline into your uterus while I perform an ultrasound."

"An ultrasound? Why, am I already pregnant?"

She shook her head, regret in her eyes. "If my suspicions are correct, you may have suffered uterine scarring from the curettage."

———

I couldn't sleep that night, the worries eating away at me until the dawn began to peek through the blinds. I couldn't imagine how Henry would react; I didn't even know how I would begin to tell him.

I decided it was best if I told him right away, ripping the bandage off and all of that.

So I headed him off at the door as soon as he came home. He hadn't even taken his shoes off before I sat him down at the dining table and prepared to tell him.

But before anything else, I'd make him some eggs and toast. And pancakes. Maybe some fresh-squeezed orange juice if I had the time.

"What's going on, Els?" he asked, coming around the counter and hugging me from behind. He reached out and grabbed the salt and pepper and seasoned the eggs in the frying pan.

I whisked the pancake mix in the bowl until my arm was frozen with fatigue. Henry flipped the eggs over and waited for me to speak.

"Does it have something to do with the visit to the OB-GYN?" he asked softly. When I nodded, he shut off the stove and unplugged the griddle, then gently turned me to face him. "What happened?"

My eyes were already watery when I forced myself to look up at him. "I have Asherman syndrome," I said, hiding the truth beneath confusing terminology.

His eyebrows drew together and he bent down to look into my face. "What's that? Is it serious?"

"It's . . ."

"Just tell me."

"It means I can't have children."

He took a startled step back, his eyebrows drawn together.

"I have scarring in my uterus from the D and C, which means that the embryo can't implant."

"Is it treatable? Is there something they can do for it?"

"There's an operation—"

"Then do it."

"You're already wheeling me down to the operating room and you don't even know what it is yet."

"Does it matter? We need to try everything."

I pushed him away. "Of course it matters. This is my body we're talking about."

"I don't understand. Don't you want to get pregnant?"

"That's not the point."

"Don't you?"

I stared at him for a long time, faced with the question that had been haunting me for the entire night. "I don't think so. No," I whispered.

He didn't say anything. He just stared at me in disbelief, but for the first time in a long time, I was actually being completely honest.

"I don't want a baby right now, Henry," I said, gathering courage with each word. "Not so soon."

"When?"

"I don't know."

He issued a snort of incredulity.

"You said you could wait as long as I needed," I reminded him.

"Not when you keep changing your mind."

"It's my body, Henry, I'm allowed to do that."

"It might be your body, but it's our family we're talking about." He walked farther away, running a palm down his face. "I've been on patrol for twelve hours. I'm too fucking tired for this."

"What about your eggs?"

"I don't want them," he said with distaste. "They've gone cold."

———

We didn't talk to each other for another five days. Henry picked up extra shifts during his days off and when he was home, he said only the bare minimum to get by.

It hurt to be apart from him, more than I'd care to admit, but pride dictated that I remain steadfast in my belief. Asherman syndrome or not, I refused to be guilted into having a baby. Period.

The chill remained until early one morning, when he came

home after a twelve-hour shift looking bedraggled and weary as he took off his clothes. The bed sagged under his weight as he sat down and rested his elbows on his knees. Something about the way he slumped over, about the weary way he held his head in his hands, caught my attention.

I sat up and turned off my alarm, which was set to wake me in a half hour. "What's wrong?" I asked, touching his bare back. When he turned around, his eyes were ringed in red and the look on his face was so heartbreaking that I instinctively crawled over to him. "What is it?"

He grasped my hand on his shoulder and shook his head. "You won't want to know," he said in a broken voice. "Trust me."

"I want to know what it is that's making you this way."

He swallowed hard as he studied my face. "You remember the case with the missing five-year-old boy? The one kidnapped in his front yard in Aurora?"

A cold chill went down my spine. "Yes."

The droop in his eyelids told me that the end of the story was not a happy one. "We found him today."

I covered my mouth as my eyes filled with tears.

"We got a tip from an anonymous caller about a house in Five Points. Sondra and I were the closest, so we took the call."

I sank to my heels as fat tears fell down my cheeks. "Stop. Please."

"We found him. He's alive."

I let out a shuddering breath.

"He's in bad shape though. The EMTs took him to the hospital, but he's dehydrated and there were signs of—"

I covered his mouth, unable to hear anymore. "He's alive," I said. "You saved him."

"He was so tiny in my arms when I carried him out of there, I felt like he might break if I squeezed too hard." He bent his neck down and buried his face in his hands. "He was so helpless."

I wrapped my arms around his neck and kissed his head. "It's okay. He'll be all right now."

When next he looked up, his eyes were burning orbs of coal. "It took everything in me not to kill the motherfucker in that house. To tear him limb from limb." As he talked, one side of his mouth curled up in a sneer and his hands formed fists in his lap. "If Jones hadn't taken him, I would have broken every bone in his mother-fucking body."

I wanted to recoil from this ugly, violent side of Henry that I'd seen only once before. Instead I continued to hold him in hopes that it would anchor him to his humanity. I couldn't afford to lose him again to the undertow of post-traumatic stress. "It's okay," I told him once again because I had nothing else to say.

"It's not okay!" he cried, shaking me off and pacing by the foot of the bed, his muscles straining against his olive skin. "There are a lot of sick assholes out there. And I'm going to take them all down one by one."

I wanted to tell him that he couldn't possibly do all of that himself—he was only human after all—but I figured that, at least for tonight, he could keep on believing that he was capable of the impossible.

Suddenly, Henry crossed the room and, without warning, punched a hole in the wall.

I slipped off the bed in shock, my ass hitting the floor with a thud.

He punched the wall again, creating another dark crater, pieces of drywall crumbling to the carpet.

"What the hell!" I cried, jumping to my feet. I grabbed his arm before he could destroy the wall altogether. "Stop, Henry. Stop!"

His arms dropped to his sides as his anger drained. "It was just a kid," he said, his voice breaking. He sat on the bed and buried his face in his hands. "Nobody deserves to die that young."

I stared down at him, my eyes blurry as it all dawned on me. I'd been so blinded by my own sorrow that I neglected to consider Henry's feelings. I thought he'd coped with the miscarriage, but what I failed to consider was that maybe he'd simply buried his sadness in order to appear strong for me.

I touched his shoulder. "Do you want to talk about . . . the baby?"

He looked up at me with lifeless eyes. "No," was all he said before disappearing into the bathroom.

6

After a long day of work, I went upstairs and lay on the bed with my laptop. I no longer worked in the nursery-slash-office, didn't even know what state it was in these days. Henry had probably painted over the mural by now and put everything back in place, but I couldn't bear to be in there knowing that just underneath a layer of paint was evidence of the hope we'd lost.

I sat there long after the computer booted up, staring at the desktop wallpaper without seeing. I was supposed to be doing work but I couldn't help but think back to Henry's outburst, at his promise of ridding the streets of every criminal.

I knew it wasn't possible, but God bless him for wanting to try.

Instead of logging onto Shake Design's FTP server, I opened a new browser window and searched for the news reports on the kidnapped Aurora boy. I didn't know what possessed me to do it—goodness knows, I couldn't bear to hear it last night—but I suddenly wanted to know, to make sure that the child was okay.

The report didn't reveal much, only that he was in stable condition, but the photograph of his mother standing by his hospital bed was enough to make my heart clench tight. I didn't know how I would stand it, knowing that my child was found but that he was not yet out of the woods. It would break my heart ten times over to see him suffer.

I'd lost a brother once; I didn't think I could survive the loss of a being I'd birthed and raised.

I pushed away from the bed, suddenly angry, and stalked into the closet. I hurriedly dressed in running gear and was out the door, running down the street before I even realized that it was starting to get dark and cold.

To punish myself, I kept going down the block, taking the four-mile running path that I'd run before. I lengthened my strides, not caring that my nose was starting to run, or that my legs were stiff and chilled to the bone. I pushed past the discomfort and ran faster. Finally, two miles away from our house, I came to a stop. My lungs burned and my cheeks throbbed from the cold air, but the endorphins were kicking in and I was suddenly elated beyond reason.

I was alive, I was married, and I had a thriving career. I was living the dream.

I stood in the middle of the quiet neighborhood, raised my eyes up to the navy blue sky and let go. I laughed and laughed until tears leaked out of my eyes and ran down the sides of my face, and then the laughter turned into sobs and I found myself inexplicably crying. I didn't know what was wrong with me, but I was out of control and powerless.

After a few minutes, I wiped at my face and started to run back home, but my muscles had cooled down and refused to move. So I trudged on instead, miserable and cold, unable to control even my own limbs.

"Elsie?"

I turned to find Henry driving alongside me in the Volvo. "Hey," I said with a tired wave.

"Are you running in the dark?" he asked with worry in his voice. "It's freaking cold out here."

I shrugged, suppressing a shiver. "It wasn't so bad before."

"Please get in."

I slid onto the passenger seat and huddled into myself. Thankfully, Henry had already turned on the seat warmer.

"Are you okay?" he asked quietly as he drove us home. He laid a hand on my shoulder and squeezed at the tight muscles there.

"I'm fine," I said, relaxing under his firm fingers.

"You've been crying."

I pulled down the visor and looked at myself in the mirror but there were no telltale signs of my tears. No smeared mascara, no dried snot on my upper lip.

"I can tell, Els," he said. "I've known you forever. I can tell when something's not right with you."

"I'm fine. Really."

"Then why does my gut say you're not?"

I forced a smile as we pulled into our garage. "That's just hunger talking," I said, getting out.

I lay on the couch, intending to rest for just a few minutes before starting dinner, but the next thing I knew Henry was nudging me awake.

"What time is it?" I asked.

"Nearly ten."

I sat up slowly, realizing that Henry must have pulled the blanket over me at some point. "Crap. I need to make dinner."

"I made it," he said, reaching to the coffee table and handing me a plate of chicken Alfredo. "It might be a little hot. I just nuked it in the microwave."

I stared down at the warm plate in my lap then up at my husband, whose face was full of worry. I reached over and kissed him briefly. "Thank you."

"Els," Henry said, his eyes blazing over my face. "Do you want to tell me why you were running out in the dark and howling at the sky?" he asked. "You're not turning into a werewolf, are you?"

I snorted. "No. On both accounts," I replied and stuffed my mouth with creamy pasta before he could ask any more questions, burning my tongue in the process.

"I'm sorry if I've been pressuring you lately," he said. "That was not my intention."

I set down the plate, my appetite lost. "Dr. Harmon said the scarring was pretty bad, that even if I have the surgery, it could still come back."

Henry sat beside me. "Then we'll just let it be and leave it up to fate," he said. "I just want you to be happy."

"I want the same for you."

He wrapped his arm around my shoulder and nestled me close. "Then we'll just take that off the table for now. You can tell me when you're ready."

I pressed my face into his chest, feeling the burn in my throat. "I feel so out of my depth. Everything keeps changing and I can't seem to keep up."

He grasped my face in his hands and looked at me solemnly. "I'll try harder, Els, I promise."

"You don't have to try so hard, Henry," I said, placing my hands over his. "You don't have to be strong all the time. You can be human too."

He blinked a few times and gave a small nod.

"I know you said I can lean on you, but you know, I can be there for you too."

He leaned forward until our foreheads touched. "Okay," he breathed. "I just didn't want you to worry about me. On top of everything else."

"I'll always worry about you. It's my job," I said with a small smile. "So if you wanted to talk about it, you can."

"Okay," he said again but didn't say anything else.

———————

Letting go is often a slow process, but sometimes, when you're ready, it happens nearly all at once. In less than a week, Henry had the office back like before. The desk and computer were in their original places. I'd asked him not to paint over the mural to hold on to some semblance of hope, so he'd just covered most of it up with the bookshelf and books so that the child's silhouette could no longer be seen.

I forced myself to start working in there again, to let go of the notion that the room was a nursery. It was just an office again, nothing more.

One beautiful Saturday afternoon, I went out into our backyard, green now that spring had come. I walked barefoot onto the grass with a white balloon in one hand and a Sharpie in the other. I wrote a girl's name across the balloon's surface and raised my hand up to the clear blue sky.

Then I let go.

The thin red ribbon slid through my fingers as the balloon rose and rose farther away from me.

As I lifted my face up to the sun, a strong hand enveloped mine. I looked over to find Henry standing beside me, his face also turned up, squeezing my hand to let me know he was there like always.

"Remember in Monterey," he said, his voice thick with emotion. "We were standing just like this the day after Jason's funeral."

"Yeah." I remembered that day like it was yesterday, when the warmth of the sunshine wasn't enough to hold off the hollow cold inside as we stood in front of that freshly covered grave.

Henry had reached between us and tried to hold my hand, but I'd wrapped my arms around me instead and continued staring at my brother's gravestone.

"Just hold my damn hand, will you?" Henry had said, his open palm extended.

I didn't have the energy to argue so I did as he asked, and immediately felt better, like I'd found shelter from the hurricane.

"I can't believe Jason's really gone," I'd said with a shaky voice.

"Yeah."

I'd looked up at him through tear-filled eyes. "I guess you're the only brother I have left."

"We'll get through this, Elsie. I'm right here if you need me."

I'd sniffed, wiping at my nose with a tissue. "You have me too."

He'd tried a grin, though it was only a shadow of his beautiful smile. "Guess that makes you my new best friend."

The death of my brother had changed everything for Henry and me, but through the shared sorrow, we'd solidified our bond and learned that we could conquer anything together.

Now here we were again, standing in our backyard, facing down another death. There was no grave, no physical proof that our baby had even existed, but we knew. We felt the loss together.

I don't know how long we stood out there that day, watching that balloon float upward until it was nothing but a white spot against the sky. And I felt it then, while blades of grass tickled my toes and the breeze played with my hair: the weight lifting off my heart and my conscience. I knew in that moment that Henry and I would get through this too.

PART THREE

ESCAPE

1

At the end of March, Henry's probationary period at the police department ended. He was given a formal oral board examination, where they reviewed his performance and offered him a permanent position in the department as a beat cop. He was assigned his own cruiser and would drive around answering calls by himself.

To celebrate, Sondra Jones threw a party for him at a bar called Shooters, inviting every off-duty police officer available. Even a few on duty stopped by to clap Henry on the back and call him a numbnuts, stiff-as-a-board rookie.

"That means he's good," Allison, one of the wives, whispered to me. "If they didn't like him, they wouldn't be messing with him."

"I'm glad being a numbnuts is good," I said, finding the thought of anyone disliking him impossible.

Allison handed me a bright pink margarita and held up her own. "Here's to you, for surviving so far."

"Thank you," I said and took a sip of the drink. I watched Henry from across the room as he talked to a few officers in uniform, and realized that he was now really one of them, part of a family completely separate from me. "Does it get easier?" I asked.

She shook her head. "For some people it does."

"Any sage advice?"

"Listen to him when he tells you about his day. Keep busy. Learn to be spontaneous. Accept that he may need some solitude," Allison said as if she'd said it a hundred times before. "And for goodness' sake, don't watch any of those stupid cop shows because they will fill your head with shit. You have enough to worry about without adding to it with sensationalist crap."

I took a large gulp of my drink. "Thank you." I scanned the crowd, searching for Henry's dark head, when I found him standing at the bar, talking to a tall blonde. She had her hand on his shoulder, leaning over him and laughing.

Allison followed my gaze and leaned closer. "Oh, and beware of the badge bunny."

I turned back to her and grinned. "We called them 'uniform chasers' in the military." I glanced back at the blonde, who was quite obviously fawning over my husband, not that I blamed her. Henry was breathtaking on a normal day. Add a badge and uniform and he was practically irresistible.

"So you know that they don't care that he's married. They'll pursue your husband like a hound dog. One time, one of them came to my house. I chased her out of there with a 44mm." She shook her head and laughed. "And Rick is nowhere near as handsome as Rookie."

As Allison was talking, the blonde ran her hand down Henry's back and pinched his ass. Henry immediately took a step back, grabbed her wrist, and said something to her. The woman just flipped her hair over one shoulder and laughed.

I watched for a few more minutes, fascinated with how Henry was dealing with being pursued. Finally, I decided I'd help him out. I finished my drink and placed the glass on a nearby table. "Okay, time for me to pee on my territory," I told Allison.

She laughed. "Good luck. Kick her ass."

I walked across the darkened room, doing a quick compare and contrast between Blondie and me. She had amazing legs encased in a miniskirt and the woman had boobs for days. I was not so endowed with my B-cups but I was confident enough with my looks to walk up and wind my arm through Henry's.

"Ah, here's my beautiful wife," Henry said and kissed my cheek.

Blondie's eyes took careful stock of me, attempting to make me uncomfortable under her scrutiny. I imagined she was gauging how well I was able to keep my husband satisfied. "Nice to meet you," she said with a fake smile. "Officer Logan and I were just talking about politics in the workplace."

I raised my eyebrow. "Oh, was that before or after you grabbed his ass?"

She had the audacity to look shocked. "I didn't!"

And that was about the time the margarita kicked in. "Listen, I was right there," I said, pointing at the table where Allison and a few other people were sitting and watching. "I saw you grab a handful of a man who's quite obviously wearing a wedding band."

Blondie pursed her red lips.

"I don't say this often because the women I've come across have been respectful of marriages, but," I said, feeling my inner bitch coming out, "if you touch my husband again, I will knock you the fuck out."

She snickered and looked down her nose at me. "Really? Threatening assault and battery in a room full of cops?" she asked with a sneer. "You'll be in jail faster than you can blink."

And suddenly, I was furious. I hated women like her who thought they had free rein to destroy relationships at whim, and I hated what they did to the image of women altogether. Not that I excuse cheating men for their behavior—far from it—but it takes two to tango.

Henry must have sensed my anger because I felt him squeeze my side. "Hey, simmer down," he whispered in my ear, then said quite loudly, "you have absolutely nothing to worry about."

I fought to control my temper, reminding myself that my actions would reflect poorly on Henry. I stood straighter and consciously relaxed my body, shook out the fists at my sides. "Marriage is hard enough these days," I told her. "Why don't you do the right thing and find someone who's not already attached? Woman to woman, I'm asking you to have some respect."

I didn't stick around to see her reaction. I just turned away and walked off, tugging my husband with me. When we'd crossed the room, he grabbed me from behind and kissed the side of my neck. "Thanks for saving me," he said, rubbing his scruff against my skin. "I wish you were always around to chase off all the badge bunnies."

"You mean this wasn't the first time?"

He chuckled. "If you knew how many times this has happened, you'd never let me leave the house again."

I wasn't sure if that was just his vanity talking, but I chose to believe he was just kidding. "And what do you do?"

His breath was warm against my ear when he said roughly, "I tell them I'm madly in love with my best friend's younger sister."

"And that stops them?"

One side of his mouth curled up. "No, but I think the fact that I talk about you for the next fifteen minutes does." He pinched my chin and brought my lips up to his.

"This probably won't help with your street cred," I whispered against his lips, glancing at the people around us. "Next thing you know, your buddies will be calling you whippednuts."

He smiled, the skin wrinkling around his eyes. "That's fine. As long as it helps with my marriage cred."

————————

A little while into the party, when most people were already three or four drinks deep, I found myself standing at the bar with Sondra Jones.

She glanced down at me with a lidded, almost condescending gaze. "Oh, I didn't see you there," she said, then barked out a drink order, needing no other tactic than her sheer presence to get the bartender's attention. When she got her drink, she turned around and leaned against the bar. "So Henry tells me that you've been having a hard time dealing with his new career."

I was already loose from two drinks and couldn't have contained the rolling of my eyes if I tried. "Of course he did."

"I'm not the enemy here, Elsie."

"No, you're just the woman Henry's spent way too much time with the past twelve weeks, the person he confided in when he should have been confiding in me." I didn't know what in the world possessed me to say it, but there it was. The ball was in her court.

"Whatever drama it is that you have created in your head, let me assure you that it's not true. I am not attracted to your husband. As you can see," she said, motioning to the tall black man across the room, "I have a very sexy man of my own. My time with Logan was spent teaching him the ropes, making sure he followed regs, making sure he didn't do something stupid that could get him killed when he goes solo."

I swallowed hard as my heart pounded in my ears. "I didn't say you were interested in him." More than anything, I was just pissed he'd confided in her at all.

"You didn't have to. I see how you look at me."

I bristled. "Believe it or not, I don't think that every woman is out to get my husband."

"Well then I apologize, but history and experience is on my side. I've been accused far too many times."

"I'm sorry you've gone through that, but I trust my husband."

"So you threatening to knock that bitch out, that was you trusting your husband?"

"That was me giving some uniform chaser the finger."

Sondra grinned. "Well then you showed more restraint than I would have."

I shrugged and looked away.

"Look," Sondra said, her usually stern demeanor softening. "I get it. You're his wife and feel like he should be confiding in you, but he's a cop now, and there are certain things that cops can only talk to one another about. Just be glad he actually talks. Some people keep all that inside. You know what happens to them?"

"They self-destruct."

She touched her nose.

I knew that better than anyone. "You don't have to tell me. I've seen it happen once and it wasn't pretty."

She eyed me for a long while. "Then it's your job to keep it from happening again."

———

At the end of the night, as I helped a drunk Henry into bed, he started singing "Wonderful Tonight" by Eric Clapton. Clad only in pajama pants slung low over his hips, he grabbed me around the waist and started to sway, crooning the tune against my ear.

I wrapped my arms around his neck, enjoying the play of his muscles against my bare skin as he moved.

"I hope you know I would never cheat on you," he said, the edges of his words softened by the alcohol.

"Never say never," I said. "Some men enjoy the attention and fall for it."

"I'm not 'some men.' I'm The Man and the only thing I've fallen for is you."

I chuckled, pressing my body closer to his. "You get so sentimental when you're drunk," I teased, but deep down in the recesses of my heart lay a thought, a suppressed fear, that maybe someday, when faced with so many other beautiful women, Henry would find me lacking.

2

They say that those closest to a person don't see the subtle changes in their loved one, but that's not to say they don't *feel* it. When you really know someone, you feel the delicate ripples that mar the surface of his personality, even if you never see the sinking pebble that caused it.

"It feels like we haven't had a date in forever," I said as Henry and I got ready to go out to dinner. I watched as he slipped on a black shoulder holster over his T-shirt and clipped in his gun and two extra magazines. He wore a button-down shirt over it to conceal his weapon from the public.

"Is that really necessary?" I asked, motioning to his getup. "We're just going to Chili's."

Henry nodded. "It seems like overkill but we live in a different time now, a new era where a fucked-up loner can go into a place like a movie theater or a mall and start shooting at random."

Yes, we definitely live in a different time, when guns are vilified as dangerous even though they're necessary to keep citizens safe. I guess your point of view depends on which end of the gun you're facing.

At the restaurant, Henry pulled out a chair for me and took the one against the wall, where he quite intently scanned the room.

"Are you looking for someone in particular?" I asked. When he didn't answer, I said, "Henry?"

He blinked and looked at me. "What was that?"

"I asked—never mind." I turned to the menu and smiled when I came across a particular entrée. "Are you going to have the lucky ribs?" I asked with a teasing smile, but my joke went right past him because, once again, he wasn't paying attention. I sighed and tried to ignore my husband like he was ignoring me.

After we ordered and our drinks arrived, I sipped my iced tea and watched him quietly. His back was rigid, his lips pursed, his eyebrows furrowed, and his eyes everywhere but on me. I wanted to shake him by the shoulders and ask him if he'd even noticed that I'd had my hair trimmed for this occasion.

Me, me, me. I felt like a selfish jerk, sure, but we hadn't gone to dinner together in months; didn't I deserve at least some of his attention?

I set my glass down on the table with a heavy thunk, causing his eyes to flick to me. "What has you so distracted?" I asked.

"I'm sorry," he said, quickly reaching across the table to take hold of my hand. "It feels like we haven't gone to dinner in forever, doesn't it?"

I tried hard to keep my eyes from rolling heavenward; I don't know if I was successful. "Yep."

I was thankful when our food arrived. I didn't know what to do with the sudden awkwardness between us, but stuffing our mouths with steak and potatoes helped fill the silence. Neither one of us, I noticed, ordered the ribs.

After two beers, Henry finally began to relax. The lines on his face eased and, I guessed, he finally decided there were no shady characters in the restaurant with us. "So I answered a call the other day about a noise disturbance at an apartment complex," he said, leaning back in his seat. "The dog had been barking all night, so the neighbors knocked on the door but nobody answered. Come to find out, the resident, who hadn't paid his rent for two months, had skipped town. He took everything with him, everything but the couch and the bed."

"What about the dog?" I asked, glad that he was finally talking.

"Animal control had to take him to the pound," he said. "Such a shame. He was a beautiful chocolate Lab, looks nearly identical to Sissy, Mr. Parson's dog in Monterey. Do you remember her?"

I nodded, smiling at the memory of the dog and of our childhood together. Sissy was an indoor dog but once in a great while, she'd escape the confines of her home and run wild through the streets. Henry, Jason, and I had helped Mr. Parson corral the dog on more than one occasion, and had a blast chasing a playful Sissy around the neighborhood.

"Excuse me, are you a cop?" a male voice asked above us.

I groaned inwardly as I twisted around to glare at the young man standing by our table.

Henry gave him a wary look. "Yes."

The man crossed his arms over his chest. "Do you know an Officer Perez?"

"I do," Henry replied.

"Well, he pulled my girlfriend over the other day and gave her a ticket."

Henry looked at him impassively, waiting for whatever it was that was so important. "Well, was she speeding?"

"A little, I guess."

"Well then I don't see the problem."

"I don't think she deserved it. She was on her way to the hospital. She's a nurse and they needed her in the ER."

Henry shrugged. "If she was speeding, then she deserved a ticket."

"But she was trying to get to the hospital."

Henry saw that my face had turned red and that I was gripping my fork unreasonably tight, so he said, "Well, I'm sorry but there's nothing I can do about that. Tell your girlfriend that she can fight the ticket in court, if she thinks she's innocent. Otherwise, I'd appreciate it if you'd let me finish eating dinner with my wife."

The guy huffed out his chest but eventually left, dragging his feet back to the table where his embarrassed girlfriend waited.

Henry shook his head, the distracted look back on his face. "Sorry," he said but our conversation was derailed and we finished dinner in uncomfortable silence.

———

During work one day, I walked into Kari's cubicle just to while away some time. "I've been staring at the screen for so long, I'm pretty sure I'm going cross-eyed," I said, taking off my eyeglasses and massaging the bridge of my nose.

She leaned back in her chair and sighed, rubbing her eyes. "I've got a case of the Mondays too."

"At least Henry's got the day shift this week," I said, leaning against her desk. "Maybe we can actually hang out."

"Or let things hang out," Kari said, wagging her eyebrows.

"I swear sometimes I wonder if you're just a horny teenage boy trapped in a woman's body," I said, laughing. I picked up the e-reader that was peeking out of her purse and turned it on. "Let's see what you're reading this week."

"Oh," Kari said, her eyes lighting up. "I'm in the middle of this novel about a girl who dresses up like a groupie to try to catch her rock star boyfriend cheating. It's pretty raunchy but funny."

I looked at the gadget in my hand and read a passage. "This is definitely not the kinky billionaire stuff you've been reading."

"No, I've moved on," she said, taking the e-reader and slipping it into her desk drawer. "It was like a gateway drug to other, more smexy stories."

I shook my head at her. "If you weren't such a great designer, I'd tell you to find a job that involves reading all day."

"Right?" she said, throwing her hands up in the air. "I would be all over that like an alpha male on a woman with a dark past."

I laughed and put my glasses back on. "You read too much."

"Not possible."

———————

That night, I decided to take a page from Kari's book and give Henry a sexy welcome home surprise. I slipped out of my clothes and wore only a tie, a trench coat, and my sexiest black heels. Then I took the computer chair downstairs and set it in the living room so that I could do a spinning reveal as soon as he walked in the front door. I even hooked my phone to the radio and put on a sexy playlist to set the mood, then dimmed the lights. The stage was set for seduction.

I sat in the chair and watched the clock on the wall, sure that he would walk through the door at any moment. But six o'clock rolled by, then six fifteen. By six thirty, I got up and checked my phone and found no messages, nothing that would indicate he was running late.

In my heels, I went to the laundry room and transferred some clothes into the drier, then folded some clothes with my ear trained to the driveway. Nothing.

Afterward, I went upstairs and put away the clothes, keeping an eye out for his car through the window. Still no Henry.

By this time, my toes were starting to pinch in my shoes and my level of desire was starting to wane. I finally called Henry at seven.

"Hello," he answered, the sound of laughter and talking loud behind him.

"Hey, are you still at work?" I asked to be sure before I jumped to conclusions. Surely my husband wasn't out partying while I waited for him at home, right?

"No. Perez and I were just at the bar, taking a load off."

"What bar?"

"The Pub on Broadway." Then he said, "You weren't waiting for me, were you?"

I kicked my shoes across the room. "Yes, I was. You told me you were getting off at six."

He sighed. "I did. But I had a rough day and needed to relax."

And you couldn't do that at home? I wanted to ask. "Fine then, go relax," I said and hung up.

I slumped onto the computer chair, spinning as I seethed. Here he finally had some time to spend with me and instead he was out with someone he works with. I couldn't understand it.

Unless it wasn't Perez's company that he was really enjoying.

The nasty thought planted itself in my mind and grew. Within minutes it had sprouted into full-grown paranoia. Before I could change my mind, I ran upstairs and changed into a denim mini with frayed edges that I hadn't worn since college and a red tank top. Then I dug deeper into the closet and found a blond wig I'd once used for a Halloween costume. I tied my hair back and put the wig on, then proceeded to put on a heavy layer of makeup.

It didn't take long before the reflection in the mirror was nearly unrecognizable.

I gave myself one more look and before I could lose my nerve, I slipped into my heels, grabbed my purse, and was out the door.

———

I'd never been to the Pub before. It was small enough that I spotted Henry, already in his civvies, sitting at the bar as soon as I walked in. For one clear moment, I realized that I was acting like a complete lunatic—I mean, really? Dressing up to spy on your man?—and was about to do an about-face when I saw the guy sitting next to

Henry getting to his feet. He gave Henry a pat on the back, threw some money on the counter, and headed my way.

I panicked and sat down on the nearest empty chair. When Perez walked by and out the door, I breathed a sigh of relief.

"Hi, sweetheart."

I turned and saw that I'd inadvertently sat with an older man of about fifty, who was wearing a white suit, a white ten-gallon hat, and an off-white smile. "Sorry. I didn't realize this table was taken," I said lamely.

He grinned widely. "Oh, you are more than welcome to sit on me, I mean, with me."

I stifled a laugh and turned in time to see an attractive young woman who couldn't have been more than twenty stand up from her table of friends, motioning to Henry. They bobbed their heads, giving her the go-ahead to approach him.

"Like hell," I said and stood up, crossing the room swiftly despite my tall heels, and sitting myself down on the empty stool.

Henry glanced at me then looked back down into his beer, dismissing me as yet another badge bunny.

The bartender stopped in front of me with a questioning look.

I cleared my throat and said in a low, husky voice, "Scotch on the rocks, please." I don't know why I said it. I didn't like the taste of Scotch and it definitely wasn't something my character would drink. But hell, it was the first thing that came out of my mouth.

"We've got two, Glenfiddich twelve and Glenlivet."

Shit. I knew next to nothing about Scotch, despite my dad's appreciation for it. "Which is your favorite?" I asked in the voice again.

"The Fiddich."

"Then I'll take that."

I braved a glance beside me and saw Henry with his head bowed, grinning to himself.

"What's so funny?" I asked automatically, then immediately wanted to kick myself. I wasn't here to interact, only to observe.

He shook his head. "Nothing."

I realized then that I was still wearing my wedding ring. I pulled my hands to my lap and quickly took it off, slipping it into a small pocket inside my purse. Still affecting the husky voice, I extended my hand and said, "I'm Lola."

He shook my hand. "Nice to meet you, Lola," he said and quickly added, "I'm married, just so you know."

I took a sip of my Scotch and tried not to cough. "Oh. Tell me about her."

His blue eyes danced across my face, warming my skin. I didn't know if he recognized me but the way he looked at me sent tingles down my spine. Even after all this time, he could still melt my panties with just one look. "Her name's Elsie," he said. "She's beautiful and loving and so giving. And a tiny bit crazy."

"In a good way, I hope."

He nodded, that smile still dancing lightly along his lips. "Yes, definitely."

"She sounds like a lucky girl, to have you."

He turned back to the beer in his hand. "I'm the lucky one," he said, taking a swig. "I almost lost her once, you know."

"Really. What happened?" I set my elbows on the bar and leaned close.

"My best friend—her brother—died and then I deployed for six months to the same place where he was killed. I lost my fucking mind after that, and I broke up with her. I broke her heart. I broke mine."

My heart hurt at the despair still in his voice. It was clear, even after all this time, that it still haunted him. "I'm sure she forgave you."

He grasped the beer bottle tight. "I sincerely hope so. I did her a favor, breaking up with her when I did."

I recoiled. "How do you figure?"

"It could have been so much worse. I could have cheated or become violent when things got rough again. I could have held on to her, even if I knew my mind wasn't right, and I might have really hurt her. We might not be together today. Can't I at least get some credit for recognizing when I wasn't right in the head?"

I met his gaze squarely and said, "She's forgiven you, I'm sure of it."

"Can I get a written guarantee? Notarized, even?"

I chuckled and tried to take another sip of my amber drink. It was clear, from repeating my words of long ago, that I was busted. Still, it didn't hurt to keep pretending. "So . . . rough day?"

"Pretty uneventful actually," he said without hesitation. "Answered a bunch of garbage calls. The highlight of the night was answering a noise disturbance call, then finding a bunch of underage kids drinking."

"Did you bust them?"

"I did," he said, bobbing his head. "But I felt bad about it. Hell, I remember being one of those kids."

"Yeah, I remember," I murmured into my drink.

"This job is . . . not what I originally thought. It's more taxing than the Air Force, emotionally at least," he said softly. "It's like I'm being dragged in a thousand different directions, but at the end of the day, I have to pull myself back together."

"How are you dealing with that?"

He gave a shake of his head. "Sometimes I'm not so sure I'm doing a good job of it. My biggest fear is that, one day, I'll come home and find her gone."

"Why would you think that?"

"Because it's happened to so many other guys at the station. My marriage is not impervious to it."

"Have you told her all of this?"

"No," he said with a rueful grin. "I've had a hard time communicating with her lately. I see the way she looks at me, with awe and adoration, but if I tell her all of this, I'm afraid that she'll look at me again with fear."

"Fear? What does she have to fear?"

"That I'll leave her again."

I swallowed hard, recognizing the truth in his words. "Well, I don't think you should keep anything from her. She needs to know all that you're going through."

"If I tell her everything, she'll have nightmares. I'd rather not put her through that."

"You don't think she can handle it?"

"She definitely can. I just don't want her to." He stood up then, signing the bill. "Well, I've got to get going. Can I walk you back to your car?"

I lifted my glass with half a finger still of Scotch. "I'm not quite done yet."

He took the glass and slid it away. "Ready?"

I held a hand up to my throat. "I'm not the kind of girl who goes home with a guy after one drink, even if he is a really hot cop."

"I'm just doing my duty, making sure you make it to your vehicle safely, ma'am."

I took his hand and we headed out the door. At my car, I reached for the door handle when suddenly he caged me in with his arms, his breath heavy against the side of my face. "I'm not normally attracted to badge bunnies," he said, his hands sliding up the back of my thigh. "But you've got something about you that gets me so riled up."

I gasped when he pushed his erection into my backside. "Officer, are you frisking me?" I asked with a smile.

His voice was impossibly raspy when he said, "Come with me and find out."

It took us approximately seven minutes and fifty-five seconds to get home. I parked and raced out of the car with my heart pounding. Henry caught me at the foot of the stairs and locked his hard arms around me. "Lola, you've been a bad girl," he said, tracing the curve of my neck with his tongue.

I froze. "Henry . . ."

"No. My name's Officer Smith tonight," he said, biting my earlobe. "And I'm here to arrest you. Unless you can convince me otherwise."

I was arrested all right, completely captivated by this man and this new game we were playing. "Then tell me what I can do, Officer."

He released me and took a step back, beckoning me with his finger as he backed into the living room and onto the computer chair. "Take off your clothes."

It struck me then that we were in exactly the same place I'd intended, only we'd taken the long route. But then again, wasn't that the story of our lives? Nobody could ever accuse us of taking the easy way to the finish line.

I started with my top, slowly lifting it over my wigged head to reveal my black bra.

He leaned back into the chair, his legs spread wide before him as he adjusted the crotch of his jeans. "Now your skirt, Lola."

I unbuttoned the miniskirt and stepped out of it so that I was standing in nothing but my underwear and heels. With the wig and makeup still on, I could almost believe that I was a different person, someone whose only goal was to seduce this sexy cop in front of me. In that moment, I *was* Lola.

"Take it all off," Henry said, palming his erection through his pants.

With one quick snap, my bra came falling away from my chest, freeing my breasts that had become heavy with need. I slung my thumbs into the waistband of my thong and began to pull it down, keeping my legs straight as I bent down to give him a nicer view of my assets. I kicked the panties in his direction; he caught them midair and held them up to his face.

"So turned on already," he said, biting his lip as his eyes caressed my entire body. He sat up and beckoned me closer. "Come here."

I slinked over to him in my heels, completely intoxicated with his obvious need and the way it made me feel so sexual. If we'd had a stripper pole, I would have gladly jumped on it to keep his hungry eyes trained on me.

He spun me by the waist and kneaded my behind. "I love this ass," he said, giving it an exploratory smack. I squeaked when he slapped it again, hard enough to send my flesh rippling. "Did that hurt, Lola?" he asked, smacking me again.

"Yes," I breathed. "But it feels good."

"Get down on your knees."

I complied, going down as he stood up and pushed his pants and underwear down to his ankles. I watched with hungry eyes as his erection sprang free, long and thick and hard as granite. I licked my lips, eager to taste him.

"You like what you see?" he asked with a smirk.

"I don't think I can fit it all in my mouth."

"You can try," he said, leaning forward and pushing the tip against my lips. I opened my mouth a fraction as he pushed in, my tongue flicking out to taste the first sign of his arousal. My hands splayed on his hard thighs, feeling his muscles straining as he inched his shaft farther into my mouth.

"Yes, Lola, like that," he said as he began to thrust, gradually pushing deeper inside. "Relax and breathe."

I did as I was told and soon I was taking him in deeper than ever. He threw his head back and groaned. "Shit, yeah," he ground out a moment before taking hold of my head and pumping in earnest.

I held on, making a vacuum with my lips as he fucked my mouth.

Before I could blink, he pulled out and was down on his knees, grabbing my hair and my chin and crushing my mouth against his. His tongue invaded the space his shaft had previously inhabited, swirling around with my own until I was breathless and dizzy. On and on the kiss went, the taste of Scotch and beer and precum intermingling in our mouths.

He stood suddenly and took me with him, throwing me onto the couch as easily as if I were a rag doll. He positioned me so that I was on my knees on the couch, my hands resting on the backrest and my ass in the air.

I twisted my head around to watch him pull off his remaining clothes, my eyes blazing across his chiseled body. God, he was physically perfect. Tall and brawny, with a wide chest and large biceps, his muscular legs balancing out his upper half. "Damn, you're sexy," I found myself saying.

He grinned a moment before he took hold of my hips and surged inside me, filling me up with one smooth stroke. I tried to reach around to touch him, but he grabbed my wrists and held them behind my back.

I leaned my forehead against the back of the couch, completely at his mercy as he pumped into me, groaning through his teeth as he did so. His fingers dug into my skin, lifting my hips higher to allow him deeper inside me, my muscles squeezing, holding on for dear life. I parted my lips to speak, but before I could tell him how good he felt, his fingers were invading my mouth. "Remain silent," he said. I sucked on his digits as he rammed into me, winding me tighter and tighter.

He pulled his hand away abruptly, then I felt him spread my ass cheeks wide and circle his damp fingers around my puckered hole. I gasped, never realizing until now how sensitive that area could be. Every stroke sent tingles straight to my core, pushing me closer to orgasm.

Then his thumb penetrated me, pushing past the burn, making me gasp at the invasion. The rest of his fingers splayed on my back as he began to rock into me once more, the pleasure now magnified twofold.

The orgasm tore through my body like an electric current, my legs nearly buckling as my entire body seized with tremors. Still, Henry held me in place as he continued to ram into me, skin slapping against skin, his cock so deep it was almost uncomfortable, until he was quavering, growling out my name.

"I love you, Elsie," he said, bending down so that his body covered mine, his arms wound around me, clutching me to his damp chest. He spun sideways and we collapsed on the couch, his semi-hard shaft still embedded inside me.

I don't know how long we lay there like that as our breathing started to slow. I'd been too caught up in the moment to even notice, but somewhere along the way, he had pulled the wig off me and thrown it into the messy pile of clothes on the floor.

He might have been able to talk to Lola, but it was the real Elsie he truly wanted.

3

More and more, having a beer with his buddies after a shift became the norm, so I too forced myself to become more social. I often stayed out with friends from work, going to dinner or attending happy hour at the bar down the street. I also started hanging out with Allison, who was quickly becoming my LEO-spouse Yoda.

It wasn't ideal, being separated from Henry in such a way, but it was the only way I stayed sane. Being alone at home, with the past there to haunt me, sometimes proved too much.

One night, while Allison and I were at my house drinking wine and watching a show, I asked if her husband was also in the habit of hanging out at the bar after work.

"Yes," she said. "It bothered me for the longest time until the chief's wife talked to me. She told me it was natural for cops to prefer hanging out with their own kind, because they've gone through the same things together. Camaraderie and all of that."

I knew it was unreasonable but it hurt to think that there were some things Henry could not—or would not—share with me. It was like a wedge between us that was driven deeper each time he kept his feelings from me and unloaded them onto other people instead.

But I had to be the understanding wife. It was expected of me.

Even when he was home, Henry seemed antsy and often went to the gym or for a run, anything, it seemed, but spend time with me. I could feel him drawing away, reminding me of the time he came back from Afghanistan a different man, of the first time I'd felt completely helpless as I watched him withdraw from me.

"Do you think you should give Dr. Galicia a call?" I asked him one night, when he actually seemed content to be at home.

He looked up from his book and frowned. "Why?"

"I don't know. To help you sort through the things you're going through."

"I'm not going through anything."

"Really?"

"Really," he said with a smile that was meant to reassure me. "Besides, we have police counselors available. Should we need them." Then he went back to reading his book, a nonfiction work called *Tactical Evasion Techniques.*

Seemed to me like he could have written it himself. "Then why have you been avoiding me?"

"I haven't been avoiding you," he murmured behind the book.

I waved a hand at him. "Exhibit A, Your Honor."

He took a deep breath and set the book down on his lap. "I'm not avoiding you or ignoring you or whatever it is you're accusing me of."

I sat on the bed. "I'm trying to be understanding, Henry. To be the good LEO wife. But you're making it so hard, especially since you're never home."

He put the book on the nightstand and sat up too, gathering me into his arms. "I know and I'm sorry. I'm just finding my footing here. It'll get easier after a while, I've been told." He pulled away and held my face in his hands, a gesture I didn't realize how much I'd missed until that moment. "Tell you what, I've got the weekend off. Let's go out of town. Let's rent a cabin in the mountains and just get lost in the wilderness."

I nodded, tears stinging my eyes. "Okay."

"Friday I'll pick you up after work and we'll just go, get away from all of this." He pressed a soft kiss to my forehead. "I promise."

Friday afternoon came and I admit I was getting very excited. My bags were packed and waiting in the car, and I had crossed off the important things on my work to-do list. Everything else would just have to wait until Monday.

At four o'clock, Conor called everyone to the break room for a surprise. We filed into the large space and wondered what was underneath the red fabric on the counter. "Ta-da!" he said as he pulled the cloth away with a flourish, revealing a two-flavor slushee machine. "As per request," he said, his eyes suddenly finding mine across the room.

I chuckled in surprise, impressed that he even remembered.

Conor handed out a stack of large paper cups. "But the best part," he said with glee in his eyes. "Is that it's filled with margarita mix and strawberry daiquiri mix."

Kari squealed beside me as she grabbed one of the cups. "Oh hell yeah," she said, then called out, "Best. Boss. Ever!"

Conor pointed at her and laughed. "And don't you forget it!"

For the last hour of work, people either drank in the break room or took their drinks back to their desks to finish working. Conor stood on the adjoining balcony and smoked with a few people, obviously enjoying the atmosphere.

I sat with Kari and a few others at one of the orange tables and shot the breeze, heedless of the high alcohol content in our cups. I kept my phone with me, watching it closely for Henry's call, but by five fifteen, I started to get that sick feeling that our weekend getaway was not going to materialize. I sipped on my daiquiri, hoping I was wrong, that the feeling in the pit of my stomach was just alcohol-related.

At five thirty, Henry called to confirm my fear. "I'm sorry, Els," he said. "They've called me in since they're short one man."

I couldn't help the whine in my voice when I said, "But it was your weekend off."

"I know. But I can't leave them one man down."

I took the call away from the break room, standing out in the hallway. "Henry, you promised."

"I'm sorry, but this is what the job entails."

"Fuck the job," I hissed, the alcohol fueling my anger. "If your job is more important than your wife, then go. But don't expect me to be home when you get back."

"Elsie," he said, his voice gritty with warning and worry. "Don't do that to me. You of all people know about duty."

"You know what duty did to me? It killed my brother, it broke my boyfriend, and now it's taking away my husband."

"I can't do this right now," he said in a terse voice. "I have to get to the station. We'll talk later."

I hung up, not bothering to say good-bye, and leaned against the wall furiously trying not to cry. I ran to the bathroom when the tears could not be contained and I cried in the stall, sobbing silently and wiping at my tears with toilet paper.

I shouldn't have been surprised. I should have known better than to place my hope on promises made of clouds.

———

When I emerged from the bathroom nearly fifteen minutes later, I'd collected myself and fixed my makeup and hoped that my red eyes didn't give me away. Conor walked by my desk with a self-satisfied smile. "So what do you think?" he asked, his hands in his pants pockets.

I think I'm not handling the LEO life very well. I think I'm not handling marriage very well.

"The slushee machine is a nice surprise," I said with a fake smile.

Conor, for all his flirtations and faults, was shrewd at reading body language. It was what made him such a good businessman. "You okay?" he asked, peering at my face.

I took a deep breath and faced him squarely, red-ringed eyes and all. "No, I'm not, and I've had too much alcohol to even bother trying to hide it," I said, then picked up my purse.

"You're not driving in that state," he said quickly. "Stick around and get sober first."

I shook my head, even though I knew he was right. I was stuck here until I got some food in my stomach and the alcohol wore off.

"We can go get some food at that new Korean restaurant down the street. We can just walk there," he said.

"Conor . . ." I meant to remind him that I was married, but rationalized that getting dinner with another man was only as platonic as I wanted it to be. If I never acknowledged Conor's attraction to me, then it would just seem as if two friends were going out to dinner. Henry had friends of the opposite sex who he confided in; why couldn't I? "I think that sounds like a great idea."

But like a guilty fool, I walked out first, afraid that people would see us leaving together. "I'll go ahead and get us a table," I said in a low voice that was a whisper that didn't want to appear so. "While you finish up here."

At the restaurant, I chose the seat with my back to the restaurant so as not to be recognized. I felt myself relax as we received our drinks and Conor made a joke about my trying to get sober with more alcohol.

"I need this tonight," I said, taking more than a sip of sake.

His shrewd eyes watched me. "I'm afraid that will get you the opposite of sober."

"So be it," I said, raising a cup in the air and taking another drink.

It occurred to me then that I'd been getting drunk way too often the past few months, which was unusual for me. I only realized I'd spoken the thought aloud when Conor said, "There's nothing wrong with that."

"For me there is. I don't like getting drunk and losing control."

"There's nothing wrong with letting go of the reins once in a while," he said, completely charming me with that slight Irish brogue. "Let loose and have fun."

"What if I'm just not marriage material?" I asked.

He grinned. "Maybe you are but you're just married to the wrong guy."

I turned a blind eye to the intimation and asked him instead, "Are you?"

"Am I the wrong guy?" he asked, laughing.

"No, I mean, are you the marrying type?"

"I was but not anymore," he said with a shrug. "These days I'm more about cultivating Shake. But should the right woman come along, I might be convinced to change."

"I think Henry is disappointed in me because I'm not ready to try for another baby," I blurted out then laughed at my uncomfortable confession. "Wow, where did that come from?"

Conor shook his head. "It's okay. You can talk to me."

I gave a short nod, feeling a sense of relief wash over me because, for once, someone was around to listen. "It's like he's married to his job and I'm just the mistress who tries to snatch up whatever crumbs of attention he deigns to give me."

"I was married once," Conor said. "But obviously it didn't last."

"What happened?"

"I was too focused on the business and neglected her. I took her for granted, basically, thinking she'd wait for me forever. Turns out, I was wrong." He gave a humorless chuckle. "It sounds like Henry is suffering under the same misconception."

I nodded with a lump lodged in my throat.

Conor's green eyes were vivid and bright, even in the restaurant's dim interior, when he said, "The next time, I'll shower her with the love and attention she deserves. Show her every day just how much she means to me."

I averted my eyes as my cheeks warmed. "Do you miss Ireland?" I asked.

"I don't give myself the chance. I try to go at least once a year," he said, moving on to the next subject seamlessly. "Have you ever been?"

I shook my head. "No. We lived in Germany when I was little, but I don't think we ever made it across the pond. Not that I remember much since I was about four years old at the time."

"It's a fantastic place, full of legends and myths. I'll take you sometime." When he realized what he'd inferred, he added quickly, "If Shake ever has business there, I mean."

His words reminded me of another man who had once promised me Prague for our honeymoon but hadn't been able to deliver due to lack of funds. Now that Henry was a cop with a starting salary of forty-six thousand dollars a year, it seemed less likely that I would ever leave the country.

The memory of our time in Key West filled me with guilt and melancholy. Was it only less than a year ago when we'd had the time of our lives, so excited for the future? I already felt a decade older than that girl who'd spent an afternoon with Henry coming up with funny names for the penis.

Determined to shake off the sadness, I filled our cups with more sake then lifted mine in the air. "To losing control."

"To losing control," he echoed and clinked his glass with mine.

———

A long while later, we left the restaurant feeling giddy and refreshed.

"It's nice to have someone to talk to," I said as we walked back to Shake's parking lot. "Thank you for listening."

"Anytime, Sherman," he said and, for once, I didn't bother correcting him. He stood by my car and waited until I located my keys in my purse. "You sure you're okay to drive?"

I waved his worries away. "I'm fine. I've had a few hours to metabolize the alcohol."

He looked at his watch. "Wow, it's already past eight," he said. "I was supposed to meet up with Julian at seven thirty."

"I'm sorry to keep you," I said.

"Not at all. I'd much rather spend time with you than with a guy any day," he said with an affable grin.

"Well, it's been fun." There was a pregnant moment when our eyes locked, when my heart pounded in my ears because even my own conscience wanted to turn a blind eye. I wanted to kiss Conor in that moment, wanted to again experience the excitement of the unknown. It was an intoxicating feeling, this being wanted.

But in the end, it wasn't in my heart to cheat. Not when my husband was faithful, and especially not when he was currently doing his job protecting the city.

"Good night, Conor," I said and got into my car, watching him in the rearview mirror as I pulled out of the parking lot. I had driven less than a block from the office when red and blue flashing lights lit up behind me. The instant panic of being pulled over throbbed in my chest, and I turned into a restaurant parking lot trying to recall just how much alcohol I'd imbibed. It wasn't a lot, but it wasn't a little either.

To my relief, Henry emerged from the cruiser. I watched him through the side mirror, hardly able to breathe as the confident and powerful man in black uniform walked my way.

"Can you step out of the vehicle please?" he said in a commanding voice.

I mumbled something about his innate ability to be so bossy and stepped out of the car. The moment I stood before him, he grabbed me by the shoulders and pulled me in for a tight embrace. "I'm sorry, Elsie," he said against my hair.

I melted into his body, forgetting why I was mad at him to begin with.

We stood like that for a few moments before he pulled away and was once again the stoic police officer. "Have you been drinking?"

I held up my thumb and forefinger. "Just a bit."

"And you're driving?" he asked, drawing his dark eyebrows together and folding his arms over his chest. "You know better than that."

"It was awhile ago. I'm not drunk anymore." When he appeared unconvinced, I mimicked his pose and said, "You don't believe me? Go get your Breathalyzer thingo."

"Say the alphabet backward then."

"Come on, nobody can do that even when sober!" I cried. "How about I walk a straight line instead?" But even as I took straight steps with my boots, I giggled at the absurdity of the situation.

He held out a hand. "Give me your keys." When I refused, he reached into the car window and pulled them out of the ignition. "Get in my car."

"A 'please' would go a long way."

He put his hands on his waist. "Now."

"No."

His jaw muscles worked and his nostrils flared as he stared at me. Then without warning, he bent down and scooped me over his shoulder, carrying me to the police cruiser. Without much effort, he opened the passenger door and dumped me inside, then closed the door before I could open my mouth and protest.

I sat back, my arms crossed over my chest, and seethed as he closed the window to my car and retrieved my purse and duffel bag.

He was silent as he drove me home, but I wasn't about to back down from a fight. Not when I had a valid reason to be mad.

"You should have just put me in the back since you're treating me like a criminal," I said. "Cuff me while you're at it. Then just lock me up at home where I can wait for you forever."

"You're acting like a child," he said, keeping his eyes on the road.

"I'm acting like a woman who's tired of being second best."

He sighed. "This is my job, Elsie."

"When you deployed, I waited for you. And when you broke up with me, I still held on to the hope that you'd come back. Now you're asking me again to wait for you while you put something else ahead of me," I said, the tears sliding down my cheeks. "When's it my turn, Henry? When are you going to make me your first priority?"

"I left the military for you, didn't I?" he asked, his jaw muscles working.

"That was for your own benefit, because you wanted to be with me. It wasn't because you finally wanted to end my suffering. It was because *you* wanted to make yourself feel better."

"You're not even making sense anymore." He stopped at the curb in front of our house and set the car in park. He turned in his seat to face me. "I left the military for you."

"Then would you leave the force for me?"

His eyes flew over my face, but his lips did not move. He didn't say anything reassuring. Instead he got out of the car, opened my door, and walked me to the porch. He unlocked the front door, set my things down inside, did a quick check of the dark house, then came back downstairs.

Finally, he faced me, allowing me to see the emotions behind his eyes. "I like being a cop. I like helping people and I'm good at it," he said, reaching out to touch my cheek. I stepped aside and let his hand fall away. "So I hope you never ask that of me."

An overwhelming urge to do just that washed over me, but seeing the look on his face, the worry that I would destroy what he'd been working for the past year, kept my lips glued together. It would be so cruel. "You know I'm not going to ask you that," I told him quietly. "I couldn't live with myself if I did."

He reached out, grabbed the back of my neck, and brought me close, touching his forehead to mine. "Thank you," he said in a voice husky with emotion. "Because if you really wanted me to, I would. I'd give up everything for you. Even my own life."

My heart hurt with his pained confession because I knew it to be true. "Just do me a favor."

"Anything."

"Don't let the past repeat itself."

His blue eyes burned bright when he pulled away and stared at me. "I would turn myself inside out before I let that happen again."

4

Relationships are like a pendulum on a clock, swinging from one extreme to another. One hour you're madly in love, unable to imagine life being sweeter, but eventually you reach a point when the relationship starts a downward sway to the center, where apathy often lies. If you're very lucky, your relationship will stop there, but for the unfortunate, the relationship will swing all the way to the point where the bond is tested beyond its limits, when you have to decide to either find a way to swing back together or bail.

As I sat on the couch that night, staring at the clock on the wall, I wondered where we were in the arc, and what we could do to prevent from reaching that dangerous point.

I tried to take my mind off things by watching a bachelor reality show, but after the guy made out with three girls in less than fifteen minutes, I turned the television off and started to read a book instead. Still, I kept glancing up at the clock, wondering what time Henry would come home.

The sound of the key in the door took me by surprise at quarter after six. I shot up off the couch, the blanket tangling around my legs, flabbergasted. "You're home," I cried as soon as he came in.

He stood at the door, half in, half out, and gave me a sheepish grin. "I've got a surprise for you."

I didn't even have time to guess. A second later, a chocolate Labrador came bounding into the house and immediately began sniffing the floorboards.

"A dog?" I asked, my eyes wide.

Henry grinned and tugged on the leash, pulling the dog toward him. "His name is Lawrence."

I approached them with my hands out, allowing the dog to sniff me. When he'd determined I was no threat, I crouched by him and scratched behind his ears. "A dog, Henry?" I asked, still unable to believe it.

Henry sank to his knees and petted the dog's back, keeping his eyes on me. "He was the dog from the abandoned apartment, do you remember? I'd been checking up on him at the pound to see if his owners had claimed him. Today was his last day," he said and added in a softer voice, "I had to save him before they put him down."

"You can't save every dog and cat you come across," I said, even as my heart sighed with his compassion.

"I know. It's just . . . this dog reminded me so much of Sissy. And he's so friendly. And I figured you could use a watchdog around here when I'm gone at night."

"'Friendly' and 'watchdog' don't really go together," I said, warming up to the idea. The dog *was* really cute, and he even smelled freshly bathed. "Has he had his shots?"

"He's had shots, and he's been microchipped, fixed, bathed. He just needs a good home." Henry stared at me for a long time, trying to read my reaction. When I didn't say anything, he put his face by the dog's. "Pwease?" he asked with a goofy little pout. The dog turned his head and licked Henry right up the side of his face.

A laugh bubbled up from my throat. "Oh God, how can I say no to that?" I asked. "You are like twin stooges."

I put my face up to the dog's and let him lick me. I held him by the jowls and looked into his brown eyes. "So . . . your name is Lawrence."

"I figured we could change it. A new name for a new life."

"How about we just shorten it to Law?"

"Law," Henry murmured. "I like it."

We spent the rest of the night playing with Law and figuring out his tricks, and for once, the pressure was gone. But what we weren't acknowledging was that this dog was a temporary bandage, a way for Henry to compensate for his absence and a way for me to make up for my inability to bear a child.

Whatever feeling of joy Law brought was temporary, because sooner or later, the pendulum would swing toward the other side again.

———————

That week, I started running again after work, with Law by my side. He was a good running companion, fast and focused. And even though it wasn't in a Lab's nature, he was fiercely protective of me. He was on high alert each time a male passed us on the sidewalk, and a few times he growled in warning as if to say, "Step off, she's with me."

At night, he slept on Henry's side of the room on a huge cushioned bed, his face always pointed toward the door. His ears would perk up at any noise, and each time Henry walked in through the front door, Law bounded downstairs like a kid on Christmas morning. When Henry was home, Law followed him around without fail. I almost wanted to change his name to Shadow.

I first agreed to take in Law because I saw in him a version of Henry, a lonely soul abandoned by his family, but I only needed to spend one night with the dog to realize that he was actually more like me. We were just two pitiful creatures madly in love with a man who was hardly ever there.

———

One night, I awoke to the sound of large dog paws thumping down the stairs. A few minutes later, I heard Henry's footsteps coming up the stairs and continuing down the hall. "Stay," he whispered and entered the bedroom, closing the door on Law.

I rolled over and even though my eyes were heavy with sleep, I was unable to keep them off Henry as he undressed. As if sensing me, he stilled and turned his head, finding my gaze in the darkness. The bright moon slipped through the blinds and cut across his face, illuminating the deep ruts between his eyebrows.

He climbed onto the bed and crawled over to me, his gaze never once leaving my face. He paused for a moment before he stooped over me, sliding his arms under my back and bending his head to my chest.

Something about the tender way he held me put a vice around my lungs, making it hard to breathe. I lifted my hand to touch the back of his head and said, "You okay?"

He shook his head, his face still pressed to the thin fabric of my T-shirt.

"What's wrong?"

His eyes were closed and his eyebrows furrowed when he pulled away. He sat back on his haunches, straddling me between his legs, and opened his eyes. "Nothing. Everything." With his palms flat against my stomach, he slid his hands underneath my shirt and worked upward, skimming the sides of my breasts, then pulled the fabric over my head. He did the same to my panties, pulling them off me in equal measures of gentleness and need.

My body came alive with his touch, my every nerve standing at attention for him. I didn't know what was going through his mind, but his light, almost reverent touch was starting to undo me.

"Henry . . ."

With a haunted look on his face, he dragged his fingertips up my thighs, along the ticklish parts of my hips, and onto the planes of my stomach. "I just want to look at you and touch you. To make sure that you're really here," he whispered, crouching over me. I felt him sigh into my skin as he pressed his lips to the valley between my breasts, then he tenderly kissed a path down to my stomach where he stopped and laid his stubbled cheek.

"I love you, Elsie," he said against my trembling skin. "I'm not going to let a day go by without telling you that."

Tears stung my eyes as desire transformed into something else: a frightened, helpless feeling I couldn't name. I didn't know what was making him hurt, but I could sense it in the air around him, feel it in the way he moved. So I held him to me, rubbing my palm against the wavy hair on his head, and hoped that it was enough.

"Do you . . . do you want to talk about it?" I asked after some time.

"No. I just need to be with you," he rasped. He moved once again, rolling off to the side and slipping a hand between my knees, sliding it upward until it reached the point where I was already throbbing with want. He lifted my legs apart and suddenly his mouth was breathing on my folds.

I arched my back, the worry momentarily forgotten when his tongue slid inside my cleft, finding the sensitive spot and massaging it. His hands cupped my ass and lifted me up as he deepened the kiss, enveloping my mound with his mouth, increasing the pressure.

The orgasm was quick and acute, racing through my entire body like an electric current. Henry groaned as my muscles throbbed around his tongue, which continued to lap at my clit to sustain the pleasure.

Then he was gone, leaving me cold. He sat up to lean against the headboard and pulled me up. He grabbed the sides of my face and kissed me, his mouth still saturated with my juices as he devoured me. He grabbed my hair and pulled me away, his eyes blazing across my face. "I can't live without you, Elsie."

Every word he said was like a hot knife through my chest, scalding the places it sliced. I wanted to know what had made him so desperately needy but knew that if I asked again, I would only get silence. So to ease his anguish—and mine—I straddled him and positioned his cock at my entrance.

He was breathing hard when I wrapped my hand around his shaft and lowered myself onto its tip. "Fuck yes," he groaned, his eyebrows drawing together as he closed his eyes. "I need to be inside you."

I slowly sank onto his hard length, moaning as a part of him connected to the deepest part of me. With my hand splayed on his stomach, I began to rock my hips, watching his expression darken, the agony and the pleasure etching deep lines into his forehead and bracketing his mouth.

He bent his neck and crushed his forehead to my chest, his hands on my back as he held me close. "I can't lose you ever again," he said in a near whisper. "You're everything to me."

I leaned back, my hips still swaying, and grasped his head. "Look at me, Henry," I said, tilting his face up to mine. I bent down and touched my forehead to his, willing him to open his eyes and just *see*. "I'm here right now."

He opened his eyes the same moment he began to move beneath me, thrusting his hips up into mine. He held me close as we made love, Henry afraid to lose me and I afraid that he actually could.

––––––

Henry awoke with me the next morning, nuzzling into my neck at around eleven in the morning. The sunlight seemed to have brightened his mood as he took a shower and dressed in running shoes, shorts, and a light blue shirt that set off his eyes.

"Where are you going?" I asked, pulling the covers tighter around me.

"Taking the dog to the park." He crouched down at the foot of the bed; a second later, his hands encircled my ankles and the next thing I knew I was being tugged through the covers until I emerged on the other side. "You didn't think I was going to leave you, did you?" he asked with a grin.

I sat up, pushing the sheets off my head, and laughed. "There are other ways to get a girl out of bed."

He raised an eyebrow. "Such as?"

"Coffee. Morning sex. Chocolate," I said, counting them off on my fingers. "Any number of those would have sufficed."

"Ah, but where is the fun in chocolate and coffee?" he asked, then suddenly bent down and rested his hands on either side of my lap, his face inches from mine. "As for the sex . . ."

———————

So we left for the park an hour later, completely sexed out. Whatever had happened last night not only made Henry deathly afraid of losing me, it apparently made him horny as hell. Not that I was complaining about the latter.

"So are we going to talk about last night?" I asked him as we walked in the sunshine. We were nearing the park as Law was starting to get antsy and tugging on the leash a little more.

His mood changed, just a tiny shift in his body that I was able to pick up. "It was nothing."

I'd thought perhaps the sunshine would seep into his skin and light up some of his dark crevasses, allowing him to talk about what was hidden there. I guess I was wrong. "So you coming home freaking out about losing me, that was nothing?" I asked, unable to keep from pushing. If I stopped now, if I just gave up, we would be lost.

He tugged on Law's leash, keeping him at his side. "I just had a rough day."

"You saw someone die, didn't you?"

Henry stopped and turned to me, his face completely still. Finally, after the longest moment, as even the dog strained for motion, he nodded.

"Ah."

"The first one I've seen." We arrived at the park then, and whatever communication I'd opened up sealed shut again as Henry took the opportunity to change the subject. He bent down and unclipped Law from the leash then pulled a tennis ball from his pocket. "Okay, boy, let's see how socialized you are."

To say that Law was excited to see the ball was an understatement. He jumped with glee, literally bowling Henry over with his excitement. The two tumbled to the ground, Henry lying on the grass laughing as the dog licked his face.

My irritation melted away as I watched them play, feeling a warm tickle in my chest. Henry would be an incredible dad.

If he were ever at home, a voice in the back of my head niggled, cooling my insides with the reality of it all.

"Go get her!" Henry yelled and I turned in time to see a ball flying at me, followed closely by sixty pounds of brown fur. I caught the ball and dodged out of the way in time. "Fetch," I said and threw the ball to the middle of the park. Law was immediately on it.

Henry was laughing when he got back to his feet and dusted himself off.

"Nice try," I told him as Law came bounding back with the ball in his mouth. "Good boy," I said, scratching the back of his head.

Suddenly, a little girl came running up to us, stopping a foot shy of Law. She couldn't have been more than three, but she wrapped her little arms around his neck without hesitation and gave him a hug. Law, incredibly, sat still and allowed the child to fawn over him. I'd even go so far as to say he was enjoying it.

It's incredibly cliché, but at that moment, my heart flipped over on itself. I looked at Henry and saw in his face the same awareness, as if we were both watching our future playing before our eyes.

The child's parents came walking up a few seconds later and almost had to pry her off Law, who sat patiently while his fur was being manhandled by chubby little fingers. I was so proud of him in that moment, and I knew that he would be just as patient with our own baby.

———

Henry and I held hands as we walked back home feeling as if the world was in its rightful place, Law trotting ahead of us. Out here, bathed in sunshine and fresh air, it was almost as if we were back to being the newlyweds who were once full of hope and promise.

"I'll do it," I said as we stepped onto our porch.

Henry froze, the key in his hand poised above the lock. He turned and pinned me with his gaze.

"I'll call Dr. Harmon about the surgery," I said, reaching out to touch his shirt, my fingers closing around the soft fabric. "I'm ready to try again."

He didn't say anything, but he didn't really have to. The reverence in his eyes as he gazed at me said it all. And when he picked me up and carried me upstairs to make love to me once more, his silence spoke a thousand truths about the man I had married, the man who'd seen firsthand the ugliness of the world but never stopped believing.

5

"At least fourteen days?" Conor's auburn eyebrows drew together and his lips pursed. He leaned back in his chair and rubbed his hair absently. "I don't know."

"It's important," I said, shifting my stance so that my legs were apart, readying myself for a battle.

"What's it for?"

"Surgery."

His eyes flickered with concern. "Life threatening?"

I sighed. "No," I said, unable to lie and unwilling to tell the truth. I didn't need one more man looking at me with pity. "But it's important."

"Can it wait?" he asked. He looked down at the calendar covering his glass desk. "Can you put it off for two weeks? At least until after we secure the Lombart account?"

I chewed on it for a moment before I began to nod. Two weeks was nothing in the grand scheme of things. "I'll have to double-check with Henry's schedule, but I think that will work."

I turned to leave and was almost at the door when he called my name.

"I want you to go to Atlanta for the pitch."

I spun around, my eyebrows rising in surprise. "You want me to go with you?"

He stuffed his hands in his pockets and flashed dimples. "No, I want you to make the presentation in my place."

"What? Why?"

"It's your baby, isn't it? You know the campaign inside and out. Who better to make the presentation?"

"But that's your job."

He laughed. "It normally is. But I think you would make a more compelling argument."

"One condition," I said, raising a finger. "If we get Lombart, I want a raise."

He grinned, unsurprised. "That was the plan all along."

"A big one."

"We'll discuss the specifics later." He looked at me expectantly. "Well?"

What could I say? This was a huge opportunity. There was no other answer than "Yes."

———

Henry had the late shift for the rest of the week, so I continued to go out after work with Kari and a few others. I figured that if I had two weeks to live it up before I was forced to give up alcohol and partying, I might as well enjoy it now instead of sitting home alone. We went out to dinner, watched movies, and hung out at someone's house and drank. I felt a little like I'd reverted to my early twenties, when partying was almost a necessity, but it felt good to cut loose a little and have some fun. I wasn't hurting anybody and goodness knows I needed to relax.

I came home that Saturday at nearly four in the morning to find Henry's car already parked in the driveway. I closed the front door behind me without any noise and winced when Law came bounding down the stairs. "Hey, boy," I said, fielding his kisses then set-ting him back down. "Quiet or you'll get me busted."

I went upstairs but didn't find Henry in the master or any of the spare bedrooms. I searched downstairs and found no trace of my husband. Then I heard a metallic clink and walked out to the garage, where he was working on his motorcycle in workout pants and a white shirt.

"Hi," I said softly, taking note of the hard squeeze of his jaws.

He continued to twist a monkey wrench for the longest time, pretending not to hear me.

"When did you get home?" I asked.

Finally, he looked up at me but the ice in his stare stole the breath from my lungs. "Two," he said tersely. "Where have you been?"

"Just out with some friends," I said, stepping into the garage and walking closer. "I was buzzing so I slept on Kari's couch until I was sober."

He looked away again, his nostrils flaring. "Check your phone."

I dug through my purse and found my phone. "Shit," I whis-pered under my breath at finding several missed calls and numer-ous unanswered messages. "Sorry. It was on silent."

He stood up then, the anger emanating from him. "Is this what you do every night when I'm working? You go out and get drunk?"

I bristled. Oh hell no. "Excuse me? Isn't that what *you* do every night after work?"

"This is different," he said in a much louder voice. "You shouldn't be out there this late at night. It's not safe for you out there."

"Where exactly do you think I go?" I asked, dropping my purse on the floor. I almost pushed my sleeves up my arms and put my dukes up but decided that was too much.

He glared at me, his jaw muscles still working. "If you only knew what I see every night, all the shit people do when the sun goes down, then you would understand where I'm coming from."

"I'd understand where you're coming from if you ever told me any of the shit you see at night," I spat out. God, I was so tired of this same old argument, of my same old plea. "You just need to open that mouth of yours and talk to me."

"Talk to you? Isn't that what we do every day?"

I shook my head sadly. "You just don't get it, do you?" When he said nothing, I continued. "What happened to you after Afghanistan, all of that shit that ate away at you, it's happening again."

He scrubbed his face with his palm. "Elsie . . ."

"I feel so closed off from you. Like there's this huge brick wall that's between us and I can't climb it." When his jaw hardened once more, I said, "You've got to help me out here, Henry."

His nostrils flared. "Fine. What do you want to know?"

"What happened the other night, when you told me you couldn't lose me again?"

He looked down at the wrench in his hand.

"For fuck's sake, tell me. Talk to me."

"You don't need to know."

"No wonder I have to turn to someone else." I spun around to leave when he grabbed my arm.

"What the hell does that mean?" he growled.

"That means I'm going to talk to someone who will actually communicate back." And I don't know why I said it, but suddenly, I wanted to take a sledgehammer to that hard facade. "Like Conor."

His face turned an ugly shade of red, his nostrils flared, and his jaw muscles clenched. "What did you say?" he asked, his fingers tightening around my arm.

I tried to pull away. "Let me go."

He pulled me against his body. "No. You're mine, Elsie."

I fortified my gaze, pretending my eyes were made of diamonds. "I'm not some object you can lay claim to."

He grabbed my left hand and fingered the metal band there.

"No, you're my wife. You agree to be mine every day you put on this ring."

I never let my gaze waver. "Then that means you belong to me. And I demand to know what happened the other night."

He walked into me, forcing me backward a few steps. Still, I held my ground, even if my heart was thumping wildly in my chest. "Fine, I'll tell you what happened," he said in a low rasp. "I answered a hit-and-run call on East Sixth. Dispatch described the victim as a woman in her late twenties dressed in jogging clothes."

I gulped as an expression flew across his features, a shadow of the pain he wore the other night. "You thought it was me," I said.

"I drove there as fast as I could, holding my breath, praying it wasn't you. And then it wasn't. But to see that woman there, bleeding out on the asphalt while EMTs tried to revive her . . . I kept thinking that it could have just as easily been you." He tried to keep his face steady, but I felt his hands trembling at my side. I grasped his fingers with my own, and brought his hands up to my face to cradle my cheeks the way he was so fond of doing.

"Why was that so hard for you to say?"

"Because the job is not supposed to affect me," he said between his teeth. "I can't afford to show any weakness."

I turned my head and pressed a kiss into his palm. "You can with me," I said against his skin. God knew I already showed him so many of my own failings.

He didn't say anything. He just rubbed his thumbs against my cheeks, staring into my face.

"I'm worried, Henry. I don't want you to lose yourself again."

He shook his head. "That's never going to happen again, Elsie," he said. "I won't let it."

"And what happened in Monterey, when you broke my heart—you allowed that to happen?"

"No!" he said immediately. He took a step back and rubbed his face again. "That was . . . a stressful time in my life. I didn't handle it as well as I should have."

"And you don't think this is a stressful time in our lives?" I asked, furiously trying to keep my voice under control. God, I wanted to shake him by the shoulders until his brain lodged itself back into its right place. "You think you're handling it well right now?"

"Are you?" he shot back. "Going out drinking, coming home at four in the fucking morning?"

I took a step back, the force of his words as powerful as a punch in the gut. I was about to issue an indignant denial, but I only succeeded in standing there with my mouth agape as his words soaked in. "Maybe you're right," I said after some time. "But at least I haven't stopped communicating."

"I'm here! I'm still communicating!" he shouted, throwing his arms out. "This is me communicating! Isn't this enough?"

I withdrew another step. "No," I said, staring at him, unable to believe that this huffing and veiny man before me was really my husband. How he had changed from the man who met me at the end of the aisle and married me in front of the never-ending ocean.

A thought suddenly popped into my head and before I could think about the repercussions, I gave voice to it. "Maybe we need some time away from each other. Maybe this trip to Atlanta is just the break we need."

I didn't know what reaction I was hoping for, but Henry didn't react at all. He simply gave me a hard stare, turned his back to me, and returned to fixing his motorcycle.

6

The day before the trip, Conor informed me that he'd be going to Atlanta as well.

"What? Why?" I put my pen down then picked it back up, fidgeting despite myself. This was not good news.

"Don't sound so enthused," he said drily.

"Sorry. I thought it was just me."

He shrugged. "I was going to let you go alone, because I think you'd rock it, but after a lot of consideration, I think I ought to be there as well. To let the Lombart bigwigs know that their business is important enough for me to attend the pitch meeting."

Of course he was needed at the pitch; he was the owner of the company. Yet something—an unknown feeling that niggled at me—felt strange about this trip. "Do you even need me then? I wouldn't want to waste an extra ticket."

"Not at all. The ticket's a business expense," he said. "Your presence will be highly appreciated. Trust me."

I stared at him, wondering if I really did. Then it struck me that the real question was not if I could trust Conor but whether I could trust myself. Going to Atlanta with Conor was in the gray, murky area between right and wrong, but its outcome was ultimately up to me.

Not Henry. Not Conor. Me.

———————

I was in the closet that night, reaching for a pair of shoes when I felt Henry's presence behind me. I ignored him, like I'd done all week, and went back to my task, picking out a pair of sexy but professional heels.

"Is that really appropriate?" he asked, his tone immediately setting me on edge.

"Really?" I asked, keeping my back to him. "This is the first time you've spoken to me all week, and it's something as douchey as 'Is that really appropriate?' Are you going to start telling me what to wear now too?"

He sighed, the melancholy deafening in the enclosed space. "I don't think it's possible to *tell* you to do anything. You are the colonel's daughter after all." He came closer, and suddenly he was everywhere, wrapping his arms around me and covering me with his body. "You're still that same old brat after all these years."

I tensed, knowing he meant it as a term of endearment yet feeling the opposite effect. I wrenched myself out of his hold and edged past him, out of the suffocating air of the closet.

He followed me out and sat on the bed, watching me pack. "If you want, I can try to take an hour off tomorrow to take you to the airport."

"No need," I said, folding a pair of slacks and placing it in the luggage. "Conor is picking me up."

"Conor?" Henry took in a ragged breath, trying to control his reaction. "That's nice of him to do that for an employee, but I can take you."

"It's fine. He's coming too." I don't know why I chose that

moment to break the news to him—I certainly could have handled it with a little more finesse—but I was just so damn angry all of a sudden.

The silence that followed was unnerving; I could have sworn I heard a vein in his forehead pop. Finally, he asked in a moderately controlled voice, "Conor is going to Atlanta too?"

"Yes."

"And you decide to tell me this now?" He got to his feet and folded his arms across his chest.

"I just found out today."

"You can't go," he said with finality. "You're not going on that trip with that asshole."

"One, he's not an asshole. Two, this is a work trip. Three, I thought you already acknowledged the fact that you can't tell me what to do," I said, folding down three fingers until only the middle one was left.

He reached out and grabbed the finger, giving me a warning look. "Why are you doing this?"

"I'm not doing anything. Now let. Me. Go."

"No." He brought my finger up to his mouth and bit it. I reached up to smack his arm when he grabbed my wrist and pinned me in place with a look of burning anger and desire. "There's no way in hell you're going."

I lifted my chin in defiance. "You can't stop me."

He grabbed both my wrists and twisted them behind me, holding me captive. His body was inches from mine, so close I could feel the heat emanating from him. He bent down and nipped at my lower lip, smirking as he pulled away. "You do realize I'm nearly twice your size? I can do whatever I want with you and there's nothing you can do to stop me."

My sex clenched at the rough promise of his words. My brain cried out that I shouldn't be reacting that way, but hell if I could do anything to help myself from wanting more. "But you won't. Because you're too much of a fucking gentleman."

He bared his teeth a second before he ripped my shorts down, his fingers cupping my mound. "I see through your bravado," he gritted through his teeth. "You're goading me because you want me inside you. Like this," he said and roughly thrust two fingers inside my cleft.

I arched my back just as he grasped me closer against his hard body.

"Go on, Elsie. Say you don't want me," he said as his fingers flicked upward to connect with that special spot. He kissed my neck, running his teeth along my jaw, his soft chuckle warm against my skin. "You can't, can you? Because you know you belong to me." He let go of my wrists and grabbed my hair, kissing me with reckless anger to prove his ownership.

I didn't want the pleasure to erase my anger, so I bit his bottom lip in retaliation.

He jerked back, his tongue flicking out to taste the blood I had drawn. "Fuck, Elsie," he said a moment before he kissed me again, letting me taste the result of my anger. His hands were suddenly everywhere, clawing at my clothes until I was completely naked, my clothes pooled at our feet. He stepped away, chest heaving, and pointed across the room. "Get on the bed."

I held my ground, daring him to carry out his threat.

"You either get on that bed on your own or I will forcibly put you there."

My heart pounded against my chest as my emotions clamored for steady ground. I wasn't completely comfortable with this Henry and yet I couldn't stop my body from reacting to his dominance. To see him towering over me with that dark look on his face, his erection straining against his jeans, turned me on even more. God help me, but I wanted to push him further, to see just how far I could go before he broke. And maybe then I'd finally get a glimpse of what he was hiding behind that increasingly domineering facade.

"Make me."

His nostrils flared before he bent down and hoisted me over his shoulder, walking over and throwing me onto the bed. He stood over me and undressed as I tried to catch my breath, only breaking eye contact when he pulled his shirt over his head.

Staring up at him, I found it hard to breathe from the unease and the lust and everything else in between. We had loved each other since we were innocent teens and now here we were, reduced to two lust-filled creatures ready to devour each other in rage.

His muscles rippled underneath his olive skin as he took one step closer to the bed. I tried to scramble away but he grabbed my ankles and tugged me toward him, lifting my legs up around his hips. He crawled on the bed like a predator and stopped when his shaft lay on my mound. He grabbed my chin and tilted my head up so he could kiss my neck. "Tell me you don't want me inside you," he said, sliding his heavy erection along my slick folds. "Tell me you don't want me to fuck you senseless."

I closed my eyes and tried to swim against the tide of pleasure coursing through my body from his words, from his actions. "I don't—" But I couldn't lie, not when he licked a path along my collarbone and certainly not when he took hold of his cock and teased my clit with its swollen head, rubbing my moisture in circles.

His voice was full of grit when he said, "Say it, Elsie. Tell me what you want me to do and I'll do it."

I threw my head side to side, trying to clear my thoughts enough to find reason. It was in there somewhere, but the fog of desire was too thick; it dulled my senses but amplified the shocks of pleasure. I grabbed his ass and hissed, "Fuck me. Please."

He gave a chuckle and in the next instant he speared me with his cock, entering me with such force that it drove the breath from my lungs. When our hips were joined and he was inside me as far as possible, he whispered roughly, "Tell me you're mine."

And it struck me then, as my insides contracted around his thick length, that Henry was not only claiming me, he was also trying to tame me, to keep me from running away. The ring on my finger felt heavy, no longer a symbol of love but a collar to which he was desperately trying to attach a leash. "I belong to me."

He locked me in his blue gaze as he thrust hard, punishing me for my reticence. He slipped his hands under my back and pulled me up to sit on his lap, but even if I was in the dominant position, he still did not give up any control. He held me by the hips and drove upward, piercing through to my center with each rough thrust.

I leaned back on my hands to regain some control and smiled when he popped out. He shook his head as he grabbed his slick cock and pumped it twice before claiming me again. He pulled me up and grabbed one of my breasts, licking and sucking on it. When I rested my full weight on him to slow his pace, he growled and bit down on my nipple.

I gave a shout and beat on his back as sharp pain radiated from my breast. He only gave me a wicked grin before biting down on my other breast. With my nipple held between his teeth, he leaned away, stretching my skin even as he yanked me onto his shaft.

I keened, caught between pleasure and pain, shocked at myself for allowing Henry to do such things to my body. To retaliate, I dug my fingers into his thighs and held them there, my nails sinking deeper into his flesh, trying to break skin.

When I didn't think I could take any more of the pain, Henry released my nipple and the relief triggered my climax. I came, my insides trembling even as I kept squeezing, holding on to him for as long as I could.

"God, Els," he growled and then pushed me onto my back as he thrust into me one last time, his hips grinding into mine as if trying his hardest to burrow inside. "I love you so much, Elsie," he said against my ear in a gravelly voice.

I gripped him to me, my heart pounding hard against his chest. "I love you too, Henry," I said, choking back the sob that bubbled up in my throat. "So fucking much."

He kissed the shell of my ear and along my jaw. "Don't go on that trip."

And just like that, I felt like I'd been doused with ice water. I pushed against his chest, the warm afterglow evaporating. "Get off me." I sat up the moment he lifted away, feeling the anger rolling over my damp skin.

"What?"

I watched him sadly, his lip swollen from where I'd bitten him. "I'm going, Henry."

He rolled off the bed and made to go to the bathroom, but turned around at the last minute. "You'd choose your job over your marriage?"

"I'm choosing myself."

I didn't know why we kept hurting each other, and for once, I didn't bother trying to find out.

I called Conor the next day to tell him I'd just meet him at the airport, even though I hadn't accepted Henry's offer. I planned on driving there myself, to take advantage of the temporary peace and think about what I truly wanted in my life.

Sometimes I wondered if Henry and I had married too soon, if I should have lived by myself in Denver for a while before even contemplating getting back into a relationship with the man who had devastated me. It hurt to think what life would be like without him right now, but I couldn't help but wonder if we'd needed that extra time apart to heal. Maybe our marriage would be different. Maybe *we* would be different.

I checked in my luggage at Denver International with a heavy heart, wishing Henry and I hadn't left things so cold before he went to work this morning. As I walked toward the security gate, it occurred to me that, for the first time since he joined the police force, I didn't tell him I loved him before he left for work. Slowing my pace, I searched through my purse for my phone.

As I eyed the long line at the gate, I dialed Henry's number and was hoping wildly that he would be available to answer, when I heard the theme song to *Firefly*. My heart leapt in my throat and I turned around to find Henry standing behind me in his uniform, holding his phone to his ear.

He gave a tentative smile as he hung up and put the phone away.

"Hi," I said, suddenly jittery with nerves.

He glanced around then grasped my hand and pulled me away from the traffic, into a quieter area by the windows. "I'm sorry," he said, his fingers still grasping mine.

"Me too." We looked at each other for a long while, lost in our own little world together. We'd changed so much. "But I have to do this, Henry. You told me once that you would let me go if I needed to find myself. So I'm going to Atlanta to regroup, to think."

"So go, Elsie. But just remember that you're my wife." He added in a rumbling voice, "And I'm not letting you go without a fight."

"Elsie!"

Henry's fingers tightened around mine almost painfully when we turned to find Conor striding toward us, looking fresh and crisp in his suit, a tan leather computer bag slung over his shoulder.

"Hey there, chap," he said, clapping Henry on the back, who flashed him a stiff-lipped smile. "You ready, Sherman?"

Henry's eyes flashed in warning. To avoid a confrontation, I said quickly, "I'll meet you inside," and waved him off.

"He's still calling you by your maiden name," Henry said through his teeth. "That disrespectful motherfucker."

I tugged on his hand and forced his gaze to me. "Hey, calm down." I stood on my toes and grasped the sides of his head. "I love you, Henry. Please be safe out there."

"I love you too, Elsie." His eyes were still glued to Conor, who was walking through the X-ray machine. "No," he said, refusing to let go of my hand.

I sighed. "I'll be back tomorrow night."

Still he wouldn't release me.

My exasperation was reaching an all-time high. "Henry, do you trust me?"

He blinked down at me. "Of course I do."

"Then you have to let me go."

The look he gave me as his hand set me free shredded me, cut me to ribbons. He looked like a man who wasn't sure if the woman he loved would ever come back.

PART FOUR

POSSESS

1

I leaned back in my first-class seat and closed my eyes, feeling the waves of emotion crash over me. I didn't know how people did it day in and day out, leaving their spouses for temporary duty assignments or work trips, but somehow I thought it would be easier than this. I didn't expect to be overcome with guilt, didn't expect to want to throw up and hold back tears and pace the aisles all at once. When I'd suggested some time apart, I'd expected to feel a little pressure lift off my chest; instead I felt crushed under the weight even more.

"You feeling okay?" Conor asked after the plane had taken off. He placed a hand over mine on top of the armrest. "You afraid of flying?"

I stared down at our hands as beads of sweat sprouted on my forehead. "No, just a little under the weather," I said, slipping my hand out from under his.

"Nerves? About the pitch?"

I nodded, realizing how close Conor and I really were, how the only thing separating us was a few inches of metal and foam. Yes I was nervous, but not about the presentation. "I've never done this before."

Conor's green eyes watched me awhile, unnerving me to the core. "Don't worry," he finally said. "You'll do great."

––––––––––

We landed in Atlanta at two in the afternoon. I felt instantly better the moment we stepped off the plane, like I could finally breathe again.

Conor and I took a taxi to the hotel and checked into our own rooms, our doors separated only by the hallway. I set my luggage down and looked around at the king-sized bed and the modern furniture, feeling an overwhelming sadness engulf me. It reminded me of the same room I'd seduced Henry in a long time ago before he'd flown to Korea, back when I'd had something to prove.

The room phone rang. "Hey, you hungry?" Conor asked without preamble.

"Yeah, actually." It occurred to me that I hadn't eaten anything since early that morning. I'd been too anxious to even bother with food.

"Meet me downstairs in the conference room in fifteen minutes," he said. "I'll have lunch delivered and we can go over the presentation."

After hanging up, I washed my face with cold water and tied my hair up into a haphazard bun. "This is just work," I told my tense reflection in the mirror. "Conor is here for work and work only."

I grabbed my portfolio and laptop and headed downstairs, my sense of purpose returning with each step. We were here to win the Lombart account from three other design companies and nothing more.

The conference room was a fairly large space on the first floor of the hotel; it held approximately twenty rolling chairs that surrounded a long table. Seated at the head was Conor, his laptop and several other electronic gadgets laid out in front of him.

"Ah," he said, flashing me a wide, carefree smile. "Just in time. I need you to look at this file Kari just sent and make sure everything's perfect."

I nodded, setting up three seats away from him. "Is it on the server? I'll take a look at it there."

"I've got it open right here," he said, waving me over. "Come on. I won't bite."

The cool scent of his cologne hit me as I leaned over his shoulder. "What cologne do you wear?" I asked, trying to breathe through my mouth. "It's very strong."

He raised an eyebrow. "I'm not wearing cologne."

"Oh."

I could feel his eyes on me as I studied the image on the laptop, looking over the information on the banner ad that we were including in our presentation. I shut the laptop, intending on addressing the uncomfortable undercurrent. "Conor, look, we have to talk."

He leaned back in the chair and folded his arms behind his head. "About what?"

"About this working relationship."

"What about it?"

I took a deep breath. "About the fact that I'm married, that you're still calling me by my maiden name, that you try to flirt with me subtly."

His expression revealed nothing of his thoughts. "And what do you take from all of that?"

I opened my mouth, unsure of what would come out, when a knock on the door interrupted our conversation. At Conor's word, a man in a starched white shirt, a tie, and black slacks came in bearing a large cloth sack with RESTAURANT MONDRIAN emblazoned on its side.

Conor stood up, waiting as the deliveryman laid out five dark brown boxes with the restaurant logo printed in silver leaf on the top. Beside them he placed a bottle of champagne and two sets of cutlery nestled inside dark brown napkins. Conor signed a receipt, slipped the guy some cash, and sent him on his way.

He turned to the spread and held out his hands. "Lunch is served." He held up a finger and retrieved two champagne glasses from a table at the other end of the room. "Mondrian is known for using only local-grown, organic ingredients," he said, taking the lids off the boxes to reveal the beautifully arranged food. "I bought two different kinds of salads, two entrees—one fish, one lamb—and dessert."

It didn't escape my attention that there was only one dessert box. "Who gets the dessert?"

"I figured we could share."

I eyed the food to avoid Conor's gaze when the scent of the braised lamb wafted up my nose. A heave worked its way up my throat, and I turned my head to avoid smelling any more.

A cold sweat broke out all over my body at the swift realization that I'd had this reaction another time, back when being pregnant was still a possibility.

No, this is not happening. It's not possible.

"Sherman, you all right?" Conor asked, walking toward me.

I held out my hand to keep him at bay. "I just need a moment," I said and raced to the bathroom.

———

I only ate the salad. I couldn't stomach much else.

Conor watched me from the corner of his eye as we ate and worked separately. He didn't say much, recognizing the change in my mood, and didn't even protest when the obviously expensive food sat untouched at the other side of the room.

I did, however, take a small sip of champagne, finding that the bubbles helped to settle my stomach. Now my nerves—that was a different story.

I tried to concentrate on the presentation but the possibility of being pregnant occupied most of my brain cells. I wasn't being very discreet apparently, because Conor called it quits around five. "Alright, your brain is obviously not in this conference room right now," he said, standing up and shutting his laptop. "Why don't you get some rest and we'll regroup early tomorrow morning?"

"I'm fine," I insisted. "You don't have to treat me with kid gloves."

"Look, I know something's wrong and you're not able to concentrate. You've been trying to write one sentence on that note card for the past fifteen minutes," he said. "So I would rather you get some rest and be fresh tomorrow than keep you working while your brain is elsewhere."

I felt short of breath as we walked to our rooms in silence, as if the hallway walls were bowing down, closing in on me.

When we reached our doors, Conor stopped and said, "We can continue the conversation about our relationship tomorrow. After we win the account."

I nodded absently and turned to my door.

"And, Elsie," he said, giving me a meaningful look. "If you need anything at all tonight, just come to me. I'm only a few steps away."

"Thanks."

"Even if you just need to talk. I'm here."

"You're there. Got it," I said and slipped into my room before he could say anything else.

———

I dialed Henry's number three times, each time hanging up before he answered. What would I tell him when I myself didn't have a definitive answer yet? Five minutes after returning to my room, I grabbed my purse, slipped out again, and went down to the front desk to ask for directions to the nearest pharmacy. Thankfully, since we were in downtown Atlanta there was one a short walk away.

I brought two tests back to the room with me just to be sure. I peed on one, intending to use the second tomorrow morning. But as I squatted over the toilet, taking careful aim at the white stick, I realized I already knew the chorus to this age-old song.

Sure enough, without even having to wait the full two minutes, the pink plus sign appeared in that tiny window, telling me that the improbable had happened. I held that stick in my hand and one by one wrapped my fingers around it, unable to think past the swell of emotions inside.

This was a sick joke by the universe, something more to mess with my already confused mind. It wasn't enough that I'd been told I wouldn't be able to conceive, that my relationship with Henry was on a fast-moving pendulum; now I was pregnant too.

I didn't need a baby right now. I needed one minute of peace to wrap my mind around my spiraling life. What I needed was a fucking break from the angst and worry of being married to a police officer, to a man who was starting to close himself off once again.

No, what I needed was one night of *not* thinking.

I threw the stick away, burying it at the very bottom of the trash can, and washed myself clean of anything to do with babies. Then I exited the bathroom and went directly to the door, without a clue of where I would go. Once in the hallway, I started toward the elevator, intending to just walk the streets and allow the night to swallow me whole, when I decided I needed to tell someone where I was heading first. I turned on a heel and, without really thinking of the repercussions, knocked on Conor's door.

He answered without a shirt, revealing a lithe but muscular torso. "Sherman," he said, more pleased than a boss ought to be upon seeing an employee.

"I just want to tell you—" But whatever it was I was trying to say kept getting stuck in my throat at the sight of my shirtless boss.

"Come in, please," he said, moving aside just enough so that I could feel the heat from his body as I edged past.

I stood in the middle of the room, which was identical to mine, and looked at anything but Conor.

"Were you heading somewhere?" he asked, pointing to my purse.

"I was coming here to . . ." I stopped, unable to remember what had brought me here.

He came toward me, full of self-assured purpose, and stopped just short of touching me. My heart was pounding in my ears as he bent his head and smelled me, his face so close to mine that I could feel his warm, whiskey-tinged breath on my cheek. "I know why you're here," he whispered.

I should have stopped him, should have stepped back and kept it professional, but I was rooted to the spot. I felt like I was underwater, my limbs sluggish, my brain too clogged to make a rational decision.

Conor's stubble prickled my neck as he moved ever closer. "I've wanted to do this for a long time now, Sherman."

Time seemed to slow as he leaned forward, his intentions clear. I felt as if I were standing on a great precipice, knowing that if I took one step closer, I would be lost to Henry. It would be so easy to just say "Fuck it" and jump over the cliff, but I had no way of knowing if I could ever make it back.

I flattened my palms against his chest and held him off. "Conor, don't."

Conor looked down, at the places where our bare skin connected. "Isn't this what you want?"

I ripped my hands away, mortified. "No."

His chest flushed red, the color quickly rising to his cheeks. "Then what the hell are you doing knocking on my door at ten o'clock at night?"

"I'm pregnant," I blurted out, not knowing what else to say.

Conor blinked a few times, the burn of my rejection giving way to a new emotion. He locked his hands behind his neck and turned away. "You're pregnant."

"Yes."

"And again I ask: What the hell are you doing here?"

"I didn't come here for you." I motioned to his naked torso. "For this."

He turned back to me, his face a mask of hurt and anger. "So why?"

"I don't know," I shouted, his anger rousing my temper. I started pacing the room, twisting the handle of my purse over and over. "I feel like Henry has closed me off, like he's sealing his feelings shut like before and that he'll break again. And we're always fighting even though . . ."

"Stop for one second." He held me by the shoulders to keep me from moving then let his hands slide down and away from my arms. "I'll be frank with you: I like you, Elsie. Beyond platonic."

"I know," I said, looking away.

"But you don't feel the same," he said with a flat voice.

"I'm married, Conor."

"Do you want to stay married?"

My eyes flicked up, and for once, I had a definite answer. "Of course."

"Then why are you talking to me about this?" he asked. "Shouldn't you be talking to your husband instead?"

"Because . . ." I began but couldn't decide on an ending.

Because I was afraid we'd only argue, like always.

Because I didn't want to get his hopes up only to break his heart again.

Because I didn't think our marriage could survive another loss.

All of the above.

Conor sat on the edge of the bed, his breath sighing out of him. "Go home, Elsie. Fix your marriage," he said, waving me off. "I'll do the pitch tomorrow."

I considered it for a moment, seizing the opportunity to fly home right that second and tell Henry about the baby, but for better or worse, I'd come to Atlanta to do a job. "No. I'm staying. We're getting the Lombart account."

Conor looked at me for the longest, most painfully silent length of time. Finally, he said, "Fine. Do what you want. But I don't want to be in the middle of your war."

My cell phone began to buzz in my purse and, seeing the caller ID, I turned away from Conor to answer it. "Henry?"

"What's the matter? Are you okay?" he asked.

"I'm fine," I said, trying to hide the tremble in my voice.

"You called me three times in a row . . ."

"I needed to talk to you about something."

"I called your room. You weren't there."

My silence was as telling as a gunshot. I looked over my shoulder and glanced at Conor, who was busying himself putting on a shirt.

"You're with him, aren't you?" Henry asked, the acidic accusation hitting the mark.

I couldn't—wouldn't—lie to my husband, so I said nothing.

"Answer me, Elsie," he said, his voice taut with rage.

I couldn't breathe. "Henry . . ." I choked out, but before I could say anything else, he hung up.

2

I screwed up.

The memory of it haunted me all night, refusing to let me rest my eyes long enough to fall asleep. The next morning, the guilt was still there, refusing to wash away with soap and hot water. It showed on my face; no amount of makeup could have concealed the misery I wore.

The atmosphere in the conference room the next morning was predictably cool as we ran through the pitch a few times. My stomach was roiling and my throat dry; I would have killed for a good, strong cup of coffee.

On the way to the Lombart head office, Conor said, "If you can't do this, you'd better tell me now."

I glanced at him, wishing we weren't stuck in the backseat of a taxi together. After last night, every moment I spent with him felt like an act of deception. "I'm fine," I said with a hard edge to my voice.

"If you're at all unsure, I can take—"

"I said I'm good," I interrupted.

"I'm sure I don't have to stress how important this account is to Shake."

"And yet you are."

"I just—"

"Hey, Conor?" I said through stiff lips. "I know my personal life is in turmoil right now, but I'm perfectly capable of setting that aside when needed."

"I'm sorry," Conor said as we ascended in the elevator. "I shouldn't place so much pressure on you. It's unfair and unprofessional."

I looked at him properly for the first time since yesterday—feeling a small tingle at the memory of his near-kiss—and gave a short nod. I'd be lying if I said I never wondered what it would be like to be with him, but wondering and doing are two different things. Just the thought of cheating on Henry twisted my stomach in knots.

The secretary led us into the boardroom, where we were introduced to three older gentlemen. I cast a sideways glance at Conor, realizing why he'd brought me in the first place. He gave me an impish shrug in response.

I should have been mildly offended that I was being used for my looks, but I was, to put it frankly, out of fucks to give. I needed to nail the pitch, get home, and make my marriage right.

So I did. I set aside every worry in my brain, shut my heart in a box, and showed those stodgy old suits why they needed to go with Shake Design. I worked that room full of men, demanding their undivided attention and receiving it. It felt good to stand up there, showing off the design concept that my team and I had come up with, proud of the work we'd put together. Conor sat in the back, wearing that smile of his that said he was pleased, and he was first to stand up when the presentation was over, silently clapping to show his approval.

"Sherman," Conor said a few hours later as we waited for our luggage to make it around the conveyor belt at Denver International. "You did good."

We had been the last of the four companies to present our pitch. Afterward, the executives had taken half an hour to make their decision, then Conor and I had rushed to the airport in giddy excitement, exchanging high fives and laughing in relief.

But the closer I got to home, the faster the jubilation fizzed out.

"Thanks. I was pretty badass," I said, feeling the joy slipping away. "But don't use me for my looks ever again."

He held his hands up and laughed. "I promise that's not why I asked you to pitch. But it did give us a definite edge over the competition," he said.

I stepped forward to retrieve my luggage, but he was quicker and grabbed it before I could. "Thanks," I said.

"It wasn't in my plan to seduce you either," he said, handing my bag over. "In case that ever crossed your mind."

"Not mine. Henry's." It was official: The mood was back to awkward.

"If ever a man deserved an ass-kicking, it would be me," he said with a shake of the head. "I misread your motives last night. I'm sorry."

"This is on both of us. I should've stopped you before it was too late."

"You did."

"Did I?" I asked. Why the hell was I drowning in guilt then?

"You did nothing."

"Exactly. I should have stopped you." I held a hand up, tired of talking about it. "Let's forget it. You're not the person I should be talking to about this."

We were lost in our own thoughts as we made our way toward the short-term parking lot, sure to walk with several feet separating us. Even though I knew he wouldn't be there, my eyes couldn't help but search for Henry in every tall man with dark hair, in every person who turned the corner.

When we reached my car, Conor said, "I hope this trip doesn't affect our working relationship. I would really hate to lose a terrific designer over my error in judgment."

"I have no plans of quitting." I unlocked the car door. "But you are giving me a raise based solely on my performance in that boardroom."

Conor smiled widely. "The paperwork was already submitted before we even left." As he walked away, he said, "See you Monday?"

I nodded, my insides suddenly trembling at the thought of being alone. "See you."

I shouldn't have been so relieved when I drove into the garage and found Henry's Volvo gone. Still, it made getting out of the car easier, made entering our house a little less daunting.

At least Law was there to give me a warm, slobbery reception as he licked my face and jumped into my arms.

"Did you take good care of Henry?" I asked, scratching the backs of his ears.

As I made my way to the bedroom, I looked around the house, trying to see if anything had changed. But nothing had moved. The used mugs were still in the kitchen sink, my book and blanket were still on the couch where I'd left them.

Our bedroom, on the other hand, looked pristine. The carpet had recently been vacuumed, the bed made, but more curious was that the lamp on his side of the bed was missing.

I unpacked, throwing my dirty clothes into the laundry basket, and placed my rolling luggage into the back of the closet. I changed into my pajamas, brushed my teeth, and washed my face. I was completely ready for bed, ready to collapse in an exhausted heap, when I finally noticed a familiar black tape recorder sitting on my pillow.

My heart held still for a few beats as I tried to wrap my brain around the reemergence of that tape recorder, the very same one that Henry had used during his therapy sessions back in California.

I sat on the bed, staring at it, trying to gather enough courage to reach out and press the Play button.

Yes, I was chicken. I was afraid of what I'd hear; afraid that contained in the ribbon was the voice of my husband saying our marriage was over. I didn't think I could ever be prepared for that.

I lay down on Henry's side of the bed and closed my eyes, smelling his scent on the pillow. Tears pooled behind my eyelids at the emotions it triggered: the surprise when he'd confessed that he loved me after we'd had sex for the first time, the overwhelming relief as he stepped off the bus on base, the euphoria when he'd dropped on one knee with a ring that rainy afternoon.

My heart hurt at the thought that I might never make those kinds of memories with him again.

I don't know how long I lay there, clutching his pillow to my head and staring at the tape recorder, but eventually I took a deep breath and finally pressed Play.

There was a moment of static silence, and just when I was beginning to think it was blank, that Henry was just messing with my head, I heard him clear his throat and finally speak.

"Elsie," he began in a low voice that raised goose bumps on my arms. It felt like years since I'd heard it. "I'm sure you're wondering what the hell you're about to listen to, but I can't tell you because I don't know what the hell I'm going to say.

"I called you tonight, worried that something had happened, but you weren't answering your room phone. I had this sick feeling at the pit of my stomach when I tried your cell phone again, this sixth sense warning me that I wouldn't like what you'd tell me. And fuck if that voice wasn't right."

His voice took on an angry edge as he continued. "I don't know what the fuck you were doing in his room—I don't even want to know—but the fact that you were in there at ten o'clock at night is fucked up, Elsie. You shouldn't have been in there. Period.

"You don't even know what that information did to me. I wanted to punch something, wanted to destroy everything in this home we've built. I went to the gym to exhaust my body, but pounding the treadmill and the punching bag for hours couldn't get rid of the mental image I have of you and Conor together. God, I want to punch that wife-stealing asshole in the face. The lamp unfortunately bore the brunt of my anger."

He took a deep breath. "That's how I found this recorder again. I was vacuuming the glass from the floor when I found your box under the bed. I didn't even know you had it, a box full of our history. The letters, our wedding invitations, pictures, the rock, that apology card I sent you in college; it was a time capsule of you and me. That box, and everything inside it, reminded me that there are some things in life worth fighting for.

"So here I am, sitting in the living room, trying like hell to figure out how to fight for you. You tell me that I've stopped communicating with you, that I'm shutting down like before. I've denied it, but I know deep down that you're right.

"I know I'm not the best at expressing myself. Talking about my feelings for you, that's easy because you're the best part of me. Those are the parts that light me up inside. But to talk about my darkest thoughts? I have trouble with that because I don't want you to know that I have that darkness in me. I don't want you to think I'm anything but that goofy boy you grew up with.

"I just . . . I find it so hard to tell you those things, Elsie. I can't talk about the shit I see every day because I don't want to take away your faith in mankind. You're the kind of person who forgives easily, who thinks that people are ultimately good. How can I come home each day and tell you that you're wrong? I don't want to take that away from you because I think that's one of the things that makes you glow: your sense of hope.

"But I understand, I really do. You need to know these things in order to feel connected to me. So I'm here, holding a damn recorder up to my face, trying to figure out how to start talking again."

I pressed Stop to take a moment to breathe. The pillow beneath me was already wet from tears I didn't even realize I was shedding. I took a deep breath, wiped my face with my sleeve, and continued listening.

"First let me tell you about Korea. I was mugged, true, but something happened before that warranted the mugging. I didn't tell you about it because I was ashamed. You have to remember that I was in a bad place. It wasn't long after you came to the hotel room, when you made love to me then left, like I had done to you. It opened up my eyes. I lied to you, pretended that I didn't want you anymore, but you saw right through it. I think sometimes you know me better than I know myself.

"In Korea I became hopeless and reckless, which is a dangerous combination. I lost myself even more. I went out partying with the single guys almost every night, getting drunk with the juicy girls. I was desperate to find a way to move on from you. So one night, on a dare, I went to find a hooker. I'm not proud of this, Elsie. I don't even want you to know that I was so fucked up, I was actually going to screw a prostitute just to get the feel of you off my skin.

"But when it came down to the wire, I couldn't do it. I backed out and tried to walk away. The guys who worked at the club followed me home. They cornered me and jumped me, shouting that I owed them money. I was stabbed twice in the side, which earned me a stay at the hospital for a week. My commander told me that it was touch and go for a time, that they didn't know if I would make it through because of the infection in the wounds. When he said that, I found myself wishing that I hadn't survived. At the time, I felt like I didn't deserve to survive.

"It was so fucked up, but I was at a low point in my life. I had just lost you again—for good, I thought—and I had nothing else but my job. The only thing that kept me from completely self-destructing was Jason's memory. He had died with honor to his name. And me? Did I really want to die in an alley with my pants around my ankles and puke all over my face? Because that's where I was headed and I could either careen toward that future or forge a path of my own.

"I hope you understand why I find it hard to talk about this, especially as I look at your face. I don't want you to stop looking at me with love. I don't want to see pity or disgust there. I don't know what's worse: the fact that I was actually considering sleeping with a hooker, or that I wanted to give up altogether.

"So I didn't tell you. How could I?

"I can't lose you again, Elsie. When I saw you in the hospital bed that night you had the miscarriage—it broke me apart to see you like that. You were lying there, looking so lifeless and pale. I panicked, because you reminded me of myself in Korea. I was scared shitless that you would give up like I did.

"I hated myself for not being there for you. You don't know how much that tears me up inside, knowing that you had to go through that alone. But you handled it, like the strong person that you are.

"I wish you could see yourself how I see you. You are my beautiful, wonky rock, Elsie. You're imperfect but resilient. It hurts me to see moments of sadness on your face. You think I don't notice, but I see it. And it kills me that I can't fix it.

"Some days I just want us to run away. I want to take you somewhere we can both be happy again, but I don't know where that would be. Some days I wonder if it's me who's making you unhappy, and I pull away to stop hurting you even more. I don't know if that's the right thing to do. Obviously not if we're at this point in our lives, where you're across the country, seeking solace in another man.

"I do know one thing for sure and it's this: I need you. It took me a long time to figure out what I wanted out of life, but I'm glad I managed to figure it out before it was too late. It's you. You're the only thing I want out of life."

The tape went silent for a few seconds then the recorder clicked off, signaling the end of the cassette. I opened up the recorder and flipped the tape over, hoping to hear more. Needing to hear more.

"I woke up this morning to an empty bed and it was like another knife in my stomach," Henry continued, his voice gritty from sleep. "Not having you here guts me. I don't know how you did that back then, when I deployed and you were left to wake up without me for six months. I never want to put you through that again. It's fucking miserable.

"But I feel some hope. You're coming home today. I've decided that I don't give a shit what happened last night in that hotel room because—even though I have a crappy way of showing it—I trust you. Whatever you were doing in that hotel room, whatever it is, I know we can work through it.

"Elsie, I don't know if I can tell you everything but I'll try. I'm not going to shut you out anymore. Even if I need to see a counselor to deal with the stress, I'll do it. I'll do anything because I'm in this for the long haul. I'm in this forever. I know I got caught up in it, in the stress of my job, that I lost sight of what is most important. I love you, Elsie. None of this matters if I don't have you.

"I'm pulling the midnight shift today, so I won't be there when you get home tonight. But I will see you tomorrow. I can't wait to climb naked into bed beside you and hold you in my arms again, to feel your skin on my lips. I miss you more than words can express. And I love you even more than that."

I turned off the recorder, my lips trembling, my eyes swollen with tears. Filled with a renewed sense of hope, I leapt out of bed and ripped off my pajamas. I ran to the closet, grabbing a pair of jeans and a sweater. It was nearly midnight, but I didn't care. The need for him burned inside me and made me jittery. I couldn't wait until tomorrow to see him.

I needed Henry now.

3

I called Henry's phone but it went directly to voice mail. I jumped in the car and drove around without aim, hoping that somehow the universe would lead me to my husband. But life doesn't work like that. I didn't find my husband just because I wanted him so badly my fingers were actually shaking. My need wasn't a beacon that would lead me to him in this dark Colorado night.

After an hour of driving around, I finally headed home. With an aching heart, I parked and locked up the house, disappointment settling deep into my bones.

I took a long, hot shower to calm my nerves, hoping that maybe Henry would choose that moment to come home and join me. I imagined him undressing and pushing aside the shower curtain, stepping into the tub, and crowding me with his large, muscular body.

I closed my eyes and ran my hand down my wet stomach, sliding my fingers through my folds. I groaned, imagining Henry's cock—its impressive length and veiny girth, its perfectly shaped head—which could only be described as magnificent.

I slipped two fingers inside me, pretending it was Henry filling me instead, but there was no pleasure to be had by myself. Not when my body craved the real thing.

Unsatisfied, I finished showering and dried off. I slipped into a black-and-white silk bathrobe and went downstairs to make a cup of tea. I filled the kettle with water and set it on the stove, washing the dishes as I waited for the water to boil.

After turning off the kettle, I was grabbing a tea bag in the pantry when I heard Law emit a short, excited bark.

"Hey, buddy," a deep male voice said.

I stepped out of the pantry and my heart fluttered. Henry stood across the kitchen, already changed into a pair of jeans and a button-down shirt folded at the sleeves, looking more breathtakingly beautiful than any man had a right to be. Our gazes locked for a long, tense second, then my body propelled itself forward, toward the object of its desire. Henry crossed the room with large, purposeful steps and met me halfway. We stopped short of touching.

He grabbed the back of my head and leaned his forehead to mine. "Hi," he said with a low, husky voice.

"I'm sorry," I said, touching the tip of my nose to his. "Nothing happened."

He gave a nod and clutched a handful of my hair, tilting my head to the side as he slanted his mouth over mine. I opened up, inviting him to sink into me, and he accepted, making love to me with his tongue. His other hand traced the curve of my waist and hip, then slid inside the robe and around to my ass. His fingers dug into my flesh as he gripped me closer, holding me against his arousal.

He backed me up a few steps then lifted me by the hips, setting me onto the counter. He pulled away, breathing hard. "I missed you," he said, fitting his fingers under the robe's collar and slipping it off my shoulders, uncovering my chest.

"Henry," I said, finding it hard to breathe when his fingers skimmed around the edges of my breasts, circling under and finally cupping them in his palms. "We need to talk."

He bent down and touched his lips to my collarbone. "No

talking. Not tonight," he said. "Right now I want to prove without a shadow of a doubt that no man can ever love you like I do."

His kisses trailed softly along my skin, along the valley between my breasts. His tongue flicked out and licked at a hardened nipple, sucked at the tender underside before moving lower down my body.

He bent down until his mouth was hovering above my mound. "I dreamed about you last night," he said with a grin, his breath warm on my quivering skin.

I moaned, leaning back on my hands as he ran the tip of his tongue along the sensitive spot between my folds. Drawing circles, he teased me mercilessly. He stood up, rubbing his palms along the insides of my thighs, flashing me a smile as he pushed two fingers inside me. "Always ready for me."

I closed my eyes and enjoyed the pleasure he was giving me, feeling myself drawing closer to the edge of climax. Then his fingers were gone and something else took its place, nudging at my entrance.

I opened my eyes and the sight of Henry completely naked with his rigid cock ready to impale me took my breath away. "Do you love me, Henry?" I asked, needing to hear it from his lips in that moment.

"With every atom in my body," he said, his eyes feverish with emotion.

I clamped my feet around his ass and urged him closer. "Then love me."

He slid into me slowly, savoring every inch as he stretched me out, groaning when he filled me completely. He grabbed the back of my head and held our foreheads together once more as he began a slow, deliberate stroke. "I do," he said in a low timbre that I felt down to my core. "Every damn second of every day."

Our lips touched and we exchanged breaths. In that moment, with our eyes, lips, and bodies locked together, I felt connected to him in a way I'd never felt before, as if it was truly possible to split a soul in two and have them find each other so they feel whole again. I never believed in soul mates until that moment, until something in me fused itself to him.

Henry had been right all along: We belonged to each other, as naturally as the waves belonged to the shore.

I wrapped my arms around his back and pulled him against my chest, holding him tight with every muscle in my body. "I'm yours, Henry," I said against his lips.

His eyes flickered with emotion and he continued the steady pace, his long strokes increasing in speed until we were on an almost desperate edge. He held me by the hips and thrust into me, his breathing becoming more ragged as we raced closer to climax.

"Say it again," he said through his teeth.

"I'm yours." I grabbed the back of his head and fit my mouth to his, kissing him long and hard before saying, "Of course I'm yours."

Afterward, he carried me upstairs and laid me on the bed like a gallant knight. He lay on his back and pulled me into the crook of his arm, holding my head against his chest.

"Did you listen to my tape?" he asked just as the sun was beginning to rise.

I nodded, enjoying the sensation of his chest hair tickling my cheek. "Thank you. For trying."

"It was . . . it's the best I could do."

"And for telling me about what happened in Korea." I traced my finger along the two scars on his side, hating the thought that he had almost died and I hadn't even known about it. Tears stung my eyes at the realization that he might have died and I would only have found out about it through mutual friends. I hugged him tighter, unable to speak past the lump in my throat.

His voice was thick with emotion when he said, "That's never going to happen again, okay?"

I didn't know if he meant getting hurt or wishing he'd die.

"The giving up part," he added, reading my mind.

"Henry," I said after some time. "I need to tell you something."

His fingers stroked my bare back absently. "Tell me."

I closed my eyes, gathering courage. I'd held back this kind of information once and it had blown up in my face and set into motion our separation. This time, I was determined to tell him the truth as soon as possible. "Conor tried to kiss me."

His muscles turned to granite beneath me but he said nothing.

I kept my cheek pressed to his chest, afraid to look up at his face. "But it was a misunderstanding. Nothing more."

His fist clenched against my spine. "What else?"

"That's all." I sat up, buoyed by relief. "Nothing else. I hope you believe me."

His face was taut, his lips pulled into a thin line, but instead of spewing angry words, he simply nodded. "Okay."

"Okay?"

He pulled me back down onto his chest. I felt his heart thumping angrily beneath my cheek, his chest rising and falling as he tried to calm himself. "I believe you."

"There's something else."

He tilted his head up and fixed his eyes on the ceiling, clearly still trying to rein in his anger. "I thought you said that was—"

"I'm pregnant."

"What?" he asked, the breath whooshing out of him.

I leaned up on my elbow and nodded, searching for any clues on his face.

"Is it mine?"

I smacked him on the chest. "Of course it is, you dickhead."

A tentative smile tugged on the edges of his lips and then bloomed all over his face. "I thought it wasn't possible, what with the scarring . . ."

I bit my lip to keep it from trembling. "I know. I thought so too. But I took a test and it came out positive." I remembered the other test in my bag. "I can take it again, if you want?"

"Let's do it."

I grabbed the test out of my purse and met him in the bathroom. I ripped open the package and uncapped the stick while Henry leaned against the sink and studied the box.

I looked at him expectantly. "Um, hello."

He looked up. "Already done?"

I flicked my eyes toward the door. "No. I need to pee on it first, and I'd appreciate it if you weren't in the room with me."

"Come on," he said, grinning. "I wouldn't mind a little golden-shower action."

"Oh my God!" I cried, pushing and ushering him out of the bathroom. "You're so gross!"

His laughter echoed through the room and could be heard through the door.

———

I opened the door a few minutes later and allowed him back inside. We stood side by side and stared at the stick on the counter with our breath held.

"Thank you," he said, taking my hand in his.

I looked up at him, instinctively knowing what he was so grateful for. That I was taking the test again, that I was including him in the momentous event. It didn't matter that we already knew the outcome, what mattered was that we were experiencing it together.

When that plus sign appeared in the window, he pressed my hand up to his chest and held it there. "There it is," he said, staring at the plastic stick.

"I'm scared," I whispered.

He turned to me. "I know. But just for tonight, let's not think about the what-ifs. For now, let's just stand here and celebrate that little thing inside you." He pressed a large hand on my stomach.

I couldn't fathom how he could be so optimistic.

"You know how I know this baby will survive?" he asked.

I looked up at him with trembling lips and shook my head. "How?"

"Because despite the scarring, this baby found a way to beat the odds," he said. "She's a fighter, just like her mom."

Tears pooled in my eyes, and for the first time I allowed myself to hope.

Henry flashed me a smile so contagious, I had no choice but to reciprocate.

4

I couldn't tell you what changed after that night, what clicked between Henry and me, but we came to an unspoken understanding. He started coming home immediately after his shifts, and even bought some weights in order to do his workouts at home. I tried my best not to hound him about communication, about wanting to know every single thought going through his head. He was right in saying I wouldn't want to know the real ugliness of the world, but that didn't stop me from wanting to know how it affected him. But he was trying, and I knew that what he couldn't say to my face, he could always say in the tape recorder.

Sometimes, I wondered where we'd be without that tape recorder, but I thank Henry's therapist in California for introducing it to our lives. It wasn't a perfect method of communication, but to make a marriage work, you have to take what you are given and make the most of it. Sometimes, an antiquated electronic device is all you have between success and ruin.

"When are supposed to see Dr. Harmon?" Henry asked one day, looking through the calendar on his phone as we stood in Home Depot.

"Tomorrow at three," I said, holding up three paint swatches. "Okay, which one: Lilac Whisper, Lavender Escape, or Morning Chill?"

Henry gave me an incredulous look. "Aren't they all purple?"

I smacked his arm with the fan of swatches. "Yes, but which one will look the best in the nursery? Which one will look best with the mural?"

He put his phone away and finally gave the colors his attention. "Something light but with gray undertones," he said then pulled out a swatch. "This one, the purple."

I laughed as I handed the swatch over to the employee behind the counter in the paint department. "You'd make a terrible paint namer."

He raised an eyebrow. "Are you kidding? I'd be awesome." He grabbed a light green swatch off the rack. "I'd call this Snot Whisper." Fueled by my amusement, he grabbed another in a brown shade. "And this is Shart Mist."

As I chuckled, Henry wrapped an arm around my shoulders and kissed my cheek. "I think we just found the name for our baby," he whispered, and I lost it, doubling over with laughter.

Several more ridiculous names were made up before the paint was ready. The employee handed us the two cans, looking none too amused by our banter.

I grabbed a can, allowing Henry to take the other, and was about to head to the cash register when he cleared his throat. "What are you doing?"

I stopped and gave him a questioning look. "Um, walking?"

"Hand it over," he said, reaching for the paint can in my hand.

I held it out of his reach. "You can't be serious!"

"Come on. I don't want you carrying heavy things."

"I'm pregnant, not an invalid."

"I'd rather be safe than sorry." He held his hand out as he waited.

I rolled my eyes and handed the can over. "God, you're infuriating."

"You're already carrying our child. The least I can do is carry the paint."

And just like that—right when I'd decided I was going to cash in a hormone card and be mad—he was back on my good side.

"If you were a color," I said as we made our way back to the car, "you'd be called Bossy Blue."

———

Henry had the swing shift for the next week and was able to come to the doctor's appointment with me. He was quiet during the internal ultrasound, watching the monitor closely for the kidney-shaped blot to appear, then focusing even more intently for the little flickering that indicated a heartbeat.

"There it is," Dr. Harmon said. "Strong heartbeat."

Henry's fingers tangled in my hair, rubbing my scalp reassuringly.

"So give it to us straight, Doc," Henry said. "What are the chances of our baby surviving?"

Dr. Harmon disposed of the condom from the wand and took her time removing her rubber gloves. She gave us each a meaningful look. "Well, you could have an uneventful pregnancy and carry the baby to full term. Or you could suffer a repeat miscarriage."

I sucked in a breath.

"Is there a way to predict that?" Henry asked.

"Unfortunately, no. The best we can do at this point is monitor the pregnancy closely."

Later, as we drove home, I asked, "What should we tell people?"

Henry placed a hand on my thigh and squeezed. "We don't have to tell anyone until you're ready."

"What about you?"

"Me? I want to get on a loudspeaker and shout it at anyone I run across," he said with a grin.

"You heard the doc, there's a good chance I can miscarry again."

"I don't care. This baby will survive."

I didn't know if it was possible to will a baby into existence, but if anyone could do it by sheer stubbornness alone, Henry probably could.

———————

"Happy birthday," I said to Kari, giving her a hug. I looked around the table, at the collection of people here to celebrate, waving to those I recognized from work. Thankfully, Conor was not one of them.

"Thank you," Kari said when I handed her a gift bag.

"I'm sorry I'm late," I said, searching for two empty spots at the table.

"No big deal. You got held up having a quickie with your hot husband. I understand," she said, winking at me across the table.

"Actually, he's at work." I looked at my watch. "He said he'd meet us here."

Kari turned to the person at her left, a Middle Eastern woman with long black hair and big brown eyes. "Her husband is a hot cop. And I'm pretty sure he's going to do a strip for me for my birthday." She flashed me another wink. "Right?"

I laughed and, noticing her half-empty cocktail glass, guessed that she'd already had a few and had arrived at the winking stage of inebriation.

I let the conversations wash over me as I looked over the menu. My ears caught the tail end of a conversation between Jerrod, a designer from Shake, and the person beside him. "Yeah, he's a good boss. He used to come out with us every now and then, but he doesn't anymore. I think the new account is keeping him really busy."

I hid my flushing face behind the menu, afraid to give myself away. Nobody knew about what happened in that hotel room in Atlanta, nobody but the three people it affected. I hated to think anyone would even suspect that Conor's sudden social detachment was because of me.

Kari joined in the conversation. "I asked him to come tonight, but he said he had other plans."

"It's probably for the best though, don't you think?" I said, unable to keep my big mouth shut. "In the military, officers and enlisted are not supposed to fraternize."

"We're not in the military, Sherman Tank," Kari said.

"Yes, but the rules of leadership should still somewhat apply."

"So you're saying we can't be friends with our superiors?" Jerrod asked.

"I don't believe anyone is superior over me," someone else piped in from the other end of the table. I fought hard to keep from rolling my eyes.

"I'm saying a boss needs to keep his distance to be a good leader, that's all. He needs to command respect from his employees and he can't do that if they've all seen him puking his guts out at a bar," I said, thinking of my dad, who'd retired as a lieutenant colonel in the Air Force. My dad had been a stickler for the rules and, as such, had been a highly respected leader.

"Not necessarily true. I'd feel more of a kinship with someone I've seen act human," Jerrod said.

The conversation continued, people arguing the difference between kinship and leadership and how it related to Conor, when I felt fingers slide into my hair.

"Hey," Henry said, bending down to give me a lingering kiss on the lips. He took the empty seat next to mine and gave everyone a wave. "Sorry I'm late."

Kari winked at him then acted put out that he was wearing a fitted long-sleeved Henley and jeans. "Where is the uniform?"

"I'm off duty now," he said, though I noticed him surreptitiously assessing the room. "Happy birthday though. I think you might like what Elsie and I got you."

Kari's eyes widened and she reached for the bag beside her. She pulled out a wad of blue tissue paper and started choking when she unwrapped a high-quality pair of handcuffs.

"You okay?" I asked.

Kari's choke-laugh continued for a few more seconds. "Oh my God, this is awesome."

"For when you find your Fifty," I said, giving her an exaggerated wink.

"Her fifty what?" Henry asked, giving us a confused look.

Kari and I shared a knowing smile. "Nothing," she said. "You wouldn't understand."

The celebration continued until well past dinner, even after the little slice of cheesecake with sparklers on it was brought out. By then a few people had gone home, but most of us remained to carry on.

Henry sat back in his seat, nursing his second beer, and rested an arm on the back of my chair. He leaned over and whispered, "Let's get out of here."

"You tired already?"

"No," he rasped against my ear. "I just want to get you home, tie you spread-eagled onto the bed, and have my way with you."

I groaned inwardly. "Then what would you do?"

He grinned. "Anything the hell I want." His eyes traveled down my body, caressing every dip and curve. His fingers traced circles along my arm, sending tingles straight down to my crotch.

Careful to keep my hand out of sight, I touched his leg, skimming my hand up his inner thigh as I kept up the eye contact. "Would you put anything in my mouth?" I asked, biting my lip.

He touched a finger to my lip. "If that's what you want, sweetheart."

"My God, would you guys stop eye-fucking each other and just get a room already?" Kari shouted across the table.

Henry and I looked up to find the entire table smirking at us, with a few other restaurant patrons glancing over in amusement. He squeezed my shoulder and shrugged. "Sorry. Haven't seen my wife all day."

We looked at each other, sharing a laugh, when the smile froze on his face.

I turned my head and found Conor standing behind us, looking a little taken aback himself.

"Uh, hi," he said, walking over to Kari's side of the table and handing her a small gift-wrapped box. "Happy birthday."

Kari jumped up and hugged him around the neck. "Thanks, boss."

Conor patted her back awkwardly and stepped out of the embrace. "I was just stopping by to greet you." He didn't even so much as look my way, which was telling in itself. I willed him to look at us, to acknowledge my presence, knowing that my coworkers were not so drunk that they wouldn't notice.

I watched Henry out of the corner of my eye and saw his jaw muscles working, his eyebrows lowering together. I squeezed his thigh. "Please don't do anything in front of these people," I whispered.

Henry turned to me with a stony look. "I'm out of here." He stood up, the chair scraping on the floor unpleasantly, and drew the gaze of everyone at the table, including Conor.

"Oh, hi," Conor said, pretending he hadn't seen us until now. He extended a hand to Henry.

Henry paused a beat before taking Conor's hand. "Good to see you," Henry said in an affable tone, the menacing undercurrent evident only to Conor and me.

"You should be proud of Elsie," Conor said, flicking a quick glance at me. "Winning the Lombart account."

Henry's grip tightened around Conor's hand as he forced a smile. "Yes, *my wife* is amazing."

The animosity flying across the table was starting to become too obvious, so I stood up and grabbed everyone's attention by making a spectacle of hugging Kari good night. "I hope you enjoy your present," I said loudly, wagging my eyebrows. "Who are you going to try it out on first?"

Kari played coy as she twirled the handcuffs around her finger. "Oh, I don't know. I'll have to see." She waved her eyebrows at me, casting a rapid glance at Conor.

"Good luck with that," I laughed, louder than was necessary. I grabbed Henry's hand and led him out.

Once outside, Henry let go and just glared at me, his chest heaving.

I stood away from the restaurant's large windows, away from curious eyes. "Henry, calm down."

"I don't want to calm down." He pinned me with livid eyes. "I want to punch someone's pretty-boy face in."

"Don't . . . please."

"You really think I would jeopardize my career for some asshole who thought he could steal my wife?" he asked with a sneer.

"Let's go home," I said in a calm voice, hoping it would influence his mood. "We'll talk about it there."

"Fine," he said and stomped off toward the parking lot. He made sure I was in my car first before slinging a long leg over his bike and riding off.

I thought the drive would help cool Henry's head, but when I walked in the house, he was standing in the living room with his hands folded across his chest, looking so damn intimidating and sexy all at once.

"You need to quit that job," he said, immediately shutting down the sexy vibes.

I mimicked his stance and shook my head. "Hell no."

"You can't keep working for that dick."

"I can't just quit my job because of a misunderstanding," I said, trying to reason with him. "This job is important to me. It's what I've been working for my entire life. I can't quit. Not this job."

"Find another one like it."

"There are no other jobs like it. Shake is one of the most promising firms out there, and I'm helping it grow. I've never been part of a company in this way before, like I'm instrumental in its success."

"But Conor—"

"It's not about Conor," I said, trying to temper my voice.

"It's got everything to do with him."

"No, it doesn't."

"Why the fuck would you let him think he had any right to kiss you?" he suddenly shouted. The volume of his voice was like a thunderclap, booming around the room, and all I could do was stand there reeling from its intensity. He had never yelled at me like that before.

"I don't . . . I didn't . . ." I said, fighting the urge to cower.

"Was it because you wanted to see me jealous?" he asked, nostrils flaring. "Well, congratulations, Elsie, you've got it. I'm fucking jealous. I'm ready to murder the next guy who touches you."

"I thought you said you could get over it."

"Well I was wrong!" He took several deep breaths. "I thought I was handling it. But seeing him tonight, knowing that you're with him every single day . . ."

I stepped toward him and wrapped my arms around his waist, trying to reassure him with my touch as well as my words. "It's not going to happen ever again," I said. "I can guarantee it."

"Damn right it's not," Henry said, wrenching away from my grasp and stalking to the garage door.

I was right at his heels, feeling the panic rising up in my throat. "Where the hell are you going?"

"To make sure Conor knows your last name is Logan," Henry said and slammed the door. A few seconds later, the Harley roared to life.

5

I didn't follow Henry. God knows I wanted to, but I knew deep down that my presence there would only add more fuel to the fire. I'd be forced to defend Conor, which would further enrage Henry, and fists would probably fly. Henry could lose his job, get sued by Conor, go to jail, or all three. And it would all be my fault.

I slumped against the wall and slid down to the floor, holding my head in my hands. I didn't know how I had gotten myself in this situation again. Was it my fault? Had I somehow given out vibes to men that would make them believe I was interested?

Or did it go deeper than that? Did I somehow get some sick pleasure out of making Henry jealous? Was that really the kind of person I was? Perhaps it had all started back in high school, at that dance when Henry had ripped my handsy date off me. It was possible that underneath the anger and the hurt, I'd somehow derived some satisfaction from the fact that Henry had obviously been so jealous he was willing to go to desperate lengths to keep other men away.

But if that was true, then what kind of a person did that make me?

I might have sat on that floor for hours, knotting my brain in circles, had I not suddenly been overcome with nausea. I scrambled to my feet and made it into the hallway restroom a second before I started throwing up my dinner.

———————

I woke up alone the next morning, though the indentation on Henry's pillow was proof that he'd at least slept there. I got up, washed my face, and slipped into my robe before going in search of my husband.

I finally found him in the basement, wearing only a pair of shorts and shoes, beating the hell out of a heavy bag with his wrapped hands. I stood at the bottom of the stairs, unnoticed, and watched him quietly as he prowled around the bag before delivering punishing combos, punching the bag twice then following up with elbow hits. Every muscle in his body flexed, his thick biceps curling a moment before striking out with enough force to send the bag swaying.

I should have been frightened by his barely contained fury, but something about the show of power from this virile male spoke to a deeper part of me, to the natural instinct of a woman to pick the strongest male of the species to mate with.

He stopped, his wide shoulders rising and falling as he tried to catch his breath. He was shiny all over from the workout, his muscles bulging from the exertion. He looked sweaty and smelly, but I'd be damned if I didn't want him to take me right in that moment.

I walked over and touched his damp back. He spun around, his muscles coiled. "Els," he said, dropping his hands to his sides.

"Tell me what happened," I said softly, fighting against the desire.

He shook his head. "Nothing. I didn't do anything to him," he said, clenching his hands into fists. "I wanted to beat the shit out of him. I wanted to hurt him."

"But you didn't." I grabbed his wrist and brought it up, unwrapping his hand and doing the same for the other.

"No. We talked. He apologized, said it was a misunderstanding and wouldn't happen again. It was so fucking civilized."

I brought his reddened knuckles to my lips and kissed each one individually, showing him my gratitude. "Thank you."

He reached out and touched a finger to my lips. "I said I could get over it, but I'm not so sure it's that easy." He took hold of my hair and cocked my head to the side, exposing my neck. "Was it here?" he asked, touching the very spot where Conor had almost kissed me.

I nodded, my heart thudding wildly from the unpredictability of his actions.

He bent down and pressed his lips to my neck. A moment later, I felt a pull, a suctioning on my skin. When he was done, he straightened, a smug smile on his face. "Now he'll know whose lips actually belong on your skin," he said, touching the warm spot on my neck.

I'd never had a hickey before. To be marked in such a way was insulting, yes, but it was also indescribably sexy. "Do it again," I whispered, pulling the robe away from my chest. I pointed to my breast, to a spot right above the hardened nipple. "Right here."

He wrapped his arms around my back and bowed down, and his mouth came down upon my chest, right above my left breast. He lifted me off my feet as he sucked on my skin, as if trying to place a kiss directly onto my pounding heart. I wrapped my arms around his shoulders, rubbing the back of his head as I moaned.

His grip tightened as his mouth descended upon mine, as he devoured me, fucking my mouth with his tongue. I kissed him back, pouring into it every apology, every bit of misplaced anger, hoping to alter it with our desire.

Henry carried me to the weight bench and sat down, setting me on his lap. He held my face in his hands, his gaze tender on my face. "Is it me you really want, Elsie?" he asked.

"Of course," I said, reaching into his shorts and stroking him to life. Then I set out to reassure him by sinking slowly onto his hard length, watching his face contort with pleasure. "I've loved you since the day we met."

He kissed my neck as his hands roamed under my robe, touching me all over while I bounced on his lap.

"Nobody else has even come close to you," I said, running my fingers through his hair and nipping along the shell of his ear. "It's only ever been you, Henry."

He took a deep breath and nodded, but something felt off, like our circuits had shorted and we were without power. But I was determined to make this work, to show Henry just how well we fit together, so I bobbed faster.

He gripped me by the hips and held me down. Breathing hard, he set his forehead against my chest and released a heavy sigh.

"What's wrong?" I asked, tilting his head up to face me.

His eyes were cloudy pools of uncertainty. "I can't stop thinking about it."

I pulled away and got on my feet. In all our times together, Henry had never denied me. "I'm sorry about what happened, Henry. I don't know what else I can say to make it all better."

He tucked himself back in and asked, "Tell me this: Did you want to kiss him back?"

God I wanted to lie. It would have been more merciful to say no, but I couldn't lie. Not to him. "A tiny part of me wanted to, just out of curiosity," I said in a small voice.

Henry rose to his feet, his face tense. "Do you want to fuck him too?"

"No, of course not!" I reached up and grabbed the sides of his face. He tried to brush me off, but I tried again and again until I finally had him in my hands. "Damn it, would you just look at me, you infuriating man!"

"What, Elsie? What do you want?" he gritted through his teeth.

"I want you to stop for one moment and look at me," I said gently.

His eyes burned into mine. "Yeah, I'm looking."

"Now tell me if you really, honestly think I'd ever want to be with anyone else but you."

His shoulders sagged as his righteous anger deflated.

"You're the only one I've ever wanted, Henry," I said, willing him to believe me. "If you don't know that by now, then I don't know if you ever will."

———————

I wore a mock turtleneck to work the following Monday, concealing the purplish mark on my neck. Hell, I wasn't Henry's personal billboard.

I was tense as I walked to my desk that morning, still unsure of what had really taken place between Conor and Henry. I breathed a sigh of relief when I turned the corner and found Conor's office empty. I sat at my desk, feeling like I'd just dodged a minor bullet, and booted up my Mac, ready to lose myself in work for a few hours.

But of course, my luck ran out almost immediately when my computer dinged, signaling a new interoffice message.

Would you come to my office, please? said the note from Conor.

I waited a good minute, gathering my nerves, before standing up, straightening my skirt, and finally walking down the aisle between cubicles. Conor's glass door was open; I walked right in and closed the door behind me.

He finished whatever it was he was typing on his laptop before giving me his attention. He clasped his hands in front of him and let out a long sigh. "So," he began, drawing out the word. "I suppose we have some things to talk about."

I took a deep breath and nodded. "I guess we do."

He stood up and walked around the desk. "Walk with me," he said and led the way out of the office.

"Where are we going?" I asked, following him out. "Why can't we talk about this in your office?" *Where we're in plain sight?*

He stopped in front of another room with a glass front wall, though this one was empty save for a glass desk and a brown leather chair. He unlocked the door and held it open for me, the smile on his face wide but guarded. "Welcome to your new office."

I walked into the middle of the room and immediately began mentally decorating it. I caught myself before I started painting the side walls. "Conor, this isn't some form of apology, is it? Because if this has anything to do with Henry I won't take it."

He shook his head. "I'd already planned on giving you this office when I assigned you the Lombart pitch. I gave you the account to prove yourself, and you have." He held out his hands. "And here we are, in your very own office."

I stared at him, trying to decide on the right move. In a perfect world, I would have done what Henry asked and quit this job. But this isn't a perfect world, and rights and wrongs aren't so independent of each other. Despite what happened and the uncertainty it would create, I believed that we could be adults about this and move on. Conor and I could continue to work together without our history mucking it up, I was sure of it.

Conor closed the door casually then turned back to me. "I do, however, owe you an apology," he said. "I shouldn't have been harboring feelings for a married woman. I was raised Catholic; I'm well versed in the Ten Commandments. I should have known better."

"I'm sorry if I gave you any indication that I was interested."

He looked down at his hands. "Your husband . . . Is he okay with this?"

"You tell me."

He snickered. "Honestly, I almost crapped my pants when he came back into the restaurant, looking like a roid-raging bull." He shook his head, laughing under his breath. "I was sure he was going to pound my face in. But we sat down at the bar and talked it over."

I shook my head in disbelief. "How did you manage to talk him down? He was out for blood when he left the house."

He smiled, that same cocky smile he was known for. "I can talk my way in and out of any situation. That's my God-given talent." He stuffed his hands in his pants pockets and looked around the room. "So, what color are you planning on painting the walls?"

6

I came home that Friday afternoon worn and weary. The week had been long; not only did I have my usual work to wade through, I also painted and moved into my new office. You just never realize how much crap you accumulate at work until you have to move it all into another space. But it was done, and it was surprising how strange it felt to be in a place all my own. No longer could I simply stand and have a conversation with my neighbors. Now I had to leave the confines of my office. I wasn't so sure I liked it, but it was, nevertheless, a step up in my career.

Still, it was tiring, this climb up the corporate ladder.

"Hey," Henry greeted me from the top of the stairs. He came down and gave me a quick peck on the lips then touched my stomach. "How are you feeling?"

I dropped my purse with a dramatic sigh. "Exhausted," I said. "I get so sleepy around two. I'm seriously contemplating putting a couch in my office so I can take naps in the afternoon. In fact, I could use a nap right now."

Henry's expression became serious. "Elsie, there's something I need to tell you."

I steeled myself, ready for whatever dire news Henry had today.

If I didn't know better, I'd say I was starting to get better at this LEO spouse thing. "Okay, hit me with it."

He burst out laughing. "You should see your face. You look so grim."

I put my hands on my hips, not in the mood for pranks. "You have five seconds to tell me before I kick you in the nuts," I said, only half joking.

He stepped back with a grin, covering his family jewels with one hand. "Okay, okay. I just wanted to tell you that I have the weekend off," he said, laughing. "And I am taking you somewhere far away."

"Where?" I asked, trying to muster an ounce of excitement but not altogether succeeding. Just the thought of packing almost made me want to turn him down.

He grinned, once again proving he could read my mind. "You don't have to do anything. You just have to get your sexy butt into the car and let me do the rest."

"But I'll have to pack."

He jabbed a thumb over his shoulder, at my duffel bag at the bottom of the stairs. "Done."

I raised an eyebrow. "You packed for me?" I could only imagine what manner of clothing he'd packed, if he packed anything other than lingerie at all. "Toiletries?"

"Done."

My adventurous streak kicked in then as a frisson of excitement wound through me. "Okay, I'm in. Where are we going?"

"You'll see," he said with a smug smile and ushered me toward the door to the garage.

In the car, I gazed at him as he backed down the driveway, still unable to believe that we were actually going to have some time alone together. A part of me didn't think it was possible, sure that he'd get called in at the last minute.

But he didn't get a call, and when I woke a few hours later, it was already dark. I squinted without my glasses, making out a mountain on one side of the road and a lake on the other. "Are we nearly there? I really have to pee."

Henry pointed to a spot across the lake. "Our destination is on the other side."

"And where is that exactly?"

"Grand Lake," he said, looking over at me. "I rented a cabin for the weekend. Just like we planned. It's a little late, but a promise is a promise."

I reached across the gearshift and squeezed his thigh.

"I want this weekend to be just about us. Nobody and nothing else matters from this moment until we leave on Sunday. Deal?"

I wasn't sure if it was possible to leave everything behind but I was willing to try. "Deal."

We parked right by the lake, beside a tiny log cabin.

"It doesn't look like much out here," he said as he carried our bags from the car. He unlocked the door and flipped on the lights, revealing the cabin's open-plan interior. It was one large room, the kitchen, living room, and bedroom all in one place. The walls were horizontal lines of wood and concrete, and against one was a large, rough-hewn stone fireplace, in front of which sat a large brown leather sofa on an Afghan rug. In the corner was the tiny kitchen, and on the other side of the room was a queen-sized bed hidden by a white, gauzy canopy that hung from the ceiling. To the right was a door, presumably the bathroom. And on the wall across from the entrance was another door.

"Where does this go?" I asked, walking over and unlocking it. The view, once I opened the door, took my breath away. Directly in front of me was a dock jutting out onto the lake that spread out in all directions for miles. Silhouettes of the mountains framed the horizon, lit only by the pale moonlight. All at once the scene filled me with a sense of peace and wonder.

"This is beautiful," I said, sure that my mouth was literally hanging open. I turned around to find Henry standing right behind me, an inscrutable look on his face as he watched me.

"Would it be cheesy if I said you're the one that's beautiful?"

I smiled, feeling like a tiny moon was lighting me up from the inside. "Yeah, incredibly cheesy," I said, fitting my body into his arms. "But who doesn't like cheese?"

He pressed his lips to my forehead and took a deep, cleansing breath. "It feels good to be here with you," he said and for the first time in a long time, I felt him start to unwind. "Come on," he said, pulling me back inside. "The owner filled the fridge per my request. Let's cook dinner."

It was late by the time we finished our dinner of spaghetti and garlic bread. After taking a quick shower in the tiny shower stall (so small, we could barely move let alone do anything fun), we snuggled into the soft bed and fell asleep in each other's arms.

"Elsie, come on." Henry's voice came from a faraway place, pulling me from a peaceful, dreamless sleep. "Wake up," he said, his voice closer.

I opened one eye and found Henry standing over me, naked and gloriously masculine, holding a blanket under one arm. "Good morning," I said with a sleepy grin, then noticed it was still dark. I checked the time on my phone. "Why are you awake at five a.m.?"

"I figured we could watch the sun rise over the lake."

I rolled over and snuggled deeper into the blanket. "No thanks. It's probably cold as balls out there."

"That's what the blanket's for." He pulled the covers away and lifted me up in his arms in one swift motion, carrying me through the house and out the back door.

"We're completely naked!" I hissed, the cool morning air taking my breath away.

"Do you see anybody else here?" he asked. I looked around at our dark surroundings, realizing that we were alone for miles.

Without missing a step, he continued down the dock, toward the two Adirondack chairs at the end. He set me down on the ground, waved the blanket open and wrapped it around his shoulders. Then he gathered me in his arms and sat down, pulling me onto his lap. I grabbed the edges of the blanket and closed it around us, creating a cocoon of warm, bare skin.

I leaned against his chest and sighed as he wrapped his arms around me. "Okay, this idea has its merits."

"Did you just say I'm right and you're wrong?" he asked, his breath ruffling my hair.

"Not in so many words." I tangled my fingers with his and held him tighter around me.

Wordlessly, we watched the sun emerge, both of us struck silent as the navy blue sky lightened to purple and the orange rays of the sun soared up and over the black mountains, bathing everything in a golden glow. The pink and yellow clouds against the cyan sky were reflected in the water, and it was as if Henry and I were alone in the world, nestled in the very center of heaven.

My heart had never felt more full, more in love with the world, than at that moment.

I squeezed his hands as my eyes prickled with tears. "I wish we could stay like this forever," I whispered, afraid to disturb the serenity enveloping us. In the distance, a bird greeted the morning with a trill.

"I love you," Henry said, his lips scraping against my ear. I knew right then that he felt it too, this magic that was spinning around, binding us together. "I could spend a hundred lifetimes loving you and it still won't be enough."

A tear escaped and slipped down my cheek. "I wish we could set things straight." I twisted around in his lap so that I was facing him, my legs hanging off the side. "Go back to being those naïve newly-weds without a care in the world."

Henry shook his head. "No, I don't want go back there," he said, taking me aback. "I don't want to be that guy because he's still in for a hell of a time. I'd rather be this guy right now, holding you in my arms even after all the mistakes I've made."

"I've made mistakes too."

His eyes flew across my face. "Then let's just forgive each other and move on."

"Can we?"

He nodded solemnly. "I don't want to have anything hanging between us. I want us to start over with a clean slate."

I didn't know if that was possible with our long, complicated history, but I so badly wanted to believe it. I nodded and buried my face in his neck, breathing in his distinct Henry scent. "I want that too. More than anything."

For a moment, I wondered what it would be like if we both woke up tomorrow morning without our memories. What would it be like to look at Henry and not know that he'd been an integral part of my life since I was a girl? Would we fall in love again without our history?

"Let's do it, Els. From this moment, it's just you and me," he said, placing a palm on my stomach, "and this being."

I shifted around and straddled him while he held the blanket around my back. I sat on his erection and slid along the length of him as I traced my finger along his angular jaw and down to his chin, pressing my thumb to the indentation there. "I love you so much," I said as I lifted and held the tip of him to my opening.

A tremor traveled over his body when I sank onto his length, joining us in the purest sense. He clutched me against his hard chest, running his warm lips along my shoulders, breathing hard. I touched his lips softly with my own, tentative little touches that promised more.

It was in this moment, as I held him tight in my womb, that I remembered the one true thing about Henry and me: that the love between us was not only emotional but also physical, as if our bodies were magnets inexplicably drawn to each other.

I held still and enjoyed the sensation of his cock throbbing inside me, warming me from the inside. I continued to squeeze at him and he groaned in appreciation. "That feels so good," he said in a raspy voice. "I could come with just that."

I kissed him, continuing to make love to him without moving my hips. I grabbed the back of his head to deepen the kiss, our tongues gliding together as we breathed as one. We barely moved as we made love, blending in with the serene scene around us.

I arched my back as Henry dipped his head to pay homage to my breasts with his mouth, wrapping his lips around each puckered nipple at a time. I threw my head back and looked up at the ever-brightening sky. I gasped when his thumb found my clit and began to draw circles, bringing me closer to the brink. Just as I was almost there, he stopped and gripped me to him, our foreheads and noses pressed together.

"Els . . ."

And then he flexed inside me, swelling as he started to come, taking me by surprise as he took me over the edge with him. My walls convulsed around him as bolts of pleasure raced through my veins. I gasped when the blanket fell away, exposing my back to the cool morning air, the contrast of hot and cold intensifying the pleasure, making the orgasm go on and on.

I held his head against my chest and waited until the throbbing subsided, until our racing hearts began to slow. He gathered the edges of the blanket and closed it around us again.

Henry looked up, the sun's golden glow illuminating the planes on his face. "God, that was . . ." he breathed.

I nodded, not needing to hear the end of his sentence, knowing in my heart what he meant to say. I wanted to stay in the moment forever, stuck in this magical little place, where it seemed like nothing could ever change.

———

After we ate breakfast, we walked to Main Street, which was lined with store facades that looked like they came straight out of old Westerns. We ate our ice cream cones and walked along the boardwalk—the sidewalk composed of wooden boards—soaking up the quaint atmosphere that was far removed from the bustle of Denver.

I stopped in front of a store to take a closer look at the old wooden Indian standing guard. Henry stopped beside me and wrapped an arm around my shoulders. I was enjoying the perfectly innocuous moment when Henry lifted his hand and touched his ice cream cone to my nose.

I turned to him with a shocked look, vanilla ice cream sticking to the tip of my nose. He grinned down at me, mirth lighting up his features making him look years younger. "I'm sorry, it had to be done," he said with an exaggerated shrug.

I grabbed a handful of his shirt and pulled him down. "Come here and give me a kiss," I said and wiped my nose all over his face, both of us laughing without fetters.

Afterward we rented a wooden boat and rowed around the lake. It was breathtakingly beautiful, being out on the blue water with the tiny sailboats and other watercraft. Near the center of the lake, we put the oars away and ate our sandwiches, breathing in the clean mountain air around us.

After several minutes of silently admiring our beautiful surroundings, I caught Henry staring at me. "What?" I asked with a curious smile.

"Nothing."

I gave him a withering look. "Come on. What?" I said. "Wait, let me guess. You were wondering how you got to be so lucky?"

He snorted. "No. I was wondering how you'd look with a huge pregnant belly."

I threw a crumpled napkin at him. "You are so not getting laid later."

"What? I was just curious," he said with a laugh. "For the record, I think you'd look beautiful, glowing."

"Uh-huh, sure."

Careful not to rock the boat, he sat beside me and gave me a peck on the cheek then wrapped an arm around my shoulders with a sigh. "I may not always be the perfect husband but I can promise you that I will be the best dad I can possibly be to our child. Or children."

I touched his cheek, touched by his solemnity. "I know you will."

"I'll probably miss more soccer games and school plays than I can make, but I'll always try my best to be there for them, to be the kind of dad they'll be proud to have."

I placed a kiss on his lips, swallowing his words in hopes they'd reach his unborn child. "You'll be wonderful, Henry," I said. "This child is going to be so lucky to have you."

PART FIVE

DEFEND

1

"It feels so good to be home," Henry groaned as he slid under the covers and snuggled up behind me. "I've had the longest day ever. Lots of garbage calls. You have no idea how many people think cops are there for their disposal. One old guy actually had the audacity to call 911 so we could clear out a branch that had fallen over onto his property."

I snuggled farther into the bend of his body. "I'm sorry."

"I only had time for a burger for lunch today," he said. "And soggy French fries."

My stomach chose that moment to rumble. "That actually sounds kinda good."

"It wasn't," he murmured sleepily. "Trust me."

Suddenly I couldn't get the idea of hot, fresh fries dipped in a hot fudge sundae out of my head. The saltier the fries, the better. My stomach rumbled again, and even though I'd eaten dinner a few hours earlier, I found myself starving suddenly. "Henry?" I whispered, but received no answer. I listened to his breathing and realized he'd already fallen asleep.

Not wanting to bother him with this craving, I slipped out from under his arms and got out of bed. I went into the closet to dress but when I came out, Henry was sitting up. "You okay? Where are you going?"

"Just going to get some drive-through," I said, slipping on some ballet flats. I gave him a kiss on the forehead. "Go back to sleep."

Even with a sleep-rumpled face, he managed to give me an incredulous look. Without a word, he climbed out of bed and started pulling on the jeans he'd discarded on the floor.

"What are you doing?" I asked. "You don't have to come with me. Just go to sleep. I'll be right back."

"Elsie. It is my solemn husbandly duty to take care of your cravings." I was about to make a quip about feminism, when he held up a hand to stop me. "I know you're perfectly capable of getting it yourself. Just humor me, okay?"

"Fine," I said, grabbing his hand. "Let's go then."

Six minutes later, I had a bag of fries and a sundae in my lap, glad I'd let Henry drive instead so I wouldn't have to wait to eat. On the way back home, he abruptly pulled into the parking lot of a neighborhood park.

"Come on," he said after opening my door. He carried the sundae and led me to the swings, sitting down and pulling me onto his lap.

"What are we doing here?" I asked, popping a fry in my mouth.

He gazed up at the full moon in the sky. "It's such a nice night," he said, holding on to the sundae so that I could dip my fries into it.

"Don't you want to go back home to bed?"

He yawned and then smiled. "I do. But I wanted to have a little midnight adventure with you while we still can." I offered him a fry and he took it. "That doesn't taste so bad."

"It's the tamest of my cravings so far," I said with a laugh. "The other day, I wanted to eat Braum's rocky road ice cream and Tabasco. I almost asked you to fly to Oklahoma to get it."

He chuckled and wrapped his arm around my waist, his palm resting against my rounded stomach. "That would have been a little tough."

When the craving was complete, I threw away the rest of the food in a nearby trash can and reclaimed my seat on Henry's lap. I wrapped an arm around his shoulder as we looked up at the bright moon.

"It's almost as beautiful as your painting," I said, tangling my fingers through his hair.

His hand slid up my neck and he guided me down to his lips. When he pulled away, he licked his lips. "You're sweet," he said. "Literally and figuratively."

He leaned his head against my shoulder and we sat there for another several minutes, enjoying the peace that the darkness afforded.

On Thursday night, I went directly from work to Maria's Cantina, a Mexican restaurant, to meet Henry for dinner. The first to arrive, I took a seat at the bar and opted to wait there.

A guy three seats down raised his glass when I received my drink. *"Prost!"*

I lifted my ginger ale and smiled. *"Salud!"* I took a sip and turned back to the entrance to watch for Henry's arrival.

"So who are you meeting?"

I turned back to the guy, who was probably in his forties, with wire-rimmed glasses and a head of wavy reddish-blond hair. He was wearing a thick sweater and slacks, looking like he'd also just come from work. "My husband," I said, noticing the odd lump at his back. "And you?"

"Waiting for an ex girlfriend," he said with a wry curl of the lips. "Trying to get back some of my stuff."

"I see," I said, and felt rather than saw Henry behind me. I twisted my head around in time to receive his kiss on the cheek.

"Hey, sorry I'm late," he said, giving my neighbor more than a cursory glance. Henry's hand pressed into the small of my back when I stood up. "You ready?"

I turned back to the guy. "Good luck," I said and walked away.

As we followed the hostess into the restaurant, Henry waved to a man sitting in the far corner with his wife and kids. "That's Franklin," he said to me as he pulled out my seat. "Veteran cop. I don't really know him. I just know he's been around the block and helped take down a drug ring last year."

"How bad is it in Denver?" I asked. Yes, it was a naïve question, but when I thought of drug dealers, I thought of places like LA or Miami, not Denver.

"Not as bad as other cities, but it's here."

I took my glasses off and set them on the colorfully tiled table, glad to be done with them for the day. "Have you ever been involved in a bust?"

"I haven't yet," Henry said softly. "But it's bound to happen."

The conversation flowed smoothly over dinner, Henry seemingly relaxed and talkative. It was a far cry from that man long ago, the one who basically ignored me in order to watch his surroundings like a hawk. The Henry of today had managed to strike the right balance between paying attention to his surroundings as well as his company.

From the corner of my eye, I noted the redheaded guy sitting at a table with a woman. They didn't order food but only had drinks on the table as they had a verbal exchange that seemed to get more heated as time progressed.

"Looks like he's not having much luck getting his stuff back," I said, trying not to appear as if I was gawking. In truth, their argument was a little entertaining and had caught the attention of several other diners.

Henry glanced over and shook his head. "They need to calm down. They're starting to disrupt the place."

I wiped the corners of my mouth with my napkin and stood up. "I need to use the restroom."

"The baby can't be sitting on your bladder already, can it?" he asked with a hint of a smile.

I pinched his nose as I walked by, feeling so fortunate in that moment. I shot one more look over my shoulder at my beautiful husband before turning the corner to head for the restrooms at the back of the restaurant.

After using the toilet and washing my hands, I looked at myself in the mirror, wondering if I was already starting to show. I turned to the side and smoothed my top over my stomach, not sure if the soft swell was caused by the baby or my dinner.

As I stared at my bump, I felt a strange sensation wash over me, like a sense of doom. Then, as if fate read my mind, a loud bang came from the restaurant followed immediately by screams.

Without thinking, I ran out of the bathroom. A moment later, Henry rounded the corner and pinned me against the wall.

"Henry!" I squeaked, finding no air in my lungs. "What's going on?"

"Hide," he whispered urgently, looking over his shoulder. "The guy's pulled out a gun and has taken a hostage."

"What? What guy?" I hissed, glad I had just peed otherwise my underwear would be soaked right about now.

"Your friend at the bar." I flinched when another shot was fired. Henry didn't even bat an eyelash. "Get back in there. Call 911. Get out through the window. Break it if you have to."

"But—"

"Do it," he said between his teeth then released me. It was only then I noticed the gun in his hand. That one image brought it all home—brought everything to a new level of clarity for me—and it left me oddly calm. No panicking, no freaking out. Henry had this.

With measured movements, I nodded. I gave him a quick kiss and said, "Be careful. I love you," before going into the bathroom and locking the door behind me. I stood by the window that didn't open and dialed 911, telling the operator with calm precision our location and the situation.

"Just stay hidden," the operator told me. "Officers are on their way."

I couldn't tell you how long I waited in that bathroom. It might have been two minutes or it might have been thirty. But as I stood there, with my back against the door, my calm reserve started to slip bit by bit. It was too quiet, so much so that everything in me wanted to go out to see if the coast was clear. But I couldn't be that person, the one in slasher movies who just can't stay hidden, and instead goes to investigate the action and gets herself killed. If I went out there right now, I might distract Henry and quite possibly put us both in harm's way.

I curled up into a ball, about ready to jump out of my skin. I'd felt like this once before, back when I'd just moved to Oklahoma and I hadn't yet experienced the tornado season.

Jason had been TDY so it was just me and Henry. It was the height of tornado season, but I hadn't been in Oklahoma long enough to look out for the signs, how a muggy, cloudy day could turn deadly in minutes. After watching the news about the developing weather, Henry finally turned off the TV and announced that we weren't safe in a third-story apartment, then drove us to the brick, one-story house of Sam Miller, a buddy from his squadron.

Sam took us directly to the interior bathroom, where we waited— me sitting inside the bathtub while they sat on its edge—and we listened to the reports on the radio. I vividly remembered the look on Henry's face, his eyebrows drawn and lips pursed, his entire body tense.

Then the lights went out and then we lost radio frequency. Henry climbed into the tub with me, covering me with his large body. The winds howled outside and it was raining so hard; we could hear it pelting the windows. I instinctively wrapped my arms around Henry's body; if he was going to protect me from debris, then I was going to prevent him from getting sucked away.

"I won't let anything happen to you, Els," I heard him say above the noise, his arms wrapped around my shoulders.

After the wind died down and the lights came back on, I glimpsed an expression on his face that stole the breath from my lungs. I remember my heart thrumming wildly in that moment, believing him, knowing even back then that Henry would throw himself in front of a bullet for me.

It was a comforting thought, but it was also scary as hell. Especially now that he was out there with a gunman, without his Kevlar body armor, with only his gun to help him. Backup was coming, but would they get here in time?

Then I heard the voice of a male shouting. I could make out, "Stay back," but the rest was a muffled mess of words. Still, there was no doubt in the tone of his voice: The perp was angry and desperate.

I flinched when another shot was fired. I wanted to hear Henry's voice, but knew that he would remain calm in a situation like this, that raising his voice meant he had snapped. I fingered the ring on my right hand, sending up a quick prayer for my husband's safety. Then I remembered Franklin and felt a small measure of relief that at least Henry had someone else on his side.

I heard sirens in the distance and felt the air releasing from my lungs. The cavalry had arrived. Henry and Franklin would have their backup.

And then a rapid burst of gunfire rang out, each report coming out sounding like a hammer against a metal door, battering down whatever was left of my composure.

I put my head to my knees and prayed hard, my tears threatening to burst out with every whispered word.

I couldn't tell you how long I sat there, praying into my lap, but a loud knocking on the door made me jump.

"Anybody in there?" asked a muffled female voice. "This is the police. It's safe to come out now."

Somehow I managed to get back to my feet and force my wobbly legs to support my weight. With trembling fingers, I flipped the lock and opened the door.

"Are you alright, ma'am?" The police officer made her way into the bathroom and looked around.

"I'm fine," I said.

She held the radio up to her mouth. "Secure back here." When I tried to walk away, she grabbed my wrist. "Be careful . . ."

"My husband's out there," I said, leaving no room for discussion. The scene that greeted me when I turned the corner made my knees buckle. There were people—cops and EMTs—walking around upturned tables and broken dishes. My eyes searched the room for Henry but he was nowhere to be found.

"Henry!" I called, circling around the commotion. I froze as, across the room, two EMTs lifted a body onto a stretcher. But without my glasses, I couldn't tell *who* they were loading onto that stretcher, his jean-clad legs and black shoes his only identifying factors.

"Please, no . . ." I said, my limbs refusing to move forward and confirm. My hand instinctively went to my stomach. "No . . ."

A hand clamped on my shoulder. It felt like a million years before I turned my head, before I saw the person beside me through the blur of tears. "Elsie," Sondra said, her normally surly expression replaced by one of concern.

I had my every thought written on my face, my every fear in my eyes. "Is he . . ." I turned back in time to see the stretcher being wheeled out of the restaurant. I about collapsed from relief when they turned the corner and I saw the red hair that indicated it wasn't Henry.

Sondra's eyebrows knotted together. "Are you okay?" The radio on her belt crackled to life. She spoke into it quickly, numbers and letters rushing out of her mouth in a way that made absolutely no sense to me. Then she turned to me. "Come on," she said, already taking long strides toward the exit. "You can ride with me."

"Where are we going?"

"To Denver Health," she said, leading the way to her police cruiser. "That's where your husband is."

2

The drive to the hospital was, quite possibly, the longest ride I'd ever had to endure. The silence in the car was thick and my worry made it even harder to breathe.

"Did they tell you what happened? Is he okay?" I asked as we got stopped by another red light. I wished she'd turn on the sirens so we could just blast through every intersection already.

"I don't know. He just asked me to bring you." She gave me a concerned look. "Cheer up. That means he's alive."

I sat back and tried to tamp down my worry, but with every light we stopped at, my imagination invented even more horrible scenarios so that by the time we arrived at the hospital, I was a hot, panicked mess.

Sondra led the way through the maze of hospital hallways, knowing exactly where to go. It struck me then that maybe she'd walked this way many times before, seen many of her colleagues shot down over the years. I started to tear up at the thought.

We walked in through the emergency-room door. Henry stood up from a waiting room seat, and I swear, my legs just about buckled from relief.

He greeted Sondra then wrapped me in a tight embrace. "Hey," he said and sighed against my hair.

I wrapped my arms around his back and pressed my face into his chest as my tears soaked into his shirt. I closed my eyes and breathed him in, the mixture of fresh sweat and his distinct smell filling my senses. I thanked every deity once, twice for keeping my husband safe.

It was tough, but I finally pulled away. "What happened?" I asked, trying to keep my voice from trembling.

"That guy, the one you were talking to at the bar," he began, his hand sliding down to hold mine. "He pulled out a gun and took a woman hostage. Franklin got his attention while I made sure every-one got out of the restaurant. He didn't want to listen to us. He was very desperate."

"What happened to the hostage?" I asked.

"When he realized he was cornered, he shot her." He closed his eyes, his eyebrows drawing together. "Then started shooting at us. Franklin caught a bullet in the stomach. They took him into the OR."

Sondra made a frustrated noise and kicked at the ground. "Fuck."

Henry shook his head. "I should have—"

"What? You should have what?" Sondra asked with a clipped tone. "Don't do that, Logan. That's bullshit. I told you never to question yourself."

I squeezed his hand, letting him know I sympathized. I realized then that she must not know Henry as well as she'd like if she thought he wouldn't question himself.

Sondra's expression hardened when another officer named Wilson approached with a grave look on his face. "He didn't make it," he said, his voice cracking. "He died on the table."

Henry pulled me into his chest and buried his face in my hair, breathing hard. From the corner of my eye, I saw Sondra closing her eyes and bowing her head, no doubt regretting her words. She took a few deep breaths and looked up, the commanding officer back in place. "Have you contacted his wife?" she asked as she strode out of the room, the other officer right behind her.

Henry's arm trembled around my shoulders as he continued to hide his face.

"Henry . . ." I said softly, but couldn't continue. I didn't know what to say, didn't know how he was even feeling. So I simply held him tighter, imagining that my own shaky arms were keeping him from falling apart.

He pulled away too soon. "I have to go back to the station. Fill out paperwork and all the standard procedure."

I nodded. "I'll come with you."

He shook his head and kissed my forehead. "Just go home, Els. Wilson will give you a ride. This might take awhile," he said, and after making sure that I remembered to lock the doors at home and keep Law by my side at all times, he made me go.

———————

It was past midnight by the time Henry made it home. He walked into the bedroom wordlessly, ignoring me and Law altogether as he headed into the bathroom. I listened for a while, but the water didn't come on, the toilet didn't flush.

Finally, after fifteen solid minutes, I crept out of bed and knocked on the door. "Henry?" I called softly through the door. "What are you doing in there?"

"Nothing."

I opened the door and found him standing in front of the sink, his palms flat against the counter, his back rising and falling heavily. His eyebrows were drawn and there was a glazed look in his eyes as he stared into the sink.

I approached him slowly, like one would approach a twitchy animal, noticing his duty belt was on the counter. "Are you alright?"

He ignored my question and reached into his shirt pocket and pulled out a pair of glasses. "You left these at the restaurant," he said, dropping them on the counter.

I took note of the empty spot on his belt. "Where's your gun?"

"I had to surrender it for tests," he said in a weary voice.

I touched his back and noticed the cotton shirt was damp. It was then I noticed the beads of sweat on his forehead and on the bridge of his nose. "What? Why?"

His eyes flicked up for a quick moment. "The gunman died," he said, his voice devoid of emotion. He could have been talking about the weather.

He turned on the faucet, pumped some soap onto his palm and began to wash his hands. "They've given me a week of administrative leave while Internal Affairs conducts the investigation," he said, scrubbing himself over and over.

I covered my mouth. "So you could be charged? For doing your job?"

He continued to wash his hands, ignoring me. Finally, I just reached around him and switched off the faucet. He turned to me, his hands dripping at his sides. "It's procedure. This is what happens with every shooting that results in death."

I closed my eyes and swallowed hard.

"A police officer died today, Elsie," Henry said barely above a whisper, as if afraid someone else would hear and judge. "Franklin was a good man. He was a decorated veteran. I should be mourning his loss, not . . ." The voice hitched in his throat. "Not worrying about having taken a life."

I held him, feeling his heart thudding against my cheek. I didn't know if there was anything I could say that would make him feel better, but couldn't think of anything meaningful.

He leaned his chin atop my head and heaved a deep sigh. A second later, I felt something dropping onto my hair, the moisture seeping into my scalp.

"I killed a man today, Elsie," he said into my hair quietly. "I don't know how to make peace with that."

My heart broke for him in that moment. How should I comfort a man who was suffering under the weight of his guilt? "Isn't war the same?" I asked, trying to give him some perspective.

He shook his head. "This is different, Els. It's different seeing the face of the person you're shooting. It's different seeing their body recoil from the blast of your gun." He pulled away from my arms and started to undress, his movements jerky and erratic. He turned away when he said, "It's different because at war, you don't see the light go out from their eyes when they die."

I held him that night, just hugged his back to my chest and said nothing. What else could I say to a man who had already judged himself guilty of murder?

———

Henry woke up with a shout.

My eyes flew open, my heart thumping hard when I found Henry sitting up, nearly hyperventilating. I flipped on the lamp and saw the panicked look on his face.

When I reached out to him, I found his skin clammy with sweat. "You okay?"

He shook his head, the motion causing my hand to slip off his back, but he didn't offer a reason. He just climbed out of bed and went to the bathroom. I waited for him, still snuggled under the covers, and watched as he came out and headed directly for the closet.

I didn't need to see him in order to know he was putting on his workout clothes. And sure enough, a minute later, he emerged in sweat-wicking shirt, shorts, and running shoes. He sat on the edge of the bed to tie his laces.

I nudged him with my foot. "Why are you running away?"

"I'm not going far. I'll be back."

"Why don't you stay and we can talk about it instead?" I said. "And don't pretend you didn't just have a nightmare. I know you, Henry. I know you're avoiding the issue again."

It was alarming, how much it reminded me of the time he came back from Afghanistan, when his sleep was disturbed and his way of dealing with his issues was to punish his body with exercise.

This time, however, I had the wisdom of history on my side. I sat up and grabbed his hand. "Please, Henry."

He shook his head as if trying to throw off the lingering remnants of his nightmare. "No," he said, pleading with me with his sad blue eyes. "Just let me deal with this on my own, okay?"

He whistled for Law and left without another word.

3

"Why don't we go for a vacation this week?" I asked as we ate a late breakfast. "I haven't taken time off in a long time. We can go to Dallas and see Julie and Will."

If I thought my suggestion would cheer him up, I was wrong. "No thanks," he said, draining his second cup of coffee.

"Seeing Will might cheer you up."

"I don't need cheering up," he said. "Besides, I have to see a counselor this week. Talk about my feelings and shit."

"It could be good for you."

He eyed me with something like disdain. "Yeah. Sure. I can talk about how I've dreamed about that motherfucker's face two nights in a row. How I keep killing him over and over but he just won't stay down."

I felt a little spark of hope from that confession. "Yes, you could talk to the counselor about that."

"So she can tell the chief that I'm a nutcase?" he asked.

"This is not the same as the military, Henry," I said. "There's not that stigma attached to getting psychiatric help."

He stood up and grabbed our empty plates, taking a long time to rinse them and load the dishwasher. When he was done with the dishes, he wiped down the counters over and over.

"Henry?"

"He can't see me like this, okay?" he suddenly yelled, taking me aback. He slammed the rag into the sink and stalked off.

I followed him downstairs to the basement where he was already laying blows on the heavy bag with his bare knuckles. "Who? The chief?"

Only the sound of skin slapping vinyl and his heavy breathing could be heard in that cool room as I stood there and waited for his reply.

After several minutes of intense jabbing, he grabbed the bag to stop its swinging. "Will," he finally said. "I don't want him to think I'm . . ." He pressed his forehead to the bag and let his words fall away.

I touched a hand to his back and kissed his shoulder. "Then do something about it. Don't go down this path again."

"What, you think I'm letting this happen?"

"I don't know what to think, to tell you the truth."

"Well I'm trying my best, Elsie," he said, eyeing me steadily. "But I don't know how to combat the nightmares or the guilt."

I didn't know how either, but slowly I could see the darkness winning, threatening to suffocate the very things I loved about my husband.

"I just . . . need you to leave me alone and let me deal with it on my own, okay?"

His words stung, but what could I do? If I kept pushing, I'd only end up angering him. So even if it was against my nature, even if it was the last thing I wanted to do, I left him there on his own, just like he'd asked.

————————

"Thanks for meeting with me," I said as Sondra and I sat down at an outdoor café.

"It's no problem." She waved the waiter over and ordered a glass of wine. "And you?"

"Just an iced tea please."

Sondra didn't waste any time beating around the bush. "Look, I know it must be tough with what Logan is going through."

"You know?"

"Yeah, with the investigation and Franklin's death, I don't know anyone who would enjoy this kind of weeklong break."

"But it goes beyond that," I said, unsure of how much I could say. Henry might trust her enough to tell her everything, but I sure as hell didn't.

Sondra watched me carefully. "Every cop goes through a rough patch, especially when they see a colleague die on the same day they make their first kill. Put yourself in his shoes."

"I have and all I can think of is that I'd be seeking some professional help."

"He's getting professional help. He's at the counselor's office right now, isn't he?"

I played with the condensation on my drink, afraid to voice my worry that it wouldn't work. He'd gone to a psychiatrist once before and it had ended with him breaking up with me. What would happen this time?

"Elsie, seems to me like you're having trouble with this yourself."

I nodded. "I guess you can say that."

"Are you afraid of him? Disgusted with him?"

"No," I replied. "I just . . . I don't think the counseling is helping."

For the past few days, Henry had come home after his sessions more shut off than before, evading even the simplest touch from me. He wouldn't accept comfort, wouldn't even let me near him sometimes. And I, in turn, suffered in silence, trying to be the strong one for once.

"I think it's happening again."

Sondra gave a nod, like she knew exactly what I was referring to.

"You told me before that it's my job to keep it from happening again."

"True, I did. But you can't blame yourself. Some things go way beyond our control." She gave a pause, eyeing me for a long, unnerving while. Finally, she said, "I went through something similar several years ago. I don't tell a lot of people because the automatic reaction is that I'm too soft because I'm a woman."

"Forgive me for saying so, but there's nothing soft about you."

She grinned. "I'll take that as a compliment."

"It was." I leaned forward. "So what happened?"

"Some gang member at a gas station just started shooting at me. Luckily he was a lousy shot and only clipped my leg," she said, her gaze unwavering. "For the longest time I couldn't get over the fact that he was so young. He couldn't have been more than twenty. I had the hardest time making peace with that."

She tore off a piece of bread and chewed on it for a moment. "I won't pretty it up: It took awhile. I don't know anyone who's invulnerable to it. We have our Kevlar to protect us from bullets, but we don't have anything to protect us from the guilt and shame."

"Then what the hell do I do?"

"Be prepared. Get ready to be frustrated and angry—sometimes so angry, you want to hurt him—and be prepared to be pushed away so many times you'll be tempted to just leave. But don't. Don't give up. Not if you want to see him recover." The way Sondra talked, the way she kept her eyes fixed on me, spoke volumes about her experience.

"Why do it? Why be a cop knowing that what you'll experience may very well fuck you up emotionally?"

"Why not? Every job has its hazards," she said, the tough police officer back. "Most of us don't enter the force out of some heroic idea, or because we like the power trip. Even if it means we carry a burden on our shoulders, some of us do it just to make a difference."

———————

On the third day of his administrative leave, I came home after work to find Henry still in his pajamas, playing Xbox on the couch. He had a dirty plate beside him and several bottles of beer on the coffee table.

He didn't even take his eyes off the television when I bent down to give him a kiss on the cheek. I ran the back of my fingers against the beard on his face, remembering that, once upon a time, it had been a turn-on to see him so scruffy. Now it was just another piece of evidence that he was starting to unravel.

"Have you even taken a shower today?" I asked.

"Nope," he said, making an obnoxious popping noise with his lips.

"You went to the therapy unwashed and in your pajamas?"

He gave me a look as if I was the one losing it. Which may very well be the truth. "Really?"

I rolled my eyes and backed off when I felt my temper flaring. Pregnancy hormones and an irritating husband should never be combined. "You got dressed, went out, then came home and changed back into your pajamas. Got it," I said, taking my shoes off and making my way up the stairs.

In our bedroom, I let out an overlong exhale, trying my best to keep from crying. *Be strong,* I kept telling myself. Henry needed me to keep it together.

I jumped when hands wrapped around my arms. "How was your day?" Henry asked, his tone much different than a few minutes before. I sank back onto his chest, taking advantage of his momentary affection. His hands slid around to caress my stomach.

"Work was fine. But my back is hurting."

He kissed the top of my head before going to the bathroom and drawing me a bath. I followed him in and found him lighting some candles.

He turned to me with a smile that didn't quite reach his eyes. "I was waiting to take a bath with you."

I turned my back as I undressed, and the little move didn't go unnoticed.

"Don't hide yourself from me," he said, taking me by the shoulders and spinning me around. "I don't care if you've gained weight."

It was a sweet thought, but my brain got stuck at the fact that he mentioned my weight at all. The scale said I'd gained nearly fifteen pounds already, due to stress-eating more than the growing fetus inside me. I was self-conscious enough without having it pointed out.

"Come on, I've seen you like this before," he said, pulling me into the bathtub. He sat behind me and wrapped his long legs around mine.

I couldn't relax, however. "When?"

"Your first year away in college when you gained the freshman fifteen. Or twenty," he said with some humor in his voice. "A lot of it went to your ass, but you had a lot to grab on to elsewhere."

I knew he was kidding; I knew this but I couldn't help but feel the sting of his words. "Shut up," I said, sitting up and sliding away from him. "Just stop talking."

"What? What did I say?"

I stood up to get out of the tub, but my foot slipped on the way out. Thankfully, Henry was quick and caught me before I fell. "Damn it, Elsie, be careful!"

I turned to him with tears in my eyes, but the words stuck in my throat. I wanted to use every curse word in my arsenal, but didn't want the situation to get out of control. So I just grabbed a towel and stomped out of the bathroom.

Henry, in his first display of good sense, stayed put.

4

Patrick Franklin's funeral was held on a somber Thursday morning with the entire Denver Police Department in attendance. Allison and I stood at the corner of Quebec Street and East Eighth Avenue along with countless others—some holding signs and American flags—to pay their respects as miles and miles of police vehicles passed by with their lights flashing.

Allison brought her husband's police scanner and we listened with tears in our eyes as the dispatcher called a status check on each cruiser. Every police officer answered the call, all but the last one. The dispatcher called his number once. When she received no reply, she called his number again, her voice barely containing her sorrow. At the last call, she said, "All units be advised, Officer Patrick Franklin has officially reached his end of watch."

It was nearly one o'clock in the afternoon by the time Henry made it home, three and a half hours after Allison and I came back from the burial ceremony. I had known Henry would have his duties during the funeral; I just hadn't counted on it taking so long.

As soon as Henry stumbled in through the garage door, I could tell he'd been drinking.

"You didn't drive in that condition, did you?"

He lifted his arm to show me the six-pack of Fat Tire beer he was carrying. "Relax, Perez gave me a ride home." He sat down on the couch and proceeded to uncap a bottle with his wedding band, not bothering to change out of his uniform.

"Where have you been?" I asked, sitting on the love seat.

"I had to go talk to Franklin's widow," Henry said then took a long pull from the bottle, drinking nearly half. "And his kids."

"Is that procedure?"

His eyes flicked away. "No. It's just something I felt I had to do, considering I was there beside him when he got shot."

"How did it go?"

"How do you think it went?" he asked, throwing his arm across the back of the couch. "It went like this. Me: Sorry I couldn't stop the guy from killing your husband. Them: Oh, it's okay. Even though it's really not because now he's gone."

"It wasn't your fault."

"How would you know? You weren't there."

His sarcastic, almost accusatory tone snapped something in me. "Why the hell are you blaming yourself for his death?" I shouted, my anger propelling me off the couch. God, I was so tired of tiptoeing around him. "You didn't kill Franklin. You didn't shoot him in the stomach."

"No, but I did kill someone that day, didn't I?"

"But he was the bad guy, not you."

He set the bottle down with a thud; it fell over onto its side and spilled beer on the coffee table, which eventually dripped onto the carpet. "I'm not the good guy here, Elsie," he said. "I'm no better than that sniper who killed Jason."

"I can't believe you'd even say that! You are nothing like that asshole." I stalked over, grabbed the sides of his face and made him look me in the eyes. "Do you hear me? Nothing."

He twisted away from my grasp. "He was just doing the same thing I was. He was just doing what he believed to be right."

That gave me pause and for the longest time, I didn't know what to say. He was right, in his crazy kind of way, but I refused to think he had anything in common with the man who'd killed my brother. "That guy shot Jason in the back of the head. Unprovoked," I said. "If you were anything like him, I wouldn't be standing here in this house, carrying your child."

He looked up at me, his eyes drowning in sorrow. "Sometimes, without meaning to, we accidentally turn into the people we hate the most."

And damn if even in his drunk state Henry's words made too much sense.

After a week, Henry's gun was returned and he was welcomed back to work. I had to admit, it was a bit of a relief to watch him walk out the door with purpose in his step. I wasn't naïve enough to think that simply going back to work would make him forget his issues, but a part of me hoped blindly for it anyway.

But I knew, as the front door finally opened four hours after his shift ended, that something was still very much wrong with my husband.

"Elsie!" a male voice called out.

I put on my robe and rushed downstairs, recognizing Perez's voice. My breath caught in my throat when I found Perez supporting a moaning Henry by the arms.

"What happened?" I asked, covering my mouth. "Is he okay?"

Perez released Henry onto the couch, where Henry slumped

over, his head bowed to his chest. I reached down to peer into his face, surprised when he smacked my hand away.

I grabbed his hair and pulled, gasping when I saw what he'd been trying to hide: a large bruise on the side of his face. I turned back to Perez. "What happened? Someone needs to start talking."

Perez put his hands on his hips and shook his head. "We were just at a bar, taking a load off after our shift. Logan was talking to a woman at the bar when her boyfriend came over. They exchanged words, Logan pushed him, then just let the guy hit him. He didn't lift a finger to fight back, didn't let me come help."

"Why didn't you fight back?" I asked Henry, my grip tightening on his hair.

Perez shook his head again, concern written all over his face. "Listen, this is between you two. I'd better go home before Allison starts to worry."

"Thanks for bringing him home."

When it was just Henry and me in the dark living room, I was at a complete loss. Here was my bruised husband before me, slipping into the waters, and the hardest part was that he wouldn't reach out and grasp the hand I had extended.

In that moment, I felt as if I had no fight left in me. My hand slipped off his head. "Why?"

He took a deep breath and pushed off his knees and rose to his feet. "It was no big deal. Just a scuffle," he said, still not meeting my eyes.

"And the badge bunny? What were you doing that would make her boyfriend mad?"

"We were just talking."

"Yeah? Were you telling her all about your pregnant wife who's waiting for you at home?"

His eyes finally flicked up to mine. "No. We were just talking."

"You should have been talking to me."

"I didn't want to talk to you," he said. "I needed to talk to someone else."

His words physically hurt. Even though he hadn't been unfaithful, it felt as if he'd slammed a door in my face. I realized then that this was it; this was the thing he'd been trying to save me from back when he was having an emotional crisis. He'd had a few different reasons why he'd broken up with me, but in the end, the raw truth of the matter was that he'd tried to spare me from this hell.

Now, to see him going through the torture, I felt lucky to have escaped it before. I wasn't sure we would still be here today if we'd stayed together and tried to brave his issues together back then. I wasn't sure I'd be strong enough to watch while the love of my life fell apart in front of my eyes.

"I can't do this anymore," I said. "I can't be with you like this."

"You said you'd never give up on me."

"I'd do almost anything for you, Henry. I'd walk through hell and back to see you better again. I'll put you back together piece by piece when you fall apart. But I won't stand here and wait for you to cheat on me," I said, tears falling down my face. "There's only so much I can take."

His face crumpled. "I would never do that to you." He wrapped his arms around me as the tears blurred my vision. He smelled of sweat and blood and his unique scent and I breathed it all in with an ache in my heart.

After a moment, I felt his hands press against my back. His fingers were shaking as he brought them up to my face, tilting my head up. "I would never, never betray you like that."

My tears blurred my vision. "You're not the most reliable person these days, Henry."

"I'm sorry," he said with a hoarse voice. His dark eyebrows were drawn, his nostrils flaring, his blue eyes full of sorrow. "I know I'm a disappointment to you. I tried to be the husband that you deserve, instead I've become this."

I stood on my toes and gently pressed my forehead up to his bruised lips. He hissed and pulled back, licking at the wound I'd accidentally opened up. I knew the second he pulled away that the moment had ended, that the darkness had enveloped him once more.

"I'd better go take a shower," he said, starting up the stairs.

I followed him, watching from the door as he undressed, taking note of the bruises blooming along his side and on his arms. "Is this how you felt? In Korea?"

He looked over his shoulder with a deeply etched frown. "No," he said, but any relief his answer gave was quickly taken back. "It's worse. The only guilt I carried back then was breaking your heart."

He didn't have to say the rest. We both knew that this time the stakes were much higher.

5

If I thought I was doing a good job of leaving my personal life at home, I was wrong. After the fifth person at Shake commented on my stressed appearance, I had to admit that maybe I wasn't doing such a hot job keeping my problems under wraps.

"How are things?" Kari asked one afternoon as she took her break by eating a granola bar in my office.

"Good," I replied like always.

Kari raised an eyebrow. "Yeah. No, they're not. You look like shit."

"You know that's really not something you say to a pregnant lady."

Kari didn't seem at all apologetic when she shrugged. "I thought things were going well with the pregnancy? Are you stressing over that?" she asked. "Or is it some sort of PTSD from the shooting?"

Little did Kari know how close she was to the truth, but even though I wanted to talk to her about it, I couldn't. Some things were best left between a wife and her husband.

"No, the pregnancy's actually progressing really well," I said and added a dramatic exhale for her benefit. "I'm just really tired all the time though."

Kari let me bow out with that lame excuse and started in on her latest read about a hardass biker with a heart of gold. "I'm looking to date a tattooed guy with a motorcycle now," she said with a wide grin. I smiled with her, sharing in her fantasy, content to forget my worries for those few precious moments.

We looked up when we saw Conor walk down the hall and stop at my door. And even though we could see him, he was polite enough to knock before cracking it open. "You have a minute, Logan?"

Kari flashed me a wink before leaving. Conor entered and stood in front of my desk, studying me quietly.

I grew impatient under that silent gaze. "Can I help you?"

Conor bit his lip, a dimple showing on his cheek. "I wanted to see where we're at with the Lombart website."

I lifted an eyebrow. "We're just waiting on design approval," I said. "Like I told you this morning."

He gave a nod. "Ah, now I remember," he said unconvincingly.

I narrowed my eyes. "What's this really about?"

"Okay, okay," he said, holding his palms up. "I'm checking up on you."

I threw my hands up in the air. "Why is everyone treating me like some sort of mental case?"

"Because you were in a shooting!" he said, his brogue becoming thicker. "And you're trying very hard to appear normal, but nobody is buying it."

"I'm fine!"

"You've just been looking—"

"If you say stressed, I'll kick you in the junk."

"Tired and grumpy," he said, sounding the same himself. "It's always been Shake's policy to follow up with employees who have had a traumatic experience, to make sure everyone is in a healthy mental space."

"You sound like a brochure."

He pulled out a small envelope from his suit pocket. "Here. I wanted to give you this on behalf of everyone at the office."

I opened it to find two gift certificates for a spa package at the Veda Salon and Spa.

Tears stung my eyes at the thoughtful gesture. "I'll be right back. I have to pee," I said and dashed out of the room before the tears could fall. In the bathroom, I took deep breaths and tried to gather myself. My hormones were out of control, magnifying every thought and emotion. It was expected that I'd be a little emotional during a normal pregnancy, but to add in the stress of Henry's issues plus the anxiety of another possible miscarriage made it so that I was an exposed, raw nerve every single minute of every fucking day.

"This is too much," I said when I came back out, finding Conor still in my office. "I don't even know if Henry would agree to come."

Conor waved me away when I tried to hand the envelope back. "Come on, it's a gift from everyone here. Just send out a thank-you email and have a day of pampering. Invite Kari if you have to."

I shot him a grateful smile. "Thank you then." I managed to hold off the tears until he left, until I sat down and tried to compose a warm and well-written company-wide email. Thankfully, my computer was large enough to block my face from view.

———————

I woke up on the morning of our first wedding anniversary devoid of any excitement or even a feeling of triumph at having survived a year. I looked over to my right, only to stare at Henry's empty side of the bed.

I stayed under the covers for several long minutes, feeling utterly and unrepentantly sorry for myself. This was the anniversary of our wedding; it should be special. At the very least, we should have woken up together. Instead, I was alone and wondering on the whereabouts of my husband.

I lifted my hand above my face and stared at my wedding ring, watching the sunlight catch on its facets. I thought back to our wedding, to that moment when we stood in front of the ocean and he promised to love me and keep me safe, to strive to become the man I deserved. It was only a year ago that we'd exchanged rings and danced under the stars on the beach in Monterey, but it felt more like a lifetime had gone by. The stars in those newlyweds' eyes were gone now; Henry and I were no longer the same people. After everything we'd been through, I didn't know how we could be.

It was heartbreaking, to look back and realize just how much had changed in the space of a year.

Henry burst into the bedroom, his face red, his shirt and hair soaked in sweat. "Morning," he said and kissed me on the forehead before disappearing into the bathroom.

I stared at the door in shock and disappointment. When the shower started running, I knew for certain that he hadn't remembered. My husband, who'd promised to love me even after his death, had forgotten the anniversary of what had been our happiest day together. I'd heard from other married people that men had a tendency to forget important dates, but I hadn't expected Henry to be one of them. Up until today, Henry had remembered every significant event in our lives.

Deciding to end my pity party, I got up and went downstairs to make breakfast. If nothing else, maybe some decaf coffee and eggs would lift my spirits.

In the kitchen, I found a huge bouquet of red roses sitting inside a square glass vase on the counter. I blinked a few times, making sure I wasn't hallucinating.

"You thought I forgot, didn't you?"

I spun around and found Henry standing in the hallway nearly naked save for the towel around his hips. His hair was slicked back and there were still droplets of water clinging to his skin.

"I kind of did, yeah," I admitted, touching a velvety red petal with my finger.

He came over and wrapped his arms around me, pressing my face into the damp hair on his chest. "How could I ever forget the day you bound yourself to me forever?"

I pulled away, wiping at my cheek, only to have him shake his wet hair at me. I laughed, feeling a ray of hope for the first time in days.

We prepared breakfast like old times; he made coffee and toast while I cooked omelets. When we sat down to eat, I could almost pretend that everything was back to normal, but I noticed that, even as he smiled, the joy never quite reached his eyes.

After breakfast we sat on the couch and watched an episode of *Southland*. "Did you have anything planned for our special day?" I asked, growing tired of the show.

"Nope. The flowers were as far as I got."

"I have gift certificates to Veda for a day of spa-type pampering. We could do that."

He gave me a dubious look. "I'm not a spa type of guy."

"Come on, it's a massage, facial, and lunch. It'll be nice and relaxing. Just what we need."

He stretched his arms above his head then draped an arm around my shoulder. "I want to stay in with you. Just enjoy each other's company. When was the last time we did that?"

"Okay," I said, fitting myself under his arm and trying to conceal my disappointment.

He sighed as he leaned his head against mine; there was a sadness in the noise, one that I felt down to my bones.

We watched another episode of the show, our problems set aside for a moment. It almost felt like old times.

As my eyelids began to droop, Henry's phone buzzed in his pocket. "Excuse me," he said, getting up and answering his phone. "This is Logan."

I leaned my head against the couch and closed my eyes, letting his deep, gravelly voice wash over me. I thought back to our teen years, back to when he was only fourteen and his voice still held that young boy's clarity and softness, often cracking at inopportune times. Then over one summer, my family and I vacationed in Virginia and when we came back, Henry's voice had deepened.

I still remembered the first moment I heard his adult voice. I'd been in my bedroom when the doorbell rang and heard a deep voice from the entrance. I thought it had been an adult, one of Dad's friends. Imagine my shock when I came out and discovered that Henry was the owner of that rough, masculine voice.

During dinner that night, my mother said to him, "So your voice finally deepened."

Henry laughed then cleared his throat. "Yeah."

"You sound like a man," my dad said, eliciting a bashful but nonetheless pleased grin from Henry.

"Thanks."

I hadn't said much during that dinner, content to just sit and listen in awe to this boy's new voice. Admittedly, I was a little confused by the way it made me feel.

And to this day, the timbre and rough quality in Henry's voice still affected me in different ways, like a fingertip trailing down my spine or a thick down coat on a cold day.

"I don't know if I can come in today."

Henry's words brought me back to the present. I opened my eyes and looked up at him; at the same time, his eyes flicked to mine then away.

"It's my anniversary. I'll have to check with the missus."

I sat up and raised an eyebrow.

He pressed the phone against his chest. "They're asking if I can come in today."

I realized with a sinking heart that he wanted me to tell him to go. The anger in me flared. This was *our* day, damn it, and I wouldn't give it up for nothing. "No. Hell no."

He nodded and talked on the phone, telling whomever it was that his wife had not given him a pass.

I stalked off upstairs, angry that he'd even asked.

"What? What did I do?" he asked a few minutes later.

I tapped my feet, trying to control my breathing. "Nothing."

"No, Elsie, tell me," he said by the bed. "I want to know what I've done wrong now."

I rounded on him. "I just hoped that on our anniversary of all days, you'd want to hang out with me instead of go to work."

"I told them no, didn't I?" he asked, exasperated. It was the first genuine expression I'd seen from him that day.

I sighed and let it out. "I don't want to fight," I said. "Not today."

It took him a few minutes to calm down, for his muscles to relax and the lines on his face to ease. "I don't want that either."

We stared at each other for a long time. Finally, I said, "Come take a bubble bath with me."

"I've already taken a shower, remember?"

I closed my eyes, feeling like nothing I did was good enough. "Fine."

I didn't know when it happened, but somewhere along the way, we'd become strangers. Acting more like roommates than lovers.

I took a bath by myself. I stayed in there with a book, soaking even long after the water had cooled. To be honest, I didn't want to suffer even more awkward moments with my husband. Then again, I supposed it was why he'd been tempted to go to work.

Unable to stand my hypocritical self any longer, I finally emerged from the bathroom to find Henry lying on the bed, his hands on his stomach, his eyes fixed on a point on the ceiling.

"You were in there for a long time," he said as he eyed me in my silk robe.

"I was really dirty." I turned to go to the closet when he reached a hand out to me. "Come lie with me."

I walked over and lay beside him, my body tense. We lay there for a long while, neither of us touching, waiting for the other to make the first contact.

Finally, he slid his arm under my neck and rolled me onto my side, gathering me into his warm body. "You're shivering," he said, running his palms up and down the silky sleeve of my arm. "You okay?"

When I looked up, I had tears in my eyes. "I'm scared, Henry."

He kissed my hair. "There's nothing to be scared of. I'll always protect you."

"I'm scared for us."

"Shh," he said and pressed a kiss to my lips, making it impossible to talk about the end of our marriage when it'd really only begun. He pulled his arm out from under me and shifted up on his elbow. He pressed soft kisses down my face, tilting my head up with a finger so he could continue down to my neck. When he reached my chest, he slid a finger along the lapels of my robe and gently drew them away.

My body reacted to his touch like an old generator humming back to life. It had been so long since we'd been intimate like this, it almost felt like a homecoming of sorts.

When his lips reached my rounded belly, he stopped and pressed his ear against it. "Can you feel her kicking yet?" he asked, glancing up at me.

"The other day. I think I felt it but I'm not sure. It could have been a gas bubble."

He nodded and whispered something to my stomach before moving back down and settling between my legs. His tongue flicked out and teased my bud with soft little laps. I moaned at the contact, so swollen and sensitive that every touch sent me reeling.

I threaded my fingers through his hair, urging him on when his tongue slid to find my most sensitive spot and began to massage it. I groaned when he pulled away. "Where are you going?"

He slid off the bed and disappeared into the closet, coming back with our wooden box of toys. He pulled out an old friend of mine—the Rabbit—from its silk bag and proceeded to lube it up.

"I'd rather have you inside me," I said, though I had to admit, it had been awhile since my old battery-operated buddy and I had had relations.

Henry kneeled between my legs with the vibrator in his hand and a grin on his face. Without a word, he slipped the silicone head between my cleft, the whole thing sliding neatly inside.

"Oh!" I was so swollen and tender, I could have come with that alone.

"Do you want me to turn it on?"

"I want you to turn me on," I said. "I'd rather have you inside me."

"No, Elsie, I want to pleasure you," he said and flipped the switch, sending rapid vibrations careening through me. I squealed when I felt the rabbit's ears massaging somewhere else, the opposite end of where it was meant to be.

Henry had a dark look on his face as he watched me squirm and moan. Then he dipped his head and continued what he'd started with his tongue.

It was an all-out assault, every nerve bombarded with pleasure. I tried to focus on one thing but all three sensations melded together to become one immense pleasure bubble until I couldn't hold back anymore and I was screaming as I exploded, feeling like I was letting go of everything that was holding me down.

When I descended from the clouds and my insides finally stopped quaking, I opened my eyes to find Henry watching me.

"Did that feel good?" he asked, running his palms along my thighs.

"Yes, but I want you, Henry," I said, hooking my ankles over his backside to bring him close.

He resisted, even though his erection was clearly visible through his shorts. "No," he said, bending over to kiss me softly. "I just want it to be about you right now."

"I want it to be about you too," I said, wrapping my arms around his neck. "I want to watch your face while you fuck me. I want to squeeze you tight as you come inside me."

He closed his eyes and took a deep breath. When he opened them again, there was anguish in those blue depths. "No, not right now," he said and went to the bathroom to retrieve a washcloth.

I dozed on and off in Henry's arms, waking up some time later to find the bed empty once again. I felt like I was stuck in *Groundhog Day*, forever doomed to keep waking up alone.

With pressure on my bladder, I rushed to the bathroom but the sight that greeted me as I opened the door took me by surprise. Henry was standing at the bathroom counter completely nude, his back hunched, his hand wrapped around his swollen shaft. Through the mirror I could see his eyes were closed, his forehead wrinkled deep in ecstasy as he stroked himself.

Was he . . . masturbating?

After hearing my gasp, he stopped midstroke and met my eyes in the mirror, my look of shock offsetting his look of horror.

"Shit," he said and pulled a towel off the rack, quickly wrapping it around his waist.

I gulped down the lump in my throat, my body at odds with the confusing feelings coursing through me. To see him pleasuring himself was a turn-on, yet knowing he'd denied me a few hours earlier was like a slap in the face. "What . . . what were you doing?"

He blinked, refusing to meet my eyes. "I was just . . ." His hands fell to his sides as he let out a resigned breath. "You know what I was doing."

"Yes, but why couldn't you do that with me?" I wanted to know if my weight gain had turned him off but couldn't quite bring myself to ask. I shouldn't care—there was good reason for my extra padding—but I couldn't help but feel insecure regardless.

He spread his palms on the counter and hung his head. "Because I couldn't."

"Why not?" I choked out.

"I just can't."

"Damn it, Henry, you'd better give me a better reason!" I shouted. "If it's because you're no longer attracted to me, then say so. Don't play these fucking games."

He spun around and grasped my arms. "There will never be a day that I won't be attracted to you. You are the most beautiful woman I've ever known. You're perfect," he said in a growl. "And I don't deserve you."

There it was, the truth laid out for me. "You think because you're having some personal issues that you're somehow beneath me?" I asked softly. "Because you couldn't be more wrong."

To prove it, I tugged the towel away from his hips and dropped to my knees. He leaned back, his wide chest heaving as I wrapped my lips around his cock. "Els, no," he pleaded.

I hummed along his length, sliding my tongue on the underside of his shaft. He held on to the edge of the counter, his entire body strained.

I put my hands on his thighs, feeling his hard muscles bunched up under the palm of my hand. I took him deeper, sucked him harder, hearing from the changes in his breathing pattern that he was already getting close.

"You're too good for me, Elsie," he said with ragged breaths. I bobbed faster to prove him wrong and all too soon, he was groaning louder. He threw his head back and arched his back, his entire body taut as he came into my mouth.

Afterward, tears stung my eyes unexpectedly as I looked up at him only to find him facing away from me. Even after what I'd done, he couldn't even look at me, couldn't even bear to touch me. It was in that moment that I realized Henry was lost to me.

6

Henry flat-out refused to go to the spa. In the end, I went by myself—not bothering to even invite a friend—and welcomed the peace and quiet that a day alone afforded. It was just too much effort to spend an entire day pretending to be happy.

I had a pregnancy massage, and even though I didn't really care for them, a manicure and pedicure.

"Would you also like a haircut and color?" the uniformed lady asked as I sat with my nails under a drier.

From across the room, I could see my reflection in the mirror. With the lines on my face softened by my blurry eyesight, I realized I'd looked the same for the past several years. My hair was long and hung in loose curls around my face. I couldn't even remember the last time I'd had it colored.

So even though it wasn't part of the package, and even though I knew it would probably cost an arm and a leg, I accepted the offer. It was definitely time for a change.

"Girl!" Kari said the next Monday as soon as she saw me walk in the door. "You look faboo!"

I grinned. "Thank you, I feel faboo." With my shorter do that ended right below my chin and new maternity clothes—a bump-hugging dress that was a little bit sexy and a little bit demure—I felt almost like a different woman.

Kari touched a lock of my hair. "Love the highlights! It really opens up your face."

"The stylist said the exact same thing."

"I know my stuff," she said with a wink. "What does Henry think?"

"He hasn't seen it yet. He came home from a swing shift this morning and was sleeping when I left. He'll see it later at our appointment."

Conor walked past us at a fast clip, a folder in his hand, but did a double take when he saw me. He gave me an appreciative thumbs-up before continuing on his way.

All day people commented on my new look, and I'd have to admit, I was vain (or was it insecure?) enough to take it all in. I thanked everyone for the spa gift once again, and though it may sound shallow, that little bit of ego boost went a long way in buoying my mood.

Henry was almost late to our doctor's appointment. He was absent during the blood-taking and waiting process and only just walked in the door as my name was being called.

"Sorry," he said, pressing his hand to the small of my back and kissing my cheek. "I overslept."

"You would have regretted it if you missed this appointment," I said once we were in the exam room. "Today's the day we find out the sex, remember?"

"I'm here, aren't I?"

I turned my back and slipped out of my dress before donning the paper robe, a little shocked he hadn't said anything about my hair yet. Henry had always been observant—once he even noticed when I switched detergent brand—so to have him ignore my new haircut was a little disconcerting. I sat on the edge of the exam table and willed him to look my way, to really see the new me, but his eyes remained fixed on a poster on the wall depicting the stages of fetal growth.

We waited in strained silence for long minutes before Dr. Harmon finally entered, bringing with her a computer on a wheeled cart and a sense of relief. She asked a few questions from her chart and examined me before finally getting to the exciting part, to what Henry and I had been waiting for since that pink plus sign.

Dr. Harmon had me lie down before squirting some warm goo on my stomach. Then she pressed what she called the transducer on my stomach, using it to spread the jelly around my abdomen.

Henry remained in his seat, his hands clasped between his knees, as the image of a fetus showed up on the screen. This was the first time we'd seen the baby in its entirety—with little hands and feet, with its beautiful little face—and it stole the breath from my lungs with each perfect little part that the doctor pointed out.

"Breathe, Mommy," Dr. Harmon said. "Baby is okay."

She took snapshots on the screen, pressing and sliding the transducer in different positions on my stomach to get a better view of the baby. Finally, she stopped and used the mouse to draw a square around something on the screen. "There it is," she said, pointing to the three faint lines. "It's a girl."

My heart swelled and I craned my head to look at Henry, to bask in this moment with the man who'd wanted a baby girl since the beginning, but he didn't seem at all affected by the news. By the glazed look in his eyes, he looked downright bored.

I swallowed the lump in my throat and focused on the image on the screen instead, giving our daughter at least one parent who was overjoyed to see her.

At the appointment's conclusion, we walked out wordlessly to the parking lot with five printouts of the ultrasound in my hand.

"So I'll meet you at home, then?" he asked, fishing for his keys in his pocket.

I gaped at him, wanting to shake him by the shoulders and ask him what the hell was his problem. He'd been hoping for a girl all along—hell, he'd been referring to the baby as a girl since day one—and now that it had been confirmed, he didn't seem at all moved by the news.

"Yeah, sure," I managed to choke out.

After he rode off on the Harley, I sat in my car for a long time, gazing at the black-and-white photo printouts. "I'm sorry, baby girl," I said, placing a palm against my stomach. "Your dad is just preoccupied right now. He wants you. I know he does."

I cried in the privacy of that car for the baby we had, the baby we'd lost, and their father, who'd apparently lost his bearings.

———

That night I dreamed of Jason. It had been so long since the last one that it was like a happy reunion of sorts. We were running together in Earlywine Park in Oklahoma, enjoying the sunshine on our skin and the crisp air in our lungs.

The oval track seemed endless as we ran and ran, but eventually we stopped. Jason looked down at me with a smile and said, "How's it going, *Smellsie*?"

Even though I hated that nickname he'd given me in Virginia, back before we even moved to Monterey, I laughed. I basked in his presence, standing in the shadow of my big brother. "I miss you so much, Jason," I said, hugging him. Even in my dream, I remembered his scent. "I wish you were still here."

"Me too."

"Things would be so different if you were still around."

He gave me a noogie but the look in his eyes was warm. "It's okay. Everything will be okay."

"But Henry—"

"Give him a chance."

I remembered then that Jason had asked the same thing of our dad, back when Henry had just entered our lives and had yet to prove himself.

"I'm trying, big brother. I'm trying."

When I woke up the next morning with the space empty beside me, I held on to my brother's words—however imagined they may be—and hoped that he was right.

I had to believe in that because hope was all I had left.

I came home late one night, tired and cranky. Some files had corrupted for a website and it had to be rebuilt from scratch. It had been a long, stressful day and my sciatic nerve was aching by the time I walked in the front door.

I took off my shoes and walked into the kitchen, enjoying the cool tile against my swollen feet. I was considering just making mac and cheese for dinner when I found Henry sitting at the dining table with a beer in his hand and a gun on the table in front of him.

I froze. "Wh-what are you doing?" I asked, hoping my voice didn't betray my fear.

Henry never took his eyes off the Glock. "Contemplating this piece of metal."

"Okay . . ." I pulled out a chair and cautiously took a seat across from him. The look on his face was foreign to me, the once familiar face of my husband now that of a stranger.

"This was the gun that helped me kill that bastard," he said in a voice that drew goose bumps on my arms.

"It was the gun that saved people from a homicidal maniac," I said.

"Did I kill him on purpose? Could I have done anything differently so that the end result wasn't two deaths?" He picked up the gun and flipped it over in his hands, his fingers running along the rough surface of the handle.

I forced the fear down, reminding myself that this was Henry. He would never, never hurt me. "I think you did what you thought was right."

He held the gun and placed his finger on the trigger, his face a horrifying mask of detachment. He might not have it in him to hurt me, but that didn't mean he would never hurt himself.

I stood up so fast my chair almost fell over. "Stop it, Henry!"

He gave me a weary look and released the empty magazine. "It's not loaded."

I held out my hand. "Give me the gun."

He glared at me. "No."

"Give me the fucking gun!"

He stood up, clipping the gun back in his shoulder holster. "This is my duty weapon. It's a felony to take it from me." He started out of the room. "And possession of a stolen firearm is a class-three felony, punishable by up to twenty years in prison."

"Henry!" I shouted at his back.

He turned around, wiping a palm down his face. "I'm so tired of fighting, Elsie."

"And what? You think I enjoy this?"

"I think you're overreacting."

I sighed and walked closer. "Henry, don't you see that you're losing me?" I asked, lifting his hand up to my cheek.

But his eyes remained cold chips of ice. "That's fine, right? Because then you have an excuse to go running off to that Irish asshole and fuck him instead."

Stunned, I lifted my hand and slapped him across the cheek, causing his head to jerk to the side.

"Do it again," he ground through his teeth, his eyes transformed into two burning coals in their sockets. "Hit me again."

"No," I said. "I'm not going to indulge in your desire for self-harm. If you want to hurt yourself then leave me and the baby out of it."

He narrowed his eyes and turned on a heel. In several long steps, he was at the front door, opening it.

"Where are you going?"

"Out."

"Where?"

"Just out." Then he slammed the door.

———————

I woke up with two arms, hard as steel bands, holding me so tight I found it hard to breathe. In that half-conscious moment, I didn't know what was going on, why it was that Henry was trying to crush me to death.

From a faraway place, I realized that this was it: Henry had finally snapped. The emotional burden he'd been carrying had proven too much and he was now going to murder me in our marital bed.

But I'm not about to go down without a fight.

I grabbed his arms and tried to pull them off me, but his muscles just hardened underneath me and wouldn't budge. I kicked at him with my legs, connecting with his thighs. "Henry. Stop," I gasped in mounting panic and clamped down on his arm with my teeth.

His hold finally loosened and I realized that they, along with the rest of the man himself, were trembling. I quickly scrambled away, turning on the bedside lamp to find him lying on his side, his face and torso covered in sweat.

"I'm sorry," he said, getting up onto his knees and making his way over to where I stood shaking at the side of the bed. His blue eyes were pleading as he approached me, his arms outstretched. "I just needed to hold you."

The pain in his voice broke my heart; I had no choice but to lean forward and let him wrap his arms around me. He gathered me close and laid me on the bed, his head bent into my neck as he took in ragged breaths.

"What is it?" I asked, running my fingers through his hair, hoping it would calm him. "Did you have a nightmare?"

"I don't want to talk, Els," he said against my skin. "I just need to hold you and make sure you and the baby are okay."

I clutched him tighter to my chest. "I wish I could help you, Henry," I said, kissing the top of his head. "It's killing me seeing you like this."

Without preamble, he slid his hand down my side and slid my panties down my legs, and used his feet to slip them off completely. Then he lifted my thigh and pushed into me, retreating and pushing until he was completely seated in me.

I moaned at the sensation of his cock buried inside my sensitive walls. I gripped his ass and pulled him closer, squeezing him and enjoying the fullness. He stilled, his muscles relaxing, and sighed. I remembered then what he'd said a long time ago, that being joined with me was the only time he'd found peace to calm the hurricane in his head. If this act would help him heal, then I would gladly give it.

"I love you, Elsie," he said over and over to the same rhythm as his hips. "I need you."

I rolled on top and straddled him, leaning over to ease the lines on his forehead with my kisses until his eyes closed and his mouth relaxed. I slowed the pace, intending to keep him inside me as long as humanly possible, soothing the savage beast with long, languid strokes.

"Elsie," he murmured, his palms sliding up and down my sides.

I continued rocking my hips while brushing my fingers through his hair, moving as gently as possible. It wasn't long before Henry's arms drifted back down to the bed and the lines on his face eased.

Finally, when he had fallen completely asleep, I went to the bathroom and wept.

7

My father always taught me never to back down from a fight, that if challenged, I lift my chin and face my aggressor. But what I've had to learn on my own is that, sometimes, when you find your back against the ropes, you have to fight dirty in order to survive.

And fight dirty I did. I wasn't proud of it, but I was cornered. One night, while Henry was asleep, I took his cell phone and downloaded a tracking application onto it, hiding it in a mess of other icons so he wouldn't notice.

It wasn't my proudest moment, but I would do it again in a heartbeat rather than sit idly by and watch my husband slide away from me.

That was how I came to be sitting in my car on East Colfax on a Friday night, staring at a building painted a dark mauve that appeared almost black in the dark. The windows too were painted over but the light above the door and the people walking in and out of the front door indicated its busy nature. Above the door was a small sign that read HITCHES & BOES.

"Henry, what are you doing here?" I checked my phone again to make sure I had traced Henry to this exact location. There were many things I no longer knew about my husband, but he still never struck me as someone who would go to a biker bar.

I got out of the car, carefully eyed the dark street, and crossed the road. In the bar's small parking lot were numerous motorcycles lined up in neat little rows. I tried to search for Henry's, but it was impossible to find in this sea of leather and chrome.

Shivering from what I was about to do, I wrapped my leather jacket around my stomach—hoping my pregnant belly wasn't too obvious—and walked up to the door. Without the presence of a bouncer, I was able to walk right in.

The smell was the first thing to assault my senses—the thick, pungent aroma of sweat mixed in with whiskey and smoke. The bar's interior was exactly as one would imagine a biker bar to look: all dark wood with a long bar that spanned the room, a pool table, and even bras hanging from the ceiling. But the patrons were not all leather-vested and bearded, with chains hanging from their belts. In fact, almost half the room was made up of people dressed in nice shirts and slacks or even dresses, like in any bar in Colorado.

It took a few moments for me to gather the courage and make my way into the dark place. I felt so conspicuous, imagining that anyone who looked my way would be able to tell that I was out of my element, a pregnant woman in a seedy bar looking for her wayward husband. If I managed to look anyone in the eye, I'd bet I'd see pity in their faces.

I walked around the room in search of my elusive Henry, but couldn't spot him. Convinced he wasn't here, I was starting back toward the front door when I noticed a tall man with broad shoulders and dark hair sitting at a table by the far wall. He had his back to me and was seated with another person, a beautiful Asian woman with straight black hair and a delicate, exotic face. She was dressed in a halter-neck top and tight denim skirt and had her hands on his shoulder as she talked.

My stomach lurched at the sight, wishing the man with the

strong jawline and olive skin was not the same one I was married to. But of course, wishes never come true. Not in places like this.

Henry was not shaking her hand off, but was in fact, leaning toward her in deep interest. I stood transfixed as he whispered something in her ear then reached into his pocket and pulled out his wallet. He handed some cash to the woman, who counted it quickly then nodded. She stood up, took his hand and led him away, the crowd easily parting for her and her customer.

I stood there, watching them go, with my mouth agape. I honestly couldn't tell you what was going on in my head at that moment, only that I was paralyzed. My body had gone completely numb—perhaps it was a coping mechanism because surely the pain would have been enough to end me.

It was Korea all over again. Only this time, I was around to bear witness as he crashed and burned.

Somebody bumped into my shoulder and apologized; the little nudge spurred me back to action. Sidestepping around people, I followed Henry's tall figure as he and his companion made their way to the back of the bar, where the woman entered through a door labeled PRIVATE.

Henry stopped for a moment and ran a hand through his hair, staring at the open door.

"Don't do it, Henry," I murmured under my breath. "Please."

But in the next moment, Henry squared his shoulders and disappeared through the entrance.

I followed them inside a hallway, catching the door before it locked behind them. I waited until they were a safe distance down the hall before following, glad I was wearing my ballet flats so as not to make a lot of noise. Deep inside me, I still held on to the hope that my Henry—that same young man with the long curly hair and the braces—was still somewhere in there and that he'd do the right thing.

I stood at the other end of the hall, watching in the shadows as the woman stopped in front of another door and asked, "You sure about this?"

Henry must have indicated an affirmative because in the next instant, the door opened and the din from hundreds of shouting people filled the hallway.

Not going to lie—my first reaction was of relief. If nothing else, Henry wasn't here to sleep with a hooker.

But then, as they entered, the terrifying uncertainty took hold of my heart. Whatever that was, whatever Henry wanted to do in that room so badly he had to pay for it, was not good.

I waited a whole minute before finally wrapping my hand around that doorknob and, with breath held, turned it. The chaos in the room was overwhelming. People were everywhere, shouting and cheering, their attention on something in the center, something I was too short to see.

I crept closer but couldn't get through the wall of people.

"Hey, Preggo Pops," a voice drawled beside me.

I looked up to find a man with long straw-colored hair leering at me.

"You wanna watch the fight?" he asked and took a step backward, indicating a pocket of space in front of him.

"The fight?" I asked and slipped in front without giving thought to what this man would even attempt. And though he did try to put his hands on my waist, I couldn't think of anything past the sight of my husband shirtless in the center of the crowd. Across from him was another shirtless man with a bald head, a fierce look on his mustachioed face.

Henry, on the other hand, wore the face of indifference. He didn't look at all perturbed as he bent his head from side to side, the muscles rippling in his torso as he stretched his arms across his chest.

"Who's the new guy?" I heard a female voice asking to my side.

"I don't know," said her friend. "But he is yummy."

"Wanna tag-team him later?" she asked.

Her friend grinned, reminding me of a shark. "Hell yes."

Oh, hell no. I twisted around but before I could give them a piece of my mind, the fight was announced.

"You all know our regular, Mr. Clean," a guy's voice boomed through the speakers. People cheered as the bald guy pumped the air with his wrapped fists.

"We have a new contender," the announcer said. "Apparently just named Mason."

The girls beside me jumped up and down and screamed while others booed.

"Let's do this!"

And just like that, without a bell or any audio cue, Henry and Mr. Clean tapped gloves and began to circle each other. Even though Henry's face was covered in padded headgear, I saw the impassive look in his eyes, as if he really didn't care if he won or lost.

Mr. Clean was the first to throw a punch, but Henry dodged out of the way. Henry tried a combo, but even I could tell it was a half-hearted attempt at fighting, and his opponent easily blocked it, punching him in the side in retaliation.

I covered my mouth and tried to look away, but I couldn't tear my eyes from the man who was throwing punches and the man who was absorbing them all.

"Hit him back!" I cried, wishing Henry would pull his arms away from his face and just defend himself.

Even the crowd was beginning to boo, insisting that Henry wasn't even trying.

"Fight back, you pussy!" I heard someone yell.

"Finish this poser, Mr. Clean!"

I couldn't take it anymore, couldn't stand by and watch as someone hurt Henry. I pushed through the crowd, my small size finally coming in handy, and emerged in the fight area.

"Henry!" I shouted. Without thought for my safety, I stomped over to him and blocked him from his opponent. "This ends here."

"What the hell? Get out of there!" someone said, the rest of the crowd calling out similar sentiments.

"What are you doing here?" Henry mumbled through his mouth guard, grabbing me by the arms. He pulled me aside, waiting for an answer.

"I'm taking you home," I said, fighting the hysteria that was slowly creeping up my neck. If he'd been hit one more time, I was sure I'd have lost it completely. I grabbed his arm. "Come on, we're leaving."

But he didn't move. He just frowned down at me and shook his head. "I have to finish this fight."

"This isn't you," I said, throwing my arms wide. "Why are you doing this?"

"You wouldn't understand," he said, wrenching his arm from my grip. "Just go home. I'll be there in a few hours."

I was shaking when I said, "If you go back in there one more time, we're done. Do you understand me? Done."

His expression was hard as he stared me down, no trace of affection or emotion in those cold, dead eyes. "I have to finish the fight."

"Then I'm done!" I stalked off with my back straight, my head held high. But he couldn't see my face, couldn't see that I was crumpling under the revelation that my husband had chosen a fight over me.

I began to sob in earnest in the dark hallway, no longer able to keep up the strong facade. Before too long I was out of the bar and walking across the street to my parked car. I stood on the sidewalk and let it out, crying like nobody could see. I honestly didn't know if I had the strength to leave Henry, but I knew I had to. He was self-destructing right before me and I was catching shrapnel.

"You alright?"

I turned to find a guy in leather pants and a matching vest, standing beside a parked bike, staring at me.

"You locked out of your car?" he asked, taking a step in my direction.

I swiped at my face with my fingers. "No. I'm fine. Really."

"She said she's fine," Henry said as he jogged across the street. He walked right up to me and cupped my cheek, a possessive touch that seemed so out of place. "You alright, Els? Was he bothering you?"

The guy lifted his hands and backed away. "Hey, just trying to help a chick out."

"Appreciate it, man," Henry said. "I got it."

I touched the hand at my face. "Are you coming home with me?" I asked, holding my breath for the answer that could make or break us.

When he averted his eyes, I knew. "I still have to finish the fight."

"Then why did you come out here?"

"To make sure you made it to your car safely."

I smacked his hand away and unlocked the car. "I can't do this anymore, Henry. I love you and I've tried my best to help you, but there's no helping someone who doesn't want to help himself."

He grabbed my elbow. "Elsie, I just need you to be a little bit more patient with me."

"I have no more!" I said, my voice echoing down the street. "I'm all out of patience and understanding and chances to give."

His expression hardened. "What are you saying?"

"I'm saying if you don't come home with me right now, then don't come home at all."

His nostrils flared and his jaw muscles ticked. "You can't stop me from going to my own house."

"You're right, I can't. But that doesn't mean I'll be there when you come home."

His eyes burned into mine, a mixture of agony and anger but beneath all that was something that looked like relief, that I was confirming what he'd thought all along: He was a loser and I would one day figure it out and leave him. "So do it."

His words punched me in the gut, shoving me further away just like he'd intended.

So I took a step back to avoid more damage.

I didn't know if casting him out would help or hurt him, but I needed him to know that the consequences were real. I needed him to feel what it was like to lose it all and maybe then he'd finally seek help. And even though it was the hardest thing I'd ever done in my life, I got in my car and drove away.

PART SIX

REVERSE

1

HENRY

I shouldn't have let Elsie go. I shouldn't have gone back inside that bar and fought again, even if I did eventually win the bout. But victory is all in perspective, isn't it? What did I gain by risking my marriage and getting the shit beat out of me? Absolutely nothing. Still, wasn't that the thing I'd been searching for, those elusive few moments when my insides were numb and all that mattered was the pain on the surface?

After the fight, I headed home even though Elsie didn't want me there. I didn't blame her for the ultimatum. If I could take a break from myself, I would.

I shouldn't have been surprised when the garage door lifted and Elsie's car was not inside. She'd told me she was leaving; I just didn't listen. I even goaded her, gave her further reason to leave.

I hurried into the house, dialing her number on my cell phone as I ran upstairs, bypassing an excited Law on the way. But Elsie didn't answer. I didn't think she would.

"Where the hell are you?" I said to her voice mail. "Are you all right? Answer your damn phone!"

I came to a stop at our bedroom door. Everything looked as it should—the bed was made and everything was in its place—but the room seemed a little dimmer now that Elsie's light was gone. It made me all the more determined to get her back. I might not deserve her, but I fucking *needed* her.

Then I saw the folded piece of paper on the dresser and all the fight in me drained out.

"Elsie, no," I said under my breath as I reached for the letter. "Not a fucking Dear John letter. No . . ."

Henry,

I'll be gone for a few days. Please don't come looking for me. I need time away from you.

Elsie

I squeezed my eyes shut and crumpled the paper in my hand. Even back when I broke up with her, Elsie never truly lost hope. But now, with this good-bye letter in my hand, I had proof that something as strong as our love—our history—could be destroyed.

I dialed her phone again and again, each time getting kicked back to her voice mail. After the seventeenth time, I finally gave up. Elsie was gone and there was nothing I could do about it.

I had finally driven her away.

I couldn't sleep that night. I thrashed around in bed, unable to find a comfortable position. Eventually, I just rolled over to Elsie's side with my face pressed into her pillow, closed my eyes, and counted the seconds as they ticked by.

At around three in the morning, I got up and went downstairs to pound on the heavy bag with my bare hands. I imagined balling up every worry that I carried around in my head and channeled them through my hands. Over and over, I drove my fists into the vinyl surface of the bag until my breath burned in my lungs and my knuckles were raw and bleeding, all the while wishing the bag could fight back and impart some hurt of its own.

In the bathroom, I stood in front of the mirror and studied the dark bruises that had bloomed on my torso and arms. The worst of the damage was along my sides where my opponent had targeted my ribs.

The battered man in the mirror should have felt disgust at the way he was treating his body, but what he should feel and what he did feel were two vastly different emotions.

After a long, scalding shower, I tried calling Elsie's phone again, to no avail. "Elsie, I'm getting tired of this bullshit," I left in her voice mail.

For the next few hours, I couldn't figure out what to do with myself. I paced the house, going from room to room trying to find things that I could actually fix. I finally patched the holes in our bedroom walls that Elsie had hidden behind a large picture frame. I fixed the leaky faucet in the guest bathroom. I washed our windows and cleared out the gutters.

But it all meant nothing because this house was not a home without Elsie.

———

That afternoon, I finally found the balls to dial Elsie's parents' house in California, hoping that it wasn't the colonel who'd answer the phone.

It was. Of course it was. "Henry! How's the beat?"

"Oh, it's fine."

"So what can I help you with, son?"

I winced at the title I didn't deserve. "I was just . . ." I cleared my throat, hoping my gamble would pay off. "I wanted to speak with Elsie."

"Huh." He paused for a long, nerve-racking minute. "She's not here."

I pinched the bridge of my nose. *Fuck.* "Then I'm sorry to waste your time."

The colonel's voice changed, took on a terse edge. "Please explain to me why you don't know the whereabouts of your wife."

I let out all the air I'd been holding. Even as an adult, I found it nearly impossible to deceive the colonel. "I fucked up, sir."

"What did you do? And please don't tell me it involved another woman."

"No, not that," I said quickly. "Never that."

"Then what could possibly make Elsie leave you and not tell you where she's going?"

"It's complicated," I said. "But I think it's an issue best left between a husband and wife."

"Fair enough." He let out a disappointed gust of air. "How many more chances can she give you, Henry?"

"I've asked myself the same thing, sir," I said. "I'm hoping one more."

After hanging up, I was more determined than ever to find Elsie. I scrolled through my phone directory list until I came upon Julie's number. Of course.

"Henry," Julie said after picking up. "What the heck is going on?"

Bingo. "Can I speak to her?"

"She's with the doctor right now."

Ice water froze in my veins. All I could say was, "What?"

"She's fine now," Julie said. "She just started feeling dizzy a few hours after she arrived and we went to the ER. Her blood pressure was too high, almost dangerously so for a pregnant woman."

"And?"

"She was told it was stress-related. She needs to eliminate any and all stressors in her life."

"Tell her I'm coming to get her," I said, taking long strides to the closet and pulling out a duffel bag.

"She doesn't want to see you, Henry."

"I don't care. I'm coming to get her today." Without another word, I hung up, threw some clothes into the bag, and marched out.

I called the station while waiting for my flight, citing a family emergency and informing them I'd be taking a few days off. If this wasn't an emergency, then I didn't know what was.

The flight itself only took two hours but it was nearly eleven at night by the time I made it to Julie's door. Missing a connecting flight was a bitch.

"Henry . . ." Julie said behind the partially opened door. After all I just went through, she still looked as if she didn't want to let me in.

I fixed her with a weary glare.

Finally, she stepped aside and let me in. "I told you not to come," she said in a low voice.

"I just need to see my wife. Please," my voice broke on the last word, and it was all I could do not to fall apart in her foyer.

Julie proved her alliance when she shook her head. "She's already sleeping."

I fought to control my breathing, knowing that misery was quickly giving way to rage. "I just need to see her."

Julie studied me quietly for a few moments, her eyes softening. Finally she nodded. "Okay, but please don't wake her. Or Will. He has school tomorrow."

I didn't need to be told twice. I went upstairs to the guest bedroom, taking two steps at a time. With breath held, I twisted the doorknob and opened the door. I meant to only peek inside but the sight of my Elsie lying on her side, her back to me while she slept, made me lose sense of myself completely. I crept inside and drifted to the other side of the bed, sinking to my knees as I took in her sleeping face. In her hand was the baby-name book I'd given her many moons ago.

God, I needed her and never more so than in that moment, when the mere sight of her allowed me to finally breathe. I bowed my head and tried not to lose my shit, taking deep breaths to calm my nerves.

When next I looked up, Elsie opened her beautiful hazel eyes and, in that moment when she was still halfway in a dream world, she looked at me like she used to, like I was the most amazing person she'd ever known. Then awareness seeped in and the look of reverence dissolved. "Are you really here?" she asked in a hoarse voice, reaching out to touch a finger to my nose. "Am I dreaming?"

"Maybe." I grasped her wrist and brought her palm up to my lips. "If I were just a dream, what would you say to me?"

"I'd tell you that I'm tired. I want to just lay everything down and rest."

"Then do it. Put your feet up and let me worry about me."

"I can't do that."

I wanted to tell her I loved her for trying. Instead I said, "This isn't your battle, Elsie. It's mine. And I'm sorry that you're caught in it. You shouldn't have to carry my burden on your shoulders."

The corners of her mouth lifted but there was sadness, not joy, in that smile. "Don't you know by now that I'm your battle buddy? Everything you've gone through, I've been at your back, watching your six."

Tears stung my eyes. And here I thought I'd been fighting alone all this time.

"You've been so busy trying to protect me, you never saw that I was doing the same for you," she said.

"I'm sorry I let you down." I pressed my forehead against hers. "I promised I'd always keep you safe, but I'm the one that ended up hurting you."

"If this was a dream, you'd beg me to come home and I'd say yes, because it's romantic," she said. I opened my mouth to do just that when she silenced me with a finger. "But the reality is that I need a break from us. You need to take a step back and examine your life, and really think about these destructive feelings you're holding on to. Are they worth losing your wife and child over?"

"I wish it were that simple. I'm not holding on to these issues because I want to. They're just there, embedded in my skin," I said. "I thought that punishing my body would help, that after so many bruises and wounds, I'd feel like I'd repented."

She shook her head. "I can't come home until you get better," she said, confirming what I'd suspected. "The stress, the fighting; none of it is good for the baby. The doctor says if it continues—"

I pressed my lips to hers. I couldn't bear to hear the what-ifs right now. "I'll try harder. I promise."

"I don't want to live like that, worrying every day," she said with a wavery voice. "I just want to be with you and have the boring, happy life we dreamed of."

"I want that too, Els. More than anything." I climbed on the bed, curling around her back and holding her close. It felt like I hadn't held her like this in years. "We'll get there. I'll fix this."

"And what if you can't?"

"I have to. I can't fail." I buried my face in her hair, losing myself in her scent. "Living without you is not an option."

———————

I woke up a few hours later on the other side of the bed, but even if our bodies were separated, our hands were between us, still entwined. It goes to show that even while unconscious, I'm unable to let her go.

I watched her sleep for long minutes, my heart clenching at the thought that she'd had to go to the hospital, and once more, I hadn't been there. I was sure by now she was asking herself if I would ever be there for her again.

When the thoughts in my head became nearly unbearable, I kissed her hand and rolled off the bed. I closed the door behind me and padded downstairs, in search for some alcohol but instead finding Julie and Will in the kitchen.

"Henry!" Will cried, jumping out of the chair and nearly spilling his cereal in order to hug me.

I picked him up, threw him in the air, then set him down soundly. "What's up, buddy?" I asked, pasting on a happy face.

"What are you doing here?"

I glanced over at his mom, who just raised an eyebrow and shook her head.

I ruffled his hair. "Elsie and I just came for a visit."

"Okay, Will, get back to your breakfast please. I'll just finish getting ready. When I come down, I want you ready for school, okay?" Julie said, putting Will's lunch box in his backpack.

"Yes, Mom."

Julie turned to me. "There's coffee in the pot and help yourself to anything in the fridge."

After she left, I poured myself a cup of coffee and Will a glass of orange juice from the fridge. I sat down at the table and slid the glass over to him.

"We had to take Aunt Elsie to the hospital last night," he said around a mouthful of colorful cereal.

"I heard," I said, holding my palms against the hot surface of the mug. "What happened?"

"She was just talking with Mom, then she said she was really dizzy. We made her sit down on the couch. I went to the fridge and got her some water. But she was still dizzy and no shoes."

"Nauseous?"

"Yeah. Mom was scared, so we went to the hospital and Aunt

Elsie saw a doctor while we stayed in this big room with lots of chairs and other people who were coughing and sick." He wrinkled his nose then brightened. "But she's okay now."

"Thank you for taking good care of her, buddy." I decided right then that, whatever happened, I would never let this little guy down.

Will set aside his empty cereal bowl and took a drink, wiping off his orange juice mustache with the back of his hand. "No problemo," he said with a proud smile.

He reminded me so much of Jason in that moment, with the same self-assured mannerisms and the same boyish smile, that I was instantly filled with longing for my best friend. If Jason were around, I knew for a fact I wouldn't be in this predicament right now. If Jason were still alive, I wouldn't be so unstable.

But then again, if Jason were around, I might never have found the courage to marry his sister.

It sucked to know I couldn't have it all—the best friend; the love of my life; the happy, untroubled life—and hurt even more to know that I might very well lose the things I did have.

"What should I do?" I asked his son instead.

Will finished his drink and set the glass down. "Make sure Aunt Elsie doesn't have to go to the hospital ever again. That place is yucky."

I nodded. "You're right. I have to do my best to make sure the rest of her pregnancy is stress-free."

"And make sure the baby is okay," he added with a seriousness beyond his years. "I want my girl cousin to be healthy. I don't want her to die like my dad."

I swallowed the lump in my throat with a mouthful of coffee. "Me too, bud. Me too."

2

I convinced Elsie to come back home the next day, with a lot of promises on my part, promises I didn't know if I could keep but wanted to make regardless. All I knew for certain was that we couldn't fix our problems while she was a few states away. We were always better together, not apart.

Still, as I sat beside her on that plane as we flew somewhere over Oklahoma, Julie's words rattled around in my head.

"She needs to eliminate any and all stressors in her life."

I knew what I had to do, knew that it was absolutely the right thing for Elsie. I just hoped she'd understand that, this time, it was different, that the past was not repeating itself.

I turned to her as she stared out the window. My eyes traced the graceful curve of her jaw down to her chest, which had grown in size over the months, and finally to the swell of her stomach. It made my heart hurt looking at her, knowing what had to be done.

"Els," I said, taking hold of her hand.

She turned to me, the expression on her face revealing that she already knew what I would say. Maybe she'd been thinking it herself.

"I'll move out." I forced the words out of my mouth, even if it was the last thing in the world I wanted.

She nodded.

"But this is not like before. I'm not leaving you. I'm just taking a step back so you can breathe."

A tear slid down her cheek. God, even when I was trying to do the right thing, I hurt her. "How long?" she asked.

I wiped away the tear with my thumb. This was absolute torture. How was it possible to miss someone this fiercely when she was sitting right beside you? "Until all is well again," I said.

She tangled her fingers in mine and squeezed hard. "And what if I need you in the middle of the night? What if something goes wrong? What if I can't do it on my own?"

"I'll be there, Els," I promised. "Just call me and I'll be there."

"This is just temporary," she said with a resolute nod. "We're not separating or divorcing."

I let out a breath at the mention of divorce. "No, we're not," I said and gave our entwined hands a shake. "Just don't give up on me yet, okay? I can't do this without you."

Her eyebrows drew together, but she nodded. Thank God she nodded.

When we arrived home in our separate cars, Elsie said she'd go next door and get Law. "To give you some time to pack," she said.

It all came crashing down on me then, that this was real. I was really moving out for an indefinite amount of time.

I went upstairs and packed my bags, moving quickly so as not to draw out the absolute heartbreak of leaving my home. I knew I was doing the right thing but that didn't stop the pain that radiated around that one muscle in my chest.

Elsie, for her part, stayed out of the way after she retrieved Law. She went into the home office, saying she needed to catch up on work. Her absence was a little blessing; I didn't know how I'd stop myself from refusing to leave if she was around.

Law, realizing that something was up, followed me from room to room, whining and making a general nuisance of himself. Finally, I couldn't take it anymore and sat down on the carpet in the bedroom, wrapping an arm around his neck. "I'll miss you too," I said, scratching his back.

I felt a tickle in the back of my nose as I said good-bye to my first dog, my first house, my first love. "Take care of Elsie, okay?" I told him. "Bark loud if you hear anything weird, and sink those chompers on anyone you think deserves it. I trust your judgment on this."

Law licked my face in response.

"I'll try to come by so we can go jogging, but don't be offended if I want to spend more time with Elsie than you. It's just . . . I need her to fall in love with me again."

I gave him one more good belly rub before rising to my feet and collecting my bags. I knocked on the office door before I pushed it open, and found Elsie hunched over the desk, crying silently into her hands.

Though it was hard, I ignored my instinct to comfort her; instead I cleared my throat. "I'm all set."

She looked up with a wretched expression on her face. "I hate this. I want a do-over."

"Me too. A marriage mulligan."

"If only."

"The time apart will be good for us," I said, willing it to be true. "But I'm not leaving you, Els. I'll still be around. I just need to take myself out of the picture to keep you and the baby healthy. I know myself, and I know what's going to happen. It might get worse before it gets better."

———————

My heart was beating out of my chest as we walked downstairs and into the garage. I busied myself packing bags into the trunk, giving Elsie every chance to ask me to stay.

But she didn't, like I knew she wouldn't.

I stood in front of her and lifted her chin with my finger. "I love you, Elsie Logan," I said, pressing a soft kiss to her forehead. "So fucking much."

"Then get better, Henry," she said, fisting the collar of my shirt. "Come back to me whole."

I leaned into her, unable to keep away. My hands slid around to her head, cupping her face as I gave her one last kiss. I tilted my head and deepened the connection, wanting to make it last forever, wanting to meld my entire being with hers so that we'd never have to say good-bye.

In some ways, she had always been a part of me ever since the day I met her and teased her about her hair. I'd once tried to run away from that truth, to shed her memory like a snake sheds its skin, but what I'd discovered was that she ran deep in my veins. She was in my cells, embedded in my very DNA. To be without her was to be incomplete.

All too soon I was in my car, backing out of the driveway as Elsie stood in the garage with her arms wrapped around herself. Before I drove away, I took a moment to compose myself, to blink away the sadness and convince myself that this was possible, that I could do this on my own again. And then I left her.

———————

I stayed at a Residence Inn, but I refused to unpack. I simply threw my bags in the closet and left it at that. I had to believe I'd only be here for a few days or else I'd fall apart.

After a long shower, I went to work. I didn't tell anybody about my marriage troubles, even if many people at the station would have been able to sympathize. But I didn't talk so it wouldn't be real. Elsie and I wouldn't become one of those LEO marriage statistics. I wouldn't let us.

Patrol that night was quiet and uneventful. Never before had I felt so lonely than in that dark car, with only the chatter on the radio to keep me company. The silence was unbearable; I sang songs out loud, recited my favorite poetry (or what I could remember), even pretended to pour my heart out to a phantom Elsie in my passenger seat. I'm sure anybody who saw me thought I had gone off the rails.

Several hours into patrol, I pulled into the nearest strip mall to find some coffee, snickering when I realized I'd inadvertently chosen a doughnut shop.

"Way to live the stereotype," I said before realizing I was still talking to myself. A few minutes later, I slid back into my car with a cup of coffee and a box of Elsie's favorite kind of doughnuts.

For the first time that night, I felt some purpose. I stopped at a grocery store then drove home, back to my fixer-upper house in Cherry Creek. I parked out front and saw that everything but the porch light was already dark. I almost drove away but pure selfishness propelled me to the front door and made my finger push that doorbell.

I needed to see her, needed the reassurance of her smile and, perhaps, her kiss.

I heard Law thumping down the stairs. A second later, he barked at the front door. "Good boy, Law," I said, letting him know I was no intruder.

After realizing Elsie probably wouldn't answer the door at eleven at night, I called her on my cell.

"Henry, there's a strange man at the front door holding a box of doughnuts and a grocery bag," she said with some amusement.

My chest warmed at the sound of her voice. "Don't worry, I'll protect you from the bastard."

Then the front door opened and Elsie appeared wearing a tank top, shorts, and a smile on her face. The shirt was tight, accentuating her changed figure. If I were a bartender, I would have spent the entire night taking her order just to see her bending over the bar.

"Hey, up here," she said, pointing to her eyes.

I grinned sheepishly. "Busted." I held out the box of doughnuts. "I have a special delivery."

She peered into the box and smiled. "Thank you."

"But wait, there's more," I said, pulling out a jar of pickles and a bottle of olives from the grocery bag. "I figured you could mix them all together."

She scrunched her nose. "That is disgusting," she said with a laugh. "And maybe perfect."

I found myself smiling, feeling a little weight lift off my chest for those few minutes. It had been so long since I'd seen a genuine smile on her face. "Anything for you."

"Do you want to come in and eat some with me?"

God, I wanted to, but I knew if I took one step in there, I would never want to leave. "Nah, I'm still on the clock." My eyes flew across her face, so fresh and beautiful even without a trace of makeup. She looked younger somehow, more vulnerable. "I just wanted to see you."

The corner of her mouth curled up into a wry grin. "Law misses you already." And on cue, our dog emitted a low whine on the other side of the door.

"Just Law?" I asked.

"No. Not just Law."

We stared at each other awkwardly for a few minutes. The entire time I wanted to blurt out my every thought in hopes we could sift through the rubble and piece something coherent together. But I didn't. I couldn't burden her with everything that was weighing me down. She was carrying enough on her own already.

My radio crackled to life just then, the dispatcher asking for the nearest car to answer a call on Downing and East Colfax. I pressed the button on my shoulder and gave a quick response. "I have to go. Domestic abuse call," I said to Elsie.

"Do you still wear that Saint Michael medallion I gave you?"

I reached into my collar and pulled it out. "Every day."

She cupped my cheek with her palm. "Be careful, Henry. I love you."

I breathed in her words and nodded. "I love you too, Els," I said and opened the front door for her. "Good night. I'll wait until you're done locking up."

———————

I was grateful to be on the swing shift for the next five nights; I was so exhausted I fell asleep as soon as my body hit the mattress. The problem, as always, was staying asleep.

That morning, the fifth day I spent away from home, I lay in bed and stared at the popcorn ceiling of the hotel room while the sunlight tried its best to steal around the blackout curtains. I called Elsie's phones—both her cell and her work number—hoping that hearing her voice would quiet the noise in my head, but she didn't answer.

I got out of bed and put on my running gear and a few seconds later I was pounding the pavement. I ran hard, pushing to feel the burn in my lungs and the ache in my legs. But it didn't seem enough. I needed something more, something to take focus away from my inner turmoil.

I don't know how it happened but when my feet came to a stop, I found myself standing in front of a boxing gym. Every self-destructive particle in my body wanted to go inside and join, to have a legitimate place to physically work out my issues.

As I stood there, staring at the vinyl letters arching across the glass window, the fog in my mind cleared long enough for me to glimpse a moment of clarity: I was standing at a crossroads. One way took me to instant gratification; the other led me home.

It really wasn't much of a choice. I turned around and headed back to the hotel, imagining each step taking me farther away from my troubles and closer to reclaiming my old life.

A little while later, I drove back to the house and let myself in, intending only to grab a few white undershirts that I'd forgotten to pack. But once inside, my feet carried me from room to room, torturing myself with memories of what I'd once had and thrown away.

I didn't know why things affected me so deeply—if I did, I would have fixed it by now. I would have patched the break in my heart that made me bleed hope and reinforced it with steel.

I paused in front of the office and saw the boxes of baby furniture we'd bought but never had the time to put together. Or perhaps we'd simply been too afraid to tempt the fates, lest something happen to the baby once again.

This time, however, I was ready to point my middle finger directly at fate. Putting together that crib would not result in a miscarriage. I wouldn't let it.

I sat down on the floor and forced myself to focus on each nut and bolt, on every piece that connected to something else, and for one precious hour, my brain was blissfully silent. No whispers of self-loathing or insecurities. All that occupied my thoughts were wood and metal and the soft bundle of flesh that would sleep in it.

After the crib was put together, I cleaned up the mess then moved the desk around. As I slid it across the carpet, Elsie's computer woke from sleep, displaying the last website she'd visited. I sat down to look closer and found it was a site about a local group for family of PTSD sufferers that met every week. It wasn't until that one moment that I finally understood how much my issues were affecting her. Apparently it was so bad, she needed to reach out to others about it.

But Elsie wasn't the person who needed the help; I was. Shame filled me as Elsie's words echoed in my head: *You can't help someone who doesn't want to help himself.*

Before I could overthink it, I sat down in the computer chair and searched for local support groups, writing down the time and place for a group specializing in traumatic stress in police officers. Then I left the website up and tacked a note on the screen:

I'm trying, Elsie. Don't give up on me just yet.

3

"My name is Henry and I'm an LEO with the Denver Police Department." A small chorus of greetings went up from the people in the room.

Unable to meet anyone's eyes, I fiddled with the buckles on my boot as it jiggled on my knee. "This is my first time here, although I probably should have come a long time ago."

I finally looked up at some of the faces in the room, at people just like me who had also seen their fair share of the world's ugliness and lived to talk about it. It gave me the courage to retell my story, starting from the day I found out my best friend had died. I talked for a long while, pausing every now and then to clear my throat, hoping that maybe someone would interrupt with a story of their own. But they were all quiet, all patiently waiting to hear the end of my story.

"So now I'm living in a hotel because I don't want to cause my wife any more stress. I don't know if I'm doing the right thing, honestly. If I'm just repeating what I did to her a few years ago."

"Do you think you're doing the right thing?" someone asked.

I dug through the layers of guilt and confusion and found the answer. "Yes. I believe so."

After the meeting, a few of the group members came up to me and introduced themselves, saying they too used to be where I was. Talking with them gave me hope, made me start believing that there was a way out of this maze.

Maybe there was hope for me yet.

———

The next day, I went by the Shake Design building to take Elsie out to lunch. The receptionist let me inside, but I wandered around, unable to locate Elsie's new office.

Kari, thankfully, found me. "Hey! Elsie didn't mention you were here!" she said, chucking me on the arm.

"She doesn't know I'm here," I said, looking around for that familiar head of curly brown hair. "I'm trying to surprise her except I can't find her new office."

She laughed. "Come on, Officer Clueless. This way." She led me down a hallway and stopped in front of a glass-walled room that was currently without its occupant. "She's in a conference call right now though, so you might have to wait."

"Thanks," I said, entering the office and looking around. The glass desk was a little cluttered with papers but the office itself was neat and full of color. I sat down on the white leather chair and picked up a framed photograph of Elsie, Jason, and me taken on Christmas Day in my senior year in high school. There was something sweet about the photograph, an innocence in our faces that we'd long since left behind. It was no wonder then that Elsie preferred to look at it on a daily basis.

"Hey."

I looked up just as Elsie was coming in. The sight of her knocked the air out of my lungs: She wore a knee-length dress that hugged her new curves in a sensual way, black heels, and bangles on her wrist. With the new way she was styling her shorter hair, she looked like a different person. It seemed almost as if being without me was becoming to her.

I tucked away that ugly thought and went to her. I stopped a foot away, suddenly at a loss how to act.

"Just come here, you big dork," she said and tugged on my belt, bringing me closer. My arms wrapped around her and my lips pressed themselves to her forehead by instinct.

I let out a contented breath that ruffled her hair. "I missed you."

"It's good to see you," she said when we pulled apart. "What's up?"

"I just wanted to take you out to lunch."

"Oh, I already ate." When she saw the disappointment on my face, she added, "But I could go for some lemon froyo with tons of sour gummy worms in it."

So that's where we went, to a place called YoYo a few blocks away. We walked on the sidewalk, our entwined hands swinging naturally as we walked.

"So, how are you?" I asked once we sat down with our yogurt.

"Doing okay."

"And the baby?"

"She's good. I almost called you the other night because she was kicking so hard."

Disappointment socked me in the gut. "I should have been there," I said, stabbing the plastic spoon into my cup.

"I'm sorry. I didn't want to bother you at work."

I reached for her hand. "I'm not angry with you. I'm just . . . I wish I'd been there. Next time call me, okay? Whatever time of day."

"Okay." She took a bite and looked at me thoughtfully while she chewed.

"Is she kicking right now?" I asked.

"No. Sorry."

I noticed a spot of yogurt by her lips and scooted my chair closer. "May I?"

She raised an eyebrow then gave the slightest nod. She didn't know yet what I intended to do but she gave me her trust anyway. Her belief in me was only one of the many reasons why I loved her so much.

I cupped her jaw with my hand and leaned closer. She tipped her head up and closed her eyes just as I touched my lips to the corner of her mouth. My tongue darted out and gently licked the tart cream away.

She was breathing hard when I pulled away, her eyes wide with desire.

"I think I missed a spot," I said with a grin and proceeded to lick her again.

A mischievous look crossed her face a moment before she lifted the spoon and swiped it across my mouth and over to my jaw. "Oops," she said with a sparkle in her eye. Then she leaned over and started at my jaw, her tongue warm and wet as it slid across my rough skin and she leisurely made her way to my mouth.

I parted my lips and invited her in, our tongues mingling with sweetness and yearning. I groaned, putting my hand on the back of her head and pulling her closer. My desire roared, my dick springing to life. It had been so long since I'd kissed her like this, and it was a relief to know that even after all this time, our bodies responded to each other with immediacy.

With my hands tangled in her hair, I kissed her, made love to her with my mouth, because God knows I couldn't do more. With my tongue and my teeth, I teased her, showed her that she'd been missed.

I stopped when I felt her hand on my chest gently pushing me away. "Henry," she breathed and licked her lips. "People are staring."

I kept my gaze fixed on the only person in the room who mattered. "I don't care."

The corner of her mouth tugged up as her eyes flicked back

down to my lips. Yes, if her dilated pupils and ragged breathing were anything to go by, she was as turned on as I was.

Unable to keep from flirting, I whispered in her ear, "Is it true that women in their second trimester are horny as hell?"

She laugh-gasped, her creamy skin taking on a pink tinge. "Very true. God, some nights I have to . . ." She paused, her gaze traveling all over my body. "You know."

It took all of my willpower to stay in that plastic seat and keep my hands to myself. I adjusted my pants, letting her know that they were already uncomfortably tight. "No, I don't know. Why don't you tell me about it?"

Her eyes flicked around the room. Our yogurt sat forgotten, melting away, as she leaned over and murmured against my ear, "I have to use the BOB just to get some relief. But nothing, not even those damned plastic bunny ears that flick rapidly, can give me what I really want."

"And what is it you really want, Els?"

The corner of her mouth tugged up. Her voice took on a raspy grit as she said almost inaudibly, "You sliding inside me, filling me up completely. I want to squeeze you over and over, want to see that look on your face when your jaw clenches and you say my name right before you come. You always make this sound like a moan between ecstasy and agony. And those deep, little thrusts at the end, like you still can't get enough."

I let out a shuddering breath. "Take the rest of the day off," I said, grasping her hand and fighting the urge to press it against my erection. "Let me take care of your needs."

"I can't. I have another meeting at three thirty. But for what it's worth, I really, *really* want to." She touched her finger to my lower lip and I pulled it into my mouth and sucked on it. "You know, you can just come home."

Reality crept in, reminding me why we were here to begin with. "I can't. Not until I'm good again."

Her eyes misted over as she nodded. "I miss you."

I kissed her forehead and sighed. "I'm working on it, Els. I finally took your advice and went to a support group the other night."

"And?" Hope broke out over her delicate features.

"It was good. It felt good to talk about it." She opened her mouth but I beat her to the punch. "To people who don't know me, who don't know my history."

"It's a step in the right direction."

I nodded, wishing I had even half of her optimism. "It is. I hope."

"I started to go to a group too," she said. "It helps knowing that I'm not the only one going through this."

"You know you don't have to do that, right? I'm the one with the issue."

"No, Henry," she said, squeezing my hand. "We're in this together, remember?"

I tucked a strand of wavy hair behind her ear, caressing her cheek with my thumb. "Okay."

On the way back to Shake, Elsie said, "Remember how you told Dr. Galicia that you never stole anything from my parents' house?"

"Yeah?"

"Well you lied," she said with a grin. But before I could issue a rebuttal, she added, "You pocketed my heart and never gave it back."

I pulled her close and breathed her in. "And I never will."

———————

On my day off, I went by the station after being summoned by the chief. I stood in front of his desk and waited with my spine straight.

He looked over a piece of paper before saying, "You've been officially cleared of the charges."

I kept my gaze ahead, to a point above his head. "Thank you, sir."

"I hope that eases your mind a little."

I didn't reply because I had none.

Chief Ross took his glasses off and placed them on the desk. "Look, Logan. Things like this, they happen all the time. You'll probably shoot many more men in your lifetime. It's only human nature to regret that, to question your choices. But I need you to get your head in the game. If you don't, it might just get you killed."

I nodded, finally meeting his eyes. "I'm trying, sir."

He didn't blink. "Try harder."

Even though it was one in the afternoon, I headed to Shooters to ponder the verdict over a beer. Was I really not guilty? Because last I checked, I pulled the trigger that propelled the bullet that killed that motherfucker.

"Excuse me."

I looked up to find an attractive brunette in a tank top and short shorts taking the stool next to mine.

"I'm sorry to bother you, but I was sitting in the corner over there and couldn't help but notice you."

Great, another badge bunny. Just what I needed. "Thanks, I'm flattered but . . ."

Before I could show her my ring, she touched my arm and said, "I just wanted to come over to make sure you're okay. You looked so miserable."

I lifted my left hand. "I'm married."

Her brown eyes looked at me in sympathy. "Your marriage is on the rocks?" she asked. "Is that why you're drinking this early in the day?"

I barked out a laugh. "No, my wife is not the reason why I'm drinking this early in the day."

She raised a perfectly plucked eyebrow. "Then what could possibly drive a man like you to drown your sorrows in alcohol?"

I leaned over, getting a whiff of her perfume. It smelled expensive. "You really want to know?" I asked with a smile playing along my lips.

She tipped her head toward me and nodded. She really was very pretty, her makeup and hair tastefully done and not trashy.

I let my mouth stretch out to an all-out smile. "I killed a man and got off scot-free."

Her recoil was so fast, she might have incurred whiplash. "Say that again?"

I laughed. "Relax, Internal Affairs deemed me not guilty."

Indecision filled her eyes; she really didn't know how to come at me. Finally, she gave a soft laugh. "You're hot, you know that? Demented but hot."

I tipped my bottle and finished the last of my beer. "That's me in a nutshell." I stood up and threw a five on the bar.

She grabbed my wrist, also rising to her feet. "You want to get out of here?" she asked with a sultry voice. "I'd like to know the reason why you're so fucked up."

I raised my eyebrows in apology. "I'm sorry but Mrs. Demented but Hot is waiting for me to come home."

————

I set the bag of groceries onto the counter, taking note of the time before getting out the chopping board. Elsie said she'd be home around five thirty, which meant I had only thirty minutes to cook a romantic but healthy meal.

She'd mentioned a week ago that her blood work showed she was low in iron, so I planned on making grilled steak kabobs. Easy and satisfying.

When she came home, I greeted her in the foyer and grabbed

her bags, setting them down on the floor. Then I immediately took her face in my hands and kissed her like I'd wanted to do all day.

She looked a little dazed when I pulled away, but she stopped and sniffed the air. "What's that I smell? Did you make me dinner?"

I kissed her again—one quick peck for the road—before taking her hand and leading her to the kitchen to show her the dining table that was arranged with place settings and flowers at the center.

"It's lovely," she said, touching a finger to the bouquet of daisies.

"Do I need an occasion to surprise my wife?"

"I guess not."

———

After she went upstairs to "freshen up"—whatever that meant—we sat down and started eating. Elsie, who's normally not a fan of steak, ate her kabobs with gusto.

"You like it?" I asked after she'd eaten half from her first skewer.

She shrugged. "Beats eating ramen noodles."

"You don't really eat ramen noodles for dinner, right?" I asked. "That's not healthy."

She laughed. "Simmer down, Officer Logan. I was kidding. Yes, I'm eating healthy. Yes, I'm taking my prenatals. And yes, I'm getting plenty of sleep. Would you like to take my blood pressure?"

I grinned. Even when cranky Elsie was cute. "No, I believe you."

I told her about the verdict during dinner, and though I knew she really wanted to ask if it alleviated my worries, she didn't say a word. I realized then that she was treading carefully around me, as if one wrong step would crack my thin surface and send me sinking back down into cold waters.

"I'm not that emotionally fragile, Els," I said as I cleared off the table. "We can talk about it."

She pinned me with a shrewd gaze but said nothing. She only stood by the counter and took a sip of water.

In two steps, I was in front of her, caging her with my arms. I leaned close until our lips were almost touching. "Come on, you know you want to talk about it."

I meant to intimidate her, to force her into opening up. Instead her eyes lit up and a familiar look took hold of her features. "Talking is not exactly what I had in mind," she said, trailing a finger from my chin and down my chest, then lower.

I was instantly hard. How could I not when my beautiful, horny wife stood in front of me, tracing lazy circles around my crotch? I licked my lips and leaned over, taking hold of the shell of her ear with my teeth. "Did you want to play Scrabble then?" I teased.

She reached around me, stuck her hands inside my pants, and gripped my ass. "Only if I can choose my tiles. I'd pick F-U-C—"

I captured her lips with a growl, grabbing a handful of her hair. I tilted her head back and pulled away, enjoying the heated look on her face. Her cheeks were flushed and her pupils dilated, and her lips were swollen from our kiss. "Elsie, I don't know if I can do slow and gentle right now."

"I didn't ask for slow and gentle." She turned around so that she was facing the counter and gave me a seductive look over her shoulder.

I slid my hands up her thighs, under her skirt, and up over the curve of her bare butt. "You're not wearing any underwear," I whispered against her ear.

"I freshened up for you."

I had my cock out in record time, my pants pooled at my ankles. I lifted the hem of her skirt, nudging her legs apart. "Hard and fast?" I rasped as I slid my cock along her wet folds.

"Stop teasing, Henry," she said. "I've waited a long time for— Oooohhh!"

I slid inside her in one clean stroke, pushing up until I was lifting her to her toes. I bent over and anchored my teeth on her shoulder, groaning at the intense pleasure radiating from my cock. I remained seated in her, feeling like I'd come home.

I felt the rapid pulsing that signaled her climax a second before she cried out, "I'm coming."

"Holy shit," I said, closing my eyes and reveling in the pleasure that one can only feel inside a throbbing woman, that extraordinary sensation of being encased in something so tight and warm and knowing that more is yet to come.

I yanked down the straps of her top to expose her shoulder, pressing kisses on her creamy skin. With my remaining self-control all but gone, I dragged my shaft out then plunged back in. I wrapped an arm around her chest and pulled her to me, kissing the side of her neck as I thrust into her over and over. My free hand snaked around to her front and cupped her mound, letting the tips of my fingers drag along my cock as it slid in and out of her.

If I had any lingering worries about hurting her or the baby, they all but disintegrated when she said, "Harder. Fuck me harder."

I gripped her hips and complied, taking all my frustrations and using it to thrust into her mercilessly. This was not making love; we were fucking and it was hasty and sweaty and glorious.

"Henry," Elsie breathed a second before she tightened around me and came again, her hips jerking back into mine. I let go, feeling the rush through my shaft and the resulting eruption inside her. I grabbed her chin and twisted her head around, covering her mouth with mine and kissing her until the surging in my dick stopped.

I held her tight against me, my heart pounding right through my chest and against her back. "I love you so fucking much."

After we'd caught our breath, I carried her upstairs to the bathroom and drew her a bath, peeling off her clothes until she was standing before me completely naked.

She looked almost embarrassed, hastening to slide into the bubbly water to hide her changed body.

I sat on the edge of the tub. "I want to look at you. Please."

She rose to her feet, the water and suds sliding down her perfect skin. My eyes traced her figure, taking stock of what had changed and what was still the same. Apart from her larger breasts and her rounded stomach, nothing else was different.

I couldn't help but gawk at her in awe, at the glowing beauty of this woman who carried our child. "You look like a goddess."

She laughed in surprise and sat back down. "You're so corny," she said, splashing me with water. She pulled up her knees and motioned to the space in front of her. "Are you getting in or what?"

"I can't," I said, glad that I had kept my clothes on. Otherwise I'd be in there right now, sliding inside her again. "I have to get going."

"You can't stay the night?"

I dipped my finger in the water and trailed it along her collarbone. "I shouldn't," I said, hoping to hear from her a reason why I should. "Not yet."

"Soon?" she asked with a hopeful lift to her brows.

I bent down and kissed her forehead. "I really hope so, Els. It kills me to wake up without you."

———

"Anyone else have anything they want to talk about?"

The members of the group all looked at one another, their faces free of judgment or expectation. Several people out of the eleven-member group had already spoken and shared their worries or experiences. It was my turn.

I took a deep breath and spoke. "I nearly died the other night."

That got their attention. "What happened?" one female cop asked, sitting straighter in her chair.

"I hesitated."

A murmur of understanding went around the group, alleviating my worries. They weren't going to judge me because they'd been in the same situation. They knew what the hell had gone through my mind during the confrontation.

"I was answering a call, a robbery in progress. The guy was still in the liquor store, hiding out in the back office. He was shouting at me and shooting wildly. Fucker must have had more than one magazine with him because he was shooting left and right. I moved around till I had a clear shot. I had him in my sights; all I had to do was pull the trigger. But I fucking hesitated. I was second-guessing my decision because I didn't know if I could handle it again. I didn't know what it would do to me . . ."

Sweat broke out over my forehead at the memory of that night. I'd literally been ready to put my gun down when the bottle beside my head exploded and shocked me back into action.

"The Grey Goose splattered on my face like a bucket of cold water, and I realized that the chief was right: My indecision was going to get me killed. So I lifted the gun and shot the fucker in the shoulder, incapacitating him until I could get closer and arrest his ass.

"If he hadn't been such a lousy shot, I might have a bullet in my head today. They'd be burying me and Elsie would be raising our baby girl alone. I'd miss everything—her first word, her first step— and all because I couldn't get my head in the game." The thought was sobering and frightening, and I hoped it was enough to wake me up.

"Are you going to tell your wife?" an older gentleman asked.

"Would you?"

"My wife and I divorced years ago, but no, I wouldn't have told her," he said. "Some people just can't handle getting a glimpse of the darkness inside us. They fear it, and then they start to fear us."

4

I went over to the house that night, my mood as black and cloudy as the night sky. As soon as Elsie opened the door, she took one look at my face and just *knew*. Without a word, she stood aside and let me in, meeting me at the couch.

I sat down, resting my elbows on my knees, contemplating what was said at group therapy that night. They didn't think Elsie should know, and once upon a time, I would have agreed with that, if only to protect her from what would surely cause her more stress.

But now, as I watched her sit down, tucking her feet under her, I wasn't so sure anymore. The need to protect her was my first and strongest instinct, but I tried to override it, to remember that she was the one who always insisted she didn't need my protection, only my honesty.

I leaned back with a sigh and fixed my eyes on her face. She was sitting up, one elbow up on the back of the couch as she waited for me to speak. She tipped her head against her hand and gave me a playful wink.

I pressed my palm against her cheek and tried my best to smile, even if inside I was aching at the realization that I could have lost her, this woman who was as much a part of me as I was of her.

Somewhere along the way I'd lost confidence in myself, but Elsie still believed that I could be whole again. It was evident in the way she looked at me, in the way she still allowed me back into her life even after all the shit I'd done. Despite everything, she still had faith I would return. And that blind hope was enough to make me believe it myself.

Without warning, she reached over and pulled the cell phone out of my pants pocket. She unlocked it and showed me an application titled TrackIt before deleting it, letting me know in no uncertain terms that she was done second-guessing me.

And that I should be done second-guessing myself.

I decided then that I would tell her, but just as I opened my mouth to make my confession, her eyes widened. She grabbed my hand and pressed it against the hard globe of her belly.

When I felt that first thump against my palm, my heart stopped. Then it happened again and again, little pulses that I could feel right beneath the skin of her stomach. It was the most incredible experience, to feel my daughter kicking me, reminding me that there was life beyond my own and that my issues were minute in the grand scheme of things.

I blinked away the tears as a laugh bubbled up from my chest. I shifted around to press my forehead against Elsie's stomach, closing my eyes and smiling to myself as I counted my blessings. Here before me were my two reasons to live: the woman I loved and the child we had created together. They were my motivation to recover, my reminders that the world existed outside my head.

A tear slid out of my eye and dripped off the tip of my nose onto Elsie's belly. I held her stomach and breathed a promise to our child that I was going to be okay, that even though I may have bad days, I would love her and her mother fiercely until the day I died.

Elsie touched the sides of my head and I looked up at her, surprised to find tears zigzagging down her cheeks. I knew then that the fog had begun to clear and she could catch glimpses into my mind again. The thought comforted me, and it brought me to my knees before her so I could hold her face in my hands and kiss her with everything I had.

She gripped my wrists, holding me in place while she returned my passion with each swipe of her tongue, each nip of her teeth. Then she stood up and, with a gentle hold on me, led me upstairs to our bedroom, where she began to peel every article of clothing off me. When I was completely naked, she ran her fingers along the contours of my body, tracing an invisible line down my stomach then wrapping her hand around my rock-hard shaft. She held my gaze as she began to stroke me, making my knees weak with each pass of her hands. I wanted to close my eyes and enjoy the sensations, but it was impossible to take my eyes off her. I guess I hadn't been able to look away since the day we met.

She started to drop down, but I grasped her by the shoulders and crouched down instead, wrapping my arms around her waist and pressing a tender kiss to her belly button before urging her backward onto the bed. She sat down on the bed and leaned on her elbows, watching me with hooded eyes as I slid her panties down. I hooked her thighs over my shoulders and blew a breath on her mound.

Her hand landed on my head, gripping my hair as she urged me closer, but I resisted. The last time we'd had sex, it had been fast and hard. This time, I intended to extend the pleasure, to make love to her like she deserved.

With my fingers, I parted her folds until she was open to me, then I touched the tip of my tongue to her clit. Her legs twitched around my neck; I smiled and licked her again, pleased at how sensitive she was.

Then I slid my tongue straight up her folds, causing her to emit a long, high moan. I did it again then quickly slipped a finger inside her cleft. She was so wet and swollen inside, so ready for me. I added another finger to the stroking, and crooking them both, massaging her G-spot while I continued licking at her folds.

I pleasured her with my mouth, keeping a steady speed, until she started to tremble. I pulled back in time to watch her muscles contracting around my fingers, and continued to pleasure her until her hips stopped bucking off the bed.

After giving her one last broad pass with my tongue, I stood up and looked at her with admiration: Her chest and cheeks were flushed pink and her hair was spread around her head like a curly halo. She was so beautiful, so unguarded and satisfied. Unable to help myself, I bent down and clamped my mouth around one breast, licking circles around the voluptuous globe. I took the hardened nipple between my teeth and bit down gently, eliciting a surprised little squeak from her. I held both breasts together and put my face in the middle, licking and sucking at the lushness of her.

She slid backward, higher up on the bed, urging me with one finger to follow as she lay on her side. On my hands and knees, I made my way to her, fitting myself around her back. I lifted her hair away and kissed along her neck, nipping at her skin with my teeth like I knew she loved while my hand caressed her down her side and lifted her leg. I fit myself to her entrance and drove inside, wrenching my eyes shut at the exquisite pleasure of being inside her.

Elsie whispered my name and twisted around, grabbing the back of my head and bringing our mouths together. I held her against my chest and kissed her like a woman ought to be kissed, letting her know that I was completely here in the moment, loving her in the only way I knew how. My other hand caressed her entire body, my palm skimming across her soft curves in equal parts desperation and adoration. Our hips moved in unison, parting and meeting in perfect rhythm. Elsie and I had had a connection since the day we met, and though circumstances had kept us apart, there was no doubt we'd always be part of the same whole.

We came together, our limbs trembling from the intensity of the climax. She gripped my hair between her fingers and stared into my eyes as her chest rose and fell in quick succession.

"I love you," she said with a ragged breath, and though she'd said it many times before, this time the words pierced me right where they were needed most.

I woke up shivering from a bone-deep chill that even Elsie's warm body couldn't stave off. As gently as possible, I slipped away from her, sat on the edge of the bed, and held my face in my hands, the nightmare still fresh in my mind.

I started when I felt a light touch on my back. I twisted around, and even without light, I knew Elsie's face was colored with concern. But by this time, she no longer asked if I had a nightmare or if I was okay. By now she knew she probably wouldn't get an answer.

This time, however, it was different. It had to be.

I lay back down and moved her hand to my chest, imagining its warmth calming my erratic heart. If there was ever a time to stop pushing her away, it was now. "I had a nightmare," I said, finding my confession hard to make even in the darkness. "But I guess you already knew that."

She said nothing, only snuggled closer and pressed her lips against my shoulder.

"It used to be variations of the shooting. The dream would always focus on his eyes. They'd be angry and volatile, but the moment I squeezed the trigger and the bullet punched into his chest, his eyes would change. He becomes nothing but a confused, lost man."

"He turns into you."

Elsie's softly spoken words raised goose bumps on my skin. "I never thought about it that way," I said. "But tonight was different.

This time I can't shoot the gun. No matter how hard I squeeze the trigger, I can't seem to fire."

"What does that mean? Why did it change?"

I flicked on the lamp and, with nothing concealed, told her about the shoot-out, sparing no details. When I was done, I swallowed hard and waited for the inevitable.

"Henry . . ." Elsie said on a sigh. The pulse on her wrist was pounding against my fingers, but there was a stillness in her features I wasn't expecting.

"I didn't want to tell you, Elsie, and make you worry about me more than you already do," I said, turning to my side to better face her. My eyes flew across her features. "But if I have to recover, if I ever want to be good for you again, I have to let you in. I have to let you see my darkness, even if it may end up scaring you off."

She pressed her forehead against mine. "I've seen your darkness, Henry Mason Logan. I've seen you at your worst. And you know what? I'm still here."

I closed my eyes and nodded, my chest tight. "I'm sorry, Elsie. For everything."

"I forgive you."

Those three words, so freely given, loosened the knot in my chest. I inhaled deeply, taking it in, allowing myself to believe that this woman could be hurt and still find it in her to forgive. Again. "Thank you," I said, lifting her hand up to my lips.

She smiled, running the backs of her fingers against the stubble on my chin. "You're welcome. Now come home."

I moved back in the very next day. It was surreal to carry my bags through the door. I wanted to kiss the walls, to thank my lucky stars that I'd been granted a reprieve and allowed back in. I kissed my wife instead and made love to her once more to make up for the lost time.

The process of recovery was slow; at least, it was for me. Recovery didn't just happen in one moment of epiphany. It happened one day at a time, getting out of bed each morning and telling myself that I'd eventually start to feel like myself again. Some days it didn't work, but little by little, the worry that blanketed my brain started to lift.

The nightmares came and went, but eventually I was able to pull that trigger again as my confidence returned. And when I couldn't, when I'd wake up breathing hard and panicked, Elsie was there to listen. It wasn't entirely in my nature to talk about my deep-seated worries, but I forced myself to communicate knowing that this was my final chance to take that rope and pull myself to shore.

I don't think the emotional baggage will ever go away, but it's just another layer of paint on the surface of who I used to be. Eventually, time will wear some paint away, but it will never be completely gone. I suspect, by the time I'm ready to retire, I'll be covered in so many layers I'll forget what's underneath.

For now, I'll take it one day at a time.

5

"Ma'am, you do know that 911 is for emergencies only, right?" I asked, trying my best to rein in my frustration.

The woman nodded and looked down at her five-year-old daughter. "See, sweetheart? When there's an emergency, you need to call 911 and a policeman will come to your door."

"But he's scary," the little girl said, avoiding looking at me.

I tried my best not to look too intimidating even as I contemplated throwing her mother in jail for wasting my time. "Police officers are the good guys," I told the girl with a smile then looked pointedly at her mother. "But don't call that number again unless there is a genuine emergency. Nonemergency calls cost resources and lives."

She gave me a look of defiance. "I wanted to teach my daughter how to call for help when—"

"Ma'am." I held my hand up to stop her, feeling my cell phone vibrating in my pocket. "I will let this one slide with a warning. Next time, you will get a fine."

I turned away and took a deep, cleansing breath as I walked back to the patrol car. I reached into my pocket and saw a missed phone call from Elsie. A second later, a text message from Kari popped up.

911. Get your ass to the hospital NOW!

I didn't bother texting back. I simply got into the car and started driving, radioing the station on the way. My heart pounded wildly all the way to the hospital. Elsie wasn't due for another ten days.

It felt like several hours passed before I finally parked at the hospital and ran inside. The nurse at the front desk saw the urgency in my face and swiftly pointed me in the right direction.

"Where is she?" I called to Kari as I ran up the hall.

She pushed away from the wall and pointed to the room behind her, her caramel-colored skin blanched. "Her water broke a few minutes ago and they said she's at ten centimeters or something."

"Thanks for taking care of her," I said, squeezing her shoulder before going inside.

The room was a blur of action. Two nurses were moving about, getting things ready, while Elsie was lying on her back with the doctor standing between her legs.

"Henry!" she said in a high, tight voice. "You're here."

I came over to her side and grabbed her hand. "Is everything alright? Is the baby okay?"

"Your wife's in labor," Dr. Harmon said, sitting down on a stool and prodding at Elsie. "The baby is coming."

Elsie grasped my hand and squeezed her eyes shut as her entire body tensed.

One of the nurses stood on the other side of the bed and petted Elsie's thigh. "Breathe," she said. "It's almost time to start pushing."

I bent down, brushing damp hair away from Elsie's forehead. When she looked up at me with those big hazel eyes, I couldn't help but press a hard kiss to her lips. "I'm here, Elsie," I said, bowing my head against hers. "I'm right here with you."

She cried out when another contraction racked her body. I held on to her, wishing it were possible to bear her pain. To see her hurting and not be able to alleviate her suffering was the most wretched feeling in the world. I would have endured any amount of this torture if it meant she wouldn't have to.

"Okay, Elsie," Dr. Harmon said, looking up at us. "At my count, push as hard as you can."

For the next thirty minutes, Elsie pushed and grunted and cursed, but the baby still had not come.

"I can't push anymore," she said, sobbing. "I don't think I can do this."

I wiped her tears away, feeling the prickle in my own eyes. God, it hurt to see her like this. "You can do it, Els," I told her, brushing her cheek over and over with the back of my fingers. "You are the bravest, most willful woman I know. If you can pull me back from the brink of disaster, then you can do anything."

"Okay, push!"

Elsie gave a mighty push and the baby's head emerged.

"One more," Dr. Harmon said.

"I see her, Els," I said, unable to take my eyes off the baby's purple face. "Just one more push."

With one last piercing cry, Elsie pushed and the baby's body slipped into the waiting hands of the doctor. There was a moment's breath of anxiety when there was nothing but silence, but then the baby began to wail and, I swear, it was the most beautiful sound in the world.

Dr. Harmon wiped the baby down with practiced ease and placed her on Elsie's bare chest.

"Oh my God, oh my God," Elsie said, tears streaming down her face as she clutched the baby to her breast. She looked up at me, her lips trembling as she smiled. "She's so beautiful."

Overwhelmed, I swooped down and kissed my wife, gratitude and love spilling over and out of my eyes. I pressed a soft kiss to my daughter's cheek and said, "You're both beautiful."

————

Later, after I cut the umbilical cord and she was cleaned up, they handed the baby to me bundled up in a hat and blanket. I cradled her tiny body in my arms, feeling like I was holding the most fragile thing in the world. I studied her scrunched-up little face, noticing she had Elsie's delicate nose and heart-shaped lips.

"You're going to be a beauty, just like your mom," I whispered to her.

Then she opened her eyes and looked up at me. In that instant, I decided that her blue gaze was my favorite feature of all.

"I've got you, kid," I told her, marveling as she wrapped a frail little hand around my finger. "These hands will take care of you. As your dad, it's my job to hold you up high so that your dreams stretch out as far as the eye can see. It's my job to hold your hand and try to lead you in the right direction, to cover you and protect you from pain. But most of all, these hands of mine are here to help you up and dust you off whenever you fall."

I gazed down at the innocent being in my arms and felt like the luckiest son of a bitch in the world.

When next I looked up, I found Elsie watching me from the bed.

"I can't believe we made something so perfect," I whispered.

"You're going to be a great dad." She bit her lower lip and a tear slid down her cheek. "These damn hormones are making me cry at every little thing."

I clutched our daughter to my chest, covering her ears. "No swearing in front of the baby," I teased.

Elsie wiped at her cheek and laughed. "So, what do you think of the name Hannah?"

I sat beside her on the bed and we searched our daughter's perfect little face for her identity. "Does she look like a Hannah?"

The baby chose that very moment to start crying.

"I guess not," Elsie said, taking the baby and, using her new-found motherly instincts, holding her to her breast like the lactation nurse had instructed. After the baby successfully latched, Elsie turned to me and asked, "What about you? Do you have a name you like?"

"I do," I said, my eyes fixed on our child. "How about Lucy?"

"Lucy," Elsie said, saying it a few more times. "It's cute. What does it mean?"

I couldn't tear my eyes away from our daughter's face even if I tried. "Light. It means bringer of light."

I stood in the doorway, leaning against the jamb as I watched Elsie sitting on the rocker, humming a soft tune to the soft bundle in her arms. I stepped inside the nursery to join them in their quiet, serene world.

Elsie rose to her feet and took Lucy to her crib, laying her on her back and tucking the blanket beneath her. My eyes traveled up and came to rest on the mural on the wall, now complete with a brighter moon and diamond-shaped stars in the sky. It was by pure luck I had managed to finish the mural in time, only a day before Lucy was born. Otherwise I might have never finished it at all.

"Let's hope she'll stay asleep for a few hours," Elsie whispered as she led me out of the room, closing the door behind us.

"I can get up with her next. I don't have to be at work until six."

We made our way down the hallway, doing a strange little hopping dance to avoid the creaky parts of the floor. "Thank God your mom comes in tomorrow," she said.

Elsie's parents had wanted to fly out as soon as Lucy was born but had conceded to my mom's request that she come first. I think they recognized Mom's heartfelt attempt at fixing things between us. Even if she and I never mended our relationship, I hoped that, at the very least, she would make an effort to be close to her grand-child.

Once inside our bedroom, Elsie and I shrugged out of our robes and slipped under the covers. I curled around her, trying to tamp down the familiar stirrings of arousal that only Elsie could incite. The doctor had said we had to refrain from sex for six weeks. That meant forty-two days of lying by Elsie every night and not being intimate with her. It didn't seem possible.

She lifted my hand up to her lips and kissed the fleshy part of my palm.

"What was that for?"

She smiled against my skin. "For being a gentleman and not pushing for sex."

"Believe me, I want to," I said, pressing into her backside to let her know just how much. "But I can wait."

"Honestly, it's a bit of a relief. I feel like a microwaved mess these days."

I pushed up onto my elbow and cupped her cheek, turning her face to me. "I don't know if you know this, but even on your worst day, you are still the most beautiful woman I know."

Her tired eyes were filled with doubt. "But my body has changed . . ."

"Of course it has," I said gently, nuzzling her neck. "You carried our child inside you for nine months. You nurtured an entire human being with your body." I lifted the hem of her nursing top and with my finger traced along the reddish lines on her stomach.

She chuckled softly. "That tickles," she said, trying to pull her shirt back over her stomach. "Stop touching my battle scars."

"No. These are badges of honor." I bent down and kissed each jagged line. "You're a freaking superhero as far as I'm concerned," I said, gazing at her in adoration.

"I love you, Henry," she said, lifting her head and pressing her lips to mine. "And I love this little family we've made."

I grasped her hair and brought her closer, opening our mouths and deepening the kiss. "I love you, Elsie," I said against her lips, feeling like the luckiest man in the entire world. So much had changed since that day last year, when Elsie had cut my hair for the police academy. We weren't the same two, wide-eyed newlyweds anymore, but even as we transformed and became different people, at the end of it all, Elsie and I moved mountains to stay together.

And in that quiet moment, when I held her close and we drifted off to an exhausted but blissful sleep, I knew we'd finally arrived at our happily ever after.

Turn the page for a preview of June Gray's
next Disarm novel

SURRENDER

Coming soon from Berkley Books

Seven years ago . . .

"I don't think that kind of love—the kind you read in romance novels—actually exists."

Jason Sherman, my boyfriend, fixed me with a skeptical stare. "You don't?"

"You do?"

"I've seen it. It exists," he said in a tone that brooked no argument. "Three words: Henry and Elsie. Those two are so in love with each other but are too dumb to figure it out."

"You said they weren't even dating."

"No. I should knock their heads together to give them a clue. Everyone else knows but them." Jason slid his arm under my neck and gathered me close. "Anyway, that's the kind of love I was talking about. Sometimes you just love someone without even knowing."

I studied his handsome face, jaw scruffy from not having shaved for a few days. I liked him, more than anyone I'd ever known in my life, but did I love him the way his sister felt about his best friend?

Was the fact that I was questioning my feelings a sign that I already did?

"Do you, um, want that with me?" I asked, afraid to meet his eyes.

Jason touched my chin and tipped my head up. "I want everything with you."

"What if I can't give you love like that?" I asked. "My parents' marriage was pretty fucked up. I don't know if I even know how to be a good girlfriend."

"You're doing fine so far."

"Fine?"

He laughed, the sound rumbling in his chest. "You're a great girlfriend, Julie Keaton," he said, cupping my face and kissing me tenderly. "And that is why I was talking about the kind of love that burns so bright it lights you up from the inside—because that's how I feel about you."

A lump caught in my throat and it took a few minutes to figure out how to breathe around it. "What if I can't love you like you love me?"

"Stop questioning yourself, Jules," Jason said, kissing my forehead. "It will happen naturally."

"Okay," I said. "I'll try."

I settled onto his chest, my muscles finally starting to unwind. Talk of love and of the future had always unnerved me. I could lay all the blame on my parents for the way I was with men, but deep down I knew that my actions were my own. The fact that I was inept at love and relationships was my own doing, but maybe, just maybe, I'd finally found the right person to trust with my heart.

"Will you write me romantic war letters while you're deployed?" I asked after some time, toying with the trail of hair below his navel.

"Email is faster," he said with a grin. "And I'll call whenever I can."

I slid my hand down and took hold of his already swollen shaft, pressing my lips to his Adam's apple. "Will you dream about me?"

He groaned, his hips arching up to my hand. "Every fucking night." Then he flipped over and crouched above me, his eyes raking my naked body. "I'll remember you just like this."

"Unshowered and smelly from hours of sex?"

He dipped his head and pressed his face to my chest, nuzzling my breast with his bristly cheek as he inhaled deeply. "You smell perfect—like sex and sweat and me."

"Jason," I said, grabbing what I could of his short hair and lifting his face to mine. "I do care about you a lot. You know that, right?"

His eyes pierced mine, so blue and bright. "Then show me."

I gripped his shaft and guided him to my entrance, taking all of him into me, loving him the only way I knew how. I gasped as he withdrew then slid all the way back home, opening my legs to allow him farther inside.

"I love you, Julie. When I get back, I'm going to take you back to Oklahoma City with me."

I stilled, my legs wrapped around his back. "You will?"

"Just try and stop me," he ground out before thrusting back into me. "Nothing's going to keep me from you anymore."

1

The lonely seagull caught my eye as I jogged, and I followed it along the water's edge, picking up speed to keep up. Eventually the bird turned to the horizon, its silhouette dark against the brilliant orange and blue Monterey sunrise. I stopped to catch my breath, the view of the ocean before me stealing the air from my lungs.

I closed my eyes and lifted my face to the wind, tasting the ocean breeze on my tongue. I gazed back out at the sea, and saw a lone figure out on the water, sitting on his surfboard and biding his time. When a large wave rolled by, he caught it and leapt onto his board effortlessly, crouching down as the ocean carried him along. He took a few rapid steps to the front of his board, looking as if he was just floating above the waves, then cantered back to the center. He rode the wave to the shore, standing tall until his board finally sank under the water.

He paddled back out again to wait for another wave, traversing the ocean as if it were nothing but air. I watched him, mesmerized, as he caught another wave and flawlessly sailed back to the shore.

"Hi there!" he called out. It was only after he said it again that I realized he was talking to me.

"Oh, hi," I said, watching as he tucked the board under his arm and ambled closer. It was only when he was a few feet away that I noticed he towered over my five foot, ten inch frame. I took in his full-body wetsuit, appreciating how it accented the slim hips that led up to his wide shoulders.

"A little early for a morning run, isn't it?" he asked with a smile in his eyes.

"A little cold for surfing, isn't it?" I countered, raising an eyebrow as I sent a teasing look down to his crotch.

He grinned, and if I thought the sunrise took my breath away, this smile inflated me with a strange buoyant feeling. I smiled back, unable to help myself. "Not gonna lie, it's pretty cold," he said. "There's definitely some shrinkage going on."

I burst out laughing, taken aback by his crude kind of charm, the kind I liked best. "Well, your board is plenty long enough to make up for it."

His eyes widened, and suddenly he was laughing along with me. "You know what they say about men with longboards . . ." he said, standing his surfboard upright beside him.

"No, what?"

"That we have plenty of wood to wax."

I let myself go as we dissolved into a fit of laughter. It felt good, laughing with this stranger. It was the first time in years I actually felt light and without a care.

He held out a hand, his dark brown eyes trained on me. "I'm Neal."

"Julie," I said, surprised to find his hands warm. I took a moment to look him over, from his wavy light brown hair tinged with gold to his straight and narrow nose, and to his boyish smile that curled up at the ends. "Have you been surfing all your life?" I asked, hoping to extend our time together.

"Yeah, for the most part. I grew up by the ocean actually. You can say salt water runs through my veins." He ran his fingers through his wet hair, slicking it back.

"I understand. I love it here."

"Where do you live?"

"I'm actually from out of town. Dallas."

"I'm just visiting for a few days myself. Born in San Diego but have lived all over."

It was only then that I noticed the sun had already risen. I glanced down at my watch and gasped. I'd been at the beach for almost two hours. "I have to go."

"It was nice meeting you, Julie," he said, flashing me that smile that was making me wish I didn't have anywhere else to be.

"I'll be back tomorrow for another run. Maybe I'll see you again before you leave."

"I'd really like that," he said, shooting me a look that warmed me from the inside.

I made it back to the Shermans' house in ten minutes, parking the rental car in their driveway. My son, Will, and I were in town for Elsie and Henry's wedding and were staying with my would-have-been in-laws the entire weekend. I'd offered to get a hotel but they wouldn't hear of it, telling me that I was family even if my son was the only one technically related to them.

I sometimes still wondered what would have been if Jason hadn't died in Afghanistan and we'd gotten married. I would certainly be a different woman today if I'd had Elodie Sherman, and her daughter, in my life for the past several years.

I'd be a lot less lonely, that's for sure.

I found Elodie in the kitchen, pouring pancake batter onto a griddle. "Good run?" she asked, turning her attention to the scrambled eggs.

"Kind of chilly, but good," I said, walking around the island counter. "Do you need some help?"

"I think I've got everything under control," she said, and handed me a mug that had an Air Force logo on it. "Help yourself to some coffee."

"Oh, me too, please." Elsie came around the corner wearing jeans and a top, her hair in a messy bun. She grabbed a mug from the cabinet and playfully hip checked me out of the way.

"And where have you been, young lady?" I asked with a wink. "Sneaking out to see a boy?"

Elodie sighed dramatically. "You and Henry live together and are getting married tomorrow. You couldn't even go a few hours without seeing him?"

Elsie laughed, her cheeks taking on a pink tint. "I just went to say hi," she said, hiding her face behind the mug.

"I'll go wake up Will," Elodie said, shaking her head at her daughter. "You two set the table."

When we were alone, I turned to Elsie and said, "He's not going anywhere. You *know* that."

She cocked her head, the easy smile gone. "I know, but I just had to make sure," she said, taking the stack of plates to the table. "I woke up this morning and for one second, I thought I was back to when he was in Korea and I was trying to live without him. I had a bit of a moment." She laughed nervously, trying to ease the tension in the room.

I hadn't known Elsie for long, but I'd immediately felt a bond with her from the moment we met. Even after his death, Jason had somehow managed to bring this beautiful, flawed, wonderful woman in my life. And for that, I was grateful. "I hear it's perfectly normal to freak out right before the wedding."

"Did you?"

I thought back to my own wedding to Kyle, to those final seconds before I walked around the corner to face the entire church.

I'd known that I didn't love the man standing at the end of the aisle, at least, not the way he loved me. "No. I didn't freak out. But that's because I had already accepted that I was making a mistake."

She nodded distractedly, pinching at her lip. "But even if Henry and I were already married, it's not like a ring on his finger will keep him from leavi—"

"Elsie," I said, cutting her off. I grabbed her by the shoulders and peered at her face. "Henry is not going anywhere, I promise you. That man regretted every day that he was without you."

She took a deep breath and nodded. "I know. I trust him."

"You two are going to live happily ever after. I just know it."

"I hope so." A moment later, her eyes narrowed and the smile on her face transformed to something more calculating. "Henry told me there'd be a few eligible bachelors at the wedding . . ."

I backed away. "Oh no, you are *not* going to fix me up."

"Why not?"

"Because."

"When was the last time you even had a date?"

"A while, but it doesn't matter. I don't want to be fixed up." When she opened her mouth to argue, I cut her off. "I've already met someone anyway."

"What? Who? Where?"

Though I hadn't been thinking of him, the guy on the beach came to mind. "I met him at the beach. You wouldn't know him."

"Bring him to the wedding."

"No thanks."

"Why not?"

"He's from out of town. If anything were to happen between us, I want no strings attached."

"You're not going to find love if you never give the guy your phone number."

"I don't want love. I just want a quick—"

I stopped just as Elodie came back in the kitchen with my sleepy-looking son in tow. "This kid sleeps like the dead," she announced.

"Just like his dad," Elsie and I said in unison then. A second later, our eyes met in horror after realizing we'd just made a dead joke about someone who was, well, dead.

"I have lots of things in common with dad, huh?" Will asked, breaking the awkward tension in the room with his excitement.

"Yeah you do," I said, ruffling his hair. "Let's go sit down and see if you eat like him too."

After spending the day running errands and making decorations for the wedding, we all walked down the street to have the rehearsal dinner at the Logans' house.

Henry had only told me briefly about his childhood, but I found his parents pleasant enough, if a little aloof. They were the complete opposite of my own parents, who had loved each other with a destructive fire, fighting and making up then fighting some more until it destroyed them both.

I'd figured out long ago, as they lowered my father into the ground, that I didn't need that kind of passion in my life, that I would be perfectly happy as long as I kept my heart guarded.

I suppose I owed my parents some gratitude because that lesson was the reason why I was able to survive the death of Jason at all.

ABOUT THE AUTHOR

June Gray is a daydreamer who, at the age of ten, penned a short story inspired by a Judy Blume novel and has been unable to stop writing since. She loves to tell stories that titillate and enrage, that break the reader's heart and put it back together again.

Her fairy-tale life has been lived on four different continents—most recently, in a two-hundred-forty-year-old castle in rural Germany owned by a graf, a German noble. She was born in the Philippines, raised in Australia, and now calls the United States home. She can currently be found enjoying the shores of Miami with her husband, two daughters, and a miniature schnauzer.

Visit the author at authorjunegray.com or facebook.com/author junegray.